The Storm

Elliot Chatima

And

Rumbi Chen

First paperback edition May 2024

Book design by Mehreen Shaukat
Edited by Alisha E

ISBN 978-1-7635933-0-5 (paperback)
ISBN 978-1-7635933-1-2 (e-book)

Acknowledgments

~ 1 ~

I extend my deepest gratitude to Rumbi Chen, a seasoned author and expert artist, whose exceptional skills and mastery of integration have brought "The Storm" to life. Just as ancient Rome owed a debt of gratitude to its noble knights, I am forever thankful to Rumbi for her invaluable contributions to this work. I also wish to express my sincere appreciation to Tafadzwa Tamanikwa for her meticulous chapter-by-chapter review and candid feedback. Her insightful comments have been instrumental in shaping this work, and I am eternally grateful for her support and guidance. Additionally I thank my wife Jane Vene N. Chatima for her support throughout the process.

Special thanks to my co-author, Elliot Chatima, whose brilliant idea sparked the creation of this book. His invitation to collaborate set the stage for our journey together. Trudy Phiri and Diana Vito played a crucial role in shaping this project, including their guidance and inspiration throughout this collaborative endeavor. With the help of my family's encouragement and support, we've navigated the challenging terrain of addressing drug abuse related challenges.

Our sincere thanks to the beta readers for their invaluable feedback and insights during the development of this book.

Chapter 1

March 2023, Bulawayo, Zimbabwe

On a Thursday afternoon somewhere in the middle of Bulawayo City, the second largest city in Zimbabwe, life is going on as usual; right in the City center, in a Fast and Furious style, a convoy of six Escalade cars in South African Plates emerged in high speed, before long, the wheels screamed to a brisk stop in what used to be Cecil John Rhode's route to Namibia, Ekupumuleni (the resting Place). The road had been intentionally widened to accommodate Rhode's horse-drawn carriage. And being a small town, people had already started gyrating around like vultures following a dying animal, albeit at a safe distance. For ten straight minutes, there was no movement, but the very inaction aroused varied feelings from the onlookers; some felt impending danger, others felt excited, and still others felt livid while others were indifferent.

Their silence was broken by a guy who was passing by selling some cosmetics yelling at the top of his voice, immediately there were some murmurings, and the excitement grew louder as they waited in anticipation. The murmurings were cut short and replaced by complete silence as that of the examination room for students taking an American Bar exam or the Cambridge check point exam as he emerged from the car, the man himself in flesh and blood in the streets of Bulawayo standing beside the third of the convoy of six cars his name, Jonathan Bowman Zuva or JBZ for short as he is affectionately known in other parts of the world. Word had swelled in town that there was something big about to happen not only in town but the country. The adoption of the United States Dollar by the Government of Zimbabwe as a transaction currency had attracted a number of traders, drug dealers and money launderers were no exception.

JBZ was wearing a designer suit made with the finest fabric; a quick glance revealed it could have been Italian style, maybe Corneliani. He was wearing a black Hat with a feather affixed to the center ribbon tucked in a bowtie like style. A horseshoe beard circled his chin and opened atop, making a half-moon like shape connecting with well-trimmed falls from both ears. The horseshoe was in a formation mimicking that of red ants at a barbeque surrounding a big piece of Countrystyle Boerwors sausage from , Colcom Meats.

The chin was distinct, and a scar on the left chic was visibly displayed with pride and perhaps displayed like a Medal of Honor awarded by the President for some good done to humanity. His eyes were blue, and he had a stare that could frighten a pride of lions to the point of giving up their territory. Further down, his Adam's apple protruded and was visible for all who cared to look, and it moved noticeably up and down each time he swallowed.

On closer inspection, the suit was made of the finest material, in the range of USD 3,000 to USD 4,000 per suit. A belt with a head made of two small guns crossed each other and was neatly wrapped around his waist. On the left hand, he wore a wrist watch, a USD 907,900 Patek Philippe made from the finest material and by the finest master craftsman, who have been making wrist watches since 1839. This watch was circa 2017, 41mm taupe brown, platinum, a round face with a baton dial and baton's hands, a perpetual calendar and moon phase indication, screw –down crown, leather strap, a pin-buckle fastening, and an automatic movement. The watch had been evaluated and authenticated by Watch Box, an in-house Swiss-trained watchmaker, and the watch came with a two-year warranty. Behind were small concealed bumps, and these could have been guns, one could speculate, as it turns out it was not any type but a Magnum, possibly a .44mm caliber, the most powerful pistol on God's earth. He had one on each side of his ass. On the right hand, he was holding a Cigar, not any ordinary type but an Inferno by Oliva Serie V Double Robusto, which had been handcrafted since 1886. This one was wrapped in a brown, gold, and purple sticker with a V distinctly marked at the center of the cigar, and it comes in a pack of 24, with each pack coming in at USD 214. On the same right hand was a signature with the letters JBZ printed on the protruding shirt. His shoes were made of real leather, possibly from crocodile skin, with patches of black and white on them to go with the classic suit.

After scanning the city like one viewing his piece of land that was purchased in his absence and for approximately three and half minutes he had taken his time to satisfy himself of whatever he was looking for, he motioned to the car in front and three men with a 350-meter effective range AK47s emerged from the car. They brought a man in his late twenties, a handsome boy, a well-known boy in the streets of Bulawayo, a promising artist who was also known to be a drug dealer; though he never had drugs on him, he specialized in recruiting youngsters into drug distribution for Manjinji a well-known local drug dealer operating at a very small scale perhaps due to capital constrains and lack of access to key suppliers. For a long time, the streets belonged to Manjinji, and there was not much use of force and violence as there was not much competition. Manjinji personally handled the authorities when arrests and interference became too much. Samson Thumelo Ndlovu was brought to JBZ, and without hesitation and any preamble, JBZ grabbed Samson by the dreadlocks; Samson screamed with pain and fear. JBZ drew a hunter knife and without brandishing it much, he cut open Samson's throat, and as he gasped for breath , blood oozed like a leaking tape, JBZ licked the blood on the knife blade and tucked it back into its position, fear gripped the onlookers and all who were subsequently told of the encounter. As Samson fell to the ground, JBZ kicked his lifeless body. He took a gallon of Gasoline, poured it on him, and burnt the body in broad day light. After that, he addressed the people with a louder voice, proclaiming the start of the new era. The streets were his, and that he would not hesitate to do to anyone what he had just done to Samson. He motioned to the team holding guns, and immediately, they started firing shorts non-stop in the air; at that point as if it were a 21 gun salute following the death of Samson, there was chaos and confusion of the highest level in the small town of Bulawayo. Four men emerged from one car, then another, and another, and there was a massive celebratory shooting in the air; no one was pointed at or threatened, and people failed to make sense of the shooting. It was a celebratory and warning shooting session. The shooting lasted for approximately three minutes, and bullets were raining everywhere while shells were scattered on the ground like Ice cubes falling from the sky on a rainy day. Disturbing screams of innocent women and children could be heard from far and near, and people could be seen running for cover while rivers of cars meandered through the roads, with many colliding and pilling up in a panic-stricken small town. Some pulled off and folded seats in a desperate attempt to avoid being hit by stray bullets, while others left the cars and took off at a speed that could have easily won the 100-meter Olympics, surpassing Usain Bolt's record of 9.58 seconds for 100 meter challenge. Then the shooting stopped, the shooters got back into the cars, and JBZ was still standing there, still like the statue of Oliver Tambo at the welcome gate at OR Tambo International Airport, still smoking his Oliva cigar; he was stable and steady as if nothing had happened. He finally gestured and got into the car, and immediately the cars screamed from zero to 100 miles per hour and hit top speeds of 180 miles per hour, leaving tar marks, smoke, little dust, and a smell of tyres, not bad for a tailor-made Escalade.

They drove past the Joshua Nkomo Statue, a national hero popularly known as Father Zimbabwe, a man of integrity, a no-nonsense man, a man of principle, a man who led ZIPRA forces and joined hands with ZANLA forces to liberate Zimbabwe from the white minority oppressive rule, resulting in independence in 1980, 18 April to be precise, yet a convoy of gangsters was passing right by his statue, one wonders what would have been his take had he been alive and active.

So there it was Ceil John Rhodes, and Joshua Nkomo; both men had mattered to the City of Bulawayo, at least the latter, and both had strong will and would not have approved what was happening in the town they had cherished. But then, times change, so are places, practices, values, and norms. The two must have turned in their graves at that very moment, perhaps had Joshua Nkomo not been buried at the National Shrine in Harare, the Capital City, per chance, his spirit might have come to protect the City; Rhodes was also buried in Matopos 37.4km away from Bulawayo City was the closest but perhaps his spirit is not in one place as South Africa and Zimbabwe divided the statue and the Grave respectively.

They drove straight to Bulawayo Colonial Collections Club, an ancient small hotel with a rich history of Zimbabwe and more importantly, where the Pioneer Column and all the Generals that Colonized and divided the country among themselves are frozen and hung in pictures on walls. Of particular importance is Cecil John Rhodes himself, General Admiral Tait, Welensky, and Rhodes' own brother. In one of the photos, Rhodes could be seen in a carriage drawn by human beings, a slave Master relationship that he enjoyed very well. Some believe that the manner he treated the blacks could be the reason why he died early while others think he died of illness and could not complete his cape to Cairo Vision, and the Mighty Victoria Falls Bridge was completed after he was gathered to his ancestors. At the age of 49, Cecil John Rhodes died of heart attack on the 26th of March 1902 in Muizenberg Cape Town, South Africa.

JBZ was standing in the lobby with his men waiting for someone, and from the passing up and down he was doing, it was clear that he was getting impatient. Just as he pulled his phone to dial a number, a man with a thin moustache emerged from the wooden stairs. He was wearing an earring and had tattoos on his back part of the neck. An eagle was carefully and skillfully drawn, and it was clear that the rest of its body and wings were further down his back. The tattooed man was in the company of two men, and when they came to meet JBZ, JBZ pulled his Magnum .44 and shot one of the men and immediately cleared his throat and said, "I am not a big fan of waiting," to which the tattooed men nodded in agreement and offered his apologies and after that, pleasantries were exchanged, and then the two men disappeared into the wooden manually operated elevator, and as soon as the door closed JBZ pulled a small paper from his pocket, it had four things; Drugs, Armed robberies, Human trafficking and any other. He handed it to the tattooed men, who introduced himself as SBU. JBZ handed him a memory stick and yelled, "Guard with your life." He also said, "I am now the boss in this town and the entire fucken country, do you hear me? I need to see all the agents tonight."

SBU replied, "Yes, Boss!" to which JBZ replied, "Fucken fantastic".

#

There was an air of contentment when JBZ emerged from the wooden elevator, a sense of victory, and for some reason, he appeared pleased with the one-sided discussion he had had in the elevator with SBU. Turning to a tall white guy among his men who were still waiting in the lobby, he uttered, "Welcome to Africa, where human rights are cut to shit size." He was oblivious to the fact that there were other people in the hotel. The men he had shot had been removed and the wooden floors cleaned, and there was no police report, no incident report, and no one was talking about it, and no one will ever will.

JBZ was picked up from the front of the club and whisked away in a Range Sport flanked by BMW motorbikes in a Russian Presidential Motorcade style and was taken to Holliday Inn where he was booked in the 16th floor in the Presidential room, but before getting there he stopped by room 312 in the third floor, and he entered the room without knocking, flanked by two men.

There were five men and one woman in the room; one was called Brigadier Cyril Napoleon Ncube, there was the Assistant Commissioner of the Police Crime Department who goes by Lesly Milton Mverechena, a Central Intelligence Agency Officer named KGB, Assistant Commissioner Operations from Prisons Rejoice Liza Robbins and last but certainly not least Director of Home Affairs known as Jack. There was a sixth person introduced as Charlie, Charlie was a state prosecutor, and it was the wisdom of the home affairs Director to bring her in. The six comprised of a strong team known for corruption, money laundering, racketeering, and espionage. None of the team members bothered what the society thought of them. Each of them had a criminal record, and it was a public secret that they had paid their way around to come out. The team was feared in all walks of life, and JBZ could not have selected a more suitable team. It is rumored that a local prophet had single-handedly put together the team and was paid one million dollars for that.

When JBZ appeared, they all stood up to greet him and sat down immediately. No pleasantries were exchanged, and while standing, JBZ started, "We all know the business of the day is to discuss three items. 1: Drug and Human trafficking and Money Laundering, 2: Supply of Guns, and 3: Armed Robbery and related activities and Recruitment of agents." After that, he handed down a memory stick to the KGB Central Intelligence guy and said, "All that you need to know is in this flush; don't be clumsy with it; the password is Napoleon's Palindrome." KGB was explaining how he was a reliable man, but JBZ was already walking to the door, then he suddenly stopped and turned to KGB; he looked at him intently and then said, "If you lose the information, I will cut your dick and feed it to the dogs, and I will cook your testicles and your brain and give your family to eat before I kill them slowly and your wife I will have goons rape her repeatedly till she dies, are we straight?" He continued, "And one more thing, I do not make idle threats." The statement caused KGB to stand up and explain further, but JBZ was gone. KGB connected the memory stick and punched the password "Napoleon's Palindrome," and it was incorrect; they spent the hour that followed trying to guess the password but to no avail. KGB picked up his phone and called Jack the Wizard, one of his fellow workmates who sent in the password as "ABLE WAS I ERE I SAW ELBA." They tried it, and it worked. In 1815, Napoleon Bonaparte escaped from exile on the Island of Elba and headed back to France in a bid to regain power. 'Able was I ere I saw Elba. 'Supposedly, Napoleon said this palindrome to Barry Edward O'Meara, who was his physician during his captivity on the island of Saint Helena. A palindrome is a word that can be read from both ends and has the same meaning. The six started studying the information, and they had to agree that JBZ was a genius, so KGB earned the respect of the rest of the room. That night, the hotel was guarded front by the PPU (Public Protection Unit), and at the back was the army.

On the 16th Floor was an angel waiting for the Prince in a shining amour, and indeed, he was on his way. Roselyn was a beautiful girl, a drop-dead gorgeous woman whom every man would want to get a number and try their luck. She was rumored to have been a Miss Zimbabwe at some point and represented that country where she eventually came second in the Miss World competitions, but it was not a mean feat, hey. To her, JBZ was a great man, and she loved him to bits, and the feeling was mutual.

Stepping into the presidential room, JBZ's attitude changed. It was as if he had passed through the seer and had had the evil spirits cast away. There, he was normal, human again. I suppose that is the power that women have over men. The moment he closed the door Roselyn jumped to him, she was wearing channel number five she hugged him and started kissing him with so much passion, the Monster that had tormented the town and killed two men in town and Bulawayo Colonial Collections Club, he was human again kissing her with so much passion as if it was his way of disconnecting with the evil way of life that he chose.

Roselyn soothed his spirit, and she was his resting place, a place of peace, a place of comfort, a place of love, a place he was seen as a human being, a place he longed to be all day. He lifted her up and took her to the main bedroom where he continued kissing her passionately, and the feeling grew stronger, and there he was, JBZ charming man; he was whispering how much he loved her, much to the delight of Roselyn. The whisper ignited the fire in her.

Looking at Roselyn, it was clear why JBZ was obsessed with her. The girl was an hour glass in shape, with a desire for all men out there; she had an appropriate bust, a good behind that sent men's heads turning each time she walked the streets, she had long hair almost reaching the waist and boy it had an effect, and she had tied her hair before, but there it was loose and free and was moving gracefully like King Augustus 11 of Poland's royal robe tail. She was wearing a red dress with a top to bottom zip and that JBZ didn't find difficult to pull down. Looking at her wearing red underwear and Bra, JBZ, who had become erect during the foreplay, certainly became harder at the sight of Roselyn.JBZ continued with the kissing, but his focus was on removing the bra and the panty, which he did gracefully. Roselyn responded to the process with groans and moans, and as he finished removing the bra, the breasts were looking at him with nipples looking like eyes, and with each touch, the movement of the breast did him good, and he whispered, *"no wonder the Bible says let the breast of the woman of your youth satisfy you"*. He might have gotten the words mixed up, but the pleasure of a woman's breast was having an impact on him. He started moving his hands behind her and pulled her closer to him, and the warmth of the breasts ignited his passion further; he moved his hand further, turned her, held her breast in his palms, and clipped the nipples with two sets of gentle fingers creating a fire that burned through Roselyn's body, and at that moment JBZ laid her to the bed and went down to the velvet and started eating it while holding her firmly by the waist in case she may jump from sensation and pleasure coming from his magical tongue. He rolled up the clitoris, gently released them, and repeated the process, and Roselyn screamed like Celine Dion singing *"You Are My Angel"* with R Kelly. JBZ immediately asked her, *"Do you want me?"*

She responded, *"Yes, yes, now come now,"* and so it was. He was inside her, stroking and each stroking, releasing an electrifying sensation down her spine; the electricity generated was enough to power a small town for two minutes. She closed her eyes and he stared at her, making melodious sounds as he made love to her; seeing her breast moving with grace and her velvet firmly clipping his manhood, he groaned in painless pleasure, and at that instant, they were both airlifted to 44 Thousand feet into the sky, a height that ordinarily require a license from the Aviation authorities but this was love hence no license was required to fly at such altitude, the flight lasted some minutes before they were thrown back to the earth in a brisk landing. The plane taxied till it came to a complete stop. The Captain and the assistant were still in the cockpit and remained in there for some ten minutes, getting feedback on the flight. They showered together, with Roselyn singing some hymns praising god for giving her such a wonderful man. They switched off the light, cuddled, and slept, at least according to Roselyn. JBZ had other plans; at exactly 22:55 pm, there was a Knock on the door, and JBZ left the room.

Chapter 2

At exactly 10:00 hours in the morning, Gerald Kapopo Lungu, the head of distribution for the African market, was quietly tucked in a Villa in Lusaka, Zambia, in the leafy suburb of IBEX; some say it is the home of thieves and politicians while others simply believe that it's a place where people with means stay, blend and hide their loot from whatever source whether legitimate or illegitimate. It is rumored that at least one in every twenty people are either drug dealers or money launderers or simply businessman making an honest living but evading tax. Gerald Kapopo Lungu could not have chosen a better place to live, but the Villa de Campre was an outstanding place with a touch of class. While Gerald was handling distribution in Africa, his mannerisms could be easily mistaken for that of a CEO of a bank or a listed entity.

At exactly 10:30 Hours in the morning, a Limo pulled in front of the Villa de Campre; the driver was in a black suit, white shirt, and a black tie, a pale figure with a firm voice and in a "Transporter" fashion; he arrives just on time and prefers to stick to his rules of engagement and wants them followed. Rule number one was that no additional passengers were communicated and agreed upon, and Rule two was that destinations are not mentioned by name but by codes usually determined by coordinates, not the address. Rule three, No Smiles, attempt to familiarize or long speeches.

As soon as Gerald appeared, the driver opened the back door of the long Limo and closed it the moment Gerald entered the car, narrowly missing the heal he had dragged as he moved with slow motion as if he were some celebrity that wanted the paparazzi to take some last minute shots.

The Meeting was being held at the D'lela, an up market restaurant with a set up like Restaurente De Popolise. The restaurant was owned and operated by an Englishmen who had fled Zimbabwe during the Land Reform Program that had taken place in the neighboring country, with many commercial white farmers having been displaced forcibly from their farms in what became a war between the landless black majority pitting the whites being the holders of vast and multiple farms. The Government of Margaret Thatcher of the UK

Conservative Party had agreed with the Zimbabwean leaders during the Independence negotiation at the Lancaster House that the UK was to compensate the white farmers for the land reform, which would see white farmers selling their land to the blacks. Earlier on, the government had tried the willing buyer, willing seller concept, but it did not yield any result. The result was a bloody conflict that followed where; after there were disagreements between the then President of Zimbabwe, Robert Gabriel Mugabe, and the then Prime Minister of Britain, Tony Blair.

The Tony Blair administration retaliated by mobilizing burdensome economic sanctions that crushed the Zimbabwean economy, with local currency losing value, with the highest note being ten $Trillion; from then on, the country Dollarized and has struggled to de-dollarize due to the lack of macroeconomic credibility and lack of support from the World Bank and the International Monetary fund some say.

At D'lela, there is free parking inside and as the Limo slowed down to enter the gate, the guests seated outside turned their heads as they could not resist as the Limo was quite a sight to be held. Business came to a standstill as the Limo entered and as it moved gracefully to a grinding halt at the main entrance to the restaurant, the driver quickly opened the door. Gerald, seeing that people were watching, decided to delay coming out of the Limo, behaving like a bride at a wedding. But he was Gerald Kapopo Lungu, or GPL, and he was popularly known by his friends. It is rumored that at one point, he shot an old man after he had called him GBL and went on to opine that the abbreviation stood for Government Blind Leaders.

When he finally came out, he stood straight and turned around as if checking to see if there were no snipers on the rooftops. He was about to walk to the restaurant when a siren screamed like Rozalla singing, *"Everybody's free to feel good."* An unusual visitor had followed the Limo into the D'lela parking bay; it was not your usual Police; it was RTSA, the famous (Road Transport and Safety Agency). A ruthless government department known for uncompromising rigidity in enforcing the Laws of Zambia. The officer stepped out of the 4x4 GD6, a highly decorated one. The officer introduced herself and did not wait for Gerald's driver to do the same; she skipped all the pleasantries and announced that the driver was doing 70 in a 40 zone. While Gerald's driver was thinking about how to deal with the RTSA, he was fixated with the officer, and he had to admit that she was in the wrong profession. Gerald announced that the officer could have been a serious Miss World contender, but the officer was not to be dissuaded by what she calls sexist remarks aimed at weakening women. The officer had asked for the license and registration, and Gerald attempted to intervene and decided to ignore and instead walked in the direction of the restaurant; just as he turned, a voice came from the direction of the restaurant calling the RTSA officer by name, the man yelling the officer's name was the RTSA provincial head, responsible for Lusaka Metropolitan province. He was among the people waiting for Gerald for the meeting. The RTSA officer was told to stand down but looked at her superior and yelled, "Another time, another place; you know I do not let go easily next time, they will not be that lucky." The superior waved her off as if he were getting rid of flies circling leftover food.

Gerald was pleased by the display of power and the flamboyance that he displayed on arrival, and now he was headed towards the meeting; his mood was very difficult to judge, and when he got to the table for six, one of the five already seated asked him "Boss what kind of mood are you in today?" To which Gerald yelled, "I am in a crab-fraying mood, gentlemen". As he settled, he complained about the lack of gender balance on the team as if he cared for women and as if he considered his Organization as friendly to the women.

Pleasantries were exchanged, and reports were discussed regarding sales; there was a noticeable decline in revenue from the sale of drugs for both retail and wholesale; this was attributable to the distributors deflecting to the rival gang and often used to burst operations. In the past three weeks, at least 15 out of the 150 distributors were arrested, while 20% of those that remained had deflected to competition, and there were rumors that the rival gang was emboldened by the communication they received from one of the local supervisors was considering joining the rival gang. As the discussions went on food and beverages kept coming as if they were paid for by the government.

When the discussions were almost over, Gerald called the waiter and asked, *"Honey, could you please bring me a well done T Born stake, and please do not forget the steak knife?"* Within twenty-five minutes, the waiter came through with the order, and as she arrived at the table, Gerald reached into his pocket and pulled K300 (300 Kwacha), announced that it was a tip, and paid another K300 as payment for the order.

At the table, there was silence, and if a pin had dropped, it could have easily been heard. Something was not right; Gerald was not happy. He took the steak knife, and with a firm grip, he held down the palm of one DZ and cut his small finger. DZ screamed with pain, but he had to admit that he was lucky to have survived. The low sales were beginning to affect the liquidity of the business, and the rate of stock turn was becoming too low with significant capital tied up in inventory; large inventory also means high chances of getting caught as huge stocks are more difficult to hide for long. For three consecutive months, targets were not being met and the finger was a punishment which was considered more like a warning, a light punishment. The meeting ended at 12:45 hours, by 12:40 Hours, the Limo had been back waiting to pick Gerald for lunch.

Gerald decided that he wanted to go to some place Informal and decided against the idea of using a Limo; he dismissed the driver and ordered a taxi using his Ulendo (a local Uber equivalent). They went straight to Broads Back Packers. From D'lela, the Taxi maneuvered and got into Thabo Mbeki Road, then into Great East Road; the driver was uneasy but managed to concentrate on driving, listening to the only woman from who men take directions (The Australian Lady who has been used in many such GBS solutions).

At the back packers, he was dropped at the entrance and straight ahead was a very basic sitting area and right at the front left, there was a big braai stand where top quality beef, pork, chicken, sausage and the famous "Zambian bream" was being charcoal grilled, a common way of preparing a bream. He ordered a bit of everything and proceeded to the bar located to the extreme right, where he ordered a Jack Daniels.

As his whisky arrived, he was approached by a woman who was clearly over dressed with splurged make up. She attempted to give him a conversation, but clearly, he was not in the mood; the woman was not his type anyway, and he thought business, a pending trip to Zimbabwe, a new market was about to be added to his African portfolio, He was increasingly getting worried about the coordination against drugs, and nations were cooperating, and the pressure was piling up. Earlier, he had mooted an idea that Africa should be split into east and Southern markets. However, the proposal required recruitment. Recruitment is a very rigorous process that takes between three and six months. The candidates needed to be honest with money but at the same time capable of using the hardware (guns) to kill when the need arose. That is a delicate and difficult balance to accomplish.

The food arrived, and Gerald said grace and devoured the food like a honey Badger, and it was clear that the food was nice and that he enjoyed it all, making no complaints at all. Another Lady appeared, and he simply waved her away. From Broads Back packers, he had ordered a Taxi using Taxi F directly to the Villa where he was staying and decided to spend the entire night sleeping. The Taxi driver had taken a wrong turn and ended up driving through a very rough road with many potholes with many of them filled with water. The engineers who planned and constructed Lusaka made many mistakes in building houses on a level plain, and there was no gradient in many parts of the city. Some places are inaccessible when it rains, but that did not matter to Gerald; he had been raised in these same streets, and besides the streets were making him a fortune, his boys and girls were lined up selling drugs and racking in good money daily though in the recent weeks business was on a downward trend.

In the evening, Gerald was ready to go out, ordered a taxi using his I Drive application, and in no time, he was dropped off at East Park at exactly 10 pm. He was accompanied by three staff members, and on arrival, the boys and girls came to the car to update him on progress regarding the distribution of the drugs on street corners. There was no hint that what was being discussed was illegal. Gerald had taught them to dress well and speak properly like business men and women. They regarded drugs as healthy products, and at some point, the taxi driver thought they were discussing known herbal food supplements Aloe Vera gel and Tians or some STC15.

At 10:30, Gerald walked towards Chicago, a local night club located at East Park Mall, earlier on he had passed through the corner Café close to Manda Hill for a crucial meeting; what a lovely place it is, quiet, classy, spacious and no hawkers loitering around just a perfect place to do business. The entrance faces Great East Road, and the road to the Café itself is parallel to Great East road. While at the corner café important agreements were signed, including renewal of leases from where they operated; communication was established regarding the launch of the Zimbabwean Market and final travel arrangements were made.

Back to Chicagos, it was a fully packed house with ladies looking for company in endless supply like water flowing from a Cistern. Girls who wanted sex for money were dotted around the entrance of the club and were constantly moving their legs and their extended eyebrows in a fashion designed to lure men. The dressing was deliberately designed to reveal the meaty parts of the body, or should we say they were wearing negligees for the business of the night for those seeking to explore the pleasures of the flesh. Yes, not many can resist the tender flesh of young girls. The dressing was designed to ensure no man shall struggle with removing clothing during business transactions. Despite all that, Gerald was very respectful of these women and girls. It was rumored that he once fired a warning shot when he came across a guy who did not want to pay a fair amount after having been satisfied sexually.

At the entrance, there were four bouncers; I wondered why they were called such because surely they were not bouncing at all. They were firm and friendly in their dealings, and one cannot accuse them of ill-treatment. In the background, DJ Maphorisa could be heard singing his Voom song, and when it ended, a streak of Amapiano music started flowing, sending the club goers into a frenzy, jumping up and down like Hordes of Welder Beast on the great migration in the Serengeti National Park in search of greener pastures, but just as there are crocodiles lurking in the river, they are certainly crocodiles looking for a weak animal to eat at night. As Gerald entered the club, he was immediately spotted by the owner of the club and was escorted to the big table right at the center of the club, a very strategic place to sit; on top of the table, there were warnings written "reserved, reserved, reserved" around the table.

Waiters started bringing alcohol, some bottles had lights flashing on top, and various bottles such as London dry Jin, and Beef Eater were brought to the table, Jacky and Jonnie Walker. Shisha was also brought to the table. Gerald was joined by 8 men and one woman, and food was supplied nonstop, pork ribs and fries, biltong, binger hot wings, nuts, bays, samosas, dumplings, fish, you name it.

At the stroke of midnight one of the members stepped out of the club to answer a call that he had kept ignoring and kept ringing. It was a call from the delivery boys; there had been some shootings, blood on the floor and two delivery boys had been shot and killed on the spot. One of the boys had their throat slit open in a sign of rage, possibly turf war, as a message was being sent across by a rival group. It was a sorry sight; no gunshots had been heard, and the shooter had silencers and was on a mission; slitting the throats after shooting was an unnecessary aggression but was probably necessary to show that the stakes were high and that it was not a pissing competition.

It was indeed time for war; Gerald and his team was informed and immediately walked out of the club and left the spoils on the table, but no one was foolish to take any of the beer, let alone sit on their table. They called the Limo Driver, who was on standby, and his wheels creamed as he responded to the call to come over. The official driver for Gerald was always on time, and in exactly 9 minutes, he arrived only that this time, he was driving a GD6 Toyota Hilux double cab with bullet proof windows; Inside were pistols 4x 0.28s, 3x.45 and two 600 meter assault rifles AK47 and some vest, the guys were loaded for war.

The team jumped into the car, and the driver did what he knew best, he made a turn straight into Thabo Mbeki roundabout he maneuvered till he was on the great east road and drove straight to grand daddies passed grand daddies and straight to the place where the opponents were and shooting started before that car came to a complete stop, it looked like the rival gang were anticipating a response but not what eventually came through. There was heavy gun fire with replies from both ends, and after 6 minutes, Gerald lost another man while he managed to down six of the rival gang members. Gerald's men retried the bodies of his men and left the scene in a huff. They returned the guns to the military barracks where they had secured them, specifically from corrupt artillery named Colonel Mupotsi Muraru. Gerald gave orders to have their man buried. In a country as corrupt as Zambia, a bribe can get you out of any kind of trouble, and so it was for Gerald and his team.

On Thursday, Gerald received Intel's message that Jonathan Bowman Zuva was on his way to Zimbabwe and that there was a meeting that night, which he was expected to attend. This meeting had been confirmed the previous night at the Corner Café. Gerald was planning to leave for Zimbabwe. He gave orders to all his men's street staff to halt any activity till the situation has calmed down. However, bulk suppliers were being shipped to Ndola, the Copper belt, Kasumbalesa and into the Democratic Republic of Congo.

At 13; 30 hours on a Thursday, Gerald was Holding his passport, all bags packed already; he was wearing a grey suit, which was easily in the range of USD 800 to USD 1000 and a Giovani Rose shoe, a pink shirt and on the left side was a USD 10,000 Rolex wrist watch which was calling all to see it. He walked gracefully, and he portrayed himself as a peaceful man. He was picked up by his Driver, this time in a Limo, and they took off from the Villa De Campre connected to East Part; from there, they drove into Great East Road and in an instant, memories of last night's shootings came flashing, and he managed to disconnect, he wanted to focus on a task at hand. Besides, it was a new day; life was for the living; as for those who died, well, some men die so others may live to fulfill their dreams.

He managed to pre-check in online using the Emirates; he was going to fly a Boeing 747, the type that developed a fault and caused the death of all on board in Ethiopia aboard Ethiopian Airways. But for now, there was no need to worry as the matter had been rectified, and the 747 Jumbo was now safe again.

They passed through the University of Zambia straight to the roundabout, then to another one where KFC was on your right. The driver was told to slow down as there was a police checkpoint, which they soon passed and they drove fast. On the right, they passed disused planes that had become obsolete and abandoned. Looking further, they could see a presidential airport.

They moved past the second checkpoint, which was manned by friendly soldiers with AK-47 rifles, and there it was looming, a giant of an Airport, and the work of Red China. The departures were on top and was accessible by a road elevated by piers, and in no time, the Limo came to a complete stop. Gerald stepped out of the Limo, and the airport marshals came running with trollies, packed his bags, and followed him.

As he was entering the first entry point, a vaccination card was needed. As he was being attended to, he oversaw the LIMO meandering the serpentine road going down from the platform from which he had been dropped.

They moved to the check-in counter, where he went to the front as there were no other passengers at the business class check-in counter. He submitted his bags, which were weighed quickly, and he was handed over a boarding pass written gate number 7. He went to the security checkpoint, where he was asked to remove his belt and any metal; his watch was one of the items he had put in the tray. He was cleared by security, and he went straight to Immigration, where his passport was stamped, and he was off to the lounge. Looking further, he could see the entire runway, and on the extreme left, he saw the air force helicopters that are always stationed there; on the extreme left were firefighting cars, the latest state of art fire equipment.

He was moving up and down, hoping from one duty-free shop to another, and a 3-litre Jack Daniels Giant bottle caught his attention. It was a huge whisky bottle strapped in a metal stand with the engineering allowing the bottle to tilt to pour out the contents. It was nice, and Gerald was tempted to buy it for himself, but he remembered his grandfather, who lives in Zimbabwe.

It was a common occurrence to have a Zimbabwean man marrying a Zambian woman or vice Versa. Gerald's Grandfather had relocated to Zambia as a young man when the liberation struggle got heated in Zimbabwe; he managed to attain a diploma in technical services and went on to study for a degree at the University of Zambia, a place where Gerald is now actively selling drugs. Anyway, his grandfather met his wife while at UNI, and they got married. They relocated to Zimbabwe after their independence. By the time they relocated to Zimbabwe Gerald's father was 22 years old.

As he was paying for the Jacky, a sweet voice came to the speaker saying, "May I have your attention, please? This is the final boarding call for Air Link to Johannesburg, South Africa and may all passengers flying with this airline proceed to gate number 6 for boarding; thank you". Gerald kept moving up and down, admiring the work of art created by yours truly Red China. As he was visiting the gentlemen's convenience rooms, he admired the awareness of cultural and spirituality as he saw prayer rooms and Muslims could be seen going into a prayer room judging from how they were dressed. Gerald could not help but admire them, making prayers at the top of the hour and he had known of a schoolmate who would take his prayers seriously.

Looking down from the gentlemen's convenience, one had to admit the brilliance of the Chinese engineers; the airport had a solar plant for clean energy in keeping with sustainability issues and the ESG issues being promoted globally. The airport had water and sewer reticulation systems. He was wondering at all this as he was shaking after peeing. He moved to the tap to wash his hands, and upon sensing his hand, the water gushed out. As he was moving out of the restrooms, the lady was back on the speaker again shouting, "May I have your attention please, announcing the arrival of Fly Emirates Flight EMKT509 from Dubai to Harare." He moved out and was now overlooking the runway, and boy, it was a giant, a Goliath of a plane with a carrying capacity of 660 souls.

Boarding was at gate number 7, ground floor, and Gerald made his way there, submitted his boarding pass and passport, and the lady gracefully waved for him to pass, going straight to the bus.

The plane took off at 16:07, and a male voice said, "Hadragadi," in some Emirati language. Later on, when the English version of the story came through, it became clear that there were safety instructions about seat belts and switching off cell phones and things of that nature. The business class and the economy were worlds apart; in the business class, one could afford to sleep, but not for Gerald. The business ahead was just too crucial, and he had to stay alert. In the business class, special food was being saved, ranging from fruits, fruit juices, various meat products and choice drinks. If one wanted anything, all they had to do was to name it, not so with the economy class, where a standard meal which was only served after the business class has been served.

On the speaker, Captain Keith announced that the plane was preparing for lending the beauty of the Boeing 747; it has maps that can show you where you are and the distance to where you are going. The captain came back saying, "Good afternoon, everyone; the weather in Harare, pretty much like Lusaka, and I am happy to announce that we are going to arrive at our destination 15 minutes before the scheduled time at no extra cost." He said this with pride as if any early arrival attracted a charge portraying a picture that he had been magnanimous as not to charge them.

The captain was in motion, lowering the Jumbo one wing down and another up as he prepares to land, but he was met with heavy crossing winds that sent the plane tumbling, and the jumbo was forced to fly up higher. Children and women could be heard screaming, but the captain managed to steady the plane and while passengers were still processing what had happened the plane opened the wheal compartments releasing both front and back wheels sending the plane screaming on the tar mark and running on the Robert Gabriel Mugabe runway at the speed of a bullet, the captain and his assistant kept applying the brakes till the Jumbo was moving slowly and announcements were being made about remaining seated and other routine things of that nature. Gerald moved from the International terminal to the domestic terminal where in between, he handed over USD500 and a 3-litre bottle of Jacky to an old man, presumably his Grandfather; they hugged and had a quick chat in the car park and parted ways. He checked in at the domestic terminal, which is used for the president when he travels; after clearance, he went to the waiting lounge and ordered a cup of coffee. By exactly 8 pm, he was ushered into an Embraer jet that had been chartered for him and sent to Bulawayo.

Chapter 3

Three diplomats were standing before the president of the Republic of Zimbabwe; their credentials had been sent through in advance. Zimbabwe had been isolated for many years due to the alleged violation of human rights, though others argue that it was due to the fact that the Southern African nation decided to take over Land from the White minority mainly of British origin and distribute it to the Black Majority. Black Majority had been displaced for more than hundred years from the fertile land and forced into unproductive reserves. The sanctions were imposed mainly by UK and USA. The UK had taken the lead in lobbying for the sanctions as a retaliation to the embarrassing dispossession of land under the land reform program by the locals. Understandably, their allies followed suit, and the rest of the EU maintained sanctions on Zimbabwe at the call of the UK. It was a widely shared belief that the reason for many EU countries agreeing to take a bilateral matter into a multilateral matter was the fear of the fact that, if Zimbabwe was allowed to succeed after the "land grab" other former colonies were going to be emboldened, and would result in a widespread land take over all over Africa and the EU would possibly be the largest casualty.

Zimbabwe was subsequently removed from the Commonwealth, which is a big market with more than 2.4 billion people providing leverage and benefits such as preferential trade, support of the member states, relaxed visa conditions and scholarships for students. The sanctions resulted in the freezing of diplomatic relations, which saw visas to the UK being processed in Pretoria, South Africa. The visa interviews are carried out at number 7 Natal Rd, Belgravia Harare and in a similar manner passports are collected from the same venue and then couriered by FedEx to Pretoria. Responses to applications are expected between two to three weeks from the date of submission.

The economic sanctions had brought challenges and untold suffering to the generality of Zimbabweans, with women and children bearing the brunt. There were local opportunities as well, but the opportunities had just become international.

Ambassador John Wayne Markey was the first to present his credentials. He moved with grace and calmness like that of a jaguar stalking an alligator laying on the sand busking in the sun. His eyes were blue; they moved slowly, circling around like that of a chameleon calculating its attack on an unsuspecting locust as he moved towards his Excellency the President, for acceptance and swearing in respectively.

The President got straight to Business, and in no time, it was over; next was William Pep Batista or Ambassador William as he is popularly known in the Diplomatic network. He was passable as an ambassador; he had all the red flags popping out like adverts on a web page, yet you could not accuse him of any wrong doing.

Third in line was Jacob Van Grooke Hreeid. As he was being sworn in as Ambassador, one wondered what the hell kind of name was that but their nation knew better and more precisely, his mother, what the name meant, but it was not a name meaning contest, so it did not matter.

All three ambassadors had their buttons on recording every moment of it, giving a live feed to Columbia specifically to the desk of the man in charge of the entire global operation. His name was Antonio Martinez, a man who was a decedent of the famous Notorious Pablo Escobar. Pablo was a Drug King pin who had grown so big that he had to die. He was a wanted man by the Interpol, FBI, Scotland Yard and all the yards as many other nations. In the United States, even the CIA, and the US Military Intelligence had been called upon to help apprehend him.

He had a drug distribution network with a net worth of more than USD 50 billion. His network ranged from distribution through Private Jets, Intercontinental Ships, War Planes, Diplomatic channels, Speed Boats, and Cruise Ships. He also used in service personnel who provided useful intelligence and tips about coast guard anti-drug operations, Interpol anti-drug and joint operations. He also employed border control teams to facilitate road transmission, especially when the streets were getting dry. Road Transportation was the most risky route, yet in some cases, things had to be done that way.

He trained his teams in a military style with Retired Lieutenant Colonel Sean Hutchinson Pompeo overseeing the military training, deployment and crime clean-up operations as well as reconnaissance missions whenever there was a need. However all, this network was destroyed when the then Kingpin was shot in the head at the age of 44 years on 2 December 1993.

The operation was carried out jointly by US Special Forces, US Military Intelligence together with the Columbian Police task force. Pablo was smoked in the head on a rooftop in Medellin while he was attempting to flee. He had been a power house, an unstoppable force that terrorized Columbia and killed anyone who stood in his way. He corrupted the government; he had become a god, invincible, and everyone was afraid of him.

On 2 December 1993, a team of armed Police detail converged at a two storey Building in Medellin Columbia. Columbia had been ravaged by a civil war and Guerrillas and Cartels emerged. Columbia spiraled into a tailspin; the country had not known peace ever since. Each day at least 5 women are raped, with between two to five people disappearing, vanishing without a trace in drug related wars and revenge. The statics like these created a real crisis.

Mexico is one country ravaged by drugs; life has become tough, with thousands fleeing the country as they attempt to get to the USA. Drugs, crime and cartels had become the order of life in Mexico and consequently would be the gate way to the USA for Colombian drugs.

The illicit drug industry in Mexico targeted foreign markets, but the industry's socioeconomic as well as political impacts inside Mexico resulted in massive corruption, militarization, violence, rape and abuse of young boys and girls in the streets. Mexico has set up a unit to stop drugs from entering the USA through its drug control unit. Mexico became a country where marijuana and heroin are produced and a gateway for the Columbian cocaine to the United States of America.

Drugs affected the Mexican Criminal Justice system, the jails, courts are filled up with drug cases. The Mexican Criminal Justice system committed most of its resources and efforts towards fighting drug laws. Surprisingly, drug use in Mexico has been over the years relatively low, indicating that Mexico is a factory for drugs and a gateway for Drugs entering the USA's lucrative market.

Jack Xi was in charge of the meetings and had the responsibility to set up the teams meeting and sharing the link as well as inviting and admitting all the participants. The team's account was set up under JMT International Corporation, a construction company with

Interests in establishing 12 countries in five continents of the world. Jack Xi was notified of the participants waiting in the lobby he clicked admit and gave access to Mexico, Columbia, China, France, Zimbabwe (AMB1, AMB2, AMB 3), and one participant was signed as a guest. All the mics and videos were muted, and no one was speaking. The meeting was due to start in five minutes time.

The plan was laid in a six power point slide presentation. Three minutes before the start of the meeting, Jonathan Bowman Zuva joined the meeting as JBZ, and Gerald was also added to the meeting. Lt1 to Lt4 were also added to the meeting.

As Jack Xi was about to start the meeting, a notification came through from Macdonald, the Tech Guy. A new link had been sent through, and everyone was to move to the new meeting, as the current meeting had been hacked into. No questions were asked. Everyone had joined the meeting and the Zimbabwe Team was struggling with Lt1 to 4. Difficult to notice was that, Gerald and JBZ were still out of the meeting due to poor network connectivity.

Zimbabwe has had power challenges, with Load shedding becoming an everyday occurrence and people would go for nearly 6 to 12 hours with no power. Industry and commerce reacted by setting up Independent Power Plants, solar systems, and Diesel Generators just to stay afloat. The country imported electricity from Mozambique's Kabora Basa and it had lagged far behind with payments, with the supplier taking a business decision to switch Zimbabwe off till payments were settled. The Country had a power purchase agreement with Namibia, which it could not breach and despite low power generation, electricity was still being exported to meet a contractual agreement with NaPower of Namibia. Whenever power was cut off, it created a ripple effect where Internet connections tripped as all major Internet connections, from fiber-based to wireless connections.

In the meantime, the meeting could not go on, so a quick call was placed through to determine the status of the team. The connection was very poor, but they managed to understand each other regarding the challenges that were being faced in Zimbabwe. AMB 1 to 3 were, however, in the meeting, supposedly joining from their Embassies. The other team members were still struggling to connect. Mr. Martinez was not in the meeting as yet but was passing up and down, clicking his figures and raising his hands up and down. Finally, the team came through.

The meeting started 15 minutes after official time; all pleasantries were skipped, and the presenter went straight to the business of the day, with no one being offered a chance to explain the reason for their lateness.

PowerPoint Slide 1

The objective is to distribute various drugs and mop up the much-needed USD. The size of the market is admittedly small from the official numbers that had been seen on World Bank, IMF and the Ministry of Finance websites. The rich mineral base, porous Border Posts, weak anti-money laundering laws and regulations, which saw the country being placed on the grey list by the Financial Action Task Force (FATF), coupled with massive corruption and theft at a grand scale, makes it easy it possible to get the easy money.

Slide 2

Usages of the funds shall involve the purchase of properties with proceeds from Zimbabwe and the rest of the region. Shares will be purchased on both the Zimbabwe Stock Exchange (ZSE) and the Victoria Falls Stock Exchange (VFX). These will be disposed of subsequently, and the proceeds will be deposited either into our London or Hong Kong based Bank, where internationally, their related fund managers will transfer the funds into Subsidiaries of JMT based in Tax havens or nations that are hostile to the USA.

Slide 3

Secure lithium export license, purchase stockpiles with dirty money, and then ship the lithium to China. China's huge demand for the minerals are used in the manufacturing of batteries increased due to the country's thrust on electric vehicle manufacturing. China was leading the world in the production of EVs as they are known. The proceeds of exports are deposited into local bank accounts; however, transfer pricing will be at play; the idea is to under-declare the value of the exports. This will be achieved through cooperation with corrupt government officials; apart from that, the carefree attitude of the government where there is no weight bridge at the Forbes border post swings the odds to our favor. Minerals such Lithium, copper, Chrome

Ore are transported and exported via the Eastern Highlands side of the country through haulage trucks into Mozambique and shipped to Red China. The country's Railway line was vandalized, all the stones, and overhead electric wires ripped off, smuggled to South Africa until the entire 500 kilometer stretch between Bulawayo and Harare was taken out. Chrome is also one of the minerals that's on the list for cleaning money. JMT decided to use various methods both fast and slow, but the ultimate objective is to push large sums from various sources. This makes tracking difficult.

Slide 4

Gold is found in Bulawayo, Kwekwe, Gweru, Rusape, and Mazoe or shall we just say in every part of the country. Gold is mined by major mining houses as well as artisanal miners. The sole buyer of gold is Fidelity Gold Refineries. The government of Zimbabwe has remained adamant in maintaining the monopoly; hence, no other actors have a license to buy gold.

However, there is a growing frustration from the mining companies as well as artisanal miners as they are paid 75% of the proceeds in USD and the Balance in the local currency, whose value continues to weaken week in and week out. The 25% is paid using the Reserve Bank of Zimbabwe Auction rate, which is determined once a week and is usually twice lower than the black market rate. This situation has caused many companies and artisanal miners to incur losses. The frustration has been exacerbated by the delays in the payment for invoices raised following delivery; the gold price is significantly lower than the world Bullion prices.

This situation has created a huge opportunity for smuggling the priced mineral into the neighboring countries through porous border posts and through International cooperation between embassies, airlines, airport staff and security teams in other nations; cooperation from local staff working in strategic places is not complex to secure due to the widespread poverty and low wages. The Staff at various border posts survive mainly from cutting deals of varying magnitude.

Zimbabwe has vast diamond deposits in Marange, which we intend to utilize as part of the scheme to clean up the proceeds from local drug sales.

The farming of Tobacco needs financing; we will launder money from outside Zimbabwe and use it for contract farming. The idea is to bring the money and pay for farming inputs and distribute these to farmers.

The farmers must be registered with the Tobacco Industries and Marketing Board (TIMB) to create a trail of clean money. Each farmer will sell their produce to the auction, the proceeds of the sale will be paid directly into our Bank account, and we will deduct all the amounts owed, take out the clean money offshore and introduce another batch of dirty money, and the cycle continues.

Zimbabwe produces high-quality Cigarettes; our main objective is to buy tobacco with proceeds of Drugs from other nations over and above the operation in slide 3 above. The Cigarettes will be exported to Red China, where the demand is very high, and not many questions will be asked.

This market is key to value preservation; the idea will be to use transfer pricing mechanisms as well as claiming credit notes from the buyer alleging damaged tobacco is not fit for cigarette making or in the event of the Cigarettes, claim defective and reduce the invoice value significantly. The profit will be retained in China and used for the purposes of Investments in much cleaner sectors such as real Estate and portfolio of funds which will be then liquidated. All this require, Bankers, Accountants, Lawyers, and these are not in short supply.

Human Traffic

This line of business requires careful planning; it's a high-risk business. Team Zimbabwe will investigate the logistics around that business. A proposal to hire beautiful girls to work in restaurants and shops overseas. Due to the crippling poverty levels, we estimate that the uptake will be a great one.

Recently, Saudis had a scheme where many girls were enticed to work in for rich families as maids. It turns out that they were being sold into sex slavery plus house work. Our model will be different; girls will be making money, and whatever they make, 25% will be sent to their families.

At the end of the presentation, the presenter asked if there were any questions and accordingly there were none raised from the participants.

#

Earlier on, before the meeting started, the BIGCAT arrived at the J. Edgar Hoover Building, a low-rise office Block situated at 935 Pennsylvania NW in Washington DC in the United States of America, the Head Quarters of the Federal Bureau of Investigation (FBI). He was part of the Drug enforcement Unit working with the Drug enforcement unit based in Springfield, Virginia United States. He was wearing cargo pants with sonny headphones placed on his head covering both two ears, shaking his head in Unison with whatever beat that he was playing. The Dreadlocks could be seen flinging sideways like a model bragging about her Brazilian long hair in show off.

From the singing along, it could be heard he was singing along to Toto's Hold that line going on he sang along.

"It's not in the way you look or the things that you say you'll do
Hold the line
"Love isn't always on time ..."

A security officer patted him on the shoulder; he removed his headphones and produced his ID; the officer looked at him and smiled to, which the Big Cat was not amused with the suggestive look as he did not take smiles from men lightly due to the increase in gay community or the LGBTQ. The officer looked at him and said, "What's the matter, babe girl? Don't tell me you are one of those men who goes to waste on a woman."

The Big Cat responded, "What's with you, LGBTQ, whatever that means?"

With a sly smile, the officer answered, "Surely we are not that bad; it just means we are unique."

The Lesbian, Gays, Bisexual, Transgender, Queer, Intersex and Asexual started as a movement for gays and lesbians, with high profile people such as Elton Johns opting to alter his sexuality to becoming gay in the 70s when it was not really a pleasing and trendy thing to do. However, he is said to have recently complained that the Laws in the US are becoming anti LGBTQ. The "I wanna kiss the girl" singer is now seen wearing pink to go with his new ways. In the United States of America, the likes of President Obama, Joe Biden were top officials to have openly promoted gays and lesbians, with Kamala Harris being a supporter of same sex marriages.

While the USA, UK, France, Germany and Australia have all agreed to same sex marriages. Africa sees things differently; it has remained adamant that it will preserve its cultural values. The likes of President Robert Gabriel Mugabe, President Emmerson Mnangagwa of Zimbabwe, Paul Kagame of Rwanda, Uhuru Kenyata of Kenya, President Edgar Lungu of Zambia, and President Museveni of Uganda have all spurned the idea of making constitutional amendments to promote a Law that will give rights to LGBTQIA.

An attempt by president Obama to promote LGBTQIA was met with stiff resistance as the then President of Kenya Uhuru Kenyata refused to budge, preferring instead to focus on the development of his nation. Anyway, that's Africa. The Americans are threatening to withhold aid if nations refuse to adopt laws that promote LGBTQ. Whether this policy will succeed remains to be seen.

The Big Cat works from the basement. He was set up by the tech team, using credentials created by Jack Xi, and he joined the meeting. From the discussions held, his work was clearly cut out for him. The Big Cat was able to secure IP addresses for AMB 1 to 3 as well as the Zimbabwe Team. However, he had a serious hurdle to overcome. Zimbabwe has been under US sanctions, specifically the Office of Foreign Assets Control (OFAC). In the list, the president and key government officials, as well as individuals that are assumed to be violating Human rights, were also added to that list.

Public organisations that are seen as perpetuating violations of human rights, as well as those that were assumed to be anchoring the "abuse of the people" were in that list. Zimbabwe has consistently been in the top five of the most corrupt countries in the world, with the greatest corruption happening between government officials and corporates regarding the awarding of tenders.

The economic sanctions have created hostilities between the two countries, and the Big Cat was aware of that. His biggest challenge was how to convince the Harare-Westgate based US Embassy to initiate discussions. The two nations had become Frenemies, cooperating and appearing on camera on certain things but maintaining their strong hostilities. There has to be a way; there had to be something that he could do. He was aware that Zimbabwe was going to ask for the lifting of the sanctions in exchange for cooperation in the investigations; this did not particularly enthuse the Big Cat as he was aware that the process of removing economic sanctions required the US Congress to debate on the matter, to even be debated it needed someone to promote it and time was not on his side. In the end, it came down to ingenuity.

He figured out that if Zimbabwe is to be convinced that the world's most organized criminal gangs were setting up shop in their country, then officials could be inclined to listening given the socioeconomic impact that this will have. But he had no idea that the most prominent political thugs had taken positions and were excited about the development.

The idea of the US negotiating with Zimbabwe was not appealing at all, but pride was to be sacrificed if the US was to get a good chance of tracking the notorious kingpin. The Big Cat had a nefarious idea, one that required him to be cleared to access Tier 5; he had Tier 4 access.

Chapter 4

"Three months no payment; I'm done being taken for a fool," snapped Stix. For a long time, JBZ had a habit of taking people for a ride, even those who bathed him. It is said, if you feed a dog milk tomorrow, it will bite you. He considered himself invincible. He ruled not only the streets, but the offices and houses too. While he was a generous thug, throwing lavish white parties and all sorts of orgies, he was stingy when it came to paying his obligations. He did everything the way he wanted and at his own pace. Sometimes, he did nothing at all. Little did he know that some disgruntlement was beginning to creep in.

Two hefty men in Aviators stepped forward, frowning their faces. Stix remained unperturbed, which made the gold-toothed man reach for his back pocket. He grinned, ready to slice his hand with a sleek okapi. The tattooed goon waved his hand, motioning for the two men to stop. "When did you grow balls of steel?" He shook his head, waiting for an answer he knew would never come. Stix raised his chin, scowling and staring at the glass doors like he had all the time in the world.

"Neptune' aha, you remind me of Neptune. Poseidon, perhaps?" Chipendo, JBZ's tattooed sidekick, murmured in realisation.

"The boss won't be thrilled; maybe you should call," the gold-toothed guy quavered in a shaky voice.

"Stupid. Only talk when asked."

Stix scowled and snarled his lower lip while raising one eyebrow. He tapped the table with the tip of his Parker, a sound which further irritated Chipendo. Agitated, he reached his hand to slap Stix. Stix grabbed him by the fingers; "Up, up there," he pointed at the CCTV overhead by the door.

Infuriated, Chipendo dropped his arm with a thud, wiping the sides of his mouth with another hand, revealing a bandaged thumb. That was a wound from JBZ. Anyone who failed to deliver orders faced his wrath not only in word but indeed. Chipendo gnashed his teeth, punching numbers into his phone. He sulked and bit his lip. As soon as the phone was answered, he nodded, rolled his eyes and sighed. He handed the phone to Stix with his back towards him. After a few seconds, he gave the phone back to Chipendo, who concluded the call with a nod. Stix smiled as a stash of crisp hundreds covered in a green handkerchief was stacked into his palm. He gestured to them where the baggage was.

"Until next time, gentlemen," Stix beamed with an exaggerated grin. He kissed the hanky and slid it into his back pocket. It seemed he had soon forgotten how some street kids had snatched his empty wallet from the rear pocket. He swore not to do it again, but there he was. In any case, he had to be stealthy since there were cameras. He knew which angle to avoid detection with. If the worst came, he knew he could have the footage vanish in seconds, with the right amount of money, of course. You had to know who buttered your bread.

This latest delivery was a key moment in the city as this would stamp his authority with international drug lords of Mexico, USA and Columbia. His credibility as a renowned businessperson was now beyond question. Stix knew this too well, hence he made the most of the moment to get his overdue tokens of appreciation. After all, he was leaning from the best. The whole country was hustling and bustling in corruption, or perhaps wallowing in corruption, whichever way, one had to make hey while the sun shined. Before the end of the day, word would be abuzz that JBZ was not a kids' game. Die hard, or die faster.

#

Svelte Roselyn slid into the hotel room with such a swagger she made passersby on cleaning duty turn their heads. She thrust herself forward, letting her torso protrude, thus revealing her décolletage. A sheer camisole with a plunging, belly-button baring neckline added a sexy detail that also camouflaged her screwdriver scar. A mark which spiraled embittered emotions toward her lover JBZ. It is said that the axe always forgets, but not the tree it chopped. She ran her fingers over her scar for a few seconds, then she sneered. As her motto was, *la joie de vivre,* she lived in the moment and for the moment.

One couldn't help but notice her tweed coat. This Burberry coat was the latest addition to her ever-growing collection. Some of these coats were lucky to be worn thrice.

She let him savor her floral, sensual scent Libre by Yves Saint Laurent, which escaped in subtle whiffs from inside her coat.

"This is new. Since when?" he whispered with his eyes still closed.

"Because I live by my own rules."

She continued, "I figured this could ignite some excitement in the engine," she chuckled, biting her lower lip.

"Are you glad I noticed?"

"You know you wouldn't dare not to," she said, clasping his crotch.

"Good girl. That same old scent had become putrid."

"But, you never complained."

"I thought JBZ would not be thrilled if you smelt differently without his or her permission."

"Enough of this nonsense," she snapped, giving him her back.

He followed her lead. He pulled her Burberry coat off her shoulder and clutched her upper arms, elevating her broad shoulders. She did push-ups religiously, and she was a karate first Kata dropout. Her Kyokushin Karate lessons were her treasure, and one day, she swore she would resume classes because it was inevitable that she would have to defend herself someday. He kissed her left shoulder in one long, sensual kiss. She tiptoed while letting her head lean backwards. As always, this was a brief ritual. They gathered themselves up and ambled to the couch overlooking the Harare Gardens. Crown Plaza Monomotapa had become their haven. Once every fortnight, they met to debrief. Well, not every two weeks, but whenever JBZ's demands on their lives. Their lives revolved around him, and it was sickening. As a human being, you can only take in so much. The elastic won't stretch the whole ten yards; it will snap. Even the elders from long ago saw it and said it. One day, the fox broke the trap.

Chipendo gobbled a whole bottle of cold still water. It gave him a sense of meaning, as he normally remarked when drunk. After all, still waters run deep. He burped and listened, following the movement of her lips. He knew Roselyn lied whenever she could, so he had to make sure he didn't miss any word. However, that didn't take away the fact that she was good at whatever she set her heart and wallet to do. She delivered on all her commitments with no qualms. She knew how to manage expectations without creating drama. Chipendo nodded, and the two ate lunch, which was their usual room service order. It was common practice in Zimbabwe not to eat and run, but to eat and chill.

Chipendo played chess on his phone, sulking and punching the air after several moves. On the other hand, Roselyn chatted on WhatsApp and commented on Facebook and Twitter with her ghost accounts. She claimed this was necessary to gain certain information on issues which could tarnish her reputation if she commented with her real identity. Her ten year old son often pestered her because she sometimes let him scroll with her when she's had too much beer. His estranged dad raised concerns over this but to no avail. He wanted peace more than anything; hence, he left the marital home empty-handed. He vowed to contest for custody once he got the legal capacity to do so. The helpless father worried about his son's future.

Chipendo and Roselyn bade each other farewell. Roselyn left first, as per routine. As soon as she was out of earshot, she rang Stix. The call lasted no longer than five seconds. She crawled off from Monomotapa basement, whistling with a wide beam on her face.

Chapter 5

JBZ was in his living room playing a game of chase with JBZ Junior, his son. JBZ had won the opening three games in a raw, with the first one being won through a back-rank mate. So it was a father and son affair, JBZ knew how to spend time with his family. JBZ Junior was a fast learner, and the father suspected so or that he was intelligent and was already good at the game of chess but was holding back.

The three games that followed JBZ had started with a double King Pawn or Symmetric or Open Game, and it ended up in a draw by insufficient material; they started another game, this time JBZ starting with Queen's Gambit, and again the game ended up as a draw by three repetitive moves. They started another game, which ended in a draw due to a stalemate.

JBZ was curious and pleased by the moves that were displayed by JBZ Junior. At that point, JBZ mooted a plan to graft him into the business in a phased approach. He had wanted his son to be smart, and there it was, his son tied up with him in a game of chess in three consecutive games. JBZ figured that some of the advanced moves that Junior displayed made it possible that the boy was capable of defeating him, and he could have decided to tie up instead as a sign of showing respect for his father. So he had a better idea; JBZ asked his son to accompany him to a friend and play a chess game with his friend. JBZ had indicated that his friend was a grand master. Junior was thrilled by this rare possibility to show off to his father.

Instead of waiting, Junior asked his father to play with his grand Master friend over the phone. JBZ had just heard about it but had not actually played any chess game over the phone or any blindfold game as it is popularly known.

In the one hour and thirty minutes that followed junior played three games with his father's friend, and it ended in a loss; they played two more games, and Junior lost them again. After that, Junior congratulated his opponent, but his rival was not happy stopping at that point. Junior sensed desperation in the old man's voice as he begged him to play another game, but to JBZ Junior, three straight losses were enough.

He placed the receiver down, and walked away. JBZ called his friend and enquired about the matches and was told the boy had lost three games in a roll; what JBZ could not understand, however was the fact that his friend was furious that his son had refused to play more games. After pressing Junior, it turns out that Junior had won two of the three games and that the old man had cheated, hence the frustration after JBZ refused to play more games.

JBZ's phone rang, picking it in an instant; he jumped out of his couch; he had been waiting for a call for the maiden trip of the first shipment of goods; it was an assortment of drugs to be introduced to the market. On the phone, however was an immigration officer who had called to inform JBZ that the renewal of his wife's permit was successful and that the processing of permanent residence was almost complete.

While leaving the Immigration office with his wife, JBZ received a call from one Manjinji, a man of few words and lethal intention almost all the time. JBZ's first test had come sooner than he anticipated. A consignment from South Africa, which had come by road, had been confiscated, not by the Police or Zimbabwe Revenue Authority but by the Big Dhara as he is affectionately known. His name was Manjinji.

Manjinji said, "Am I speaking to JBZ?"

JBZ snapped at him, "It depends on who the fucken hell you are and whatever you have to say, make it quick."

Not to be outdone, Manjinji retorted, "I have been warned of your arrogance and stupidity—"

Immediately JBZ interjected, "I do not have time for monkey games; what the hell does a piece of chicken shit like you want from me anyway?"

Soon after saying that, JBZ heard screaming that disturbed him, and in an instant, he knew that his men were in trouble, so he paused and then continued, "What do you want?"

With a dry laugh, Manjinji stared at the top of his spectacles, "I thought you were a tough son of a bitch; I did not know that you were going to give in so early. Honestly, I am disappointed that you had no fighting spirit in you; maybe you are just overrated. Anyway, I need USD 300k of $100 and $50 brand new non-sequential notes half each by the end of the business day (EBD)."

JBZ was stunned that his men had been captured, and the initial investigations indicated that there would be light or no resistance in the local market. Now, the word "light" needed to be given a new meaning in this context. Occurring in a manner it did, JBZ had to admit that he had underestimated the local Mafia.

JBZ made a few calls to three local banks that he had understanding with. He made a request for the ransom money. The banks needed to know the purpose of the money in keeping with the Know Your Customer requirements of the Bank or KYC in short in the banking circles.

Manjinji had given three hour timeline to JBZ to deliver the requested ransom, but JBZ had asked for 24 hours; the request was met with stiff resistance, with Manjinji promising an unspecified action if his demands were not met at his appointed time and in a Nigerian Movie style he had only said "we shall see" and in Africa that is a packed statement which is used to threaten, sometimes the threats are not be carried out, but when they are, they will be significant. It is, however, a serious offence to threaten someone with unspecified action, but this was a war of the underworld in which national laws and regulations do not apply. As he was processing the payment, he was fuming with anger. JBZ had operated in far more complex markets, coming out on top almost all the time and losing to a little-known guy in a third world troubled country did not sound well for him.

By 08:00 am the following day, JBZ received a parcel; in fact, it was left at his front door. His heart raced with his heart rate shooting to somewhere above 120 bits per minute. He was anxious, and his guess was that it had to be related to the Manjinji guy.

He rushed to open the parcel, and to his shock, there was a half-hand with all five fingers arranged in the box; the edges of the half-hand were uneven, suggesting it was cut with a blunt object, with the sole purpose of inflicting pain.

There was a note that read, "I took the liberty to cut one finger each hour that you delayed coming with the money; when I saw you were long coming, I got bored and decided to kill him, but I chose mercy and thought of cutting other fingers, but then that would have meant creating a dependent and a burden for society, so the goodness in me decided to cut the left hand instead. This is all on you JBZ, you could have avoided this sort of situation, but you are used to having things going your way, and here I am doing things your way; it looks like you are a man who likes it rough", "now who is the Chicken shit now?", "if you delay then what's coming will be equally on you.

JBZ immediately hid the parcel and called his colleagues; they met in the 20 minutes time at the Café DuShvile. Information regarding the three members that had been ambushed by Manjinji was shared; they had the exact location. Calls were made to the military connections, and the police and four hours later, the team was being briefed that a high-level national security threat was detected and that his name was Manjinji; their orders were to secure him and bring him alive.

At 03:00 am, the team moved into Manjinji's Beitbridge compound; the team moved swiftly and captured Manjinji, who was in the company of three-necked women supposedly keeping him company and giving him pleasure. Two of the three of JBZ's members were recovered alive; however, the leader who had his hand cut off had his head decapitated, and the head was again set to JBZ's house; they recovered a hacksaw in the room where the members were being held hostage, this tied in with the description that Manjinji had made in the initial letter sent together with the half hand. The team searched for drugs, but they never found them.

JBZ was not sure how to report such an innocent ten year innocent school boy failure; it was like a fatal mistake, a back rank mate. In his career, this had to be the most embarrassing moment of his life. Manjinji was to be killed, but somehow, one of the Police within the team voiced concern, stating that the man needed to be tried; JBZ was informed that Manjinji would be put to trial and sent to jail, after which JBZ would get a chance to be even.

At 8 pm that same night Manjinji's story was televised, the reporter who covered the story indicated that there were some people who wanted to frame him and that all the charges that had been brought before him were dropped, and he could be seen walking on the streets as a freeman, the state had no tangible evidence. At that point, JBZ realized that he was dealing with something big, something up there where the Popo hits the Lolo. JBZ thought about Military intelligence, where he had been taught that there was nothing such as a familiar face or coincidence. At that point, he concluded on one thing, that there was a mall in his team, and he was determined to fish it out.

Meanwhile, a consignment that had come through Malawi was successfully received, and all the distribution centers were activated. The main centers being Harare, Bulawayo, Zvishavane, Mutare, Chitungwiza, Bindura, Chipinge, Masvingo etc.

By 9 am on a Monday, the trials had started; the drugs under trial were in three main categories such as Cocaine, Heroin and Fentanyl.

Cocaine – a stimulant which became prominent in the United States in the 1970s. The white substance, which is distributed as a powder, killed 5070 people in 2011 alone, with this number rising to 5319 in 2013, topped 7324 in 2015 before soaring to 11316 deaths in 2016. By 2021, all drug deaths from overdose of various drugs peaked at 107,000 people. The use of Cocaine has increased in recent times; similar to Heroin, Cocaine releases a large amount of Dopamine in the brain, triggering a feeling of Euphoria upon use.

The abuse of cocaine can cause cardiac arrest, convulsions, stroke or death. Those that have used Cocaine have experienced a feeling of paranoia, excitability, extreme weight loss, anxiety as well as depression.

Cocaine is highly damaging to the body as well as the mind. The euphoric feeling it produces can create an emotional dependency for those that are battling depression and stress. It can make someone high and make a person temporarily forget their troubles and create a feeling of invincibility and life's cares and burdens. With unemployment at 80% in Zimbabwe, this is one of the reasons why the country has been the fastest-growing drug abuse zone. Once the sensations disappear, the person is left wanting more amounts, creating a pattern.

Heroin

A very addictive synthetic opioid, popular for its fast-acting properties. The morphine derivative origin are from poppy seeds like other opioids. The drug is commonly sold as a white powder; it, however, has other types, such as Heroin Black Tar known to be brown in color. In the United States of America street names of Heroin be like Big H, Black tar, Hell Dust and smoke and Thunder. These street names are to reflect the nature of Heroin one can find.

According to the CDC, Heroin killed 4454 people in 2011, with this number increasing to 15961 in 2016, a very worrying trend indeed. Heroin continues to be the leading killer for people struggling with substance abuse. The highest number of disorders have been reported to be caused by Heroin among those that abuse drugs. Some tend to mix Heroin with Cocaine or Methamphetamines and Fentanyl. This substance, this substance is very addictive and can be taken as a cigarette, snorted or injected. It affects the mind by producing intense euphoric sensations.

In the Heroin euphoric rush, addiction is easy, but quitting is extremely difficult, and withdrawal symptoms such as cravings and heavy extremities can cause some to continue to abuse Heroin.

Those that are suffering from overdose symptoms can experience bluish lips, shallow breathing, convulsions and coma.

Fentanyl- this drug is very powerful and is mostly used as a pain killer with 50 to 100 times the potency of Morphine and 50 times potency of Heroin. 18335 Fentanyl related deaths were reported by the CDC for the year 2016; this represented 28.8% deaths of all drug abuse-related issues.

The drug is highly addictive, and quitting could be very difficult without treatment. Even with treatment, some may fail to go through all the treatment process required.

Fentanyl is a powerful Opioid; it was once used in hospitals as a prescription drug. It can be used to treat severe pain and has been used as an anesthetic in the 1930s. It can be inhaled through the nose, it comes in tablet forms as well, and it can be synthetically manufactured as well; results are dangerous, such as analgesic that can be injected, snorted, swallowed or bottled on paper. Fentanyl is even more lethal when combined with other drugs such as Cocaine, Methamphetamines, and even Heroin.

JBZ rolled out a training program for distribution, measurement, handling, as well as customer service and product knowledge; this was considered crucial as part of the sales program.

The drugs were also targeting school boys and girls, especially those in the Rugby leagues. There was market intelligence obtained in the run-up to establishing a branch in Zimbabwe, and it revealed than many Rugby coaches wanted their boys to Bulk, but they did not have access to the strong staff that they needed to achieve the results they needed within the shortest possible period.

Chapter 6

It's a Friday night in the city of Harare; in recent times, the sunshine city, as it is popularly known, has seen a massive transformation in the area of entertainment, with places that were formerly preserved or built up for residential purposes being changed to business areas. It is exactly 17:45 pm, and JBZ's men are lined up on the strategic street corners in and around the city center. There are bars and Hotels dotted around where young girls and mature empowered men hang out. At Five Avenue shopping center a well-known place in the evil avenues' Sodom of the City of Harare, boys are lined up in the streets selling illegal sex stimulation drugs. The shopping Centre has five retain shops, three beauty spas, two main music areas and three bars that cater for various classes and ages through various genres. The Medicine Control Authority of Zimbabwe had been trying so hard to curb the infiltration of illicit drugs, but judging from the ever present traders, it appears that the regulator has lost the war against the highly organized gangs.

At 18:00 the games began, the drugs were being distributed in already filling up drinking places, and the revealers seemed to have heard the gossip that something new was on sale in town and were excited. At Five Avenue, a live band was planning, and prostitutes were already lined up. Along Fifth and Central Avenue, the ladies of the night had also signed up for distribution of the drugs, promising what was dubbed double pleasure of the flesh and the euphoric experience that the drugs would bring. The main drugs in the sale were mainly cocaine and heroin. The Golden girls along 7th street also joined in the new trade of the white euphoric money making substance and were clearly excited about the revenue mix and increased business that was anticipated due to the new drug, at least according to those that marketed the idea a day before.

In Places like Avondale, Central Town, the Blue Lagoon, Green croft, Pomona, Helensvale, Chisipite, drugs were being distributed discretely. Belgravia shopping Centre was taking care of the recently returned University of Zimbabwe who had been on a semester break and were now frequenting the place wearing negligees looking for companions of empowered men looking for a tight and narrow passage of pussy tender thighs and erect breast. By 19:00 pm, the supervisor reported that sales were going well as 5kgs of cocaine had been sold nationwide; this was considered to be a great start as this was achieved in a few hours. Sales were high in elite suburbs with house parties as well as houses converted into drinking places topping the list. These were small and secretive, normally gated, such as Three Home Gates in Borrowdale.

In Bulawayo, sales were going well, with places such as bars, brothels, hotels, universities, polytechs and shabeens topping the sales.

An elite school rugby tournament had been organized to take place in three months' time. The Coaches had been approached, and at least nine schools participated in the purchase of Heroin; this was achieved through their sports Directors sharing information for the team members to "bulk".

So there it was; the drugs had infiltrated the country, cities and villages, with places like Mutare, Masvingo and Beitbridge contributing their fair share of the revenue. At the three Home Gates, the party was going on forever, with party goers dancing one song after the other, spending two hours dancing nonstop, to the surprise of the DJ Manyama.

At 12 midnight, JBZ received another report that the product had topped 10kgs in sales; this was welcome news to JBZ. The Tech guy was instructed to use their system to record the sales by sales person, sales by place, city, and sales by product. This information would be analysed to determine future allocations. The Tech guy also employed data collection methods, which saw data such as the estimated average age of buyers and sellers to determine the age group with the most sales. Tech was also instructed to collect information regarding weekly sales, weekend sales, month-end sales, monthly, quarterly, and half-year and annual sales. This would then be used to determine trends and reorder levels.

At 00:30 Saturday, an ambulance was called to a hideout in the Avenues area; this was a makeshift drinking place which offered alcohol, drugs as well as sex. Four People were down, two men and two women, and they were seemingly unconscious. First to be called was the City of Harare ambulance, which responded, promising to send an emergency rescue in five minutes; when twenty minutes lapsed, they called MRA and Mars ambulance services; these were private operators who responded with swiftness, storming the coordinates within three minutes. The comparison of responses shows the extent of the collapse of service delivery in the county.

The EMRA ambulance team made an assessment, touching hands and the neck, checking for a pulse; they decided that one-two of the four would be taken in as the other two were not responding or rather did not have a pulse and in summary, were presumed dead and could not be helped. However, the crew advised them to take them to the hospital.

The EMRA ambulance took off at great speed; all this time, it had been idling, and its beacon was flashing as patients were being assessed, but when it took off, it left skid marks. As people were reacting, the Toyota Quantum ambulance siren screamed as it maneuvered into the third street before making a quick turn into Josiah Tongogara; the road had been named after one of Zimbabwe's Most decorated soldiers who commanded the guerrillas in the fight against independence, pitting Rhodesian army. At the corner of Montagu and Third Street, a swarm of ladies of the night were purposefully and strategically positioned with the young and the old making moves each time a car approached. The act may have been repeated for eternity to the extent that when the ambulance was approaching the intersection, ladies made their signature moves, swinging in a model-like catwalk and in the process, opening up their jackets, revealing the fine-creating that was waiting to be explored. But this time, the urgent business was to save lives.

The ambulance rushed to Parirenyatwa, turning into Old Mazowe Road at great speed and slowing down as it reached the gate of the once revered Group of Hospital. The gates were opened in a fashion exhibited in Clive Owen's King Arthur movie when gates to the north of the wall were opened by order of Bishop Jamanos in the final quest for Arthur and his Knights as they journeyed to rescue a very high-ranking family of importance to Rome, their orders were to secure their safety and return in particular with Alecto who as far as Bishop Jamanos could remember, god's favorite child and pupil who was destined to be a Bishop or Pope.

The ambulance sped through the gates, which were quickly closed as if to prevent enemies from entering a City in an ancient Greek style.

The driver sped straight to the outpatient, parking the car at the receiving bay, and the team retrieved the two patients. Upon lifting, they noted that the woman was heavier than before. A quick handover process was done, and the woman was taken to the resuscitation room, but after several attempts, she was pronounced dead on arrival; the police got to work to determine where the patient had been taken from, and the gentlemen who had accompanied the patients assisted in responding to some questions.

Meanwhile, temperatures and blood pressures for other patients were being taken; the guy was boiling, and blood pressure was high, averaging 220. The Doctor who attended to the patient requested a blood test, among several other tests. These tests could not be done at the facility, so the parents of the patient arrived, and they made arrangements for him to be taken to the Avenues University Hospital.

Upon arrival, the patient was tested for a number of things, including full blood count blood. The Patient was admitted to the intensive care unit at a cost of USD 3000 every three days. The collapse of the Public Health system caused a huge strain on the private healthcare system. The government of Zimbabwe had been accused of venturing into fruitless and wildcat spending while healthcare was falling apart. However, the government was steadfast in stating that the impact of economic sanctions made it difficult to invest in public health.

At the hospital, the patient was determined to be James Matare, but the man was struggling. Doctors who visited him at 05:00 were concerned about his condition as he had deteriorated rapidly. At 06:00 am, James' condition was assessed as critical but stable. A nurse was assigned to monitor him 24/7, and visitation was slashed to shit size with only two close family members being allowed at a time. At 09:00 routine visit, a meeting was held with the Lead Doctor for James to discuss the results of the tests. Doctor Willson Scott Tavonga explained that the patient had persistent high blood pressure, and the scan had revealed tinny blood clots. James had suffered a Brain Aneurysm; the doctor went on to explain that brain surgery was to be done within 24 hours. The doctor continued stating that the patient had what seemed to be traces of Cocaine and Heroin in their blood streams.

However, the samples had been taken for further analysis since it was their first time to deal with such properties. The affected part of James' brain was located at the bottom of the brain; this meant that the surgery was going to be a delicate process, the doctor continued. The lead doctor indicated that the process would not take less than 8 hours and went on to suggest an inch by inch, making sure that there were no errors. Unlike the first world, where such operations are now done using laser technology, this part of the world was a messy and bloody drilling process.

A meeting was proposed with the spouse of the patient, and upon learning that James was single, his mother and father were called to a meeting. In an African fashion, the meeting ended up being attended by six people; the term "close relatives" has a different meaning in Africa, where cousins are considered very close relatives. The lead doctor explained to the family that James had suffered a brain aneurysm. He went on to state that this developed through excessive consumption of drugs, which, based on the results of the test, and appeared to be Cocaine and Heroin. The doctor indicated that they had sent the samples for further analysis and independent opinion.

The doctor indicated that his heart was enlarged as well, indicating that he had lived with high blood pressure for some time. At that point, the relatives were stunned, with the mother bursting into tears and crying uncontrollably while the Father lifted his head up with a clenched fist and gritted teeth. The father managed to say, *"Zvakanaka Shumba munokunda rwisai semurume"* meaning it is well, Lion (his totem), you will overcome. Be brave like a man, he said as if James was there at the meeting.

The operation was scheduled to start at 3 pm after payments had been made; the procedure required USD4500 for the doctors, USD3500 for the doctors' team, and USD3300 for the anesthetics, and USD7, 000 for the hospital. The family struggled to raise the 50 % that was requested by the Hospital Accountant.

Meanwhile, post-mortem for the two victims who were pronounced dead by the EMRA and the woman who died on arrival at Parirenyatwa Hospital were all confirmed to have succumbed to excessive consumption of substances, which could be cocaine and Heroin based on description; the girls said that the drugs were new in the market.

At the Mutare General Hospital, three girls were fighting for their lives, admitting to have smoked a cigarette with a heavy white substance. The samples were sent to Harare for analysis as there was no functioning Lad at the Hospital. The tests were sent to a private facility to do the testing. The Doctors were waiting for the results and managed to stabilize the patients somehow.

At Plus Five Trauma Hospital in Harare, Mpilo, and UBH in Bulawayo, cases of patients brought in from parties either fully unconscious or in a Comma or dying at the party had been reported.

Three accidents occurred in Harare, with drivers sustaining critical head injuries; the police have recovered white substances as well as cigarettes at the scene of the accident.

The coming in of new drugs in the market had been a long-awaited development by those who complained of lack of variety in the market. The high unemployment rate and idleness created the longing for something strong to make the youth forget about their sorrows on a daily basis, and Cocaine and Heroin were doing exactly that. It created a pumba's *"hakuna matata"* the problem-free philosophy.

Back to the Hospital, a team of five doctors, 3 aids, three student doctors, medical pharmacists and anesthetics were having a meeting. The latest results were brought in, and discussion regarding the surgery stated that the Pharmacist and the Aesthetician raised concerns about the high blood pressure and the sugar level, which were both on the high side, as well as the general frailty of the patient, arguing that the patient may not manage to wake up. After much discussion, it was agreed that the patient should be monitored for the one hour that followed, and at exactly 8pm, the surgery commenced.

Hours before the operation, the doctor met the family and communicated that James was indeed very lucky to have survived; he indicated that the brain Aneurysm, also known as intracranial aneurysm, was a weakness in the Blood vessel in the brain that balloons and fills with blood. The greater cases of intracranial aneurysm occur between the underside of the brain and the skull. The aneurysm can leak or rupture, causing life-threatening bleeding internally. The treatment is usually based on the severity of the case. The treatment of a ruptured aneurysm includes careful control of the blood pressure, and a procedure can be administered as a preventative measure. In case of a ruptured aneurysm, then an immediate medical procedure is required.

During the procedure, James' family had been waiting with unabated breath; cigarettes were smoked, coffees were taken, and teas were brewed; stories were told as minutes seemed to tick slowly as relatives waited anxiously for news of the success of the procedure for their beloved James. At 04:30, the doctors came to see the family and proclaimed that the operation had been successful; only two relatives were allowed in. The mother and father came back rejoicing, but the father could not hold back his tears; this time, they were tears of joy, not sorrow or sadness.

Four days later, James' Blood pressure shot up. The doctors tried hydrochlorothiazide, amlodipine besylate, and inhibitor lisinopril, but none of it worked. The blood pressure remained high. The patient was constantly in pain despite a higher dosage of a powerful pain killer. After Investigations, they picked that there was too much alcohol in the system, and this increased metabolism and drugs were being flushed out through urine too early; this created a scenario where drugs could not have the intended impact. The doctor sought to flash out the alcohol, and Jet fuel was administered. Jet Fuel is named after its vibrant, luminous yellow color, and has been used for many years as an intravenous Vitamin Drip with various and extensive health benefits.

Jet Fuel contains a cocktail of all the B Vitamins, Magnesium and high doses of Vitamin C, suspended in either a small 200ml normal saline sachet (which is used as a general system booster and runs faster over about 20 minutes) or in a 1000ml mega-fuel also containing electrolytes and some glucose (this takes longer to run in, and is best used as a booster and hydrator before or after races or times of extreme exertion).

After administering the Jet Fuel, the Blood pressure went down to 40 and at some point during the night of the fifth day after the operation, the body experienced a major event. In the morning, James's relatives were informed of the worst news they had ever anticipated. James was not going to be able to walk again; he developed a major stroke due to high blood pressure; he also sustained damage to his brain and was going to always have jerky movements as the brain was not able to control some of his movement due to the damaged nervous system. His reasoning was, unfortunately, affected. And so it was, the man who grew up vibrant, a dreamer full of hope, was ruined by a cigarette of Heroin and Cocaine; what a loss, what a waste.

In the meantime, police were investigating cases of a suspected overdose of what seemed to be cocaine and Heroin. The doctors treating James had to report the matter to the police, and this was part of their ethical duty.

Chapter 7

The death toll stood at 10 people by Sunday end of day. In Murehwa, specifically at Murehwa Centre, a fight erupted in which Tino a 27 year old man had insulted his mom, and this caused a spectacle at the small growth point as the mother decided to retaliate in public causing a stir with business coming to a standstill.

Tino erupted, his voice sharp with disdain. "What kind of a silly girl are you?"

His mother, taken aback but firm, responded. *"Handipenge ini ndirimunhu akakwana.* I am not silly, and I am not a girl. I am your mother, and you need to treat me with respect."

Tino scoffed, his tone mocking. "Well, you look like a girl to me, and I will call you whatever I want."

His mother raised an eyebrow, a mix of frustration and astonishment in her voice. *"Wambo puteiko iye nhasi* (what did you smoke today)?"

Tino's retort was cutting. "Young lady, you are becoming a nuisance. Why don't you go home and do the dishes and cook for me?"

His mother's patience waned, her words laced with exasperation. *"Madhakwa ka mavakurotomoka* (you are drunk and have lost your mind)."

Tino's threat was met with defiance. *"Nhasi munotiza pamusha pano* (Today you will leave the homestead)."

His mother stood her ground, her resolve unyielding. "I will not be intimidated at my own homestead. I am not going anywhere, young boy. It's funny how you address me as a Young lady. I remember carrying you for nine months and the pain and agony I went through to raise you after your father deserted the family. You are such a disappointment to humanity."

Tino's anger flared, his tone menacing. "Play by my set of rules or else"

His mother's challenge was unwavering. "Or else what?"

With a dismissive wave of his hand, Tino retorted, "I have called the police."

His mother's frustration was palpable. "To do what? What crime have I committed now?" Her concern shifted to her son's well-being. "I think you need a doctor."

Tino's response was cold and cutting. "Young lady, you are the one who needs a doctor because you are sick."

The next thing Tino woke up at Murehwa District Hospital. He was hand cuffed. Tino was weak and powerless eyes were red and blood stained visibly. One wondered how he was even seeing. Tino could not remember what had happened to him or the scuttle he had had with his mother at the growth point.

A man in a Black suit was standing close to his bed. He was Honourable Matunzi, the member of Parliament for the area. He was informed about the incident and decided to see it first-hand. This incident was important to him as he was a member of the Parliamentary Committee on Health and Sanitation. The increase in cases of drug abuse and violence and deaths attributable to drugs had grown steadily and worryingly.

Right in the City of Harare, a base for drugs was set up. Young boys and girls were lured, promises of instant money and good life were enough to attract the Generation Z which strives on doing nothing other than being on Twitter, Instagram, SnapChat, Facebook and TikTok. The character of these *ama 2000* (2000s babies) was the same in America, Australia, Africa and other countries like Pakistan, Khuzestan, Uzbekistan. Tajikistan, Turkmenistan and all the STANS.

Girls were enticed from Glenview, Chitungwiza, DZ and Mabvuku mainly. What started as a drug distribution experiment created a downstream viable lucrative brothel business just like medicines by accidents. Viagra was created to cure hypertension and now it's a multi-billion dollar business curing erectile dysfunction.

It all started when the City of Harare condemned an entire block of flats in Jambare resulting in the immediate evacuation of all the occupants due to the imminent danger of collapse cited by the engineers. The plan was to destroy the building within two weeks' time, but then council being council with all the bureaucratic and incompetence, nothing was ever done, and no one asked why as the City Fathers fell into slumber land while the city was falling apart. So, there it was, the Storm was brewing. The six floors on the abandoned flat has 50 rooms, an amazing open place just like in the movie Hotel for Dogs directed by the German Director Thor Freudenthal.

Initially JBZ was skeptical about the set up as Jambare was a dirty and unpleasantly smelly place and for that JBZ's doubts were justified. Neglected Garbage could be seen pilling up with no viable plan from the authorities. JBZ reluctantly agreed to the pilot project especially after the initial cash flow projections revealed that one girl could serve 20 people per day at USD 100 per client, this translated to USD 2000 cash per girl per day and with 50 girls targeted, USD 100,00 would be raised per day amounting to USD 3million per month. Certainly, Numbers don't lie. JBZ was not emotionally connected to the work he did, the use of the word "project" was selected as if there were no human beings being violated in the process.

One of the hurdles they had to pass through was the Jambare Police station which was a stone's throw away. Thanks again to poor salaries and terrible working conditions of service as well as the set up at the top where corruption was systematic and entrenched into the operations.

The Police force was effective, but the corrupt cultivating behavior saw middle and junior ranked officers taking part in the process. Corruption was being rewarded instead of being punished. The number of clean officers in the force was like a spit in the wind. So, there it was, a deal was struck between the Jambare Police and JBZ's men. It was a very simple deal the police were supposed to merely turn a blind eye to the operations and inform JBZ's men whenever danger was coming their way especially when the anti-drug teams were being dispatched. In return JBZ was generous with money, bottomless beer as well as groceries among other feather beddings. The deal was sealed, the member in Charge briefed his men that any matter relating to drugs and sex offences was to be directed to the member in charge the moment it is received with not further delay.

#

Josephine left Chitungwiza at 4am every day to look for her missing daughter. She had been looking for her daughter for the past three weeks. A police report had been made with a missing person poster pasted on walls. News on radio and TV was awash with the matter. After three weeks of no clues, a girl from the neighborhood knocked at the door, she was 14 years old, looking drunk and weak. She narrated her ordeal at the Jambare camp. She narrated that she was introduced to the Jambare flats where Young boys and girls were making money and living an independent life. She continued highlighting that initially they would get money to pack some drugs and then go home. They were warned never to speak about it to anyone. The girls would sleep at the flat if they knocked off late and security was provided for them.

One day girls were screened with all the young and beautiful girls being escorted to the new packing floor within the same flat. The wing was newly spruced up and girls were moved in there and she was one of them. Unlike the packing rooms where packing was being done in an open space, here there were small single beds, the type that one is given at the mine meant for one to sleep overnight with no extra comfort whatsoever. The girls were given some drugs and tied to the beds. That night all virgins were violated and were asked to bathe under guard. The rape had nothing to do with desire for pleasure but to ensure that come the following day no client would struggle to penetrate as the girls were to service a certain number of clients per day. The following day men lined up paying USD 100 to sleep with any girl that was free.

As the girl narrated her story, Josephine was cut to the heart like the congregation that Peter was preaching to in Acts Chapter 2 verses 36 to 37. The girl explained to Josephine that her daughter was there and that she was one of the most preferred ones and that she was serving more clients over and above being abused by the ones managing the brothel. Josephine was emotional when she heard this, she started sobbing uncontrollably like a little girl, she tried to imagine what was happening to her beautiful girl who had won all the 16 beauty competitions she had participated in. It was difficult to accept that her daughter was being put through such an experience in her own country. She used to read that in the news and hear of Albanians and other Asian countries where girls would be taken into sex slavery as portrayed in movies such as Taken first released in 2008 followed by Taken 2 and 3.

Now it was no longer in the movies, she was the mother of a girl being abused physically by men she does not know at least 20 times men with no protection ceased her and raped her thrusting into her helpless body and dumping semen and leave. One after another they came through with no time to wash or eat, all along she was tied to the bed and undressed, no fore play no caressing or touching to allow lubrication of her virginal muscles, she screamed in agony of the dry entry but there was no one to help. It seemed, the more she screamed the more the men thought she was enjoying, mistaking screams of pain and agony for pleasure.

The girl was being reaped apart, torn apart, she was being destroyed each and every day. More drugs were administered on her and not much time was allowed to rest or recuperate. The fact that she was young should have made men to feel pity for her, but it created an opposite reaction. All men wanted underage girls. Josephine's wished to die, the treatment she received made her lose her mind and lost any dignity left in her.

The following date Josephine arrived at the Jambare Police station at 05:22am reporting what she had been told by the girl who had escaped. Josephine was tall and Beautiful late thirties woman who could easily compete in a beauty contest with 18 year olds. She demanded to be taken to the Flat to look for her Daughter but the Police knowing the protocol, they delayed for 30 straight minutes. Meanwhile the officer in charge was informed and operations at the flat were swiftly moved with all the girls being moved out and whisked away.

The beds were heaped in a disorderly manner to give the impression that there was no life at the flat. When Josephine arrived at the flat, she carefully examined the place from floor to floor and did not see anyone, she told the police that the warmth in some of the floors suggested that there were people staying there who could have been tipped off. She demanded answers and threatened to expose the entire Police station if their daughter was not found within 24 hours.

Around midnight Josephine was called by the Jambare Police Station to inform her that her daughter had been found. Josephine wasted no time, she arrived at the station within 20 minutes for a journey that takes 45 minutes. When she got to the police station, she immediately demanded to see her daughter, the officer in charge wanted to counsel her before showing her but she could not agree to that. The door opened and a tiny, wasted girl in tattered clothes with multiple cigarette burns and what looked like a swollen face. She struggled to identify her as her daughter. She almost denied her, but she saw a peculiar wart on the girl's left ear. She fainted.

Josephine was shocked with what she was seeing. Her once vibrant girl was pale and speaking with a husky voice. Josephine then moved towards Gloria, her eyes filled with tears of relief and concern. "Thank God, I have found you, my babe! Where have you been? Who did this to you? Tell me, baby."

Gloria's response was harsh, her demeanor cold and distant. "What the fuck do you want bitch, if you want to fuck do it quick, do not waste my time, I have a long queue to clear. My pussy runs around the clock so get your dick, so we get over and done with it, you look like a two minute mother fucker anyway."

Josephine's heart sank at her daughter's words. "I am your mother, and I have come here to take you home."

Gloria's tone turned defensive. "Get something clear here, bitch, we fuck here no takeaways here. So, you are a lesbian bitch hey, I have fucked three and I can tell you they are better off getting a dick, they are going to waste fucking their pussy on another. I advise you to get a dick in your life."

Confusion clouded Josephine's expression. "What are you talking about, Gloria? I am your mother."

Gloria's response was a painful revelation. "I have no parents. They died in the war, and I was dumped by the roadside. I was picked up by a good Samaritan, and they are now my family. Please go wherever you came from; I am not your daughter."

Josephine's world shattered at Gloria's words. She sobbed at the sight of her daughter, unable to comprehend the reality before her. She had the guilt of failing to protect her daughter from the passions of the world and now she was facing the consequences of not instilling principles of hard work and dignity. She somehow believe that had she taught her well, she would not have fallen victim to drug dealers. She was full of regret and wished she had been a better parent. She told her that she wanted to take her home.

Gloria remained resolute, accusing Josephine of attempting to kidnap her. "Take me home, my ass. I am no fool. You want to kidnap me."

Josephine reached out to her daughter, her voice trembling with emotion. "We will get you some help, my baby."

She immediately resisted the charm and attempted to run away but the rope used to tie her stopped her, she fell face down, bleeding instantly. She was a mess. Gloria was taken to a hospital whereupon her case was treated as an emergency. Josephine wanted to press charges, but the police just indicated that Gloria was found in a pit meaning the only witness is the person who made the discovery.

At the hospital the doctors performed full blood count and many other tests and after four hours it was time to get an official report. Three doctors emerged from a swinging double door. Dr Ginya was the first to speak.

"I am Dr Ginya the gynecologist you are already aware the circumstances surrounding Gloria's health. I am here to report to you that Gloria is pregnant. I am so sorry. Our assessment shows lacerations on her female organs, she has suffered significant damage, her body was not yet fully developed to withstand the level of sexual activity she was put through, and we believe that she was raped several times in a day. She will need surgery. Given the pregnancy, we have also tested her to determine the safety of the child and that of the mother, ordinarily these results cannot be disclosed but given Gloria's state, we are having to inform you so that you are aware when taking care or her."

The doctor paused, then continued saying that the mother was in danger as she had developed a strong Sexually Transmitted Infection (STI), and given that she was pregnant, management of the disease would be delicate and most likely to affect the baby. She had lost a lot of blood. The doctor continued to state that Gloria's immune system was weak, test results revealed that she was HIV positive, and she would have to be treated immediately.

Second to present was Doctor Sean Desmond Martin. He introduced himself as a physiatrist. At that point, Josephine was praying in her heart, but the doctor immediately stopped talking, the prayers became loud, and the doctor allowed her time to finish. After two minutes she stopped praying.

Dr. Sean went on to state that according to the assessment they had done, Gloria was going to need a lot of counseling and when he realized that the family was not getting it, he told them that Gloria was now mentally ill, and that the family had an option to admit her into a facility where she could receive help.

Despite Gloria's various conditions the doctor's had assessed and diagnosed, Gloria did not die from any of them. A postmortem was performed, and the results collected indicated that she had traces of various drugs such as heroin, cocaine, fentanyl and methamphetamine. At times a cocktail would be formulated, and these girls would be injected before they had sexual encounters with men at the brothel.

However, the drugs were not the cause of her untimely death. Gloria had to be poisoned in a way that would not expose the JBZ's team, she was already a witness of drug abuse and prostitution besides the girl from the neighborhood. Gloria was a loose end which had to be tied before going to bed. Among the traces of drugs found in Gloria there was a fifth chemical trace known as Strychnine, which is a poisonous drug which if given in high doses it leads to an untimely death once exposed. At the hospital, JBZ had one of his team members watching the developments, giving update on a real time basis as events were unfolding, and this person was personified as a female nurse. She was giving JBZ information regarding Gloria's state and the investigations at the hospital.

The moment Gloria was left alone on the ward bed, this was the nurse's chance to eliminate Gloria. The nurse had a syringe which contained some unknown solution of which she then administered into Gloria's vein and immediately vanished away into thin air. This occurrence exposed the lapse of security and the carelessness that hospitals sometime expose patience to. Stories of babies missing soon after birth were a common occurrence in many of the hospitals. There were even stories of babies being swapped, especially when a mother gives birth to a deformed child.

Within a time space of 15 minutes, Gloria had experienced a respiratory failure which led to death. A nurse on duty walked to Gloria's bed 8 minutes later to find her body not responding, with froth on her mouth. Immediately one of the doctors on duty was called and pronounced her dead.

It was difficult to mourn Gloria without thinking about the pain and agony that she experienced in all the process of being kidnapped, introduction to drugs and cases of forced sexual intercourse and other worse things.

Chapter 8

Simon had spent six months in a facility fighting his way through, the use of drugs had gotten the better part of him and each day he had confessions and positive reinforcements to the fact that he would leave the life of addiction and drinking.

A local Pastor visited and prayed for him twenty two times while his Pastor visited him at least three times a month. He had a solid support system and there was no doubt in the mind of the team of doctors, counselors and co-addicts that Simon would be a success story. He was booked for an interview on national television during the week he was released from hospital. The scene was palpable and his piousness was so real that even the interviewer was left with no doubt that the man had repented and convinced that he would never return to consuming beer or drugs again in his life. Many addicts called in and asked a lot of questions on how to overcome the addictions. Simon was able to respond to the question with ease and with no emotional attachment, making it clear that he was speaking from the bottom of his heart.

Three days went by, it was time for Simon to leave the facility for good. He knelt down and prayed to God and thanked all the team of experts that had assisted him in his quest for rehabilitation. When he walked out, he started meditating on how he had overcome the addictions.

He was picked up by Aunty Cecilia who was so excited to see a changed man he had become. They passed through a shopping mall to pick up supplies. Simon went to the bathroom and on his way back he lost his bearing, he ended up in a bar accidentally and there were cheers. While he was still trying to figure out what had happened a mug of beer was placed right in front of him with the bar man exclaiming, "It's on the house buddy, it's my birthday today and the guy over there is treating everyone".

He looked at the mug full of beer and instantly remembers the teachings and the positive reinforcements as well as the many prayers and visitations by the priest, the radio and television interviews he had given. While doing so, small bubbles started popping out at the middle while the edge frothed with a whispering sound like that of carbonated beverages. The glass became moist outside and his throat became dry but still he resisted the drink in front of him. In an instant the mug started tearing small cold tears from top going slowly to the bottom of the mug, Simon was shaking and there were two voices fighting in his mind one was so vocal asking him to partake of the rare gift while the other reminded him of how far he had gone.

He finally said, "What can one mug change in the history of a man's life," and so it was. He grabbed the mug and lifted it clicking cheers with fellas nearby and it was bottom up and back to drinking ways. What a waste of time and effort.

Chapter 9

The number of drug related violent cases had reached 50 nationwide and still more were being recorded and, in those cases, at least 15 people had died and 20 had sustained various degree of injury. Meanwhile the number of number of cases for overdose of drugs had topped 25 nationwide as per reported numbers with actual numbers expected to be more.

The police commissioner was concerned about the increase in cases of drug related violence and deaths. The streets were increasingly becoming a battle ground with turf wars becoming common place between gangs selling drugs. The police had received Intel that a man named JBZ was part of a drug cartel and was the main man in charge of the Zimbabwean market. His teams were considered highly efficient in their distribution and selling of drugs. JBZ was everywhere yet nowhere, the man had his influence, power and fear in all street corners, but he was a ghost. No one in the police force had ever seen him or at least spoken to someone who knows his personally, yet his name was spoken of in the underworld.

There was no evidence against him or anything that could link him to the drugs yet each time the drug business was discussed his name would always pop up. JBZ had an 8 to 5 job, he was a family man who would go home straight after work. According to the police team he had been assigned to look for information under cover for two weeks and hence was entitled to some rest. The community loved him. They found nothing sinister about his movements. Neighbours were interviewed by the police discretely as part of the investigation and accused the police of wasting taxpayer's money on the wrong man instead of fighting crime and real criminals as part of their responses. The neighbors described him as a family man who took time to be with his family and a man who actually preaches the word and works with youth counselling them against drugs and bad behavior. What the police was looking for did not fit the description. There were even claims within the police service that JBZ was a myth that the government had created in order to frame someone for something that was about to go wrong where a culprit was to be blamed to appease the masses.

#

It was a lazy day, detective Mike was out for a picnic with his girlfriend Lisa. They had come with a brown rug and laid on top was a checked new blanket. The spot they selected was circled by Mopani and other trees shielding them from the sun in what seemed to have been a seal of approval for the two love birds. Mike was wearing khaki shorts revealing his hairy thighs that often sent Lisa crazy each time she set her eyes on them, and she was so fond of them. She loved to gently rub the thighs and feel the small, coiled hair making a tiny bumpy feeling.

Detective Mike had a scar on the left thigh and another one on top of the right thigh. He had sustained these injuries in the DRC and the other one in the Darfur region war respectively. Mike was wearing soft rubber heal shoes that allowed him to climb the rocky Matopos.

Detective Mike was the born in a family of 5, his father was a peasant farmer throughout his entire life sustaining his family and sending them to school. Mike lost his parents during the liberation struggle. His father and mother were accused as sellouts and for this they were beaten and buried alive in a brutal show of force and bid by the guerrilla fighters to create real examples of what would happen to anyone who would sympathize with the Rhodesian army.

The allegations were said to be false, it was an act of jealousy taken too far but once accused of such a crime then the die was pretty much cast and only death could save you from the fear. At that time mike was still very young but till today he has a vivid recollection of how his parents were killed and this has created a string desire to make protect the civilians, Mike had a higher purpose for joining the military.

Detective Mike and Lisa were enjoying the moment. Lisa was wearing a yellow dress with bulky side pockets and large buttons. For Detective Mike between him and Lisa's perfect body were giant easy buttons. But the barrier was in Mike's head, he was a fine detective and ex-soldier, but he was a shy one.

Earlier on Detective Mike had visited Pomongwe Cave, a site believed to be the cave that the Great Chaminuka Mufemberi used to hide on his way to Nyamandlovu. The cave had been officially opened on 1 July 1994 by Honourable Vice President Comrade S.V. Muzenda MP. Before visiting the cave, a tour guide had offered them a lecture about the area and the rock paintings that were done by the now extinct San people. The San were hunters and gatherers and were driven off their land when war broke out between the Bantu and the San. The San people are believed to have used inferior weapons made of wood while the Bantu had improved technology ahead of the San.

In Ancient history, the place is believed to have been home to elephants, lions, and cheetahs. However, Elephants have migrated so are the lions though it is said that from time to times elephants visit the area after every two years to show their calf their history and where they used to live many years ago. The place is now home to one cheetah per square kilometer as well as the notoriously poisonous black mamba whose venom can kill a herd of elephants in a matter of minutes. The small head 2 to 2.5 meter long average weight snake is grey in color with a lighter lower part. This grey serpent which is black inside of its mouth can grow to 4.3 meters long. The serpent loves to stay in rocky areas and its main food is mainly young ones of the Rock Rabbit.

After the lecture they proceeded to the cave and immediately left the place after viewing the picket fence protected national heritage. Detective Mike drove his Toyota Mark X to Matopos specifically the place where the "Sun, Steel and Spray" dreamer was buried. Detective Mike paid USD 4 each to access the rich history cast in stones on top of the mountain.

At the reception, great men were frozen in history hung on the wall in form of images and folk tales. These were indeed great men according to the history of the white minority and to blacks there could be many other names to describe them given the acrimonious relationship that existed between the blacks and the whites which led to enslavement of the black majority, the driving of the Blacks from their ancestral land. There had been a raging debate where whites contends that they have developed the country and so their invasion was to be seen as god sent while the blacks disagree with the assertion. This debate is a chicken and egg or better still it can be likened to Bruce Lee versus Jack Chan in the karate circles.

First of the great men was Sir Charles Patrice John Coghlan who was born on the 24th of June 1863 and died on the 28th of August in 1927. Coghlan studied Law and met Rhodes in Kimberly in 1882. He always detested the power of the big business and would clash with

Rhodes and later on with representatives of the British South Africa Company (BSAC). Coghlan arrived in Bulawayo in 1900 founding the Law firm Coghlan and Welsh. He was later involved in politics and was appointed the first Premier of Southern Rhodesia in April 1924. Without Coghlan's courage and dedication in the cause of self –government, Southern Rhodesia could have been a fifth province of South Africa and there would be no independent nation of Zimbabwe. Coghlan was a Catholic, he was buried in Bulawayo, but his fellowmen petitioned that he be reburied alongside Rhodes and Jamerson. This matter was settled and achieved after parliamentary debate and on the declaration of a sacred Catholic area on the Hill.

Second on the list of brave men was Sir Leander Starr Jamerson who was born on the 9th of February 1853 and died on the 26th day of November 1917. Jamerson had met Rhodes in 1878 and they became lifetime friends. He was Rhodes' right hand man in the occupation of Rhodesia (Zimbabwe).

In December 1895 Jamerson led the ill-fated invasion of the Transvaal named the Jamerson Raid. Killing 17 men with 55 wounded and 35 missing. This embarrassment led to Rhodes resigning as the Cape Prime Minister and Jamerson became Prime Minister to the Cape Colony from 1904 to 1908. He died in the United Kingdom in 1917 and was reburied on the 18th of May 1920 at the "View of the World" in Matopos Hills, the delay in his burial was due to World War One.

Allan Wilson was third on the list of frozen brave men hanging on the wall of fame at the Matopos reception. A military patrol was dispatched to capture King Lobengula who had fled north. In seeking to capture him, a patrol numbering 34 Men led by Majors Allan Wilson and Henry Brown were killed by the Matabele warriors on the 4th of December 1893 at the Battle of PUPU on the Shangani River North of Lupane.

Right at the middle a wooden frame was hang on the wall with the first line of the contents written "Summary of the life of CECIL JOHN RHODES."

Rhodes was born in England at Bishops' Stratford England in 1853. He relocated to Africa for health reasons, joining his brother Herbert in Natal. In 1871 Rhodes visited diamond digging at Kimberly, Northern Cape. He later enrolled at Oxford University in

1873. By 1890 he became the Prime Minister of the Cape Colony, later he occupied Matabele (now Matabeleland province in Zimbabwe) in 1893.

Rhodes resigned from Prime Minister of Cape Colony in 1896, he made peace with the Matabele people at Indabas in Matopos Hills and chose his burial place.

Rhodes received a Doctorate of Common Law from the oxford university in 1899 and died in 1902 in his cottage at Muizenberg, Cape Town on the 26th of March. Rhodes had left the following wish "I admire the grandeur and loneliness of the Matopos in Rhodesia and therefore I desire to be buried in Rhodesia on the hill which I used to visit and which I called "the view of the world" in a squire to be cut in the rock on top of the hill, covered with a plain brass plate with these words thereon", "there lie the remains of Cecil John Rhodes."

After that lecture, Detective Mike and Lisa proceeded uphill to see the grave of Rhodes, Jameson, as well as the mausoleum where Allan Wilson and his men where presumably buried with names engraved, four faces of the Mausoleum had names of Allan Wilson and his brave men.

Back to the picnic they were both tired and retrieving their picnic basket they removed their shoes picked up some snacks from the basket. Detective Mike was talking to Lisa face to face or *uso kwa uso* in Swahili. He was gently touching her and the face to face talk and the attention that she was getting had a desired effect on her. She was responding with her body becoming powerless and surrendering to Mike, who continued to tell her how much he loved her and that she was the most beautiful woman in the world. Mike kept moving his hand and this time he was caressing the thighs and from time to time venturing to the upper part squeezing the waist folds gently and briefly touching the velvet.

He continued to talk to her looking at her directly into her eyes, mike continued to talk to her but it was clear she was no longer listening to him but she cherished every word he spoke and the touch brought a sensation that rushed through the spine and producing electric shocks that griped the head. Lisa was tongue-tied as Detective Mike continued to speak to her. Her breasts were erect, and she held on to his waist and quickly directed his left hand to hold her tight. Mike became aroused and Lisa could feel him even with clothes on.

Mike was holding her by the waist the big buttons had been opened Lisa was wearing bra and an underwear she wiggled with pleasure as Mike kissed her and holding her and squeezing her tight at that time she reached to his short, opened the zip and in one motion brought out his manhood she rolled on top of him and pushed her underwear aside, holding his manhood firmly she trusted it inside her producing as sound that could have raised alarm but people were minding their own business, she was working on him going up and down before Mike rolled and going on top of her, pumping slowly and gradually increasing the tempo looking directly into Lisa's eyes and telling her how beautiful she was, it went on till there was a sudden wind that lifted them up in the air, they were up in the heavens feeling light and crying with joy and in an instant they came falling down to earth and were all totally spent.

Then Mike attempted to pull out to get some juice, but Lisa resisted and urged him to stay inside. She wanted to be touched but Mike was in another world altogether. In fact he was thinking of going but Lisa was insistent.

Lisa whispered, "You screw like a demon."

"I have been told," Mike whispered back.

"I have never had a man holding me and making love to me like that."

"Then things are about to change."

"You keep saying that, but you are not committing to a clear plan of marriage, I am not getting younger, I need more children, matter of fact I need four more children."

Mike was taken aback, "Four children, that's a lot honey."

"Well, well, well come and see, come and see a soldier is scared to start a family," Lisa chuckled softly.

Mike kissed her forehead. "I accept the challenge."

Mike started kissing Lisa as if to embark on the new challenge right away, Lisa took it lightly but soon Lisa could not resist the touch and the kissing, Mike was back inside her. This time Lisa was doing the talking telling him how it was sweeter and nicer, and those words of encouragement made Mike stronger and firmer and Lisa responded with loud moans that Mike had to kiss her in order not to raise alarm. They went on it for some time with Lisa telling him that she was sure she had conceived and Mike becoming firmer with this encouraging sentiment till they both ran out of steam and rested. They fell asleep for two hours, they were awakened by Mike's phone. Mike yelled, "Hello who the hell is this I am on vaca—"

A firm and authoritative voice came on the phone, it was Senior Inspector Thomas G Mawire. " I am goddam Senior Inspector Mawire, I have a situation here we need your combined military and police skills here, there is a helicopter leaving in 1 hour for Harare, its headed to Manyame Airbase and you are to be in it. Don't be late."

Mike was blunt as he squeezed Lisa's hand, gazing at her. "On condition that Lisa comes with us—"

"Negative," interrupted Inspector Mawire.

"Then hold on," Mike responded.

The Inspector was holding on to the phone and he heard everything, Mike started by clearing his throat and said, "Lisa I have known you for some time now and I would want to come back home to you, I want to wake you up in the middle of the night and kiss you, I want to hold you in my arms every night, I love you."

He pulled a small box and knelt down, lifting the   ring said, "Will you marry me?" Mike was not aware that other people had gathered the time he started talking.

Lisa kept quiet for thirty seconds, she then burst into tears and said yes three times.

Inspector cleared his throat and said, "Well done, now the Chopper is small get on the Fast Jest leaving in 2 hours' time. You will be staying at the military barracks. You are to report to Major General Israel Phiri. He is head of Military Intelligence, he is the Vice Chair and Joint Chiefs of National Security and International Cooperation. Be there by 08:45, he will be waiting for you. One more thing, take care of Lisa, it's an order."

Mike saluted and responded with a "Yes Sir."

Chapter 10

As birds sang the dawn chorus, another disruptive sound ruffled the morning air. The sound grew louder as the trees became taller and close-knit. The first rays of sunrise painted the sky with soft hues of orange and pink, leaving a beautiful backdrop behind JBZ's Aston Martin Vanquish. He had several fleets of luxury and low-end cars. They all served specific purposes. He was that organised. This Vanquish was one of the once-in-a-blue moon cars that he drove, along with his vintage Jaguar MK7 and a 1980 Mazda 323. The latter was his first car, so he held it with sentimental value. It was his from dust to grass story. Today, he found himself on the road so early the dew wasn't yet forming. It was so still that only birds and JBZ's roaring Aston Martin Vanquish pierced the serenity. His sleek matte Vanquish sliced through the quiet streets with an occasional Jacaranda leaf or two falling on the car. JBZ. Behind the wheel, JBZ, the notorious drug lord with an apparent heart of gold, gripped the leather-clad steering wheel with knuckled intensity. His veins stuck out as he grabbed the steering, whilst his face looked straight ahead. Soft undertones of Joe Cocker's With a Little Help from My Friends echoed. If it wasn't for the time of day, JBZ would have put this song on maximum volume. For those who knew him, low volume meant he was either troubled or thrilled. With a raucous personality like his, it was a common sentiment that he was always thrilled, never depressed.

This morning, he seemed rather unusual and off-tempo. He dropped with both hands in their recommended 10 to 2 position while observing all traffic rules to the tee. He focused so hard on his driving one would assume he was in a driving test. He also tended to tap his fingers as he drove, but today, he was like a good student. He looked into the distance as he drove as if making sure he missed nothing on the road ahead. It was his custom to shuffle his playlist and never repeat any song. However, the Joe Cocker song was on repeat. While he maintained a straight face, repeating this song meant he was enjoying listening to this soothing soul music. His lyrical taste ranged from hip-hop to afro-jazz and rock. Today was a smooth sailing morning with crooning music, unlike JBZ.

All the thirty minutes that JBZ drove, his phone rang six times. He sulked at each missed call. That was, in any case, too early to phone anyone unless it was a wife or husband missing each other while away from each other. Otherwise, it was also a good time to chase after debtors since they would still be dazed from sleep and answer the phone on impulse. JBZ continued driving without checking his phone, something he did every now and then. His phone was so important in his business that his son once complained that he loved it more than him. Although this infuriated JBZ, it hurt him that his boy had spoken the utter truth. In another fight with his son, he said, "If I have to save either my phone or you, I'd take my iPhone. Let you rot, and then I'd smoke some pot." Even his employees knew too well how crucial his phone was. In the event that JBZ's phone wasn't reachable and it was urgent, his business partners knew by default they would phone Roselyn. For all community-related services, his right-hand man was the go-to person. Those two handled almost any situation equally well. There are a few incidents where they ended up either losing deals, being fined or shortchanged. It didn't bother their boss to have these kinds of mishaps because he ultimately had his by hook or crook. One such incident was the Manjinji scenario.

JBZ was startled when a car making a U-turn hooted. He honked back, not fully aware of who it was. He only caught a glimpse of what seemed to be a woman's arm adorned with a wave of black, clanky bangles and oversized sunglasses. Her teeth looked like they could glow in the dark. A smile beamed from the corner of her right lip. JBZ slowed down while opening the remote-controlled towering two-metre gate. It was his practice to reduce speed but not come to a complete halt at the gates for security reasons. Even the sharks he dealt with were familiar with that habit. His mate, a black Aston Martin, rolled into the long, winding driveway. There was no house in sight for about thirty metres. Along the way, he had practised his opening lines, which he would say after ascending the three steps to the front door and ringing the doorbell

At last, the Vanquish pulled up to a charming, grey house nestled under a canopy of ancient indigenous trees. JBZ stepped out, his custom-tailored trousers accentuating his imposing presence. A frail woman with her hands on her sides stood at the garage entrance, blocking him from proceeding to park. She looked pale like a ghost and as if she would collapse at any second.

She cleared her throat and spat. JBZ clenched his fists on instinct for a split second. He hated anyone who spat in his presence. That's also the reason he stopped watching soccer. He claimed only he could spit whenever, wherever and at whoever. He went a step further; he enjoyed spitting on unruly subordinates. They complained in their small chats until they became resigned to their boss's rascal behaviour.

Staring at him, she said, "What brings you to Rolfe Valley?"

He dropped a tear.

Chapter 11

The hair on the back of Nobesuthu's neck stood on end. Beads of sweat formed on her nose and eyebrows. She flared her nostrils as fumes escaped from her nose. She breathed heavily, tapping her legs. While her visitor, JBZ, still sobbing, stepped a few steps back, almost treading on his other foot, she raised her eyebrows, frowned, sulked, folded her bonny arms and looked aside. For the first time in decades, since the days he proclaimed himself king of the streets, JBZ was humiliated, belittled and diminished to a nonentity. He was weakened, cheapened and stripped of all his street glory in seconds by an armed, frail woman whose collar bone made holes in her shoulders so deep they could hold spoonfuls of water. She moved to the side of the garage for support as her legs couldn't carry her for long. Nevertheless, her stern demeanour grew stronger as she scowled, waiting for an answer from this sorry excuse of a human being intruding on her space and breaking the chatter of the birds in her home. She often enjoyed early mornings listening to birds singing and watching daybreak with the sun rays glistening through the foliage in her tree-studded home. If the day darted like this, its progression would be interesting. He was used to a life where he dominated the conversation, popping champagne on yachts with beauties scantily dressed swarming around him, calling shots even with international dignitaries. But here he stood, powerless, arms hanging listlessly on his sides. No gun in sight or hand. This woman exuded so much power on him it drained all his energies. He looked like a puppy, except this puppy wasn't waging its tail to play. The streets respected him because he ruled them, not this pale, petite woman in her body-hugging black joggers and a black tee. Whether she had just returned from a jog or not, there was no sweat to show for it on her tee. Her composure was of someone who had long anticipated this very moment. A memorable moment of undressing this ruthless man in front of her. She clenched her fingers to prevent herself from perhaps spurting something that she would regret. The outline of her t-shirt showed her laboured breathing, with her chest falling up and down.

After a palpable silence of sixty seconds, JBZ wiped a tear. He had last cried when he was eight years old after he fell off a mountain bike he had stolen from his neighbour's gate. The bicycle was too high and long for him to handle, so he lost both balance and control of the handles. He broke his arm then. He cried because he was stuck under the heavy weight of the bike and felt helpless to free himself. Being a kid, he fully recovered within a mere four weeks and had the plaster cast off. He vowed never to place himself in a situation where he became so vulnerable, he was unarmoured. The bicycle and the plaster both symbolised his loss of power in those moments. That irritated him, which also contributed to establishing his criminal empire. He stole the bike not to keep it but to ride and return it. His parents couldn't afford even a small second-hand bicycle for him. He accepted his fate, but that wasn't going to be his fate. He acknowledged that his parents provided the best they could for all their children with no partiality. He vowed to give shower them with a luxurious old age. He targeted his anger and dissatisfaction with life in the universe.

He forced a smile through clenched teeth. The ten minutes they stood seemed like an eternity. JBZ stepped forward, hesitated, took a step back and turned to look behind as if in search of an Invisible Hand to propel him forward. With arms outstretched, his lips slowly curled and opened to reveal a gold tooth. Even his eyes beamed.

"Nono, I need you."

She rolled her bulging eyes, which enhanced her oval face. JBZ shortened her name to Nono as an endearment. That was once upon a time.

Seeing that no reply came, he continued, "Forgive me."

"Jonathan," she murmured his name, her voice barely audible. The air grew heavy with unspoken words as they stared at each other.

She made another sotto voce utterance in her native Ndebele language. An insult that was popular in her hometown of Njube.

"I've missed you," JBZ humbly admitted, his voice a low, raspy growl. It was a shame his crew didn't witness these rare moments of their boss behaving like a hatchling at the mercy of the elements and all the predators.

"You have the nerve? You walked out fifteen years ago. I am shocked you still remember this house. You remember me! No! No!" she shook her head, letting her wavy hair fly across her face.

Nobesuthu's eyes hardened, and little lines formed at the edges. She stroked her furrowed forehead.

"You can't just come up my driveway after all these years, Jonathan."

She gestured him towards his Aston Martin and the gate. Each time her index finger moved, his gaze followed her without moving his head. It was as if he was looking at a fading image which he wanted to admire forever. Just another touch. It didn't amuse her that he drove that matte Vanquish; she had been exposed to a life of luxury cars from a young age when her dad worked as the chief electrical engineer for Volvo. Besides, she knew well enough to realise that he only drove certain makes of cars when going for a pilgrim or an orgy. For long, it had frustrated her that he was such a conceited hook-nosed hypocrite. That was one of the factors that led to their subsequent separation. About thrice a year, he hosted exclusive drunken orgies where he drove a special car depending on his pick from the select range. Another three times, he went on pilgrimages with his top brass sidekicks and a chosen few community leaders, and again, he chose a car from the special collection. A separate pool of cars in an elite fleet was for occasions like todays. These were vehicles in which he isolated himself, shut all the hustle and bustle of his routine, and embraced the universe bare.

A one-sided battle of wills commenced under the canopy of trees near the garage entryway, her past grievances bubbling to the surface, frothing like a mochaccino. She threw harsh words at him, harsher truths were revealed, and disgruntlement and anger engulfed her like wildfire, flaring up an outburst. She flung her arms up and clapped her hands before raising them in surrender. He let her speak. It is said that when you are guilty, you don't go about building cities. He bowed and nodded as she blurted her disapproval of his sudden appearance. He was fixated on the ground like one, begging the earth to swallow him. There is an old adage that says, 'not all days are the same'. The great JBZ stood here insignificant like lice. Mice would be prancing at this extraordinary sight.

But then, as the minutes stretched into hours, Nono's resolve softened. She maintained eye contact and saw the pain in his eyes, the regret etched on his face. She couldn't deny the lingering love she still felt for him despite all the pent-up emotions of wounds he had inflicted on her. In the past, by now, he would have slapped her and flown her around numerous times. But he remained meek, showing his puppy eyes. He also wrung his palms each time she paused from shouting. To her, his genteel disposition signalled there could be hope that he was a changed man, sincere in his apology. Another sign was that he left his phone in the cup holder of his Vanquish, which was rather strange considering that he fiddled on his phone all the time. Rumour had it that he slept holding his phone in case he woke up during the night to sneak a peek. JBZ obsessed over his phone so much that he often fought with his son about it. Apart from that phone problem, they got on pretty well. For Nobesuthu, to see his hands free of his phone was a positive sign. She had his attention, and that's the conviction she needed. She extended her hand, and he held it with his fingers and kissed the back of her hand. For years, this had been their tradition of agreement, unity, and little acts of love. JBZ sighed with his eyes closed, letting his torso rise and fall in tune with his broad shoulders.

Her eyes were a turbulent river of emotions. Tears welled in her large, round eyes as she placed a gentle, small hand on his chest. Her eyes were a turbulent sea of emotions.

"I can't change the past Jo, but maybe we can find a way to heal," she whispered, gripping his brown Bottega Veneta nubuck jacket. He stroked her hair and kissed the top of her head. He wore some of his best clothes and drove one of his favourite cars not to impress this woman who wasn't easily swayed by material things but to enhance his features, for he considered texture, colour and detail when choosing an outfit for the day. A subtle dash of Jacques Bogart's Silver Scent Deep and a spritz of aftershave complemented his clothes that morning. He often has a scent for every occasion, with a few signatures that are favourite. Today's deep conversations and recollections called for a deep scent.

Nobesuthu caught a whiff of his fragrance, and at that moment, all their tension evaporated like fog under the morning sun. They embraced and squeezed tightly with their love rekindled by the rawness of their emotions. In the quiet of the early morning, two souls, scarred and imperfect, found solace in each other's arms once more, under the sunlight and chirping birds that bore witness to their tumultuous reunion.

However, she didn't invite him into the house. Instead, she grabbed his hand and strode towards his Vanquish. His eyes lit up with a smile covering his face from corner to corner. Without thinking twice, he opened the door for her and ushered her in with a bowed head. He meandered out of the driveway, driving with one hand on the steering wheel whilst the other held her small palm. Once outside the gate, he let go of her chamomile-scented hand. He navigated through the winding roads of the quiet, lonely town, laughing at some wild memories of their marriage, which was marked by both violent extremes and quiet episodes. It had been fifteen years since he last set foot in Rolfe Valley, and his reason for returning was this frail yet petite wonderful woman named Nobesuthu—a lady he had once loved with a begrudging passion and yet abandoned without explanation. During his absence, she tried to cling to memories, but they hurt so much it was like reliving the hell he put her through. All the same, there were memorable happy times, too, but dissecting the good and the bad proved to be a struggle. Despite his deafening silence, she knew his stints from the news, social media and hearsay. Right now was a moment to soak in the sunlight glistening through the car windows.

Meanwhile, JBZ ignored the few calls that rang. Nobesuthu smiled each time he ignored the phone. Perhaps time indeed changed people for the better. Whether she had really forgiven him was a question for another time. Cruising in his Vanquish with Nobesuthu and sharing happy memories took centre stage. Roselyn rang him twice, and still, he ignored her. His goons knew that to get his attention, ring twice within 30 seconds; the timing was of the essence. Still, he ignored this SOS. Roselyn needed his go-ahead for a methamphetamine consignment from Argentina, which he had put on hold because his team hadn't finished its due diligence. For once, he was happy being just Jonathan. An ordinary man next to his lover. They say the first cut is the deepest.

Chapter 12

D etective Mike had been chasing the elusive drug baron lord, JBZ, for years. The crime boss was notorious for running one of the largest drug cartels in Sub-Saharan Africa. He forged his way into the Southern African Development Community (SADC) region by paying his goons above market rates. Over the years, he weaved his way and penetrated international markets syndicating with oligarchs, yet with all this knowledge, no substantial evidence implicated him. Moreover, his community loved and adored him as their saviour. If he ever chose to contest as a Member of Parliament, he would have a landslide win in his constituency. As such, some people from his hometown nicknamed him Honourable. Despite having several plush houses north of Samoa Machi Avenue and across the country and even overseas, he often visited his childhood suburb, where he performed benevolent acts like drilling boreholes, installing solar systems for community halls, and making educational donations at all the fifteen schools in the locale. The looming water shortages resulted in water rationing with closures from Friday to Monday at Morton Jeffrey Water Works and Warren Park Water Works. This saw residents in most high-density suburbs queuing for water at the few boreholes that dotted the communities. Furthermore, after the last cholera outbreak of 2013, there was a general outcry to the city fathers to provide safe drinking water, but the council were bankrupt, and the provision of safe water was at the mercy of donors. Hence, the Honourable stepped in and commissioned boreholes not only in his hometown but in surrounding townships too. Again, he won the hearts of the masses. It's a pity he showed no interest in politics. He could easily be a senator, MP, mayor, you name it. On a needs basis, he was also patching up the pothole-marred roads and providing bus service on the city and Jambare Musika routes for the relentless women who sold at the fresh market stalls. He also erected streetlights to assist in creating a safe neighbourhood. His charitable acts were almost countless, and there were other ad hoc activities he did. In addition, he established panel discussion panels and monthly support groups for substance abuse recovery. He collaborated well with the local council and municipality. JBZ also revamped the local football club into a commercial club in Division 1. It kept the youth active with an opportunity of earning an honest living from soccer as a side hustle. Being the philanthropist that he was, he often won accolades. However, he declined all offers to grace events as a keynote speaker. In the end, organisations stopped inviting him; he answered as bluntly as he could be.

"I give to help; I don't give to be on TV."

Also, his sweet-tongue, charisma and generosity attracted many people to him. It was a north and South Pole magnetic attraction. The public was ever ready to pounce on anyone laying nasty accusations on him. Father Christmas could never harm children or anyone at that, just as they viewed JBZ. As often is the case, a basket carries both good and bad apples. A few enlightened people saw JBZ for who he really was. They saw through his veil of disguise that behind that sacrificial lamb was a roaring hungry lion. A stealth lion masquerading as a lamb. The city, leaving a trail of destruction in his wake. Mike relied on his intuition to follow JBZ's trail. He had seen the devastating effects of his operations firsthand and was determined to bring him to justice.

Around 8.30 am Mike received an anonymous call about a lead on a shipment of methamphetamine from Mexico arriving from the Port of Beira and entering Zimbabwe side through Nyamapanda Border Post for onward distribution to night clubs in the major cities and towns, the rest to be buried underground in Shurugwi. Coincidentally, Shurugwi had Zimbabwe's largest number of artisan miners, illegal, dangerous miners known for their ruthless killing splurges. They were known as the machete gangs, and they brandished their machetes with the click of a finger. Arrests were yet to be made. Only their blood trail remained, decapitating men and women as they ravaged the small town. Mike didn't pursue any of their alleged cases because he was fully aware that they had connections in the police force. Rumour had it that Lesly, the Assistant Commissioner of the Police Crime department, had some vague links with their leader. As long as it had no apparent link to JBZ, Mike didn't lose sleep over it.

#

Mike paced the long corridor at work, running his sweaty palm over his shaved head. He glanced at his watch every now and then, went into his office to look at the car park, then at his watch again, then back up and down the quiet corridor. It was a Friday night, and most police officers had knocked off for the day, but a handful remained to man the station. Only Mike's timed footsteps echoed in the passageway.

Mike conducted several operations which had led him down a dark and dangerous path especially during undercover or unauthorised missions where he risked his life. His ego sometimes clouded his fair judgement. His fiancée threatened to break up with him once, and that was his wake-up call because he loved her and had already proposed to marry her. She, on the other hand, feared for her life, his safety and their peace, let alone spending quality time together without call-of-duty interruptions. Sometimes, his hunch would lead him to abandon a picnic or a steamy romance episode, and that infuriated her. She would sulk and throw tantrums, and he ignored her, just giving her a peck on the cheek and taking his pistol and jacket out the door he rushed. Today, he had promised to take her out for dinner, but he now wanted to have an early night, so he leaves for Mutoko before dawn. That was another tantrum loading, perhaps a break-up since he had accepted her ultimatum without objection.

The recent spate of sexual and drug abuse cases at Maloweni flats in Jambare triggered a hunch in Mike. He could smell JBZ in all that except that these recent crimes seemed careless and lacked that meticulous touch that he suspected was JBZ's trademark; 'kill them smart' was his motto. To corroborate his instinct, the deaths that the coroners and doctors certified as overdoses and traumas were all related. Nevertheless, he couldn't convince his boss that he had a lead. A witness in Mutoko.

#

After her daughter's demise, Josephine relocated to her rural area not only for a change of scenery but also for a safe environment for her teenage boys, away from the influence of social media and so-called influencers. She dropped her jaw when she asked her son what he aspired to be after school, and his answer paralysed her.

"When I grow up, I want to be a boss at Zimmex Mall, with large sunglasses, designer leather belts and big wheels."

Although this disturbed her, at that time, she let it pass. Only after her daughter's tragic experience and subsequent death at the hands of ruthless drug 'jazzmen' she packed her few belongings and headed to Mutoko, the village where she grew up. Her youngest son was only eight. He would start a new life on a clean and fresh page.

Chapter 13

Whilst still in his office, Mike sighed when he spotted Lisa's red Volvo XC90 slowdown in the parking lot. She didn't like Mike's low car, and whenever possible, she preferred to ride in her own car. Mike often rode it when they were together on some lazy weekend driving around. His salary wasn't enough to save for such a luxury car. He had other priorities, and although he could qualify for a loan to buy one, he was risk averse in money matters. Lisa, on the other hand, was privileged enough to take over her successful father's architectural company, which had offices all over Africa. The moment Detective Mike saw Lisa's red beast, it took him less than thirty seconds to grab his jacket and keys and fly down the staircase from the first floor.

"Hi babe, you look beautiful as always," Detective Mike greeted Lisa with an abrupt peck on the cheek.

Lisa raised her eyebrows, looked at him over her spectacles and shook her head. She then rolled her eyes as she spoke.

"You…spied…on me, didn't you? I thought I'd surprise you in your office…but…well, here you are…out in the car park," she drawled with a smirk.

"Babe, come on, what do you mean? Are you not happy to see that I missed you a lot? I couldn't wait in that lonely office any longer?" He kissed her as she held onto his arm.

She sighed, drooping her head, "Mike honey, you may be a great detective, but with me, you suck at that," she said, winking at him and tapping at his shoulder. An old African saying states that 'a small mountain is worth high value to those far off, those who stay in its foothills see it as a plaything'.

Mike chuckled and complimented her nails, but she brushed him aside.

With a wry smile, she said, "Shall we go?"

With a resigned shrug, Mike pulled his goatee. Each of them went to their car, and Mike drove out first as his car was already in reverse parking. Lisa knew that whenever Mike generalized his compliments, like saying '…beautiful as always' '…looking good', it indicated he was absent-minded, or there was nothing worth complimenting on. She preferred him to keep quiet in such instances than to annoy her.

After what seemed like an endless trip to Avondale, they arrived at Winding Valley Avenue Restaurant. Mike held his fiancée's hand and went in to ask for their reservation. On Fridays, the joint was sometimes packed, so it was safe to book in advance. The couple sat across from each other at their favorite Italian restaurant, the soft candlelight casting a warm glow on their faces. It was meant to be a romantic evening, but something was clearly bothering Mike. His usually sharp mind seemed absent, lost in a cloud of worry. Lisa, concerned, reached across the table and gently touched his hand.

"My honey bear, you seem distant tonight from the time I arrived at your workplace. What's bothering you, Mike? This is supposed to be a happy night?"

He looked up, his eyes reflecting a mixture of exhaustion and preoccupation.

"Huh? Oh, sorry, Li. Yes, there's something troubling me."

Lisa leaned in, her eyes filled with compassion. "You can tell me, you know. We're a team, remember?" She said, rubbing her engagement ring.

Mike sighed and took a deep breath. "It's this case I'm working on. It's a death from drug abuse with apparent links to a man on our wanted list, and I can't seem to piece it all together. It's consuming my thoughts, babe."

Lisa nodded. "I know your dedication to your job, Mike, but you can't let it eat you up. It's clear you are distracted. After all, we're here to enjoy each other's company tonight."

Detective Mike forced a weak smile with his lips hardly moving. "You're right, my sweetheart. I should focus on us, not work. I'm sorry for being so absent-minded."

Their dinner continued, and the Old Italian classic music and the general ambiance of the restaurant slowly melted away Mike's worries. Lisa made sure to keep the conversation light and engaging, steering it away from the grim realities of his work. For the first time since the ultimatum she gave him, she talked about their wedding plans. She had shelved that topic until there were tangible changes in Mike's attitude towards their relationship and his work. He had to be decisive and set his priorities right; otherwise, it was not fair to their relationship. His work had a way of disrupting their plans, almost taking center stage and importance over their plans. She was uncertain anymore if she could marry a guy who was already married to his work. It would be impossible to raise a family together with Mike's divided attention. She became so tired of fighting and competing with his job that she issued him with an ultimatum. At times, she told him it would be better if he cheated than fight this losing battle with his occupation.

As they enjoyed their meal, Mike appeared more relaxed than when they arrived. He reached across the table and tapped his fingers like they were walking on her hand. He then held her hand in a soft caress and murmured, "Thank you, gorgeous, for always being there for me, for bringing me back to the present. I love you, Lisa."

Lisa squeezed his hand and smiled affectionately. "I love you, babe, that's what partners do. We support each other through thick and thin."

Mike told her that despite the weight of his work, she was someone who cared deeply for him, someone who could help him find solace amidst the chaos of his demanding job. Their love was the anchor that kept him grounded, even in the stormiest of times, and for that, Mike was grateful.

Mike and Lisa's dinner had gone well so far, with laughter and conversation flowing naturally. Yet, as the night wore on, Mike's inner turmoil grew stronger. He glanced at his watch discreetly, realizing that he needed to leave early to pursue his lead in Mutoko. However, he couldn't bring himself to tell Lisa, especially with how their date had turned out. She had given him an ultimatum last time, asking him to choose between his demanding job and their relationship. He knew that leaving early tonight would only reignite those tensions and erase the evening's wins. As they finished their main course, the waiter approached with the dessert menu. Lisa, eager to extend their time together, suggested, "How about we share a dessert, honey? I hear the *torta della nonna* here is incredible, and even their *panna cotta too.*"

Mike hesitated, gasped, mumbled and then looked at his watch. He desperately wanted to pursue the case and potentially prevent more tragedies, but he also cherished his quality time with Lisa. In the end, as usual, his commitment to his job won. "Actually, Li, I think I'll pass on dessert tonight. I need to wake up early for something important tomorrow."

Lisa's face fell slightly, and she couldn't hide her disappointment. "Mike, again? We've talked about this." She threw her napkin on the table.

Mike felt a pang of guilt as he looked into her eyes. "I know, my sweetie, and I'm sorry. But this is something urgent, and I promise I'll make it up soon. I always do."

She sighed and shrugged. "I just hope you remember to balance your priorities, Mike."

Their conversation grew strained, and the once romantic evening now hung in the balance. Mike was once again torn between his duty as a detective and his love for Lisa, but there he had an ultimatum, which could have dire consequences for their relationship if he had made the wrong move. As the tension escalated, they found themselves in a heated argument. Her disappointment and frustration boiled over, and she raised her voice, saying, "Detective Mike, it's always something urgent with you! You promised we'd have this evening together, and now you want to leave just like that!"

Mike, feeling cornered and defensive, shouted back, "I can't help it, Lisa! Lives are at stake, and I have a duty to protect this community!"

Their voices echoed in the restaurant, drawing the attention of nearby diners. The argument continued, with emotions running high as they both struggled to reconcile their love for each other with the demands of Mike's job. It was a painful reminder of the ongoing conflict in their relationship, leaving them both emotionally drained and on the verge of tears. Amid their heated argument, Lisa suddenly leaned in and planted a gentle peck on his cheek. Her eyes were filled with tears as she whispered, "I love you, Mike, but I can't keep waiting for you to choose. Take care."

With that, Lisa got up from the table and left Mike alone in the restaurant. He did not have time to grab her hand. The room seemed quieter as he turned and watched her walk away. He clutched his temples, then buried his head in his hands. This time, the weight of his choices and the impact they had on the woman he loved seemed heavier than ever. As she stormed out, she paused for a moment. Her hand trembled as she hesitated, and then, with a heavy sigh, she slowly slipped her engagement ring off her finger, held it in her palm for a second, and then walked towards Mike. She carefully placed it on the table near his elbow. He looked it up just as he let go of the ring. It was a silent gesture, but it spoke volumes about the depth of her pain and her uncertainty about their future together. Lisa continued to walk away, leaving behind the symbol of their commitment, and Mike sat there, staring blankly at the ring. He sat there in the dimly lit restaurant, eyes still fixated on the ring. His heart ached, and he felt a mixture of regret and longing. For a long time, he knew that his dedication to his job had strained their relationship, and now, Lisa's silent but powerful gesture had left him speechless and listless.

After a moment of reflection, Mike stood up. He reached for the engagement ring, slipped it into his pocket, and took a deep breath. Leaving some money on the table for their meal, he rushed out of the restaurant and sped to his car. He drove, telling himself loudly that he needed to find a way to balance his demanding job and his relationship with the woman he loved and that the case in the village would have to wait; his heart had become the priority.

Chapter 14

JBZ continued to ignore his calls, much to Nono's happiness. They had no care for the world. What gave JBZ assurance that his empire was running efficiently regardless of inherent occasional hiccups in the day-to-day running was Lesly not calling him. If anything threatening his business or life were to ever happen, Lesly was under obligation to inform JBZ by phone or through their secret SOS system. Whether chaos or wins that were taking place and deals being struck, JBZ took pride in his capable team of goons and Roselyn and the grotesque tattooed guy Chipendo. Besides, before he left, JBZ had concluded all major deals with Argentina, South Africa, Mexico, Mozambique and the US. The minor ones that cropped up could be safely handled in his absence. Nobesuthu was what his mind needed; otherwise, he would lose his sanity.

Nobesuthu stood in the doorway, light passing through her chiffon dress that hung loosely on her. She fanned her face since the overheard fan made her cough and sneeze. It was too hot for early September. JBZ opened one eye, forcing his eyelid to stay open, both eyes shut. He yawned rolled over, and threw the sheet to the side. Patting the bed, he gestured to Nono.

"Come here, my chocolate frog."

He always had the famous kid chocolate Freddo in his bags or in his house. The chocolate he wished he ate more in his childhood, yet it cost a meagre five cents then. His parents couldn't afford luxuries daily, which would spoil their children. As kids, they got Freddos and Chomps once a month unless it was Christmas.

"Are you ready to tell me the real reason that triggered your journey? Penance or expiation?"

"Is that not the same word?"

"That is beside the point. I want to know what made you want to come here to your Vanquish fifteen years later. You have hardly been on your phone during the two days you have spent here. Are you hiding from cops, the mafia, the government or another estranged wife?" she spoke in a crescendo.

He tried to coax her into sitting on the bed. She refused and remained at the doorway. JBZ conceding defeat to anyone was breaking news. He let her have her way. She went to the kitchen. He spread the bed, freshened up and followed her.

"Thank you for preparing breakfast," he said, entering the kitchen. He could smell the strong aroma of coffee.

"I remembered my childhood, all that I couldn't have. Then, I met you when I had nothing in high school. We fell in love. I got into a good deal because I was cunning and resourceful. I ousted the then infamous local drug baron, Jazz. I married you. I became the boss. I cheated. I hit you. I flaunted money on you, thinking it soothed the harm I inflicted on you. We decided we didn't want kids. I fathered a son with our maid Trish.

You found out. You chased Trish away. I became a wounded lion and treated you like trash. Our house became a warzone. You broke down into depression. You didn't tell any of your relatives or friends. You lose weight and your appetite for life. I walked out. I was scared you would sell me out to the police, so I had a plan. Yet, all these years, you didn't. You knew all my moves back then. Fifteen years of living with you, we had half happiness and half bad times. It made me ponder why I did all this to you. My empire wouldn't have been this massive if you chose to report. I am human. I needed to come back to my senses before I lost myself."

She sipped her coffee, staring at him with a straight face.

He continued, "Maybe it's time I let my son take the lead. I want to retire with you, and we can go far away and stay on an island. I bought one in Maldives. You will like it. Well, I have insomnia; I became worse until the doctors suggested I have a change of scenery because the medication isn't working anymore. After weeks of thinking of a haven, I thought of our home. Rolfe Valley. I was prepared to be chased away, and then I would go to Norway. My uncle, the priest, lives there. That would be a sanctuary. But here I am. You are still kind. I remain unworthy of your love. I will always love you, my Nono."

He walked over to her, gently took her cup, and placed it on the table. He hugged her. Despite being here for two days, sharing laughs and a bed, this was their first intimate touch. A hug. She hugged him back, feeling all her bones squeezed as he tightened his embrace. His phone rang; this time, it was Roselyn's ringtone. He had to answer this one. She hadn't looked for him on this special phone since his arrival. Something was wrong. He looked at his phone, still embracing her closely. Answering would question his sincerity, especially during their first physical contact. He bit his teeth closed his eyes, and smirked his lips. Nobesuthu smiled and ruffled his hair. The call timed out.

#

Mike spent the night at Lisa's house. She forgave him. However, he fidgeted all night, perhaps fixated on James' death and the Mutoko lead.

James was once a promising musician known for his talent and vibrant personality. But as the pressures of life or fame mounted, he turned to crystal methamphetamine (crystal meth) for an escape from his problems. This drug went by other names such as *guka makafela* or just *guka, mutoriro, dombo* or ice. Little did he know that this decision would set him on a harrowing journey of self-destruction. He upgraded to cocaine and heroin, which led to his death from overdose. It was up to the police to apprehend the drug suppliers and put an end to this menace. Yet, there were many moving pieces which complicated this puzzle. Mike finally slept but with one eye open. Sometimes, love stands in the way of work and vice versa. Those are some of the difficulties of growing up. Lisa went to sleep with a happy woman. But whether that would last for long would be a test of time.

Chapter 15

James' descent began innocently enough. Feeling overwhelmed by his financial troubles and the weight of expectations from his fans, he was introduced to meth by a friend. The initial euphoria was like nothing he'd ever experienced before, and he was hooked. He later moved to crystal meth as it was stronger than ordinary meth. Like methamphetamine, crystal meth also contains a stimulant drug called amphetamine. However, crystal meth is made from meth produced in a lab, and it is a pure form of methamphetamine. Crystal meth can be snorted, smoked, injected, or swallowed. It takes about one hour for the drug to reach its full effect once consumed. Lately, it was discovered that users like James were flushing up their anuses for faster gratification. While both methamphetamine and crystal meth can damage the body and brain, crystal meth is believed to be more addictive. Moreover, crystal meth is generally more expensive than methamphetamine.

As James' substance abuse continued, his life started to unravel. His once-thriving music career came crashing down as he neglected his work, lost touch with his fans, gave dismal live performances with revelers throwing bottles at him and alienated his friends and family. When he showed up well on stage, his lyrics were so offensive it wasn't safe for children under the age of eighteen. Within a few months, his appearance deteriorated, and he became gaunt and unrecognizable. He bragged that he kept stock of approximately fifteen grams of crystal meth, about one gram of fentanyl, worth an estimated street value of $400. His addiction isolated him from everyone who cared about him. He became paranoid, convinced that people were out to get him. He withdrew from society, spending days and nights in the company of fellow users who shared his addiction where they all 'heard voices'.

The toll on James' physical and mental health was severe. He suffered from extreme weight loss, dental problems and chronic insomnia. His body was deteriorating, and his mind was plagued by hallucinations and anxiety. He shouted and ran from invisible people chasing him. As fate would have it, one fateful night, James found himself in a dangerous situation when a deal with a drug dealer went south. James owed him so much he refused to lend him even one milligram. He narrowly escaped a violent encounter, leaving him traumatized and more desperate than ever to numb his pain with narcotics. He had to get a fix, and soon. He had run out of his precious stock as he was broke. He stumbled upon a man at their usual joints who wanted to test some concoctions on him. That's where cocaine and heroin were mixed with other household substances, and this contributed to his overdose and ultimate death.

Mark's story serves as a cautionary tale of the devastating effects of methamphetamine abuse. Once a promising artist, he was reduced to a shadow of his former self, isolated, tormented by addiction and prematurely dead at the height of his career.

Chapter 16

One night, as Mike sat in his unmarked car, watching a known drug front in Jambare, he received a tip from an informant. JBZ was rumoured to be attending a high-stakes poker game at an upscale casino along Samoa Machi Avenue. It was a risky move for him, and Mike saw it as an opportunity he couldn't pass up. It had been months since JBZ's return from his short sabbatical. All else seemed normal, with Roselyn over-excited that her master was back and impressed with her work in his absence. Perhaps she would receive a salary rise and other pecks such as a penthouse in high-end Cape Town.

Detective Mike called for backup and, along with his partner, Detective Mark 'Razor Wire', headed to the casino. Dressed in elegant tuxedos to blend in with the crowd, they entered the casino. Inside, the opulent surroundings contrasted sharply with the danger that loomed. Both discreetly scanned the room, spotting JBZ at a poker table. With a silent nod, they approached, joining the game as players. Hours passed, tension mounting as the game unfolded. JBZ's reputation for ruthlessness was well-earned, and he played with a cold, calculating demeanour. Mike could feel his eyes on him, sensing something was amiss.

Finally, the moment of truth arrived. Mike and JBZ found themselves in a high-stakes hand. The tension was palpable as the cards were revealed. Mike held his breath, and her heart raced. He had to win this hand to catch JBZ off guard. With a poker face to rival his, he revealed his winning hand, a flush. JBZ's jaw clenched in frustration as he laid down his cards, realising he'd lost. It was an exclusive game for specially invited guests from JBZ's crop. Detective Mark had hacked into the invitation database and replaced two new counterparts with himself and Mike. They didn't call him 'Razor Wire' for nothing. This night's jackpot winner takes the "surprise bag" stashed with packets of powders and other narcotics. Technically, this was enough grounds to arrest JBZ. Caught in action. The casino's security team moved in to apprehend him, but JBZ wasn't one to go quietly. A chaotic scene erupted as he attempted to flee. Mike and Mark pursued him through the casino, adrenaline pumping through their veins. Glass broke as they flew past waiters and tables. There was a gunshot outside.

After a harrowing chase, they cornered JBZ in a dimly lit alley in the CBD. It was a rainy night, which made it difficult to camouflage in the Harare night crowd. The streets were deserted, with a few cars trickling in the city centre. Even the vendors who often sprawled the streets till midnight were nowhere to be seen. JBZ drew a weapon, but Mike and Mark were quicker. Shots rang out, and JBZ fell to the ground, arrested at last. As the handcuffs clicked into place, Mike looked at the man who had eluded him for more than a decade. For now, justice had been served, but the cost was high. He punched him, saying that was disturbing his relationship with Lisa. His colleague restrained him from further beating the culprit. One would be forgiven to wonder if the pursuit of criminals like JBZ was worth the personal sacrifices officers made along the way. Detectives Mike and Mark had finally captured the criminal drug lord, but Mike knew that in the world of law enforcement, the line between right and wrong could sometimes blur, leaving scars that ran deeper than the ones on the surface. Detective Mark had hacked the invitation file and replaced two newbies, Mike and himself. They didn't call him 'Razor Wire' for nothing.

That night, other drug seizures included 10kg of methamphetamine buried at a farm in Mutoko, 15 litres of GBL (gamma-butyrolactone), the party drug and a $3 million haul of cocaine hidden in the hull of a cargo ship seized at the Port of Beira from Mexico. This was evidence of a global crime network behind the smuggling and distribution of these illegal drugs.

Chapter 17

Detective Mike drove home a happy man, and he drove straight to his fiancée's apartment. Although it was almost midnight, Mike still proceeded to let himself into Lisa's flat. They both had full access to one another's residences. He disarmed the alarm and sneaked into the house with minimum noise so as not to startle his sweetheart. He was so ecstatic he had to share the news with his other half that he didn't care if she scolded him in the process.

Lisa, being the light sleeper that she was, grabbed her teaser, which lay in her second drawer as that was a strategic place and also picked her mobile phone, ready to phone Mike if the need arose. She slid out of bed, tiptoed towards her door, and lay flat behind it. She froze when footsteps approached her room. All her strength seemed to suddenly vanish as an adrenaline rush sped through her, and she shivered and shook involuntarily. She fought hard to maintain a normal breathing pace. Her heart pounded so hard it showed on her black silk night dress. She held her phone in position to press her speed dial, then shaking her head, she stretched out her pepper spray instead. As a detective's woman, Lisa had learnt a few tricks for self-defence from Mike. He taught her what he termed 'the fundaments of dating a detective'. He promised to teach her some extras if time permitted. Now, all those annoying lessons of repeated defence movements were paying off, not that it was a good occurrence having to use them. Mike had also recommended that she avoid placing her defence equipment in conspicuous places like under the pillow or the first drawer. He had also bought a baseball bat and a gold stick for her, but she refused both, citing those were weapons that could easily be used on her.

Mike turned the door once as if trying to check if it was locked or not. He then knocked softly while calling Lisa's name in a soft undertone.

"Lisa, Lisa, Cleopatra and Tut," he said, then waited.

He knew she slept like a dog, and if anything, she had heard that. He used that as their code whenever she wanted to verify his identity. For him, she only changed the order of the words, "Tut and Cleopatra, Mike, Mike." Sometimes, Mike exhibited signs of being paranoid, which he denied, but he also rubbed into those he loved. He was both a finicky policeman and lover. So, he repeatedly stressed the same points when talking about protection, criminals, burglars and vigilance. Perhaps that is why Lisa sometimes gave him ultimatums so there could be a clear distinction between works, life in general, and their love life. Mike's family outnumbered him; hence, he spent all his energy on prepping up his beloved fiancée.

Lisa shrugged, looked up, and then took a deep laboured breath. She then opened the door with her eyes closed. She pulled her bedroom door slowly and inhaled deeply to take in Mike's scent, which also verified that it was him. They immediately embraced. Mike lay his head facing her neckline, where he savoured her sweet scent while his nose brushed her ear.

"Babe, it's late. Which one is it, sadness or joy?" Lisa said, turning her head to face him.

"Ecstasy! That bugger, J, what nonsense, I pinned him down."

"What! You did?" She took a step back and then hugged him again.

"Yes, babe, you heard right. I am a man of my word. I don't entertain nonsense from nuisances," Mike said, looking up at the ceiling.

He continued in a diminuendo, "Come here," and clutched her tighter, closing her mouth in that instant in an engulfing kiss. She stood on tiptoe, and her shoulders arched upwards as she grabbed his head tighter.

Lisa then led him by the hand as she moved with a sensuous slink towards her bed.

"Cuff me," she begged in a sensual whimper. Mike was not as adventurous as Lisa in those areas. He was reluctant and looked at her silhouette and then at his handcuffs. He threw his snips behind him and crawled to her.

"How about removing your tie because I wanna tie you down with my hands. When you lie down, I will tie you down and ride you, no lie," she continued.

Lisa moaned and groaned as he made his way along the crevices of her bikini line. She worked her way up and down his groin until he moaned. She was ready for him.

Chapter 18

JBZ had the finest lawyers in the land, no doubt. He needed them. Sandking and Centurion were renowned criminal lawyers who knew no bounds and left no stone unturned in their quest for justice or injustice, depending on where the facts and money lay. Unlike in "The Merchant of Venice", where Portia won the case for Antonio by wit, these lawyers won most cases by guile. Hence, they charged premium pricing for their valued services. Sandking and Centurion representatives had already made phone calls and transfers to their bank accounts. This story could have gone quietly, but since JBZ was involved, it quickly caught media coverage. Social media was awash with videos, photos and memes of his dramatic arrest even though it happened in a lonely alley. The two men and a lady who were in the vicinity took their amateur photography skills to task and captured as much as they could. Alleys were common for ladies of the night to feed clients who valued service rather than comfort.

#

Detective Mike stood in front of the drug baron, JBZ. He was still cuffed to the table, bowing his head. Senior Inspector Chris entered the room as Mike addressed JBZ.

Gritting his teeth, Mike hissed, "You are responsible for so much suffering in the ghettos, the whole city, and Africa at large, you J nonsense."

Smiling smugly, JBZ muttered, "You know you can't touch me, lover boy. I have friends in the right places. Friends who pay you not to play with me, you understand?"

Meanwhile, Inspector Chris stood and watched in silence. He stepped forward and shouted, "That's enough, detective."

Detective Mike glared at the inspector, but he gave him a stern look in return. Inspector Chris turned to JBZ and told him that he was free to go. The culprit, JBZ, winked at the dejected detective, who then looked sideways. Detective Mike's forehead furrowed, although he tried to put up a neutral face. Sneering, JBZ was escorted by junior officers out of the interrogation room. Detective Mike clenched his fists while his begrudging gaze followed JBZ as he swaggered out.

Mike watched with his mouth aghast as JBZ walked out, and the door closed behind him.

Mike turned to stare at his superior, "You can't be serious, Chris."

Inspector Chris sighed and shoved one hand into his left breast pocket while he pushed the other hand into his trousers' pocket. At that same time, he attempted to balance on one leg with his eyes closed. Detective Mike was perturbed for a moment.

One would be forgiven to assume that this was a scene by Jackie Chan from the kung Fu classic movie "Shaolin the Drunken Master". Inspector Chris staggered for a few seconds while the detective looked in amazement. Inspector Chris was an illustrative person, but this was on another level. Detective Mike, in all his astuteness, couldn't figure out what the intended lesson could be. Inspector Chris sighed, and spoke through his breath, "It's not my call, Mike. Sometimes, we have to play by their rules. You saw what I just did? That's how we dance to their tune, whatever the tune may be at that time." He patted his shoulder and paused, as if to speak, then strode out. Mike dragged his feet to the nearest chair and sunk sluggishly into it, hiding his head in his beefy arms. This intensified the tension between Detective Mike, who wanted justice, and Inspector Chris, who followed orders from higher offices.

#

JBZ stepped out of the police station and into a dark alley. A sleek, unmarked vehicle pulled up, and the tinted window rolled down. There were two shadowy figures at the rear of the vehicle. JBZ jumped in, and there was a loud greeting in the car. The vehicle sped off into the night, leaving behind a bewildered and tense atmosphere.

"Good to see you, JBZ. You won't hear from me again," bellowed one of the passengers at the back. The vehicle sped off into the night, leaving JBZ standing at his gate.

Chapter 19

In the heart of Zimbabwe's pristine savannah, a place of unparalleled beauty, JBZ sought refuge from the hustle and bustle. A place called Suwojena. Legend said this was where the elders of old gathered and entered through a white door that appeared on 'the tree without a name' situated at the cliff top. This was the very land that housed this stunning resort. Nowadays, it represents those who want to experience the purity of nature by pampering them like royals. It was a place where the price was the prize. Unless one won the lotto or a hefty inheritance, only those who counted their change in thousands could stay at Suwojena since the price per night could easily pay a term's school fees in an average group a school or buy a 1.5-litre Japanese preowned car. For JBZ to treat his main team like that was indeed a generous feat. A few brought their partners, while the majority brought their 'small houses' and hook-ups. The drug lord had extended the offer to each member and a partner or anyone else willing to go through a rigorous background check. Despite being in a giving mode, JBZ prioritised vigilance, especially after his disgraceful arrest by detective Mike and his colleague. Whether he was attending a wedding or a funeral, his security detail had to be on point. One hundred percent at any time, all the time.

JBZ had fled the concrete jungle and law enforcement agencies of the city, hoping to find solace in this remote African paradise. Lately, so many mistakes have been happening in his syndicate. He had to break away and regroup. As he made his way deeper into the wild, the vibrant colours of the savannah came alive. Towering acacia trees stretched their branches towards the vast African sky, and the golden grasses swayed with the rhythm of the wind. In the distance, a herd of elephants meandered along the horizon, their silhouettes etched against the setting sun. In the near distance, down in the gorge, the Bade River reverberated with the epic symphony of hippos honking in unison. There was a bask of crocodiles lying on the shore, winding down for the day. Also, a float of crocodiles could be spotted semi-submerged in the water near the river shore. There was an array of aesthetics to capture in the charming scenery. However, it's the bloat of hippos that caught JBZ's attention. While talking to a tour guide, he learnt that contrary to popular belief, hippos don't swim; in fact, they cannot swim because of their weight. Rather, they walk or run under water till they reach shallow water and step out onto land. Even more surprising to him was that they cannot breathe underwater, too. Instead, they survive underwater by controlling their breathing and body position. This new information intrigued him to the point where he paced the deck with his eyes closed, something he did when in deep thought. He also clicked his fingers, another sign of contemplation for JBZ. Suppose he could apply some of these fascinating adaptive traits to his threatened empire. Mistakes were happening at a confidence level higher than anticipated in his strategic planning. He had to nip this menace in the bud. Rightly so, it was justified to suspect anyone as the possibility of a snitch had become apparent. Nobesuthu's voice startled him back from oblivion.

"Honey dear, how can you walk with your eyes closed at a height of 300 feet?" she said, enclosing his shoulders in an embrace, thus guiding him away from the deck. He rested his hand on her waist, and they joined the others.

As the sun dipped below the horizon, casting the wilderness resort into a tapestry of amber and crimson hues, JBZ and his guests gathered in the common area, huddled around the flickering flames of a campfire. Nestled high upon a cliff that faced the gaping chasm of the Bade River gorge, the resort offered a breathtaking panorama of untamed nature. JBZ wore his safari shorts, which hugged his bum in a way that made him sway like a lady. His men giggled, but no one would live to his face for fear of the repercussions. While he was genteel to the general community and to his crew, JBZ was a revered and feared man who, unless he told you to laugh, you wouldn't even chuckle, worse still, think of laughing. Men like Manjinji had challenged him, but no one in his vicinity dared approach him, well, at least without the necessary reinforcements.

Laughter dotted with course jokes engulfed the atmosphere. JBZ had paid a premium to have the entire place to himself and his entourage. Apart from wanting the time and privacy to make as much noise as they wanted in their planned drunken brawls, he did it for security. JBZ never liked surprises. He planned his moves like Garry Kasparov, the chess grandmaster of Kasparov's Immortal fame. And like Kasparov, he won almost all his games. Amidst the murmurs of appreciation for the resort, there was talk of a man whose notoriety echoed far beyond the remote paradise of Suwojena. His name was Ivan Lilydale, the founder of Suwojena. Ivan was a figure that was both enigmatic and mystifying, and he looked like a rugged adventurer. His eyes gleamed with an intensity that spoke of the wild. Yet, it was his source of inspiration that set him apart – the hippos down the gorge in Bade River.

Earlier, the tour guide had briefed them that Ivan had spent years studying hippos. He was enchanted by their grace beneath the water's surface and their ferocity when threatened. But what truly fascinated him was the rigid dichotomy of these animals, this is, their capacity for both gentle nurturing and unrestrained rage. JBZ drew parallels between these traits and his. Although he joked that he was similar to a hippo in some ways, he scanned to see his team's facial expressions and body language. There seemed to be pure laughter and merriment. As the daylight faded, the resort's manager, a stout middle-aged man with a curled moustache, amused the eager guests with stories of Ivan. He spoke of how Ivan would sit for hours, silently observing hippos in their native habitat. It was said that he believed the hippos held a secret, a hidden wisdom that he sought to unlock and integrate into his life's work.

The scent of the evening's meal wafted through the air, and JBZ and the team savoured a delicious feast of venison under the night sky studded with stars. This was a place where luxury met the untamed wild, where guests could savour gourmet cuisine while feeling the heartbeat of the natural world. Even the mosquitoes knew not to disturb guests at night. The night grew still, save for the occasional distant call of a night bird and hippo grunts, which became more distinct than in daytime. The stars shone brilliantly, casting their glow on the cliffside resort, and the gorge below Suwojena was a place where guests could experience the beauty and the danger, the tranquillity and the fury of the wilderness.

JBZ glanced at the fire's flickering flames, his gaze momentarily lost in the dance of the orange and red embers. He turned to the group, "Tonight, friends, is a night I've been waiting for. I've brought someone very special to share this place with us." Nobesuthu stood by his side, her expression a mix of curiosity and unease. After being estranged from Jonathan for fifteen years, this journey into the wilderness was their first real adventure after reuniting at her Rolfe Valley residence a few weeks earlier.

She spoke with a smile on her face, and it shone in her bulging eyes, "Jonathan, you've always had a penchant for the extraordinary, but I never thought I'd find myself in such a magnificent remote place. Maybe all of us, right? What's the significance of this?" As she spoke, JBZ stole a glance at Roselyn, who was hearing about Nobesuthu for the first time. Roselyn almost choked on her tequila and struggled to swallow another sip. Her jaws seemed locked, too. She dug her barefoot deep into the wooden floor, pinching it harder with each second. For a long time, she was JBZ's lover, and all other one-night stands, escorts, and flings he had time and again were fleeting and didn't bother her, but not this. A wife.

JBZ's computer geek chimed in with a thoughtful tone, "JBZ is like those hippos, ma'am. Powerful, mysterious, and at times, dangerously unpredictable. But he's also fiercely protective of what's his, just like the mother hippo with her young." When desperation or greed strikes, men are known to sing for their supper, just as the nerd deed. Even though JBZ was the community's sweetheart, he was slowly killing future generations and at times, instantly killing them. Another man nodded in agreement. JBZ smiled, and he reached for Nobesuthu's hand.

As hours turned into days, Nobesuthu couldn't shake the bitterness that had long festered in her heart. The memories of past wrongs and betrayals had resurfaced, and she found herself consumed by a burning desire for revenge.

One evening, as the moonlight bathed their Cliffside paradise, Nobesuthu retreated to her room. Her partner, Jonathan wasn't in. She had been secretly probing into his affairs, determined to uncover his motive for coming to this distant place. The man she knew and fell in love with back in high school was a schemer, shrewd as a snake. She spotted a glistening object in her drawer. She had stumbled upon a trove of information that shook her to the core - he had been spying on her, tracking her every move since they arrived at the wilderness resort. With a mix of anger and despair, Nobesuthu confronted Jonathan under the same starlit sky that had once seemed so romantic.

"Jonathan! I can't believe you've been spying on me. Is this how you maintain your control over everything, even me?"

Caught off guard, JBZ struggled to explain. "Nono, my love, I never meant for it to come to this. I just wanted to make sure you were safe in this unfamiliar place. Please, let me explain, Nono." But the words fell on deaf ears as her shock intensified. JBZ tried to coax her with money and professed his undying love for her, which made him overprotective, especially now that he was back in her life. He moved forward to kiss her, but she slapped him and jumped onto the bed, covering her head under a pillow.

"Have I ever given you reason not to trust me? Huh? You are still the screwed-up person that you have always been. You will never change—"

He interrupted her with his hand gliding under her nightie. She jerked with a loud no and tried to free herself, but he pinned her to the bed, whispering that she must keep quiet. His dominance sprung back while she lay helpless.

As the night wore on, despite being exhausted and irritated, Nobesuthu hatched her plan and jotted it in her journal in way only comprehensible to her. In the days that followed, she quietly began to gather information that could tarnish JBZ's reputation and ruin his endeavours. The time came to leave Suwojena, and the group embarked on their city-bound journey. The winding road down the cliff was a breathtaking path filled with hairpin turns and vibrantly decorated mud houses of the Shangani tribe. Towering trees on either side cast dappled shadows on the road while the distant echoes of the gorge's

waterfalls accompanied their descent. The hippos seemed to honk in farewell while the

view of the lush wilderness receded as they wound their way down. Ahead of them lay a

captivating array of fauna and flora that painted a vivid picture of Midland's natural beauty. Midlands was well-known for its steep, scenic winding roads, such as Boterekwa. It was no doubt that Suwojena was nested in such grandeur. The flora along the road was a lush tapestry of greenery that mesmerised JBZ's team. In the midst of this breathtaking landscape, JBZ read a book. He flipped pages to reach his folded

page in the book "The Art of War by Sun Tzu".

Chapter 20

Three days after returning to the city from the enchanting savannah at Suwojena, JBZ found himself back at the magical resort in the company of Roselyn. He had to appease her; otherwise, she threatened to spill the bins on his shenanigans with her to Nobesuthu. JBZ always played his cards right and being with Roselyn back at Suwojena was a gimmick at play. He had important visitors to entertain. All his top aides in high places needed some pampering to be innovative. This time, it was going to be a one-night stay with serious business operations.

Meanwhile, JBZ and Roselyn sat together by the campfire, the flickering flames casting a warm glow on their faces. She lay on his shoulder, her face beaming while he played with her faux locs. JBZ had instructed that she put on that hairstyle as the feel of silk-like plastic hair extensions, Brazilian or Peruvian hair, nauseated him. On her, he liked a rough feel to excite his imagination, as he claimed. Sometimes it was difficult to understand him as, at one point, he liked Indian hair on her. Since he was in charge, she complied and only complained about the wind. The courage she had to arm-twist him into a savannah escape with him pleased her. It was her first victory against her new rival, Nobesuthu. While Roselyn was tough on fellow gangsters and any other menaces, she was meek to JBZ. With him, she humbled herself so much that she turned from rigid to flaccid in seconds. She cowered at him, but when making love, it was a different story. Someone had also told her that to win a man's heart, one had to act like a toddler. With all that effort, then boom, a so-called wife appears from the blue. She had to make her move, pretty fast. Roselyn smiled when he complimented her fragrance, Libre by Yves Saint Laurent. She chose it out of defiance; she liked to spice up her life whenever JBZ would let her. He leaned closer to her face, gave her a peck on the forehead, and caressed her cheeks before speaking in hushed tones, "Rosey, you know why we are here? Apart from your seductive moves, you temptress, you're crucial to the success of our new operation."

Nodding, she replied, "I understand, J. This magnificent resort provides the perfect cover, and the beauty of the savannah conceals our true intentions. What's the plan, though?"

He smirked, "This hidden gem in the gorge will be our remote location as a premium experience escort point." Roselyn raised an eyebrow; then he explained further. "In fact, I could buy this place. I want to buy it. Come to think of it, its obvious Ivan won't be willing to sell this place which he has nurtured and cherished, but what do I care? I can take the shit out of him. Then again, he's such a good man. Let's see what deal we can strike without shoving any sticks up anyone's ass. They don't call me JBZ for nothing. Wait till the guys get here." Taken aback by his words, Roselyn stared at him open-mouthed. Then she sat up straight, trying to make sense of it all.

JBZ's suitable team of notorious six high-ranking officials he met in Bulawayo months back was en route to Suwojena for the night. A team is known for corruption, espionage and anything in between. Roselyn had done the needful by organising a bevvy for them. Of course, she had sent a catalogue, and each man had to choose their finest stallion. The local prophet who single-handedly established that amazing yet dreadful team was also among those visiting. Apparently, his entertainment for the night was the Assistant Commissioner Operations from Prisons, Rejoice. It was rumored that the two were having an affair and that the prophet had silenced the commissioner's husband with a spell. With so many churches mushrooming, it was not surprising to have church leaders with no moral compass or calling at all. In fact, most churches were an investment scheme, easy for money laundering too. This prophet made a good living from shady deals. His association with JBZ, the community man, was a gift he cherished. It was also necessary as it boosted JBZ's charity work. JBZ knew how to keep his circle satisfied and silent. After all, it was a symbiotic relationship. Dog eat dog. Carry me, I carry you.

After collecting herself and gulping some water, Roselyn spoke. This time, although her eyes bulged, she remained nonchalant, "It's a bold move, J, and a brilliant one. This land, with its vast, uncharted territory, will be our advantage. I wonder what your nemesis will do."

"Which one, that brat Mike or—"

His phone rang him, and he stepped out to the deck to answer, leaving Roselyn frowning and rolling her eyes. "Damn, Nobesuthu," she muttered under her breath and sulked.

Chapter 21

Late in the night, the city had a few vendors remaining for that last-minute customer. The hustle was real. A few blocks away, the roar of powerful engines echoed through the streets as a high-speed chase unfolded. The suspect's sleek, black sports car weaved through trickling traffic of possibly late-night revelers. With adrenaline pumping, Detective Mike and his temporary partner, a determined police officer, pursued the runaway car. Their patrol car's red and blue lights flashed in a frantic dance. The chase led through narrow alleys, across isolated intersections, and onto the highway off Rodrick Mayor Street, where speeds reached a dangerous 110 kilometers per hour. Given the poor state of most roads, especially with the rainy season coming up, any speed above 60 kilometers per hour was tantamount to a sure fatal accident, if not death.

The police duo in their outdated cruiser struggled to keep pace as their vehicle jostled and bounced along. Looming fuel shortages meant that even the police, at times, were incapacitated. Their odometer flashed as it was past the reserve tank since afternoon. The pursuit continued into the pitch-black night, with the only sounds being the revving engines and the clattering of gravel beneath the tires. With no backup officers to assist, it was a gritty, old-fashioned chase through the unforgiving terrain, a test of both the officers' determination and the suspect's ability to navigate the treacherous, pothole-laden roads.

The inevitable happened, and the police cruiser sputtered to a halt, leaving the suspects with a significant advantage. With their engine dead and no backup in sight, the officers were forced to watch helplessly as the suspects' BMW disappeared into the night, leaving behind nothing but the echo of its engine fading in the distance. The chase had come to a bitter end, with the suspects making their escape due to the unforgiving combination of poor roads and dwindling fuel supplies. It was a frustrating and challenging night, especially for Mike. He promised not to jeopardize his life over avoidable duties, but she would never understand the commitment a police officer has pledged to the nation. Worse still, the trauma they went through in the name of duty. Most underwent post-traumatic stress disorder (PTSD) treatment. All Mike wanted was support, but then again, the standards had fallen, and the prestige that had once accompanied the job had washed off like soap. His fiancée was right; he needed to make better judgement calls. Lisa was his chocolate, whereas the police force was his calling. He could call while eating chocolate, and he could still eat chocolate while calling. The two Cs had to coexist amicably, somehow, like in the old times when he first met Lisa, and fuel and resources were abundant.

His partner suddenly jerked in remembrance. He had a two-litre coke bottle of petrol in his bag, which he bought during lunch for use on his small car stuck at home. They refilled the car. Mike reprimanded him for storing fuel in a dangerous container and place. An explosion could happen at any time with such carelessness. However, it was the norm for people to carry fuel around in such plastic containers, too. They went back on their way.

#

Detective Mike lay in a hospital bed at Parirenyatwa, looking bruised and bandaged. The first person he saw when he opened his eyes was his fiancée. "Lisa, I didn't expect to see you here."

Worried, she held his hand, "Honey, you scared me half to death. What happened out there?"

"It was a high-speed chase; our fuel ran out on our way back, a haulage truck smashed into us. We are all lucky to be alive," Mike said, gently squeezing her hand.

Teary-eyed, Lisa continued, "I can't believe this. You promised me you'd be more careful."

"I know, babe. I'm so sorry. But we had to catch those suspects. They were dangerous. You know, the recent kidnapping and the dug offences were those guys. I'm sure it's that son of a bitch behind it all."

She squeezed his, too, "I understand Mike, but your safety matters too. You mean everything to me."

Smiling weakly, he said, "I love you, Lisa. This is a wake-up call. I'll be more cautious from now on."

With a teary smile, "I love you too, Mike. Just promise me you'll come back to me in one piece next time.

Lisa withdrew her hand and, with a determined tone, said, "Babe, I'm so relieved you're alive, but I can't keep going through this. If you put yourself in danger like this again, I... I can't do it anymore."

"What do you mean?"

Still teary-eyed, Lisa continued, "I'm saying that if you don't prioritise your safety and our future together, I can't be a part of this anymore. I can't live in constant fear of losing you.

"I understand, sweetheart. I promise to be more careful, not just for the job, but for us. For our future."

Lisa grabbed his hand and kissed it, "I want to support you, honey, but I need to know you're committed to making this work." The two shared some lighter moments until the nurse came to dress Mike's wounds, and Lisa left.

Chapter 22

“ “I am Poseidon, ruler of the seas. I shape the destiny of mortals. Though I have my failings, I will not let you see them. I will let you see as far as you can sip the sea,” his voice echoed.

Waves crashed against cliffs, and gradually faded.

Even in the small concrete jungle of Harare, the essence of Poseidon lingers, manifesting in unexpected ways. JBZ stood outside by the large sliding doors of his lavish house. The night had subtle hints of the distant sounds of sirens and the low hum of cars. Suddenly, a figure emerged from the shadows – Poseidon, god of the sea, appeared before JBZ.

With a disapproving gaze, Poseidon spoke, “JBZ, your empire is built on the suffering of many. The seas themselves weep for the lives you've drowned in misery.”

JBZ sneered, “Who is this? Another moral guardian? I built an empire where others feared to tread and where my feet led.”

Poseidon scowled, “Your Empire is built on greed and destruction. The seas, unlike your empire, are timeless and eternal. Stop comparing yourself to the sea, for you have yet to see what the sea holds. Quit your seesaw with people’s lives. Your past should not define you. Rather, it should refine you or nothing at all. You let it confine you to bitterness. Unless you are at peace with yourself, you will not be at peace with the world.”

JBZ raised an eyebrow, “Eternal, shit, huh? Well, I control my destiny. No one's higher than me. I choose to be bitter; I will not beat about the bush. My life was shit, and not even a pair of sheets on my bed. Sometimes, I slept on the floor, but now I run the floors from the Atlantic to Antarctica. You can’t tell me a jerk.” He puffed his Cuban cigar, savouring the smoke.

Poseidon, smiling with disdain, spoke, “You mistake power for true greatness. The sea is powerful, yet it nurtures life. What have you nurtured, JBZ?”

JBZ waved his cigar, revealing its gold label; I've built a legacy that'll be remembered. For good or bad, that’s none of my business.”

"Legacies built on suffering are forgotten with the tides. The sea, on the other hand, endures," Poseidon said, shaking his head.

As Poseidon vanished into the night, JBZ shuffled back into the house, bewildered. He woke up shaking from this dream. He sometimes compared himself to Poseidon of Greek mythology, especially when bragging.

#

JBZ was about to outwit by duress Ivan, the Suwojena owner, to sell his resort to him and use it for premium pimp or escort services. But after his strange dream, he seemed to have changed his plans.

One late summer afternoon, Roselyn entered as he poured himself a shot of his favourite whiskey. She cavorted towards him in such a way that his whiskey overflowed.

"I know that smile; what are you planning now?" Roselyn asked, caressing his head while giving him a peck, which left an imprint of her lipstick.

JBZ sighing, snapped at her, "Not today, Roselyn. I've sent a driver to fetch Nobesuthu. I also have an important call with Mexico and the US. So, I don't need drama. You hear me?"

Raising an eyebrow, she murmured, "Someone needs sexual healing. Too much stress." Then she walked out in an exaggerated strut. Meanwhile, JBZ sat behind a massive desk, where he reached for a high-tech communicator. He activated it to initiate a secure call. Hushed whispers from the other end of the conference call filled up the room. Once Jack Xi started talking, silence ensued. His opening words signaled his dissatisfaction.

"It's survival in a world that will crush us if we show weakness. We don't make the streets kind; they make us powerful." He continued, while everyone followed, and wanted feedback on their previous discussions on the new ventures.

While he talked, JBZ had sudden flashes of his distorted dream featuring Poseidon.

Chapter 23

Detective Mike engrossed in his investigation, studied a board covered in crime scene photos and notes. His desk phone rang, and it was his boss.

"I've got a lead on the drug trafficking and human smuggling case. It might tie back to JBZ for real this time, beyond reasonable doubt," Mike shared the update with his boss.

"Listen Mike, you are now paranoid, and I am taking you off that case. This is bordering on obsession now. You may also need PTSD counselling. I am also booking you in with the nurses at CityMed Psychology Partners." Mike was left speaking alone on the phone. He sank into his chair, clutching his temples. He crumpled up little notepads and flung them onto the wall. He then banged his desk and stormed out of the office. Once inside his car, he called Lisa. Just as she answered, Mike's partner Mark rushed to his car, banging the window frantically.

"We have a match. It is all connected, and this goes beyond our city, our country," Mark spoke, gasping for breath in between words.

Staring straight ahead nonchalantly, Mike replied, "Great, how about you go and tell that to your boss. I'm sure he will be impressed, and I believe so." With that, Mike rolled up his window and drove off, leaving Mark with more questions than answers. He stood there wide-eyed, his gaze following the direction of Mike's car. After a few seconds of bewilderment, he shook his head and dawdled back to the office.

#

Cleopatra was the last active ruler of the Ptolemaic Kingdom of Egypt, and she was known for her charisma and her alliances with influential figures. Cleopatra, known for her intelligence and ability to navigate complex political landscapes, made Mike more hopeful that he could find his way back into the case and crack it. He had to search for the big fish in his sphere of influence without bypassing his boss. To Mike, Cleopatra represented the cunning and strategic approach needed to ace the investigation. On the other hand, Mike viewed the "Boy King", Tutankhamun, who ruled during the 18th dynasty of ancient Egypt, as the symbol of mystery and the quest for hidden truths. Detective Mike and Lisa's use of Cleopatra and Tutankhamun's names as code words reminded him why he joined the police force. He had to get back onto this important case. But to do that, he had to be discreet and shrewd.

Chapter 24

Noel James was in his living room, and his wife figured out that he was far deep in a place far away. Noel James was deep at the center of the international waters near the strait of Taiwan, a major trade route that the US protects with Aircraft careers. James had been in the Navy for 20 years; he had joined straight from college as a family tradition; his great Grandfather was in the Navy, and so was his Great Grand Father, a World War 11 Hero, and so was his father before him.

NJ, as he is affectionately known, was working with the FBI anti-drug Unit. During his days in the Navy, he had lost a close friend through an attack from the Red China, which Beijing disputed to have initiated with the USA army, saying that they only responded to provocations. The Chinese suffered heavy casualties in the confrontation, and little was said about the matter, and little is known about the matter till today.

It was in October 2021 when the Chinese were battling an increasing number of Corona Virus, better known as Covid 19. At that time, Millions of people died, and governments reacted by imposing hash lockdowns for periods extending to as much as three weeks in succession. Business came to a standstill, and employees were released from work, with companies struggling to reopen after each successive lockdown.

Companies entered into lockdowns with weak cash flows and emerged much weaker; supply chains were strained, with cargo movement curtailed to a snail's pace, sending prices heavenwards. A crisis of vaccines ensued, with the developed countries accused of hoarding the anti-virus while poor nations could not afford to manufacture their own drugs, thanks to China and Russia, who offered Sino Pharm and SinoVac to African countries, especially in Zimbabwe. The Chinese and the Russians have always been close friends of Africa, dating back to the time of the Liberation struggle when Africa was battling with the yoke of burdensome evil colonial rule that saw thousands being killed and some driven off fertile lands. It was a time when China itself was considered a poor nation. So, the bond between Africa and these two "great" nations cannot easily be broken.

Speculation was rife globally that China had lost as much as 1 Million people to the Wuhan-originated virus, which president Trump at the time called it the Chinese Virus. The Chinese refuted that 1 Million people had died, with Beijing scoffing and offering only three hundred thousand as the total number of fatalities.

At that time, the Chinese ruling Communist Party started making threats against Taiwan under what the Chinese called the one China Policy. A long-standing political plan that was aimed at uniting Taiwan as part of China, unlike the current status quo where Taiwan wants to be independent of Red China. The Threats and rhetoric got the US government rattled; the US used the Strait of Taiwan for significant Trade. Predictably, the US decided to support Taiwan. The US made its position clear that should the need to support Taiwan and the request to do so is made, they would support them without hesitation.

The US Reacted by deploying aircraft Careers into International waters close to China; tensions escalated when the US secretary of state made a stopover state visit to Taiwan. China saw the move as a direct provocation by the US and acknowledgement that Taiwan was an independent sovereign state, a position opposed by China. China reacted with a show of force never seen before in the history of Mankind by circling Taiwan with Aircraft Careers with both air and marine drills taking place daily.

The US's response was an announcement of a raft of measures aimed at restraining China from ceasing control of Taiwan; this was achieved through the ban on the export of Microchips to China, among other crippling restrictions meant to beat China into submission and obedience.

Noel James was reflecting on the old tradition of sailors dying at sea and the protocol that was followed throughout his career; he had lost a number of good friends and witnessed the standard procedure being followed when one dies aboard an aircraft carrier. The crew follows a strict protocol to ensure that the diseased is treated with the utmost respect and dignity that a human being deserves; then the crew attending the funeral must wear the uniform of the day, and where possible, the ship will be brought to a halt, and all the flags on board will fly it have must as a sign of morning and respect for the distinguished fellow.

The casket bearers, the firing party, and the buglers assemble on the deck all the other crew members. The casket beers consists typically of six to eight individuals positioned on both sides of the coffin, lining up in order of height they carry the casket which bears the deceased who must meet specific criteria such as being a member of uniformed officer in active duty, a retired navy sailor or an honorable distinguished charged veteran. Burials are seen as a rich and honorable tradition that is desperate to the career of the earlier days of sailors venturing into the open seas.

This tradition dates back to the ancient civilization of the Egyptians, Greece, and Vikings, who are known to have conducted maritime funerals in honor of their dead.

These have been adopted by various Nations; the deeply rooted and rich tradition has been talked about in many nations, inspiring many to become sailors. The stories have been talked about in many versions for centuries and have inspired many sons and daughters to become sailors in defending their territorial waters.

In the past, the deceased would be sewn into a sailcloth and sent overboard. This would be accompanied by a religious ceremony according to the individual's faith. In recent times, many options have been explored for the disposition of the deceased's remains, including placing them in a coffin or an urn or even scattering the remains at sea. There are instances when the cremated remains are mixed with cement to create a concrete block which is dropped into the ocean to form a man-made reef.

Whatever the disposition method, the ceremony is conducted with full military honors, including the Riffle salute and the playing of Taps, the specific details of the ceremony vary according to the deceased service history and personal preferences. After the ceremony, the body is placed into the ship's front tail and placed on canvas litter. And slid into the sea. As the body reaches the water, crew members salute, and the ship's bell rings and the body is allowed to sink to the floor of the ocean; in situations where the body is to be transported to land, the body is placed into a body bag and stored in a freezer.

Noel narrated how each time he was deep in thought, he flushes with ceremonies at sea that he had been a part of and this brought a sense of sadness each time he thought about it as he wanted to be buried at sea but retired before he could accomplish death.

He was now working with the Big Cat, an FBI agent known for his non-formal approach to work. Actually, he was never seen wearing anything formal clothes. Noel did not notice that he was literally talking to himself; while in a trance his wife had been calling him, but after getting closer and hearing some murmurings, she decided against the idea and instead was keen to learn what was going on.

#

James Brown was a man in his early forties and had a distinguished career. He had been trained at the world's most prestigious military Academy in the history of mankind. He had worked on the most dangerous missions in Iraq, and Afghanistan, to name just a few. He flew the F-16 F-35 lightning and was one of the few who had laid their hands on a multi-billion dollar B spirit bomber. He was tactical and smart in dangerous mountainous areas, able to maneuver, and he was key in the hunting and capture of the notorious drug lord such as the Gaintanistan Gulf Clan a manhunt for Colombia's most wanted men, the drug lord called Otoniel, a man who needs no introduction in the realm of illegal Legal drugs, he too was coopted into a team working with the FBI.

At exactly 14 hours, the big cat Noel James and James Brown were ushered into the office of the director of foreign missions and in the office where two men and one lady only referred to as Charlie. The director welcomed everyone skipped the pleasantries, and went down straight to business, saying, "Gentlemen, you have selected to go to Africa into a nation hostile to ours. The mission is contacted side by side with the national police of that country. You are to leave within 24 Hours as your travel details are being worked out and diplomatic discussions are taking place. You will be briefed in full on your way there. Am I understood?"

Noel quickly responded, "No, Sir!"

"Did I hear no Sir?"

Again, Noel answered, "Yes," his voice was strong and firm.

"I run no soldiers necessary here. I am the one in charge, and we will hear no "No sirs here, am I clear? Does anyone have a question?"

"Yes, Sir!" Noel shouted.

The Director leaned forward, his demeanor expectant. "Spit it out, son."

Noel hesitated, then corrected himself. "I wouldn't say 'spit' is an appropriate term, maybe 'retch'."

The Director's brow furrowed, "Cut the soft soap, son. What is it?"

Noel squared his shoulders. "What is our mission, Sir?"

The Director leaned back, a smirk playing on his lips. "Need-to-know basis, son. You're a sailor; sail with the tide until you can see what's going on."

"What tide might that be, Sir?" Noel inquired, his tone tinged with uncertainty.

The Director's expression turned grim. "Shit. Rain. Tide, son."

Lesly, the seasoned veteran, entered the room, his eyes scanning the group with a mixture of skepticism and disdain. "So, these are the kids I am to lead in a charge? I thought they were real men."

The Director interjected smoothly, his voice carrying authority. "I assure you; their CVs are impeachable…"

Lesly waved off The Director's assurance with a scoff. "I am sure they are, but what I see are frightened men who have come to Mama for protection. Don't worry, boys, I will protect you." He then guffawed.

Noel, ever the curious one, couldn't help but interject. "What's your point, honeybee?"

The three gentlemen were excused, and outside the office, they wasted no time expressing what was on their hearts.

Noel James added, "I hate that bitch with all my passion, power and strength."

James Brown snapped back, "I don't waste my energy that way. I like her; I like her tough talk bitchy tongue and matter of fact, by the end of this mission, she will be mine, and I will make love to her…"

Lesly, not to be outdone, said, "I am sure you will; what's stopping you from doing that now, little boy? I see fear in your eyes; it's written all over your face. I tell you what, how about I challenge you to a Judo fight, and if you win, I am all yours?"

The Invitation was irresistible in two parts, James Brown had made a remark before his colleagues and was to prove that he actually could walk the talk, and secondly, Lesly was a beautiful senior officer, and the offer carried a border line disciplinary threat and the possibility of being in love with Lesly. Lesly was a beautiful woman who could effortlessly win a beauty contest wearing a military uniform with no makeup, and all judges scored her 10 out of 10.

While James seemed to be pondering over the invitation and its possible outcomes, Lesly held his upper body and the next thing he was down.

She bellowed, "From now on, you know who the boss is; I will send you wherever I please."

Chapter 25

The detective Mike was coiled on a couch with his head gently on Lisa's lap. His phone rang, and he picked it up at once. It was Chief Inspector Paul Nyathi. Without greeting him, he simply said.

"Report to KG6 at 10 PM, son. Do not be late," Paul Michael's voice crackled through the phone before abruptly cutting off.

Lisa appeared from the kitchen, concern etched on her face. "Who was that, Mike?" she asked, her tone urgent.

"Some Paul guy," Mike replied, his tone strained. He ran a hand through his hair, trying to shake off the unease settling in his chest.

Lisa's eyes narrowed. "Some Paul guy?" she repeated incredulously. "He sounded like someone in authority."

Mike shrugged, "Yeah, I guess you could say."

"You guess?" Lisa's voice rose slightly, a mix of frustration and fear. "Mike, this isn't some casual call. Whoever he is, he's serious."

Mike met her gaze, seeing the concern etched in her features. He reached out to her, pulling her close, his arms wrapping around her in a protective embrace. "Hey, I don't know the guy," he murmured, his voice soft but determined.

Lisa leaned into him, her grip tightening as if she could anchor him to the safety of their home. "Please, Mike," she pleaded, her words barely more than a whisper. "Be careful. Come back to us. We need you."

Mike swallowed hard, the weight of her words sinking in. "What do you mean?" he asked, the fear in his voice palpable. "What do you mean, 'back to us'? You mean you and me, of course. I will be back for you, Lisa," he assured her.

But Lisa's response stopped him in his tracks. "No, Mike," she trembled. "There will be four of us. I'm pregnant. I was going to tell you in a special way, but I guess I had to break the news this way. First-time pregnancy doesn't show easily in the early days."

Mike's heart raced as he processed her words. He knelt before her, feeling a mix of emotions swirling inside him. "To you, Lisa, and our two unborn babies," he vowed, his voice filled with determination. "I will be there for you. I will raise our children with you, provide for you, and protect you. Know ye all men to whom it may concern: the family of Detective Mike is a no-go area."

Lisa's tears turned to urgency as she pointed to the wall clock. "You'll be late, Mike!" she exclaimed, a note of panic in her voice.

Immediately after that, the phone rang, and Mike answered after the first ring. The man on the phone simply said the President and US embassy Staff are waiting for you, son; you better bring your ass here now. Soon after that, Mike had the sound of a Bell Jet Ranger hovering above the house, and the rope was dropped. He picked up the rope, and the Hit Scope was moving upwards. The hit scope was up in the air, just like when Augustine Gibbons picked agent Stone in the triple X movie from the US military maximum Prison. Stone had been brought to prison for two offences, with each carrying a nine year Jail Term, one for disobeying a direct Order and one for breaking the General's Jaw.

Mike arrived at the King George the Sixth Barracks, popularly known as KG6, and immediately sensed that there was a problem. He was used to being told how the president was interested in some of the cases that he was working on, but he had not actually seen the President actively being on a case. Yet he saw the presidential motorcade. And heavily armed soldiers. The security was heightened and a little bloated. Considering that it was at KG6, a secure Military facility already.

Detective Mike was met by the chief of Police himself. Mike was briefed on how to handle the protocol and US faster than bad if you are frustrated by the process. He asked you to ask the police chief why they had called him specifically, and he was informed that the President. Had personally requested that she be involved in the case at hand.

Mike was ushered into a crisis room full of dignitaries and Amy, general Air Force official commander of the national army. Air Marshall, air commodore or wing commanders and noticeably, the SAS Team, the director general Central intelligence. Unit heads ahead of the military intelligence with all present.

At the same time Mike arrived at KG6, a fleet of duty cars arrived at Mike's house, took photos of the house, went inside where Lisa was sleeping on the couch, and asked her to wake up the team. They had come to take her to a safe place as the authorities feared that she would be an easy target. She resisted, but the men were more persuasive.

It was exactly 00:00 hours when they arrived at the safe house with her two unborn babies. The events that took place from Mike being called for a meeting with the President to discussion about the pregnancy and the manner in which Mike left in a huff in a hero style as well as the manner she was whisked away from the house to a safe house brought both fear and excitement.

She was happy that she was pregnant with twins, not any other men's but Mike's twins, and she was willing to tell everyone who cared to listen, but she was not allowed to make any calls, and her phone was taken in, and she would communicate only through a secure approved line. She feared that if Mike died she would never see the perfect family she had been dreaming of since she was six. She did not want to be a single parent and raise deficient children.

At the instruction of JBZ Mike's house, phones and car were all bugged, and every conversation he made was being listened to 24/7, 365. The man who was in charge of such responsibility was none other than T1; this name was a shortcut for Tendai picking the T and I in the name to make it T1. T1 once complained of how Mike and his wife were so much in love, and he expressed his desire to be in a relationship based on what he listened to, from general conversations to love to foreplay and making love and even to the way they fought over different matters always managing to find each other in the process.

T1 was falling in love with the couple, and he began. He always looked forward to listening to them, and he had so much respect for Mike as a man, for how he protected the nation, how he loved his wife and how he managed to achieve a delicate balance between work and life.

Mike would switch from attending a crime scene and dealing with hardcore criminals, having a shootout with the armed robbers who were either caught in the act or hot pursuit. Mike would change from a King Kong protecting his nation to a sweet and lovely handsome man that any woman dreamt of.

JBZ was receiving real-time intelligence and was the one to throw the first punch. JBZ was a master planner and executed his plans with the precision of an Eagle spotting a fish in the water from miles away, grabbing an unsuspecting fish, and soaring to the heavens while its claws dug deeper into the flesh, sending excruciating pain throughout the body while breathing becomes more difficult.

JBZ managed to track Detective Mike, and as soon as Mike was out of the house, he received reports from T1, and the collaborating confirmation came from one Senior Police Officer who had been cooperating with JBZ. JBZ was a man who feared no one and had no regard for religion or authorities. He was used to having his way almost all the time, but there was something about Detective Mike that made him uneasy. He managed to assure himself that he was a great man who needed to be worried about low-level Detective Mike, but his mind had a way of always fucking with him, creating nightmares. JBZ knew that Detective Mike was an ordinary Detective who did his work underfunded and without much support from most of his colleagues, who were either corrupt or too motivated to follow through on matters, especially where there was added Risk to life without a clearly defined benefit to self.

JBZ had a great eye for great talent, and the moment he had an encounter with Detective Mike, he was sure that he was either going to have a great employee in Detective Mike or a rival whom he was to fight till the very end. He was able to read the minds and measure the degree of a man's ability to set goals and peruse them given what the Detective accomplished. JBZ never had a chance to reach out to Mike and he was aware that with his propensity to commit crimes, it was only a matter of time before they met in the field.

JBZ intercepted the radio communication concerning the security arrangements for Lisa and assembled a team that got to Mike's home just a few minutes before the real corps arrived. The kidnapped LISA, without much force, and though she was afraid in the process, he believed that she was in the hands of the Police.

Mike requested to call his wife at 0400, and the call was answered by JBZ himself.

JBZ said, "Put me on the speaker, son. So we avoid the kachandra's kachandra. I have your wife and the twins. What happens from now on is up to you. Do not be on the investigation team, son. I know how much you love your wife; you guys are such a great couple. It would be a tragedy if anything were to happen to LISA and the two babies.

Mike's jaw clenched as he listened to JBZ's ominous words. "I do not take idle threats," he retorted, his voice laced with defiance.

JBZ chuckled darkly. "Oh, poor Mike," he taunted. "You think this is a pissing competition? Don't be stupid, Mike. Don't do it, and all shall be well. If you agree, then I will let go of your family, and you will live happily ever after. But if not..."

The unspoken threat hung heavy in the air, and Mike felt a cold chill run down his spine. "I'll never agree to your terms," he declared, his voice firm. "You can't manipulate me with empty promises."

JBZ's laughter echoed through the phone, chilling Mike to the core. "We'll see about that," he sneered before the line went dead, leaving Mike with a sinking feeling in the pit of his stomach.

Mike roared, "Have you not heard that you can take a man's wealth and everything that he has, but if you threaten his family, then there is no measure of how fast and how hard the man will pounce on you. You have had your act on the stage, JBZ it's time you leave the stage and disappear and never come back, or else I am coming to take you down."

JBZ sneered again, "You have some set of balls, son, talking to me in that manner; I have always believed that you are talented. I could use a man like you on my team. Come work for me. By the way, greet the baggers who are listening."

"Come and see my face JBZ, so that when I hold your head in my hands, piece your chest and retrieve your heart, my face will be the last thing you see before you die. I will put you on a makeshift Spit-rotisserie. Will you die? All this I will do before your staff and upload the video of you begging for mercy. I can do a movie on that."

JBZ had not had any man speak to him like that, and it really got to him. He screamed loudly, kicking things around and throwing things missing one of the staff members. Mike was concerned that JBZ might hurt his wife but was pleased with how JBZ reacted as Mike spoke like someone with something of value that belonged to JBZ, and while JBZ was ruthless, he never acted out of emotions and without full information.

Detective Mike was aware that any sign of weakness would mean JBZ was going to either kill LISA or keep advancing. Either way, he was advancing somehow, so buying time was necessary at the time.

"Enough of this foreplay, Detective; let's talk business here, but there is a sound that may jump start you here."

Immediately after that, there was a deafening screaming sound; Mike could not believe that his Lisa was being tormented. Lisa was being tortured by two men and one woman. She was suspended on an iron rod with legs tied together, and they were pulling her nails one after the other with some pliers.

Mike seemed unmoved in his voice, "Wow, you are good but not that good. They say men are great planners and achievers, but their downfall is the same. So I thought why men do anything? It's all about the money, women, power and religion. Men go down the same way; bragging gives a man away. You and I have the same thing in common, we both love our families."

"I want your word that you will stand down; however, I will keep your wife as insurance, Detective."

"I knew that you bitches were listening to my conversations with Lisa, and I found a traitor inside your team, and I have been tracking you in real time; if you think Lisa means anything to me, then you must be joking."

"So, I can do whatever I want with her?"

"Go ahead and do the most despicable things you can ever think of."

"You are such a drug dealer, Mike; you and I have a lot in common; all these people are just pieces on a chess board which I can exchange or dispose of at any time without emotion."

"Yes, we both do drugs. You trade in drugs, and I trade in stopping the trade in drugs, so we are bound to have commonalities."

In the background, Lisa could be heard screaming louder and louder, and Mike was tempted to speak with her, but he gritted his teeth and managed not to speak.

Lisa pleaded, "Mike, you promised to look after me. I am pregnant with your children; I love you, Mike. Please save me and the kids. We need your help."

JBZ responded with a loud, sharp laugh, "Mike, I must have underestimated you. I will do whatever I please to Lisa. I will start by cleaning her up and treat all her wounds. When she is healed, she will be my girl, and when you our twins, are born, I will graft them into family business. Lisa is a sweet girl, and I will have her."

Mike was quiet for some time, and then he responded softly. "I have a song I want you to listen to JBZ."

"Your wife and your unborn child are going to be taken as slaves, yet you want to sing."

"Why are you in a hurry? You are scared of music, too?"

"Ok, make it quick I have a new ass to try not sure what kind of positions she prefers, so we have a long day trying positions, hey."

Soon after saying that, JBZ heard a troubling sound of his son screaming on top of his voice and his wife crying. JBZ was shocked.

"What do you want? Don't do anything to my family; I will kill you if you touch her."

"Please don't squash creativity, let's enjoy the game here. It's a check, mate my Drug Lord. What next? Turns out my Drug Lord has a weakness. It's a pity your son plays good chess, and he can make a good Detective and hunt down criminals like you."

Mike had requested that JBZ's wife and son be tracked and that, at any given point in time, the Police should have the ability to capture the family as insurance for any eventualities.

Chapter 26

The US embassy houses 30 Marine Corps; the Marine Corps are elite soldiers with special Military training. In Zimbabwe, these are charged with protecting the Ambassador who, in diplomatic protocol, represents the President of the United States. The security arrangements are such that wherever the Ambassador goes, there has to be an advanced team. So, the Calendar of Activities is released for the whole year, and security will be arranged in accordance with that.

When the Ambassador is on the move, the security teams create security circles of armed Marine teams. The circles can be larger or smaller and mainly consist of three to four Marine Corps. Closer to the Ambassador, a security perimeter is established. This security system was designed by the US Department of Defense.

The security arrangements are made depending on the assessment of a particular nation's peace and security risk. Other nations have tighter security due to their high-risk nature. In the case of Zimbabwe, the rating was assessed as medium to low risk due, though there were moments of heightened risk.

The Radio (new code name for cable) came in from Zimbabwe at 20 2:44 PM. It was a nail-biting moment as the US Ambassador's wife and Son had gone to the high-density suburb of high fields, and they had not been seen or heard from by the end of the business day. A small Marine special unit was assembled at the multi-million dollar. The embassy is Africa's largest US embassy, and it was constructed at an estimated staggering amount of USD 292 million.

The team had one mission: to locate, secure, and safely bring the ambassador's wife and son. Olivia had gone to performing arts at Raps Theater in Borrowdale at the same Levy's Village afterwards, she was to be the guest of honor at cultural Heritage in the afternoon in Harare' oldest suburb of Highfield. She asked her son to come along.

The ambassador could not resist being part of the rescue team. He could not sit and watch and entrust other men to go out and look for your wife and child while you pass up in the office waiting for other men to secure your family.

Knowing that the elite Marine squad would decline, the ambassador, who was a soldier as well, decided to drive the Car. And nobody noticed it was wearing his combat gear. Steven McMillan was in charge of the operation. He was the mission discharge with an impeccable CV, and he took this role as the defense attaché was on leave. Having fought battles in Iraq, Afghanistan, and many other special operations, He was the most capable man to manage such a volatile situation.

They drove out of the gates on the east. The gates were opened in a fashion like that in the movie "King Arthur" when Arthur and his Knights were asked to go north of the wall by Bishop Jamanos. North of the wall was a dangerous place; at the same time, the Saxons had come. Their order was to secure the safety of a high-ranking family, which was of great importance to Rome just like Clive Owen was charged with a task to bring Amarios son Alecto, who was destined to become a Bishop or even Pope one day.

So was Stephen and his men were to return with Olivia and Brian, the Ambassador's wife, and son. The mission was a silent night mission as it was not sanctioned or approved by the authorities in Zimbabwe.

The Jeep they were travelling in rolled into Lovernum with tires screaming. As the beasts of the car moved sideways and steadying as it took off at a great speed, there was a moment of silence and one a Mark remarked.

Mark: What kind of an ambassador anyway, who would leave his wife and children and attend it to and be rescued by other men? Maybe he was observing protocol.

John: Mark fuck protocol, this is his family; if I were him, I would be in this fucking car driving it myself, proving that I am not one to wait in some 3 m perimeter wall at the embassy waiting for other men to rescue my family.

Mark's voice cut through the tension in the car, his tone laced with concern. "Careful, men," he cautioned, his words a sharp reminder of the gravity of their situation.

The driver nodded in acknowledgment. "Yes, careful, man," he replied, his voice holding a note of urgency.

As the driver spoke, everyone in the car recognized the familiar voice of the ambassador, and a sense of alarm swept through them.

Stephen Macmillan, sensing the seriousness of the situation, wasted no time in acting.

"Ambassador, sir, please stop the vehicle," Stephen urged, his voice firm but respectful. "We must take you back to the embassy, sir."

The car slowed to a halt at Stephen's command, the tension palpable as they awaited the ambassador's response, their hearts pounding with the weight of the unknown dangers lurking outside.

The Ambassador snapped, looking past his shoulder while maintaining his grip on the steering wheel, "So that I can wait there and sit in the embassy? Perimeter wall three meters high, waiting for other people to save my wife and son? No, it's not going to happen!"

Steven McMillan coughed, hiding his embarrassment, "No, Sir, you can't be here. You will compromise this operation, and your judgment will be clouded by your emotional feelings."

Steven McMillan: No, say you can't be here. You will compromise this operation, and your judgment will be clouded by your emotional feelings.

There was a big shattering sound, and in an instant, the Jeep rolled 4 times; all the team members were killed, and the ambassador was taken alive. There was a live feed to the control room at the embassy, and up to the time the ambassador was taken, the live feed died. The ambassador was kidnapped, and that is the only information that the control room managed to get.

The Jeep had some gasoline sprinkled; the car was bent beyond recognition. Witnesses at the scene stopped to help. But we're both shot in the head and chest. The gunfire was reported to the Mabelreign police station which quickly reacted and reached out to Harare Operations Team. The matter was escalated to the criminal investigation team CID, the Homicide team was also called, and forensics was also called to the scene.

At the embassy, the staff was gripped by fear and sadness. The ambassador had been kidnapped, his wife and son missing as well. There was no official word. The kidnappers had not reached out to demand anything, which was an unusual situation.

The ambassador's wife and son had been accompanied by two embassy staff and one of the members escaped and managed to inform you that there was a commotion and a shootout. Men with heavy combat gear prepared for war, very experienced and very smart, could be ex-military or some such.

The defense attaché was on leave; he had become withdrawn of late and missed a number of embassy events; he had complained of illness and had visited the Doctor frequently. The Ambassador was concerned about his recent change of behavior, but there was nothing out of the ordinary. JBZ had managed to secure records of all Embassy staff, and for one, he was looking for an opportunity to get up close and personal with the Marine Corps. He got his chance after waiting patiently. It was In June 2023 when JBZ met with the defense attaché. The Embassy had held a dinner, and invitations were sent through based on a list approved after rigorous vetting and yet there he was JBZ in the flesh and Blood at the embassy function.

JBZ spoke with his upper-lipped snarled, "So you are the defense attaché here?"

The Defense Attaché, unperturbed and looking straight into his eyes, said, "Yes, Sir, and you are?"

"I am a man talking to the Defense attaché."

Eyes widened, and tilting his head back a moment, the Defense Attaché stared intently at JBZ, "Temper, temper."

"I am kidding; hey, the name is Jonathan."

The Defense Attaché spoke casually, "As in JBZ?"

They both laughed out loud, then JBZ added, "Who would invite the most wanted man to an American Embassy? I am sure your sophisticated systems and machines would have picked that up."

Defense Attaché: You have no idea what goes on these days; people have mastered the art of deception; beating systems is not very complicated, but only pros can do that.

JBZ: so, where are you from? Louisiana?

"Never. I am from Chicago, the Mighty Chicago," the Defense Attaché chuckled.

"And what are you doing here? Honestly, you seem to me like a man cut out for better things. Why Africa, and why come to Zimbabwe of all the places on God's Earth? Your contribution to your country is immense; you deserve something better."

"Deployment is from above, my dear; we are soldiers; we go wherever duty calls."

"I see at your level, you should be in Europe or Australia."

"You have an American accent. Are you an American?"

JBZ laughed, muffling his answer, "Among other nations."

"Which part of US are you familiar with?"

The conversation went on for minutes, and JBZ managed to strike friendship with him using Information that he obtained from his sources from his inside men at the FBI. Turns out that the Defense attaché was due for a promotion to be posted to the European Union as a top Diplomat responsible for US –EU relations. However, things took a turn, and the promises made were never fulfilled. The president had hand-picked him contrary to tradition that only career diplomats are appointed to the ambassadorial role.

The Vice President is rumored to have preferred someone else, and he decided to plant false evidence of espionage, and while investigations were going on, someone was appointed to the position.

After he was cleared of all charges, to save him from total embarrassment, he was offered to be in Zimbabwe. He was an unhappy man and was actively looking for an opportunity to cooperate with anyone who would help him get his revenge. To make matters worse, the Current Ambassador was part of the panel that disciplined the staff members that were used in the smear campaign.

Later on, JBZ established communication, and they agreed on a deal trading information such as activities of the Embassy in Zimbabwe and the events and activities of the Ambassador.

On the day of the incident, the defense attaché had called in sick, he, however had access to the schedule of activities, and JBZ paid USD 4, 5 Million USD into St Helena Bank Account and USD 6, 5 Million into a Dubai Bank Accounts. These accounts were in the name of the Defense attaché's mother-in-law's cousin, which was a perfect cover. The money was for upcoming operations and for assistance with the Ambassador's movements. The Defense attaché had cut down security around the Ambassador and his family as part of the deal. JBZ's man who attacked the embassy Jeep was tracking the car in real time.

Chapter 27

The United States had been hunting for the elusive Martinez, who was in the USA expanding his territory, and his connection with JBZ had worried the FBI when funds traced from Drugs, Tobacco, Gold, Platinum and illicit Cigarettes sales were tracked and for the first time the FBI listed JBZ and his men involved in the money laundering. The FBI tracked the movements of funds, and these were seen in tax havens and nations hostile to the USA.

JBZ had partnered with Martinez, with the later securing the product for the former and the later also clearing his personal funds through various schemes. JBZ ventured into farming, where he would give cash to the farmers to buy inputs and would, get proceeds from the sale of the produce and pay all the applicable Taxes, apply for foreign Exchange approval to transfer the funds; some would be sent as purchase on inputs while as repayment of Loans to service the input farming scheme while others are paid off as dividends to foreign shareholders.

Sometimes tobacco is exported, and funds are not remitted back to the country as debit notes are sometimes raised to indicate that the product was damaged and are worthless. He was also involved in the exportation of Platinum to South Africa processing as there is no plant that does that in Zimbabwe; the ore content and the percentage of secondary minerals such as gold and silver would be under-declared. JBZ has recently embarked on the exploration and mining of Lithium to supply the battery-hungry sustainable energy new industry. The export is being made through the porous Forbes border posts. JBZ's companies are estimated to have 3900 gold mining claims in Zimbabwe, a country where gold is found in every province. Zimbabwe has more than 285 minerals, including precious stones. JBZ's favorite is Gold, and he was doing an average of 22 Tons of gold per month, smuggling 60% of it through diplomatic links while the balance would be sold through formal channels and funds invested into real estate and then sold.

JBZ collected consequence notes in Zimbabwe and sent these notes using different airlines. His web of businesses would come up in investigations from time to time, and some of the dealings would coincide with companies that were suspected by the FBI to be owned and controlled by Martinez.

According to the FBI, the value of business dealing between JBZ and Martinez grew from a mere USD 10 Million to USD 4.5 Billion annually, revealing again the fact that the Southern African country is probably suffering illicit financial flows that are more than the official GDP figures. The FBI had a reason to believe that Martinez was supplying JBZ with Coke and a cocktail of other drugs, a suspicion they managed to prove recently.

The FBI believed that there was a Link between JBZ and Martinez. But there is a problem, a very big problem. They say most life complex problems can be solved by a simple solution; however, there may be no simple solutions to complex problems. The USA and Zimbabwe are enemies; the US has maintained a cocktail of economic sanctions on Zimbabwe, which crippled the country's economy and impoverished its people over the last two decades.

The difference between the hostilities between the USA and North Korea and that of the US vs. Zimbabwe is that while the US had slapped the teapot-shaped Southern African Land Locked country with economic sanctions, Zimbabwe had been willing to engage the US in recent times to resolve the matters raised by the US as the basis for economic Sanctions.

Zimbabwe maintained diplomatic ties with the USA. The US also built its largest embassy entire Africa in Zimbabwe; however, some say the size, location and timing of the construction of the Embassy has nothing to do with the relationship between the USA and Zimbabwe but an expression that Zimbabwe is a strategic location in the American Vision as it serves its Interest. So Harare maintained its embassy office in Washington DC while Washington DC moved its office from Takawira to the newly established Westgate office and continued mainly to exchange insults.

JBZ's operations were now strong in Zimbabwe as well as neighboring countries such as Zambia, South Africa, Namibia, Botswana and Mozambique. His well-nit network of suppliers, distribution informers at government, police, Interpol and even the CIA and the FBI was a complete one thanks to the inspiration from his distant cousin, Pablo Escobar and the "great" of Otoniel. JBZ had taken things a notch higher; he had hired software engineers to develop an ERP i.e Enterprise Resource Planner to manage his business.

He had companies that paid Taxes, in all jurisdictions, had financial statements prepared under the International Financial Reporting Standards (IFRS) and have invested heavily in Sustainability and Sustainability reporting; the companies invested in Corporate Social Responsibility whose events were attended by Presidents, Government Ministers, Permanent secretaries, governors etc.

His financial statements were audited by ZZZ Accounting, a firm of Auditors based in the USA, but outsourced audits of nations to small one to two partner firms despite the size of their operations. Companies have been receiving adverse opinions about significant cash handling and lack of paper trail, especially for cash transactions. An extract from the audit Opinion of one of the companies was as follows:

Basis for Adverse Opinion
The company's had a revenue of USD 366 Million, 69% of which came through cash payments from walk-in customers, the Organization was unable to furnish the auditors with the cash summary report and end of day print out to reconcile cash received and the till cash balance. The inventory was counted without the supervision of the auditors, and since these constitute 60% of the value of total assets, the potential misstatements in inventory could be both material and pervasive.

JBZ used to interfere and get clean Opinions but later decided against the idea, opting instead to allow the auditors and allow the company to look like it had weak internal controls, yet it was due to the fact that the revenue was from illegal activities. The remainder of the revenue came from two clients, who, suspiciously, should have been related parties designed to be customers.

JBZ had increased activity in his bank accounts since the string of the Russia –Ukraine war. The CIA, FBI and Scotland Yard suspected that Martinez and JBZ were supplying weapons in the Black market; surprisingly, the weapons have an American Origin. Investigations revealed that some of the weapons came from Afghanistan. The US had had an embarrassing defeat in Afghanistan when the Taliban advanced, and President Joe Biden ordered what could be said to be an embarrassing withdrawal, which resulted in Billions of Dollars' worth of war equipment that included the Apache helicopters, jets, and ammunition.

JBZ has always acknowledged the need to strengthen the software, and in his response to the management letter, which detailed a list of internal control weaknesses he had instructed his teams to appoint a consultant who would communicate with the auditor and then disagree with them midway, and in the end nothing would be done.

The FBI had allocated an agent to monitor JBZ's operations at arm's length; they must have underestimated JBZ. He had grown to be a big man with colleagues and friends in high places who owed him a lot of favors. JBZ now had senior Civil servants that that he had helped with money to send their children to school; some needed Bank statements to show proof of funds, while others had terminally ill parents or spouses who urgently needed medical attention. Some had children who were offered partial scholarships and needed to pay a certain fee by a particular date.

JBZ had men who specialized in gathering intelligence of highly placed people in need and offering them the relief they were looking for, and in return, they were willing to climb the mountain barefooted for him.

At some point, JBZ asked his network to organize meetings with Presidents in five countries in one week, and they pulled it off; this showed the power of his connections. Sometimes, he would ask for an exemption for the export of prohibited minerals, and he would get the approval in a day.

If he sensed a weakness in the network, he would look for real decision-makers and give them gifts; those who refused would disappear, resign or later change their minds after being persuaded. JBZ was able to focus on some personal needs that employers were not able to meet.

In recent times, JBZ and Martinez decided to join hands to beef up "security" of their operations by building a formidable team to shield their cash, gold and other high-value drugs.

Chapter 28

The weak started with the Minister of Healthcare visiting various institutions across Zimbabwe; the visit to Ingutsheni left the Minister heart broken and in shock about the degree of drug abuse and the impact that this was having on the younger generation.

The minister was informed that more than 65% of the cases of mental health were due to drug abuse, with crystal math and cocaine being the leading drugs. The sister in charge also narrated how cases involving young girls were found to lead the statistics on sexual abuse in the process of taking drugs; some young girls were first-time consumers and were abused once they got high. Others were forcibly raped while under the influence of drugs and could not recall what had happened to them.

The use of drugs had become widespread in school, with drugs coming in cigarette form, and candy, sweets like, the list is endless. The Minister was given alarming national statistics for suicide involving young adults and teenagers who had given up on life.

Somewhere in the capital City of Harare, at a place called Pa House, along Harare drive and between Borrowdale Road and Enterprise road, a party was starting. It had taken three weeks to organize the bacchanalia. It was an exclusive party only for the elite, children from very wealthy families, and those who were in government.

The exclusivity nature of the party meant that those from the Ghetto could not attend the party, and this meant that all wannabes had to pay bribes of as much as USD150 to USD180, depending on who they talked to, just to be invited. Others offered sexual favors in exchange for the invitation, and the abuse of young girls who wanted to be invited but fell short of meeting the criteria was rife. The organizers could not have chosen a better time to host the Party; the house was on a hill overlooking the east. The swimming pool, which was easily 20 meters by 30 meters, was an attraction right in the middle of the property. The house was built on an area of 1000 Square meters while the stand size was a staggering 10,000 Square meters.

The party started on a low note, with those who arrived early talking in pairs, picking some eats that were brought by waters who moved around with some placed on different points for self-service. The deco was done by Jolly white events company, a leading events company, and it was not difficult to see why they are the best in the country when it comes to deco and impressions. The deco was impressive and lived up to the expectations.

The elite could identify with each other while those who had bribed themselves into the party found themselves gathering in groups, though they had tried to blend in by wearing the most expensive dresses, but their accents limited style and lack of natural fair and rhythm made it clear that they did not belong, a conclusion that even they managed to reach sooner than later and they never ventured much into creating many friendships and so they enjoyed the party in their own way and mostly surrounded by their kind.

The music grew louder and louder, and so did the crowds, with genres changing from time to time with Yang Money, R. Kelly, 50 Cent, Nikki Minaj, Justine Bieber, Rick Ross, Akon, topping the international playlist with Davido and mostly Nigerian musicians topping the African variant while Amapiano proving to be the most popular of all the selection on offer by any measure. On the local music scene, Chibaba, Chi Gaffa popularly known as Winky D or Big man wowed the fans with songs such as "Happy Again", "Happy Happy" while on the naughty side the *"Babe Rako Raroorwa"* song took center stage with everyone singing the song word for word. Not to be outdone was XQ with *"Mai Mwana Itsvigiri"*, Jar Prayzah with *Chiremerera"*.

Surprisingly the sungura Champion was popular among the elite with songs such as *"Amake Boy", "Tafadzwa Nyarara", "Madhuve Ndewangu"* topping the list and sending the party goers into a frenzy, with most performing the Alick Macheso Invented Borrowdale dance. Amapiano continued to overshadow any other genre, and this was understandable given the heavy presence of Ama 2000, a phrase used to describe those born from the year 2000 popularly known in the global arena as generation Z.

This age group is very independent, experiences sex and relationships at a very young age and does not have strong relationships. They are easily bored, and as a result, they create a lot of friends, but very limited meaningful bonds exist. This category does not suffer long, does not stay in one job for far too long, is techno survey among, and does not take instructions well.

At 11:30, the complexion of the party started changing rapidly as the sons and daughters of Ministers of Foreign Affairs, Home Affairs, and Health Ministries started coming through. These were treated with dignity and were mostly protected through and through by a team that was very vigilant and kept an eye on proceedings.

At the stroke of midnight, a team of ten people arrived amid pomp and funfair, sending all the ladies and guys screaming and whistling with admiration as the daughter and two sons of the President of the republic of Zimbabwe, Mr Kufazvinei Wellington Junior. There were cheers as they mixed and mingled with others.

After 20 Minutes, the drugs were brought to the tables, and immediately, the music went wild as the party goers wasted no time, moving to the tables and buying and immediately consuming. Some made cigarettes while others snorted, others getting injections, with others doing anything in between all this for the love of the party. The beers kept coming like the party was catered for; in fact, the entrance fee, at USD 350, was steep enough to buy any liquor popular among the average group. Besides, this was a civilized crowd; they needed no restraining as they were modest.

They took to the dance floor in twos, and some disappeared into the house. Four men loitering around the pool as if they were following the proceedings; they tried so hard to stay under cover; they were holding cell phones in their hands like everyone else would do from time to time.

They seemed to have been communicating something, and they were dressed well to blend in with everyone and avoid raising suspicion. The lads were after girls at the party, and their communication seemed to have been about who would go after which girl; they were probably trying to avoid clashing, so they probably decided to divide the girls among themselves. So the plan was in motion; the lads would pick a girl each at different intervals, disappear and later on come back without the girls. This happened five times, so in an hour, five girls were taken, and nobody seemed to notice.

At 2 am, 10 Girls had gone missing, but again, everyone was too busy to notice; no one looked for them, though friends casually asked about them but figured that they might have found a corner to entertain themselves and that in the morning, they will see then when the time came to go home. In any case, they were adults and were able to look after themselves.

The last act was rather violent as there was gunfire sending the party goers crazy and the music growing louder and louder. The guns are a symbol of happiness and confirmation that the party is now at its peach; however, it took a few minutes for the crowds to realise that the guns were actually blazing and the President's daughter was taken together with the Minister's daughter, they did not resist much as they were wasted. The abductors faced resistance from the body guards, but the body guards were easily overpowered in a shoot-out were the abductors had 700-meter range AK 47s. The car screamed, and the tyres marked the road with threads as they took off at high speed.

The girls were drugged, and at the instruction of JBZ, 8 of the girls were sent to the Brothel in New Lands, where they were used to entertain high-level guests. Being under the effects of drugs, the girls were stripped naked and were placed in rooms where they would be visited by men and asked to perform all sorts of sexual acts.

At least five of the girls had nor had sex before, and losing virginity under such cruel circumstances was more painful than anything they could ever experience in life; the young girls screamed with excruciating pain as the ruthless abusers pieced their perfect bodies, breaking them down with their oversized manhood, the abusers were thrilled to have slept with a virgin, an encounter so rare in modern times given that girls start having sex in grade six or seven there about.

The virgin girls were abused more and more as their screaming caused the abusers to tear them apart, assuming that they were screaming with joy, yet they were in paid, innocent children well-mannered who had preserved themselves but due to peer pressure and the desire to fit in, had gone to a party they were not supposed to go, thus they were at the wrong place and the wrong time.

Men kept coming with, each paying at east USD 800 for an act, and for that amount, they demanded anything they wished, and if they did not get what they wished for, some would resort to beatings and even biting and yelling all sorts of insults. This new way of entertainment was new to Zimbabwe, and most participants were excited about this new innovation; however, brothels are illegal, and that makes the game even more interesting.

The act made one sick as the girls were treated like toys, and photos were being taken while they were forced to perform unimaginable sexual acts and other unthinkable things.

JBZ had instructed that the girls be treated in the cruelest manner to send a strong message to government officials who wanted to act against his operations. JBZ wanted things to go his way.

By six am, each girl had been raped by 20 men, each paying USD800, with JBZ making a cool USD128, 000, or was it cool? The girls groaned with pain when the effect of drugs had weaned off. Each of the girls was given food to eat; it was difficult for them to eat, as they were each deep in thought about the events that took place, how the hyped party ended up being a kidnapping ground, and why they were the only target, "why me " they each must have been asking. They all complained of severe pain, with most having so much pain in the genitalia.

Later in the afternoon, the girls were screened, 3 had tattoos, so they were sent back to the Brothel, where they went through the same ordeal of being abused as sex toys by very unkind strangers who had paid to be thrilled. They cried and screamed as they were raped and ripped apart, beaten and insulted, but they were powerless, they were tied to the bed, and one of the girls asked for the drugs as she could not come with the pain and emotional abuse without the aid of the drugs. The girl was given the drugs on condition that she extend her shift with two more clients than the usual 20.

The demands from the brothel customers were high, and the cries and resistance made some customers pay more to further damage the young souls; in their minds, the cries were cries of excitement, yet these girls were traumatized and in great pain.

At a secure facility somewhere in Harare, the President's daughter and the Minister's daughter were undressed, two men could not resist the temptation to rap them before selling them, but then they learnt that this was business and they had no business fucking business inventory as doing so would reduce the value of the inventory. The fact they would always get one or two girls to pass around among themselves after every raid managed to calm their nerves. The girls were in an inventory that was waiting to be sold, and these three girls were joined by girls taken from the Brothel.

At exactly 3 pm, the Auctions started. The screens were on, and all the girls from the brothel were sent to stand before the screens; the Camera was on, and bids started coming through; the opening bids were for USD180, 000, and all other girls were sold for not less than USD280, 000. One girl, seeing what was happening, took a razor blade and cut her throat after the auction as they were taken to the car for transportation to their owners. By the end of day one, all the girls from the Brothel were sold and transported, with only one committing suicide.

The President's and two minister's daughters were not sold on the first day. The next day, all three were paraded; however, only the Minister's daughters were sold for USD380,000 each; this was no longer a market for sex but a ransom market. The president's daughter was sold the day that followed, and transportation was organized in advance of the sale.

The President was talking to the Commander of the Zimbabwe Defense Forces regarding the progress that had been made in the Sango Border post when the chief of protocol came literally running, and without greeting anyone, he simply asked to speak to the president.

Chief of Protocol spoke, "Sir, I need to talk to you right now in private."

The President said, "You can speak here."

Chief of Protocol answered, "No sir, it has to be in private, and it has to be right away, sir; I am afraid it's very urgent."

While they were still debating, the police chief arrived flanked by his two deputies responsible for Crime and Operations. At that point, the Central Intelligence Boss, the SAS, and the Military Intelligence arrived. The president sensed that there was danger. Last to arrive was the head of Correctional Services.

The chief of police broke the news to the president, and there was serous panic; the President was notified of the disappearance of the US Ambassador and his wife, Olivia, as well as their Son Brian. The president was aware of the diplomatic challenges that the story brought. In public, the president managed to keep a straight face; however, he authorized USD11, 5 Million to hunt down, and recover his daughter and that of Ministers as well as "killing all the mother fuckers involved".

The President managed to set up a task force to investigate the US embassy incident and the disappearance of the Ambassador under what the President said to be unclear circumstances.

The matter relating to kidnapping was confusing as three days had passed with no contact and no demands being made. The US was making all efforts to engage Zimbabwe to assist in the investigations; however, the illegal operation was an issue they were still to explain.

Chapter 29

In the Pentagon crisis room were general McMally, Jack Williams, Directors of the CIA, and FBI, and the President was chairing the meeting. The purpose of the meeting was to agree on the way forward on the Zimbabwe crisis. The president wanted further details and was willing to explore all diplomatic channels to start the process. There were four presentations to be made, and the first was the Directors of the CIA, DR John Williams.

John Williams said, "Mr. President, Ladies and gentlemen, I would like to begin by starting what we know so far…"

The President sighed before speaking, "Has the intelligence community gathered new information from last night?"

John Williams was the one to respond, "No sir, but if I may—"

The President interrupted him, "You may proceed with your proposal."

John Williams scowled and slightly shook his head, "Mr. President—"

Again, the President cut him short, "John, please call me George Norman, we are in a crisis, and I don't have time for ass-licking protocol bull shit language."

John Williams spoke with a straight face, "Yes, Sir, Mr. President, I will. So far, we know that Olivia and Brian were kidnapped in Highfield at a local school where they were attending a cultural show, and one of the aids managed to escape to the embassy in Westgate; the others did not make it. It's a real crisis."

The President added, "Hold on, John what's the distance from the embassy to the Highfield?"

John Williams coughed before saying, "About 30 km, Sir. We do know that at this point the kidnappers have not demanded anything from us; they have not called the embassy; we are not sure why, but based on the intelligence gathered so far and the style of kidnappings, we believe that it's the same people who took the ambassador. These people don't play defense, just offensive, whatever they are after, and they are loaded for war."

The President urged him, "Go on, John."

John Williams seized his moment to shine and cleared his throat, "Sir, we believe that the men who attacked the ambassador could be a part of an international organized criminal group, maybe ISIS, ELSHABAB or even the Wagna Missionaries or some such bandits. Judging from the swiftness of the team, the Zimbabwean authorities are far behind."

Mr. President continued, "And you know this how?"

John Williams responded swiftly, "Its classified Information, Sir."

"I hereby declassify," instructed the President."

John Williams raised both his chin and torso as he explained, "It's not that simple Mr. President; we have information that some of the members here are not authorized to have access as the story is still developing."

"I hereby authorize," added the President.

General McMally almost stood up but decided against the idea and chose instead to reach for the bottle of mineral water, but John got the message loud and clear.

John Williams added, "At this point, we have gathered intelligence confirming a pattern that the FBI has been observing for years now. I will let the Director of the FBI take it over from now."

William Gross was the Director of the Federal Bureau of Investigations; he took over from Jullian Bright Wagner, who resigned after a committee of congress found out that he had shared classified information with a long-time distance lover, and this leaked in the British Telegraph.

Gross spoke, "We have been looking for Martinez, a notorious drug Lord, a criminal involved in drugs, prostitution, kidnaping, human trafficking and money laundering. The man is a Ghost, but he has been sloppy a few times."

Gross continued while staring blankly at the wall, "We have managed to track a criminal and remote cousin of Pablo Escobar and an admirer of the notorious Otoniel. He has been emboldened by the stories of the two; his name is JBZ and he operates in the enemy territory of Zimbabwe."

The President bit his lower lip and asked, "So why Zimbabwe, of all the places, why not South Africa?"

Gross pulled his belt up, pretending to fix it, and held his head high, "Zimbabwe has gold in every City and Province, the weak judicial system with artisanal miners actively trading in Gold. The level of corruption has reached heaven, and the borders are so porous. The country is said to be losing more than four times its Gross Domestic Product (GDP). However, the real draw for JBZ in the teapot-shaped nation's adoption of the multi-currency system with the USD dominating trades; the country has its allegiance to Red China and Russia, and these two nations are bitter rivals of our Great nation."

Mr. President, still looking puzzled, asked, "Still, that does not explain why you think Martinez is involved, does it."

Gross, without wasting time, jumped to the facts, "We have tracked funds from Zimbabwe linked to a character we believe to be JBZ, and there are transfers between companies that are controlled by JBZ and Martinez, their trade has increased from a mere USD 10 Million three years ago to 2 Billion per annum."

The President snapped at Gross, "So?"

Gross remained nonchalant and said, "So I will call the Big Cat."

Mr. President chuckled, "We have Cats in the FBI?"

Gross murmured, "Careful, Mr. President, the Big Cat has claws."

Mr. President looked around the room, "Who is the Big Cat?"

Gross was quick to answer, "Mr. President, I warn against revealing the identity of the Big Cat."

Mr. President nodded and said, "I am under no obligation not to reveal, but I will consider your advice."

He walked in from a door behind General Macmilay, who made no effort to hide his disapproval of the appearance of the Big Cat.

The Big Cat spoke, "Mr. President, Ladies and Gentlemen, we have infiltrated the operations run by Martinez. While we have intelligence of some of his operations, we have Video recordings of Martinex logging into a Teams meeting where matters relating to drug supply to Zimbabwe and money laundering were discussed."

Mr. President's ears twitched, "Did you see him, Son? Did you talk to him? Show me something."

The video was placed, but no images were displayed. Big Cat continued, "He uses a code, he never speaks in meetings, his runner does all the talking for him, and we have Videos."

Mr. President paced the room with one hand clutching a pen, which he was squeezing hard, almost like a stress ball. His steps echoed off the walls, his grip on the pen tightening with each stride. Then he said, "I am with you, but this is not enough." Commander Maxwell, a man taller than David Cratenden, was a US Naval forces leader for Africa who took over from Adam Robert P Burke. The man was considered firm and fair.

General Macmilay's words brought relief to the whole team, "Mr. President, we are able to send the Navy Seals supported by our stealth unmanned Arial vehicles should there be a need to soften the ground."

However, the Secretary of State dismissed him, "Negative Commander, we cannot attack a sovereign nation, we hear the Southern Africa region and the African Union stands in solidarity with Zimbabwe, any unprovoked aggression will backfire as Red China and Russia are willing to support nations in Africa. The African Union has united on the calling of the removal of the "illegal sanctions" on Zimbabwe. Any attack reduces our chances of overtaking China in Africa. Zimbabwe is so strategic and central to our 2060 Vision. The relations maybe bad, but they are still cordial, we still have an embassy, and we engage diplomatically, and that is to be safe guarded at all costs."

Mr. President turned to look at him, "Secretary, what would you have me do?"

The Secretary of State responded, "Mr. President set up a diplomatic channel and replaced the ambassador with an interim war veteran with diplomatic training to manage the situation. Pick up the phone and speak to President Kufazvinei and agree to agree."

Mr. President retorted with a frown, "Agree to do what?

Secretary of State masked his annoyance and spoke with great composure, "Agree to set up a combined Investigation team, a task force of some sort to rescue the ambassador and his family. The Joint Operation is to be chaired by both countries —"

Mr. President spoke sharply, "Zimbabwe is our enemy; their President may refuse. We have actually asked X to pull down messages portraying the USA as having started some military operation to rescue the US ambassador without going through the authorities. This kind of news is damaging to the operation."

While the secretary of state was still speaking, the Director of the CIA's pager received a message; the message was from his secretary telling him to watch the news on CBBC channels. The Director grabbed the remote and switched on the TV, and there it was. Disaster in Zimbabwe, young girls had been abducted at a local party, and the Ministers and the President's daughters were taken among other 10 girls.

The reporter was narrating that at least 10 girls were kidnapped at a party, and three girls were later found at a Newlands' newly established illegal brothel. One girl was found dead with her throat slit, and supposed blood gushed out through the main vein till she was cold. The President and Ministers of Health and Home affairs Daughters were not found; the rest of the girls had been sold and already shipped out of the country. Detective Mike was in charge of the Investigations, a man who had been personally hand-picked by the president, too had just had his wife kidnapped by JBZ himself.

As Mr. President ran his fingers through his hair, the tension in the room seemed to thicken. His brows furrowed as if in contemplation, his gaze piercing as he pointed a stern finger at the general, his voice resonating with authority, "General, please tell your men to stand down, Secretary. I need you to reach out to Zimbabwe ASAP. I need you to discuss the idea of the US getting authorization to Investigate and rescue the Ambassador and his family."

At that moment, a call was placed through; it was the Zimbabwean Ambassador to the US, and he wanted an urgent meeting with the PRESIDENT IN THE NEXT 30 Minutes or earlier. In fact, he was waiting at the white house; given the circumstances, he had to come without an appointment.

Chapter 30

The US and the UK had imposed economic sanctions on Zimbabwe, and for the past two decades and counting, the people of Zimbabwe had endured economic hardships; it is estimated that more than 100 British companies closed shop with Billions of Dollars leaving the country most through illicit financial flows. Development stalled after annual inflation reached heavens while people languished in poverty as unemployment reached 80%; the Zimbabwe Dollar deteriorated to a point where a way fare for commuting into town cost ZWE 7.5 Billion, with one needing ZWE 15 billion for a return fare.

The people migrated to the neighboring South Africa, Botswana, and Zambia, with some migrating to the UK mostly to do care work, with a few migrating to Australia. The country became economically and socially unstable, with the vast majority of people living under USD 2 per day. Children dropped out of school with the girl child bearing the brunt as some girls were forced into marriage at a tender age as poverty continued to bite. Girls as young as 12 were married off to polygamous arrangements, a practice common in The Manicaland Province Of the country.

The socio-economic challenges that ravaged the country created a restless nation that lived on the edge each day. The country had all the attributes of a nation at War, yet the people of the Republic of Zimbabwe were commended for peace and tranquility. The volatile socio-economic situation created a political risk. Many opposition parties emerged and threatened to topple the ruling party, with the ruling party pointing fingers at the western powers, accusing them of interference in the internal affairs of the country. The government accused the US and the UK of fanning factionalism in the ruling party and funding the opposition to achieve a regime change agenda.

Key government-related networks and politically exposed players were added to the sanctions list, creating a travel ban. Companies that were suspected of propping up the "corrupt "government were slapped with economic sanctions as well.

Zimbabwe's President and key government officials were placed on travel restrictions to the EU, UK and the US, while companies that were considered complicit in aiding abuse of human rights under the UN Global compact 10 Principles were also restricted in their trade and investment activities.

In the Banking sector, banks scaled down, with International Banks such as Barclays and Standard Chartered exiting the Zimbabwean market as business became too low and the number of rules and regulations they had to comply with in view of the sanctions had become too high. The Know Your Customer requirements from Legal and compliance had become a major risk as the economy became more informal, creating massive ethical dilemmas; the KYC became a high ethical issue, prompting banks to de-risk not only in Zimbabwe but in Africa.

Global Insurance giants pulled out of the country and suspended covering any foreign companies doing business with Zimbabwe.

The internal and external debt ballooned to highs of USD 18 Billion for external debt, with the official internal debt being a moving target. The World Bank and the International Monetary fund suspended lending money to the country, drying up all Budgetary support as well as affordable infrastructure funding. The suspension of lending to the country continued even after the country had cleared its debts with the Bretton woods intuitions, with existing debt to other nations being cited as the reason for suspending lending, a position that the government maintained as a continuation of hostilities.

The country initiated a staff monitoring program with the IMF with key monetary targets being set, but none was ever achieved.

Foreign payments became difficult to make as most local banking lost their correspondent banking relationships, and this made it difficult, if not impossible, to facilitate business; critical spare parts could not be procured for industries, mines and important processes.

The National Railway system came to a standstill with the electric wires looted for a 450 km stretch; this created strain on roads as all goods ranging from fuel, goods, Agricultural produce and raw materials.

On the Human Capital front, the nation lost the best brains and continues to lose Human Capital with engineers, doctors, Lawyers, Nurses, and Accountants to name a few.

The state of the health delivery system deteriorated, with major public health institutions failing to cater for critical services and, drugs being in short supply, low staff morale among Doctors and Nurses.

The nation has been hit by repeated cases of typhoid and Cholera year after year, and lives lost needlessly.

Councils have been failing to provide water, refuse collection, and street lights. Council infrastructure is old and is frequently bursting. Roads became death traps due to numerous potholes that have not been attended to.

Put together, the impact of the economic sanctions has severe social-economic implications as the gender-based violence has spiraled out of control, child-headed families are on the increase due to abandonment or parents simply dying, and relatives are not economically empowered to look after the orphans with the government's social welfare safety net underfunded due to budgetary limitations at the tax base have dwindled over the years. Marriages are breaking up before the ink used for signing has dried up.

The Secretary of state had been reading the above report; he was aware that the US had on numerous occasions embarrassed Zimbabwe at United Nations meeting by refraining from attending the address by the head of state and government of Zimbabwe.

The secretary had been looking for points to start the engagement with Zimbabwe how tables have turned now. Zimbabwe had put a raft of measures to reengage the WEST, but its best efforts were received with scorn and disdain from what the government termed the "unrepentant west". The Secretary managed to obtain the details regarding the US activities in the Republic of Zimbabwe; first was the revelation that the much liked belvedere teachers collage was a donation to the people of Zimbabwe by the USA in 1985. A financial Aid package from the US was compiled, and this was considered a good starting point. The secretary needed to show the President of Zimbabwe that the people of USA were friendly to the people of Zimbabwe even though there was tension due to differences in opinion.

The Secretary was aware of the sentiments by one popular Takura Mugoni that the aid from the states was to be received with caution as he likened the USA as one who shoots innocent civilians with one hand while the other hand delivers food handouts, and blankets. It was clear that the rest of the government distrusted the US programs. In reviewing the reports, he came across a report where a US ambassador was forced to suspend activities planned for a particular day and was escorted back to the embassy along Chitepo by then; this was before the Westgate embassy was built.

Having looked at these reports, it was decided that an engagement strategy be crafted. The US was not willing to remove the sanctions in exchange for permission to partner, but the Secretary of State was very much aware that all options had to be on the table. The US needed to rescue its ambassador as they did not want a repeat of what transpired in Afghanistan.

According to some sources, In 1978, Dubs was appointed United States Ambassador to Afghanistan following the Saur Revolution, a coup d'état which brought the Soviet-aligned Khalq faction to power. He was being driven from his residence to the U.S. embassy shortly before 9 a.m. on February 14, 1979, on the same day that Iranian militants attacked the U.S. Embassy in Tehran, Iran, and just months before the Soviet invasion of Afghanistan. He was approaching the U.S. Cultural Center when four men stopped his armored black Chevrolet limousine. Some accounts say that the men were wearing Afghan police uniforms, while others state that only one of the four was wearing a police uniform. The men gestured to the car to open its bulletproof windows, and the ambassador's driver complied. The militants then threatened the driver with a pistol, forcing him to take Dubs to the Kabul Hotel in downtown Kabul. The abduction occurred within sight of Afghan police. Dubs was held in Room 117 on the first floor of the hotel, and the driver was sent to the U.S. embassy to tell the U.S. of the kidnapping.

At the hotel, the abductors allegedly demanded that the Democratic Republic of Afghanistan (DRA) release "one or more religious or political prisoners. No demands were made of the American government, nor did the DRA ever give a complete or consistent account of the kidnappers' desires. Some accounts state that the militants demanded the exchange of Tahir Badakhshi, Badruddin Bahes (who may have already been dead), and Wasef Bakhtari.

The U.S. urged waiting in order not to endanger Dubs' life, but the Afghan police disregarded these pleas to negotiate and attacked on the advice of Soviet officers. The weapons and flak jackets used by the Afghans were provided by the Soviets, and the hotel lobby had multiple Soviet officials, including the KGB security chief, the lead Soviet advisor to the Afghan police, and the second secretary at the Soviet embassy. At the end of the morning, a shot was heard. Afghan police then stormed Room 117 with heavy automatic gunfire. After a short, intense firefight, estimated at 40 seconds to one minute, Dubs was found dead, killed by shots to the head. Two abductors died in the firefight, as well. An autopsy showed that he had been shot in the head from a distance of six inches. The other two abductors were captured alive but were shot shortly afterwards; their bodies were shown to U.S. officials before dusk.

The true identity and aims of the militants are uncertain, and the crime "has never been satisfactorily explained" although U.S., Afghan, and Soviet officials "were all but eyewitnesses" to it. The circumstances have been described as "mysterious" and "still clouded." Several factors obscured the events, including the killing of the surviving captors, lack of forensic analysis of the scene, lack of access for U.S. investigators, and planting of evidence. Soviet or Afghan conspiracy was not proven.

Some attribute responsibility for the kidnapping and murder to the leftist anti-Pashtun group Settam-e-Melli, but others consider that to be dubious, pointing to a former Kabul policeman who has claimed that at least one kidnapper was part of the Parcham faction of the People's Democratic Party of Afghanistan. Disinformation that was spread in the Soviet and Afghan press after the murder blamed the incident on the CIA, Hafizullah Amin, or both. Anthony Arnold suggested that "it was obvious that only one power… would benefit from the murder—the Soviet Union," as the death of the ambassador "irrevocably poisoned" the U.S.–Afghan relationship, "leaving the USSR with a monopoly of great power influence over" the Nur Muhammad Taraki government. Carter's national security adviser, Zbigniew Brzezinski , stated that Dubs' death "was a tragic event which involved either Soviet ineptitude or collusion", while the Afghan handling of the incident was "inept." The Taraki government refused U.S. requests for an investigation into the death.

The Carter administration was outraged by the murder of the ambassador and by the conduct of the Afghan government and began to disengage from Afghanistan and express sympathy with Afghan regime opponents.

The incident hastened the decline in U.S.–Afghan relations, causing the United States to make a fundamental reassessment of its policy. In reaction to Dubs' murder, the U.S. immediately cut planned humanitarian aid of $15 million by half and canceled all planned military aid of $250,000, and the U.S. terminated all economic support by December 1979 when the Soviet occupation of the country was complete.

The Afghan government aimed to diminish the U.S. presence in Afghanistan and restricted the number of Peace Corps volunteers and cultural exchange programs. On July 23, the State Department announced the withdrawal of non-essential U.S. embassy staff from Kabul and the majority of the diplomats as security deteriorated, and the U.S. only had some 20 staff members in Kabul by December. Dubs was not replaced by a new ambassador, and a chargé d'affaires led the skeleton staff at the embassy.

In another case that the Secretary of state was looking at, sources informed about the matter say that on December 23, 1972, Noel was appointed U.S. Ambassador to Sudan when Sudan and the U.S. reestablished diplomatic relations severed as the result of the 1967 Arab-Israeli War. The outgoing Charge d' Affairs, George Curtis Moore, was asked to stay on as Deputy Chief of Mission until the new Deputy arrived in March.

On the evening of March 1, 1973, militants from the Black September faction of PLO stormed the Saudi Embassy in Khartoum, where a farewell ceremony for Moore had just concluded. Noel was wounded during the taking; he and Moore were among the ten diplomats taken hostage by the militants. The next day, March 2, the hostage takers shot Noel to death. Also murdered were his deputy, Moore, and Belgian diplomat Guy Eid.

Another matter the Secretary of state looked at took place on August 19th, 1974; recently appointed Ambassador to Cyprus, Rodger Davies, was shot dead during a Greek Cypriot protest outside the U.S. Embassy. The demonstration brought out over 300 people who were protesting against the U.S.'s failure to prevent the Turkish invasion of the northern part of the island the week before. Davies was seeking shelter in a hallway at the embassy building in Nicosia when a sniper struck him in the chest. When Antoinette Varnava—a Maronite consular employee—rushed to his aid, she too was struck dead with a bullet to the head.

James Alan Williams, a political Foreign Service officer, was at the embassy in Nicosia when events unraveled. He served in Cyprus from 1973 to 1975 — the height of the tension between Greek and Turkish Cypriots, the coup which ousted democratically elected leader Archbishop Makarovs III, and the Turkish invasions — all of which define the sociopolitical landscape of the divided island today. He was interviewed by Ray Ewing beginning in October 2003.

The last matter to be reviewed was in relation to Libya attack

During the 2012 Benghazi attack, a fire was set against the wall of the main consulate building while three Americans were inside—Stevens, Sean Smith, and a security officer. According to U.S. officials, the security officer escaped; the staff found Smith dead. They were unable to locate Stevens before being driven from the building under large arms fire. Local civilians found Stevens and took him to the Benghazi Medical Centre in a state of cardiac arrest. Medical personnel tried to resuscitate him, but he was pronounced dead at about 2 am local time on September 12, 2012. Later reports suggested that the attack was coordinated and planned, with any protests either coincidental or possibly diversionary. Libyan president Muhammad Magariaf blamed elements of Ansar al-Sharia for the killing, linking them to Al-Qaeda in the Islamic Maghreb. Libyan officials suggested that it might have been a revenge attack mounted by loyalists (of deceased Libyan leader Muammar Gaddafi) who were defeated in the Libyan Civil War the previous year. The doctors who tended to Stevens said that no visible physical wounds were found on his body and that he died from smoke inhalation, making hypoxia the cause of his death.

The US Secretary of State needed to carefully study previous instances of death or kidnapping or US diplomats dying in a foreign land.

Chapter 31

It was exactly three hours after the kidnapping of the US Ambassador and, subsequently the kidnapping of the Zimbabwean President's daughter. Both the US and the Zimbabwean authorities were kept informed about the progress that Investigation team was making, and both parties were not happy with the pace of progress as they were facing severe pressure, mainly from the International community and relatives of the affected. All global network channels covered the story on an hourly basis with commentators brought from various Institutions; leading commentary was from the Institute of African Studies, an international Organization that focuses on African history and major war and transformative events.

The meeting was called to order, and discussions started almost immediately. US Secretary of state: we are aware that Zimbabwe has been on the global map for all the wrong reasons, and now you have just created an unsafe environment that has endangered not only the US Ambassador and his family but also the residents of Zimbabwe, specifically the President and the Ministers' daughters. You have left us with no option but to reconsider reassessing the necessity of opening diplomatic lines with your countries.

The US holds the Zimbabwean Authorities personally responsible for the Kidnapping of the Ambassador and his family. The action taken was an act of seeking a solution before your incompetent people ruin the investigation and put the Ambassador at risk.

The Zimbabwean Ambassador spoke, "With all due respect, Secretary, your arrogance and hypocrisy will threaten the progress we seek to accomplish, and may I remind you that we have a very tight deadline and that you Americans are looking at three stripes from the inside of a very small cell."

US Secretary of State snapped, "What's your point here, Amby?"

The Zimbabwean Ambassador smiled and frowned. "There is no big brother here, and I don't answer to you; the name of the game is Cooperation here. Keep this dip dap *kabugila balas kachandras kachandra* attitude of yours, then let's see how you are going to achieve your goals."

US Secretary of state retorted, "It is clear that your man is not making critical gains in obtaining the intelligence required within the time available. We can dispatch a special team which can achieve the results we seek in record time.

Zimbabwean Ambassador, not to be outdone aid, "I am holding the greater part of the stick here, remember. So let me guess, your man will do a better job, I suppose?"

US Secretary of state put a straight face, "Your country has just become a terrorist nation, and we do not negotiate with terrorists. You know our position on that, Amby, don't you?"

Zimbabwean Ambassador replied, "You see, this is the thing that got your Ambassador into trouble. You are a very disrespectful nation, and you even think you know better than the locals and can run an operation in a sovereign nation at will. Your Ambassador made a poor judgment or, shall we say, an arrogant decision, running an operation in a foreign Land without informing the authorities. I can charge him with Treason or anything I so desire, or I can keep him in prison while thinking of what to charge him with."

US Secretary of state suggested to move forward for the sake of progress. Then, the Zimbabwean Ambassador reminded him that, "Your nation is considered an enemy of our people and that there is no goodwill. The US is our enemy, and that will not change. We have offered you a chance to thaw the relations, but you decided to be more hostile to our nation, to our people, our leaders and our companies. I thought I could clarify things here a bit. What's your proposal?"

US Secretary of state was civil. "We propose three names from the list of sanctions, increase our International Aid to USD500 Million for the next three years in exchange for independent investigations and carrying out Military operations necessary in an attempt to rescue the Ambassador and his family and bring them to our own soil. We also want to hunt down JBZ and secure information about Martinez.

The Zimbabwean Ambassador declined the proposal with no explanation.

US Secretary of State then asked, "Won't or can't?"

Zimbabwean Ambassador explained, "Your nation has placed burdensome illegal criminal economic sanctions on us; we need total non-conditional removal of the illegal economic sanctions without delay. Repeal the ZIDERA and all administrative measures placed against our sovereign Nation and sign a cooperation agreement with us that commits to not sanctioning our country in the next 200 years to come."

US Secretary of State's disposition changed; he became loud. "No way, Ambassador, that matter requires congress, we hold a view that the matters that called the sanctions into existence are still unresolved."

The Zimbabwean Ambassador was not flinching, too. "Then the Ambassador and his family's blood is on your head. Congress better get started now. The clock is ticking; with or without you, we will do our best to rescue the Ambassador and his family and charge him with treason upon sight."

US Secretary of State explained that he had a mandate to agree on the terms he presented, not any further.

The Zimbabwean Ambassador was stern. "Then get a fresh mandate, Secretary, or bring your principals to the negotiating table. We will not be bullied on our own soil. We are not backing down here."

US Secretary of State became irate. "I detest being insulted."

Zimbabwean Ambassador snapped, "Not so thick-skinned as portrayed on TV, huh? Someone has been feeding your ego. If we can endure criminal, Illegal, and burdensome economic sanctions for more than two decades, then I am sure you can take an insult."

US Secretary of State was suddenly calm. "I am giving you a deal of a lifetime; you will get a promotion if you take this deal; you will be seen as a winner. My government will give you a house by the Beach front, free education for kids up to PHD, a salary of USD55,000 per annum till you die, a lump sum of USD5 Million paid upon signing, a green card, and you can bring as much as a 5 family members and extended family on green card. What do you say?"

Zimbabwean Ambassador spoke with pride written in his voice. "I am here to represent my country Mr. Secretary. Your bribe and corrupt practices are not tolerated. Any attempt to divert attention from the real matter will be met with the condemnation that it deserves."

US Secretary of State shook his head as he answered, "That's pathetic, and Africa is a shithole and can't be helped. You have seen the light, take the deal and secure your generations to come. You will be seen as a great man. You have lived your life in the US; what are you fighting for? The people you speak of don't know you. When was the last time you were paid? Have I not offered assistance to your offices countless times after you had run out of resources? Are these the people you so wish to protect?"

Zimbabwean Ambassador raised his voice, "Tell me something, Secretary, why is it so difficult for you to come to the table and talk objectively about the situation at hand? It would seem that you are afraid of engaging in real negotiations. Your desire to dominate discussions is baffling. You can't even save lives first."

US Secretary of State told him that was classified, and the Zimbabwean Ambassador rubbished that off, saying, "Classified my ass."

US Secretary of State chuckled, "See, you even speak like one of us; take the goddam deal and walk away. Do not be foolish. Do what is best for you. Present the deal to your president as the best deal there is for the nation. We can't be seen to be negotiating with Zimbabwe. The world must see a consistent treatment of the country. Any sign of weakness will embolden other enemies of our great nation."

Zimbabwean Ambassador answered, "I wonder what they saw in you making you Secretary, a man who can find time to play in the middle of a crisis. You are not serious."

US Secretary of State asked if that was a yes to his proposal, to which the Zimbabwean Ambassador replied, "I believe we are running out of time here, and we need to make progress, lest we wait for those on the ground to accomplish."

US Secretary of State reminded him, "Mr. Ambassador, should we fail to agree here, then I'm afraid that the US has other options that you may find less appealing."

Zimbabwean Ambassador spoke with revived energy. "Here we go. That took long to come. Your nation has threatened us for the past decades, and we have remained resolute in looking after our people under the circumstances; your regime change agenda has failed and talking about it now won't help in any way. What are you going to tell the world? That the US had always resented Zimbabwe in the International arena, the provocation did not yield the desired result, and you have ensnared the country by staging the kidnapping of your own Ambassador and his family, planned the killing of the US Marine

Corps who were part of the covert operation. Hired Mafia to kidnap some girls in what seemed to be a random inclusion of the President and Minister's daughters. This will be a story we will take to the whole world. We need sanctions removed in totality, and then we will talk."

US Secretary of state again reiterated that they were not prepared to adjust the deal, which they believed was a great deal for both parties. The Zimbabwean Ambassador declined, stating that his country could not accept the deal, as it was bad for his people.

The Ambassador was standing up to leave when the Secretary commented. "The moment you walk out of that door, you know that there won't be any diplomatic privileges for you. We are shutting your embassy and closing all diplomatic channels. We will use force, and we will achieve our objectives with or without you."

Zimbabwean Ambassador, seemingly unperturbed, said, "We have lived with these threats for years, and we are not going to start fearing your rhetoric now. We will work with whatever we have to solve the situation." The Ambassador then left the building. When he got to the Embassy of Zimbabwe, the place was cordoned off, and reporters were asking him about the terror attack. There was a press conference held, and the US Secretary informed the public that they had searched and obtained evidence that the current Zimbabwean Ambassador to the US was linked to the kidnapping of the US Ambassador to Zimbabwe and that he was going to be interviewed by the police.

The US Secretary of State called a meeting, and this time, the meeting was attended by at least 13 members. He addressed the meeting first. "Speak to your President; you have 30 minutes; if he agrees, then well and good; if not, we have already set the tone, and the media is waiting to see how the story will unfold. It's up to you."

Seeing the silence, he continued, "Here is what we will do, we will remove your Biggest Commercial Bank from the sanctions list only. That allows you to trade at a much higher level than before."

The Zimbabwean Ambassador clapped his hands. "New speech, huh?" then the Ambassador sat down and was quiet for some time as if considering a bride price for his first born master's degree holder. "I agree with the removal of our Commercial Bank from the illegal sanctions, and we would need the removal of all private sector companies listed to be removed In exchange for a cooperation deal for a joint operation. We do not have a deal on JBZ as yet."

US Secretary of State added, "I believe that we are making progress; however, if JBZ is what we think him to be, then these two things could be linked."

The Zimbabwean Ambassador scratched his beard and pouted. "What's your point, Secretary?"

US Secretary of State shook his head, puzzled at the pout. "Well, that we conclude the deal as we are running out of time."

The pout vanished as soon as it appeared, and the Zimbabwean Ambassador replied. "We have USD12 billion worth of government assets frozen in your country. 1.6 billion Of corporate funds are trapped between banks due to economic sanctions, and the funds cannot be moved to the destination bank, nor can they be moved back into the originating bank."

Annoyance is getting the better of him, the US Secretary of State bellowed. "Do you know that we have an easy option of just declaring war on Zimbabwe and bomb the shit out of you?"

Unmoved, the Zimbabwean Ambassador answered, "Yes, you do, but you will not pursue that option; your Vision 2060 places Zimbabwe at the center of regional strategy. Besides, do you really want to destabilize the country? Whatever you are doing in surrounding countries, just know that Zimbabwe has more than 280 mineral resources, including diamond, gold, platinum, uranium and huge deposits of coal, which you like so much to the extent of exempting it from the sanctions list. You need to champion the removal of the economic sanctions."

Seizing his moment to shine, he continued, "We are aware that there is a taskforce that reviews the status of progress in the resolution of matters giving rise to economic sanctions and recommends to congress for ratification; you need to influence this process."

US Secretary of State listened intently. "I make no promises; let's get the Ambassador and his family first."

The Zimbabwean Ambassador, with a slight smile emerging, said, "Is that a yes?"

US Secretary of State responded, "You could say we need immediate control of the investigations and chair the Taskforce." The Zimbabwean Ambassador then said it was for the President to decide, but to avoid delays, he proposed that they have a jointly chaired task force.

Chapter 32

The team that was tasked to review the economic Sanctions on Zimbabwe had one task, to meet and propose the lifting of sanctions. The US Congress had been called for an urgent meeting to address an urgent matter, but no specific details were given. However, murmurings in the White House had gossip leaking some details to the press.

Reporters were gathered at the White house waiting for the presidential press conference, as is the custom. When the president arrived, he gave a speech about his views regarding the war in Gaza. Israel had continued the onslaught on Palestine on the back of "provocations" from Hamas after Hamas allegedly launched missiles into Israel and abducted at least 250 people, including women and children, who were attending a cultural show.

The paparazzi had been screened, and each was wearing their White House pass, dangling like a gangster's necklace.

Mr. President said, "We have reiterated our support for the people of Israel; we are, however, concerned about the developing humanitarian crisis. We would want aid to be allowed to reach vulnerable groups such as women and children displaced from their homes.

The White House Press Secretary stepped in and announced that the president was taking questions.

One Tony asked, "I am Tony with the Free Press International. Mr. President, is it true that the highest number of people dying in Gaza are mainly women and children? How does your support for Israel sit with your recent discussions regarding military cooperation with Saudi Arabia? Given that the Middle East is not happy with the stance on Gaza by Israel, how do you plan to manage the relationships between the Middle East and the US?"

Mr. President answered with composure, "That is a delicate situation; it is my belief that Israel has the right to defend and protect itself from an act of aggression and provocations from Hamas and from anyone for that matter. We are, however in discussions with the leadership in Israel to do so, giving regard for human life, specifically to protect the children. The complications come from the claims and evidence submitted by Israel where they claim that Hamas is hiding weapons in clinics and hospitals and in aid trucks."

Another lady asked, "Mr. President, I am Regina from City Press. With the upcoming elections in Taiwan, China has upped her threats and has started aggressive propaganda to swear the decision of the People of Taiwan. What is your reaction to that?"

Mr. President answered, "We stand with the people of Taiwan, and if we should see that their sovereignty and territorial integrity is being threatened, then we would intervene with such a force that the People of China has never seen before. We have already deployed two aircraft carriers in response to China's dangerous drills near and Around Taiwan."

A lady in red asked, "I am Gertrude from Global News Agency. Mr. President, can you tell us the details regarding events in Zimbabwe where it is rumored that the Ambassador was kidnapped while on an unsanctioned and unauthorized mission to redeem his wife and son who had been kidnapped earlier on."

Mr. President sighed first, "We are looking into the trickling Intelligence, and as there are potential threats to human life, I would say it's not the best time to comment now."

The President was visibly shaken despite having tried to put up a brave face. The last question made him unaware, and he almost refused to answer.

Later on, Congress met and received the recommendation to lift the sanctions on Zimbabwe and pledge not to reverse or impose same for the next 30 years, though the Ambassador wanted 200 years. Congress did not agree to the matter. The Democrats wanted the deal to be approved without conditions; however, the Republicans wanted the approval of a USD12 billion package for the US Mexico Border wall; the matter dragged on for three hours, with recess being called for in between. After agreeing to a USD3 billion on the US Mexico Boarder funding, the deal was eventually agreed upon, so it was a deal inside a deal. Congress only lifted sanctions on the Commercial Bank, and money trapped in the bank accounts while frozen assets would be released upon completion of the mission.

Chapter 33

In the Orange Brick building, a task force was set up in the City of Harare.   The Zimbabwean team of Investigators consisted of Detective Mike, Silver and Detective, popularly known as Malaika and six other assistants. There were members of homicide, violent crimes, hostage negotiation, narcotics, communication specialists, military intelligence and human trafficking who had been working with Interpol. Since the Kidnapping of Mike's wife Lisa, there have been arguments about whether Mike was the best person to lead the charge.

The Team from the Military Intelligence and ZRP Support Unit had raised concerns over Mike's suitability, especially in decision-making and the ability to remain calm and objective during the operation.

The Zimbabwean Police force is highly regarded when it comes to their discipline and high IQ, as well as advanced investigation skills, which have been demonstrated through the solving of many mystery cases; some cold cases have been raised to life.

The Force has resolved some of the most daring Murder and Robbery cases that were well planned and, in some cases, where former uniformed forces who went bad were involved, and they emerged victorious.

The Force is credited with solving a number of cases, such as the Harare Airport road Armed Robbery squad that had terrorized travelers, robbing them of goods and cash, the Marondera robbers whose signature was to rob and ask the victims to remove all their clothes before leaving the scene, more recently the recent armed robbers who nabbed in Beit Bridge Town.

The Force has created such a great relationship with societies, and this has helped them get tip-offs. They have generally connected with criminals serving long sentences to get information leading to the new crimes, methods and schemes, as these are well-informed and are often consulted by inmates inside and outside who intend to commit armed robberies; once released, they are usually informed of latest success stories as they are looked up to.

The force is probably credited for solving what seems to be the greatest victory in the history of the fight against crime. The notorious Masendeke and Chidhumo, a duo of serial killers so cruel, was the duo that Chidhumo was code-named Cold Storage in an apparent reference to how he killed people in cold blood. He never hesitated to kill, and to him, spilling human blood was not anything out of the ordinary.

The two started their criminal activities in Zimbabwean Prisons and managed to kill many victims. Chidhumo and Masendeke were hanged in 2002. They were put on the same death row because Zimbabwean Law still allowed the death penalty.

The Duo were hanged just before the hangman retired from active service, and since then, the country has operated without a hangman.

Chidhumo and Masendeke met in Mutimurefu remand prison in Masvingo in 1995, where each was on a 16-year sentence. They became friends and hatched a Prison Break style escape from incarceration in November 1995 along with one Langton Zano, Langton Charumbira and Maverudze Musara. They overpowered the prison guards and forced them into cells before they escaped.

The freaky four fugitives who liked the refugees fled to Mozambique. It was there where they saw a spate of armed robberies in the mountainous Manicaland Province and frequently venturing to Masvingo, then retreating to Mozambique through the porous Border. This happened for two straight years.

The Zimbabwe Republic Police remained committed and steadfast in their investigations and cooperating with the communities. The robbers had several encounters with the police, and with each encounter, they became more experienced in handling fire arms and always managed to escape and evade arrest.

After two years of committing horrific crimes, Chidhumo was apprehended by the Police in Mozambique in what was a great display of investigative skills and dedication to eradicating crime and ensuring a crime-free society.

The ZRP has for years worked tirelessly to make Zimbabwe one of the safest countries in the world where one can walk in the streets at night without fearing to be robbed, unlike South Africa, where one can be robbed in a shopping mall and sometimes in front of the police.

The ZRP has managed to investigate and arrest most criminal cases that have been reported.

Masendeke escaped in August 1997; Chidhumo managed to escape from Chikurubi maximum prison, where he had been incarcerated; he managed to rejoin Chidhumo in Mozambique.

The Zimbabwe Republic Police launched a massive manhunt codenamed "operation Masendeke" in Mozambique. A bounty of USD60, 000 was placed on Chidhumo's head. He ran for effective 29 days till the well-trained detectives crossed over to Mozambique, pursued him, and shot him in Beira.

In 2020, in a separate encounter, the Zimbabwe Republic Police, with assistance from their dog section, nabbed an 8 member gang of armed robbers who went on a spat of robberies in Chitungwiza. Blue Circle, Glen Norah B and Marlborough in Harare. This happened when the detectives had done thorough investigations and acted upon information from the community, a team of detectives and support Unit, and the Canine teamed up in an operation. This high-impact team learnt that the suspects were using a BMW and planned an ambush. Initially, they had a shootout, and the robbers managed to escape.

However, the following day, a massive manhunt was initiated, with every road within a net mile radius being locked down, and all internal dirt roads closed off.

The operation took 12 hours till the robbers decided that it was now safe to move, and they were caught in a chase that lasted 30 minutes. Shots were fired, and there were replies from both ends, with guns being handled professionally and the fire for fire encounter lasting for 20 minutes till the robbers ran out of ammunition after being wasteful in random shooting initially. The Robbers were arrested, and AK47s were recovered.

The Zimbabwe Republic Police has been the pride of Zimbabwe, and for years, they have demonstrated commitment in and out of the country, setting international records for professionalism and dedication to service by winning peace keeping mission prizes and commendations in Darfur.

The Zimbabwe Republic Police has cooperated in many operations, including Interpol and the African Union Mechanism for

Police Cooperation (AFRIPOL), its first joint operation, which resulted in 1000 suspected smuggling of Migrants and victims.

Coordinated with the participation of Law enforcement in 54 countries, including Zimbabwe, in the operation "FLASH-WEKA" took place in May and June to dismantle organized crime networks behind human trafficking and migrants smuggling in Africa and beyond.

According to INTERPOL, at least 1062 were arrested, while 823 trafficking victims were identified. At least 2731 irregular migrants were detected while 801 merchandise were ceased, and these included stolen firearms and vehicles.

Chapter 34

The FBI is an elite force trained in various tactics with degrees such as behavioral sciences, Criminal Justice, Criminology, Cyber security, emergence management as well as forensic science and Law enforcement being some of the programs that staff at the FBI is required to have completed.

The FBI is trained in special weapons and Tactics, Hostage rescue, Intelligence gathering, public corruption, organized Crime, Violent Crimes, as well as cyber-crimes.

The FBI has a track record of investigating dangerous international Criminal cases involving drugs, and terrorism. They have swift and well-resourced training schools, and its staff are the best in what they do.

The FBI is credited with gathering. The Federal Bureau of Investigation, America's national law enforcement agency, didn't emerge overnight. It evolved in the early decades of the 20th century, ultimately dominated by its ambitious chief J. Edgar Hoover.

By the end of the 19th century, as settlers populated more of the American West, the U.S. Census Bureau declared the frontier "closed." But that didn't mean law and order reigned nationwide. On the contrary, bank robberies, corruption, and new threats like anarchist violence overwhelmed thinly staffed and undertrained local police forces.

In the early 1920s, the discovery of oil under Osage land in north-central Oklahoma made members of that tribal nation among the wealthiest people in the world. By 1923, the Osage people were sharing what amounted to $30 million in royalties. But scores of those wealthy Indians began dying—in mysterious shootings, stabbings, explosions and suspected poisonings. Out of inertia, indifference or corruption, local law enforcement did nothing.

Members of the Osage turned to Washington for help, appealing to what was still known simply as the U.S. Bureau of Investigation. Under the leadership of a young, untried J. Edgar Hoover, the Bureau used undercover informants to identify some of the white Oklahoma residents who had tried to marry—and murder—their way to oilfield riches. Agent Tom White, a former Texas Ranger, led the investigation, which ultimately convicted William Hale, a prominent cattle baron, his nephew Ernest Burkhart and others in a vast conspiracy. Many other Osage homicide cases from the era remain unsolved.

On the evening of March 1, 1932, one or more kidnappers abducted the toddler son of famous aviator Charles Lindbergh. They left behind a ransom note demanding $50,000, some muddy footprints and a broken ladder. Two months later, the boy's broken and decomposing body was found partly buried near the Lindbergh mansion.

The next day, President Herbert Hoover directed the Bureau to coordinate the murder investigation. Crucially, special agents flooded the region with notifications of the serial numbers of the gold certificates paid as a ransom. More than a year later, a German immigrant carpenter named Bruno Hauptmann used one of these to buy gas at a service station. After his arrest, another $13,000 worth of the securities were found in his garage. When Hauptmann stood trial, Bureau agents testified that his handwriting matched that of the ransom note. He was convicted in 1935 and executed in the spring of 1936.

When the infamous crime spree of Depression-era outlaws Bonnie Parker and Clyde Barrow ended in a barrage of gunfire, it was local police officers who staged the ambush. But it was the Bureau that helped those officers determine just where to lie in wait. By May 1934, when the couple were linked to stolen cars transported across multiple states, prompting federal involvement, Parker and Barrow were already responsible for a series of brazen robberies and murders across a large swath of the United States. Eventually, bureau agents in at least eight cities would collaborate with law enforcement in as many different states, sharing tips and fresh leads. The pursuit prompted early Bureau efforts at profiling, as special agents tried to anticipate where Bonnie and Clyde might be heading next. Ultimately, it was an FBI agent who tracked them to a remote corner of Louisiana where the successful ambush took place.

As the Cold War heated up in the late 1940s, U.S. military intelligence agents working to decode Soviet "diplomatic" cables made a stunning discovery. When they finally cracked the cypher, messages revealed a spy network burrowed deep inside America's top-secret atomic development program at Los Alamos, New Mexico. FBI agent Bob Lamphere, who supervised numerous high-profile Cold War espionage investigations, followed the trail of clues in these decrypted messages, tracing the links that led from Los Alamos scientist Klaus Fuchs to a nondescript engineer named Julius Rosenberg in New York.

The FBI interrogated and arrested several members of the spy ring, including Julius and his wife, Ethel. FBI head Hoover, who declared the Rosenbergs guilty of the "crime of the century," clearly viewed their 1951 conviction as justice. But it also was controversial: Later revelations show that the FBI only pursued the case against Ethel in order to make Julius confess. Neither did; both were executed in 1953.

Some FBI investigations wrap up quickly; others, like the attempt to bring the murderer of civil rights leader Medgar Evers to justice, drag on for decades. A bullet felled Evers on the front doorstep of his Jackson, Mississippi, home in June 1963, but it wasn't until 1994 that evidence collected by the FBI finally helped convict white supremacist Byron De La Beckwith for the assassination.

The Bureau almost immediately connected the murder weapon to the culprit: De La Beckwith had dropped the firearm after its recoil drove the rifle scope into his eye, and it had been located by police. But two all-white juries rejected the testimony offered by FBI agents and other witnesses. As Evers' widow prodded local prosecutors to reopen the case, the FBI helped locate new witnesses. De La Beckwith was finally convicted in 1994 and died in prison in 2001.

The FBI began investigating a series of mysterious bombings in 1980 after one of the homemade devices exploded in the cargo bay of an American Airlines flight and another device was sent to the president of United Airlines. The FBI, teaming up with postal inspectors, quickly noticed design similarities between the two bombs. They also found links to similar attacks throughout the 1980s and into the 1990s; of the 16 incendiary devices placed or sent between 1978 and 1995, many caused severe injuries, and three proved deadly. Since the bomber used scrap materials, and left few if any forensic traces, by the mid-1990s, all the Bureau had to go on was a rudimentary profile. Only when the agency and the Justice Department green lit newspaper publication of a 35,000-word manifesto by the so-called Unabomber did a social worker named David Kaczynski alert the FBI to similarities between the screed and the thinking and writing style of his brother Ted. The FBI led the team sent to arrest the Unabomber at a remote shack in Montana, discovering a live device ready to mail under his bed. Kaczynski pled guilty and died in prison.

Owen Hanson, who often went by his nickname, "O-Dog," led a charmed life. He had been a popular high school athlete who found some athletic success—and even more popularity—at the University of Southern California.

After graduating with a business degree, he got his real estate license and, over time, undertook several seemingly successful business ventures that enabled him to buy a luxury home in Redondo Beach and a number of vacation properties elsewhere, drive expensive cars, travel routinely to Las Vegas to gamble, and party with professional athletes and celebrities.

However, as law enforcement came to discover, Hanson's most productive "business venture" turned out to be a violent international drug trafficking, sports gambling, and money laundering enterprise that operated in the U.S., Central and South America, and Australia from 2012 to 2016. Late last year, Hanson was sentenced in U.S. district court in San Diego to more than 21 years in federal prison for heading up that criminal enterprise. He was also ordered to pay a $5 million criminal forfeiture, which included $100,000 in gold coins, his luxury vehicles, jewelry, vacation homes, a sailboat, and interests in several businesses.

Twenty-one of Hanson's associates were also charged in this crime ring, and all have pleaded guilty—the most recent one in April 2018.

So how did a one-time talented and well-liked school athlete turn into the mastermind behind a major criminal operation? The story of Owen Hanson's illicit activities actually began in the early 2000s in college, when he sold recreational drugs and steroids to his teammates. But it wasn't until early 2014—on the heels of an international sports gambling investigation that the FBI worked in partnership with the New South Wales Police Force in Australia— that some of Hanson's post-graduate activities got the attention of federal law enforcement. And once again, investigators from the FBI and New South Wales joined forces to uncover a second gambling—

and, ultimately, drug trafficking—enterprise that would lead all the way to Hanson.

Through the use of sophisticated investigative techniques, including court-authorized electronic surveillance, informants, and undercover agents, investigators learned the following:

- **Hanson built and managed a multi-million-dollar gambling** business that operated in the U.S. and internationally and employed an accountant, a private detective, enforcers, bookies, and money runners. He and his co-conspirators concealed their activities by using sham bank accounts and offshore web servers.

- Hanson's gambling business ensured prompt payment of losing bets through threats of violence and actual physical violence against its customers. One individual who ran afoul of Hanson was threatened constantly—he received pictures of his deceased mother's defaced headstone from Hanson via e-mail and regular mail, pictures of his wife along with her personal information, and a video showing beheadings.

- Unsatisfied with the tremendous financial success of his gambling business, Hanson expanded his growing empire to include international drug trafficking, which would put even millions of dollars more into his organization's coffers.

- The drug operation started small but evolved into a sophisticated, diversified, and complex trafficking organization that smuggled thousands of kilograms of illegal narcotics—including cocaine and methamphetamine—throughout the U.S., Canada, and Australia.

- Hanson's willingness to engage in the drug trade knew no limits—he sold every drug in any amount to anyone who wanted it. He routinely shipped large quantities of cocaine from Los Angeles to Australia, he provided an FBI undercover agent with five kilograms of cocaine and five kilograms of methamphetamine, and he sold recreational and performance-enhancing drugs to professional athletes.

The federal judge who sentenced the former college athlete explained that the severe prison term he handed down was warranted because of the "staggering" and "astounding" size and scope of the criminal enterprise's activities. And referencing all of the advantages Hanson has had in his life, the judge said, "It is difficult to understand how you got here, other than greed."

Hanson bragged about his aspirations to be an even bigger player, and he continued his criminal activity right up until the night before his arrest in September 2015, when he coordinated a drug deal with an undercover agent. He only stopped because law enforcement stopped him.

Assistant U. S. Attorneys Andrew P. Young (619) 546-7981, Benjamin Katz (619) 546-9604 or Mark W. Letcher (619) 546-9714

<u>NEWS RELEASE SUMMARY</u> – January 10, 2016

SAN DIEGO – Owen Hanson, leader of the violent "ODOG Enterprise," pleaded guilty today to conspiring to operate an international drug trafficking, gambling and money laundering enterprise in the United States, Central and South America and Australia from 2012 to 2016.

According to his plea agreement, ODOG Enterprise trafficked hundreds of kilograms of cocaine, heroin, methamphetamine, MDMA (also known as "ecstasy"), anabolic steroids and Human Growth Hormone ("HGH"). As Hanson admitted, ODOG Enterprise's drug operation routinely distributed controlled substances at wholesale and retail levels, including selling performance-enhancing drugs to numerous professional athletes. The ODOG Enterprise also operated a vast illegal gambling operation focused on high-stakes wagers placed on sporting events. The Enterprise used threats and violence against its gambling and drug customers to force compliance.

Three of Hanson's associates also pleaded guilty today: Giovanni Brandolino (aka "Tank"), Marlyn Villarreal and Jeff Bellandi.

In one instance discussed in court papers, an individual who owed the ODOG Enterprise more than $2 million received a DVD showing a beheading and a photo of his desecrated family's gravestone in an effort to collect the alleged debt. Hanson pleaded guilty today to conspiring to operate the ODOG enterprise in violation of the

Racketeer Influenced and Corrupt Organization ("RICO") statute and to conspiring to distribute controlled substances.

Brandolino, the second-highest ranking member of the ODOG Enterprise, pleaded guilty to conspiracy to violate RICO and conspiracy to commit money laundering. As part of the plea agreement, Brandolino admitted that he assisted Hanson with the importation and distribution of hundreds of kilograms of cocaine and heroin. Brandolino specifically admitted establishing a drug distribution network in New Jersey and New York. Villarreal and Bellandi also pleaded guilty to conspiracy to commit money laundering.

So far, 16 of the 22 defendants charged in connection with this case have pleaded guilty, including Daniel Portley-Hanks, Jack Rissell, Kenny Hilinski, and Rufus Rhone. Portley-Hanks, a Los Angeles-based private investigator who assisted Hanson with tracking down delinquent gamblers and other individuals who owed the enterprise money, pleaded guilty to extortion on December 27, 2016. Jack Rissell, labeled as an "enforcer" in the Superseding Indictment, also pleaded guilty to extortion on December 17, 2016. Kenny Hilinski, Hanson's associate, pleaded guilty to the RICO conspiracy on May 24, 2016. Hilinski operated much of the gambling apparatus from Peru, where he maintained various gambling websites, coordinated the collection of payments from various bookies and gamblers, and directed the organization's runners to distribute the proceeds to Hanson through shell companies and cash deliveries. Portley-Hanks, Rissell, and Hilinski are awaiting sentencing.

Rhone, who pleaded guilty to conspiracy to distribute methamphetamine and cocaine early last year, was sentenced on September 19, 2016, to 72 months in prison.

The remaining defendants are set for trial on February 14, 2017. Luke Fairfield, a San Diego-based Certified Public Accountant, is accused of assisting Hanson with laundering the proceeds of his various illegal endeavors by, in part, setting up shell corporations and advising members of the Enterprise on how to structure bank transactions to avoid detection by bank security and law enforcement. Derek Loville, a former professional football player, is accused of distributing retail quantities of drugs for the ODOG Enterprise in Arizona. Dylan Anderson and Khalid Petras, the other two remaining defendants, are accused of running an illegal gambling business. Charges against these four defendants are merely accusations, and they are considered innocent unless and until proven guilty.

The case arose out of a joint investigation by FBI, IRS and the New South Wales (Australia) Police Force in conjunction with the New South Wales Crime Commission. Hanson was initially indicted and arrested on September 9, 2015, after arranging the delivery of five kilograms of cocaine and five kilograms of methamphetamine. Eight individuals in Australia have been arrested in connection with Hanson's global organization. Assistant U. S. Attorneys Andrew P. Young, Benjamin Katz and Mark W. Pletcher are prosecuting the case.

Miguel Ángel Rodríguez Orejuela (born August 15, 1943) is a convicted Colombian drug lord, formerly one of the leaders of the Cali Cartel, based in the city of Cali. He is the younger brother of Gilberto Rodríguez Orejuela. He married Miss Colombia in 1974, Marta Lucía Echeverry.

The Rodríguez brothers and "Jose" formed the Cali cartel in the 1970s. They were primarily involved in marijuana trafficking. In the 1980s, they branched out into Cocaine trafficking. For a time, the Cali Cartel supplied 80% of the United States and 90% of the European cocaine market.

The Cali Cartel was less violent than its rival, the Medellín Cartel. While the Medellín Cartel was involved in a brutal campaign of violence against the Colombian government, the Cali Cartel grew. The cartel was much more inclined toward bribery rather than violence. However, after the demise of the Medellín Cartel, the Colombian authorities turned their attention to the Cali cartel. The police campaign against the cartel began in the summer of 1995.

On August 6, 1995, Rodriguez Orejuela was arrested when the Colombian National Police broke down the door of his apartment (Hacienda Buenos Aires) in the exclusive Normandia neighborhood in Cali, Colombia, as he was about to slip into a secret closet called a Caleta. Rodriguez was betrayed by Jorge Salcedo, his main bodyguard. Rodriguez Orejuela was not eligible for extradition to the U.S. for crimes committed prior to December 16, 1997. However, while he was detained in Colombia, Rodriguez Orejuela continued to engage in drug trafficking. As a result, the United States requested his extradition.

On March 11, 2005, Rodriguez Orejuela was extradited to the United States. His brother, Gilberto Rodríguez Orejuela, had already been extradited. On September 26, 2006, both Gilberto and Miguel were sentenced to 30 years in prison after pleading guilty to charges of conspiring to import cocaine to the U.S. in exchange for the United States agreeing not to bring charges against their family members. Their lawyers, David Oscar Markus and Roy Kahn were able to obtain immunity for 29 family members.

On November 16, 2006, the brothers pleaded guilty to one count of conspiring to engage in money laundering. Both were sentenced to an additional 87 months in prison. The two prison terms were set to run concurrently.

Miguel Rodríguez Orejuela is serving his 30-year sentence at FCI Loretto in Pennsylvania. His inmate number is 14022–059, with a release date of July 15, 2028.

The United States Navy Sea, Air, and Land (SEAL) Teams, commonly known as Navy SEALs, are the U.S. Navy's primary special operations force and a component of the Naval Special Warfare Command. Among the SEALs' main functions are conducting small-unit special operation missions in maritime, jungle, urban, arctic, mountainous, and desert environments. SEALs are typically ordered to capture or kill high-level targets or to gather intelligence behind enemy lines. SEAL team personnel are hand-selected, highly trained, and possess a high degree of proficiency in direct action (DA) and special reconnaissance (SR), among other tasks like sabotage, demolition, intelligence gathering, and hydro-graphic reconnaissance, training, and advising friendly militaries or other forces.

Depending on the availability of platforms, threat level, and environment, different methods can be used for the insertion and extraction of SEALs into a target location. This could include nuclear-powered cruise missile submarines equipped with dry deck shelters, SDV submarines, surface vessels, surface swimming, or other vehicles.

All active SEALs are members of the U.S. Navy. The CIA's highly secretive and elite Special Operations Group (SOG) recruits operators from SEAL Teams, with joint operations going back to the MACV-SOG during the Vietnam War. This cooperation still exists today, as evidenced by military operations in Iraq and Afghanistan.

Although not formally founded until 1962, the modern-day U.S. Navy SEALs trace their roots to World War II. The United States Military recognized the need for the covert reconnaissance of landing beaches and coastal defenses. As a result, the joint Army, Marine Corps, and Navy Amphibious Scout and Raider School was established in 1942 at Fort Pierce, Florida. The Scouts and Raiders were formed in September of that year, just nine months after the attack on Pearl Harbor, from the Observer Group, a joint U.S. Army-Marine-Navy unit.

Scouts and Raiders

Recognizing the need for a beach reconnaissance force, a select group of Army and Navy personnel assembled at Amphibious Training Base (ATB) Little Creek, Virginia, on 15 August 1942 to begin Amphibious Scouts and Raiders (Joint) training. The Scouts and Raiders' mission was to identify and reconnoiter the objective beach, maintain a position on the designated beach prior to a landing, and guide the assault waves to the landing beach. The unit was led by U.S. Army 1st Lieutenant Lloyd Peddicord as commanding officer and Navy Ensign John Bell as executive officer. Navy Chief Petty Officers and sailors came from the boat pool at U. S. Naval Amphibious Training Base, Solomons, Maryland, and Army Raider personnel came from the 3rd and 9th Infantry Divisions. They trained at Little Creek until embarking on the North Africa campaign the following November. Operation Torch was launched in November 1942 off the Atlantic coast of French Morocco in North Africa.

The first group included Phil H. Bucklew, the "Father of Naval Special Warfare," after whom the Naval Special Warfare Center building was named. Commissioned in October 1949, this group saw combat in November 1942 during Operation Torch on the North African Coast. Scouts and Raiders also supported landings in Sicily, Salerno, Anzio, Normandy, and southern France.

The second group of Scouts and Raiders, code-named Special Service Unit No. 1, was established on 7 July 1943 as a joint and combined operations force. The first mission, in September 1943, was at Finschhafen in Papua New Guinea. Later operations were at Gasmata, Arawe, Cape Gloucester, and the east and south coasts of New Britain, all without any loss of personnel. Conflicts arose over operational matters, and all non-Navy personnel were reassigned. The unit, renamed 7th Amphibious Scouts, received a new mission, to go ashore with the assault boats, and buoy channels, erect markers for the incoming craft, handle casualties, take offshore soundings, clear beach obstacles, and maintain voice communications linking the troops ashore, incoming boats and nearby ships. The 7th Amphibious Scouts conducted operations in the Pacific for the duration of the conflict, participating in more than 40 landings.

The third and final Scouts and Raiders organization operated in China. Scouts and Raiders were deployed to fight with the Sino-American Cooperative Organization (SACO). To help bolster the work of SACO, Admiral Ernest J. King ordered that 120 officers and 900 men be trained for "Amphibious Raider" at the Scout and Raider school at Fort Pierce, Florida. They formed the core of what was envisioned as a "guerrilla amphibious organization of Americans and Chinese operating from coastal waters, lakes, and rivers employing small steamboats and sampans." While most Amphibious Raider forces remained at Camp Knox in Calcutta, three of the groups saw active service. They conducted a survey of the upper Yangtze River in the spring of 1945 and, disguised as coolies, conducted a detailed three-month survey of the Chinese coast from Shanghai to Kitchioh Wan, near Hong Kong.

In September 1942, 17 Navy salvage personnel arrived at ATB Little Creek, Virginia , for a week-long course in demolitions, explosive cable cutting, and commando raiding techniques. On 10 November 1942, the first combat demolition unit successfully cut cable and net barriers across the Wadi Sebou River during Operation Torch in North Africa. This enabled USS *Dallas* (DD-199) to traverse the water and insert U.S. Rangers who captured the Port Lyautey airdrome.

In early May 1943, a two-phase "Naval Demolition Project" was directed by the Chief of Naval Operations "to meet a present and urgent requirement". The first phase began at ATB Solomons, Maryland, with the establishment of Operational Naval Demolition

Unit No. 1. Six officers and eighteen enlisted men reported from the Seabee's NTC Camp Peary dynamiting and demolition school for a four-week course. Those Seabees, led by Lieutenant Fred Wise CEC, were immediately sent to participate in the invasion of Sicily. At that time, Lieutenant Commander Draper L. Kauffman, "The Father of Naval Combat Demolition," was selected to set up a school for Naval Demolitions and direct the entire Project. The first six classes graduated from "Area E" at NTC Camp Peary. LCDR Kauffman's needs quickly out-grew "Area E," and on 6 June 1943, he established NCDU training at Fort Pierce. Most of Kauffman's volunteers came from the navy's Civil Engineer Corps (CEC) and enlisted Seabees. Training commenced with a grueling week designed to filter out under-performing candidates. Eventually given the name "Hell Week" by NCDU recruits, this rigorous course was integrated into UDT training and remains a part of modern-day Navy Seal training today.

By April 1944, a total of 34 NCDUs were deployed to England in preparation for Operation Overlord, the amphibious landing at Normandy. On 6 June 1944, under heavy fire, the NCDUs at Omaha Beach managed to blow eight complete gaps and two partial gaps in the German defenses. The NCDUs suffered 31 killed and 60 wounded, a casualty rate of 52%. Meanwhile, the NCDUs at Utah Beach met less intense enemy fire. They cleared 700 yards (640 metres) of beach in two hours, and another 900 yards (820 metres) by the afternoon. Casualties at Utah Beach were significantly lighter, with six killed and eleven wounded. During Operation Overlord, not a single demolitioner was lost to improper handling of explosives. In August 1944, four NCDUs from Utah Beach, plus nine others, participated in the landings of Operation Dragoon in southern France. It was the last amphibious operation in the European Theater of Operations. Once the European invasions were complete, Real Admiral Kelly Turner requisitioned all available NCDUs from Fort Pierce for integration into the Underwater Demolition Teams (UDTs) operating in the Pacific Theater.

Thirty NCDUs had been sent to the Pacific prior to Normandy. NCDUs 1–10 were staged on Florida Island in the Solomon Islands (archipelago)during January 1944. NCDU 1 went briefly to the Aleutians in 1943. NCDUs 4 and 5 were the first to see combat by helping the 4th Marines at Green Island and Emirau Island. A few were temporarily attached to UDTs. Later, NCDUs 1–10 were combined to form Underwater Demolition Team Able. Six NCDUs, 2, 3, 19, 20, 21 and 24, served with the Seventh Amphibious Force and were the only remaining NCDUs at the end of the war. The Naval Special Warfare Command building is named after LTJG Frank Kaine, CEC commander of NCDU 2.

Much like their brethren in the US Army Special Forces (aka Green Berets), the Navy SEALs claim a lineage to the Office of Strategic Services (OSS). The OSS was a paramilitary organization and also a progenitor of the CIA. Army Special Forces, founded in 1952 by former members of the OSS, established the first military special operations combat diver units nearly a decade before the SEALs were created in 1962. Some of the earliest World War II predecessors of the Green Berets and SEALs were the Operational Swimmers of OSS.

The OSS executed special operations, dropping operatives behind enemy lines to engage in organized guerrilla warfare as well as to gather information on such things as enemy resources and troop movements. British Combined Operations veteran LCDR Wooley of the Royal Navy was placed in charge of the OSS Maritime Unit (MU) in June 1943. Their training started in November 1943 at Camp Pendleton, California, moved to Santa Catalina Island, California, in January 1944, and finally moved to the warmer waters of The Bahamas in March 1944. Within the U.S. military, they pioneered flexible swim fins and diving masks, closed-circuit diving equipment (under the direction of Dr. Christian J. Lambertsen), the use of Swimmer Delivery Vehicles (a type of submersible), and combat swimming and limpet mine attacks.

The OSS MU mission was "to infiltrate agents and supply resistance groups by sea, conduct maritime sabotage, and develop specialized maritime surface and subsurface equipment and devices." The MU operated in several theaters. In the Mediterranean, a fleet of hired Greek wooden fishing vessels – called caiques – covertly supported OSS agents in Albania, Greece, and Yugoslavia. After Italy surrendered, the MU and Mariassalto, an elite Italian special operations naval unit, operated against the Germans. In the Far East, the MU operated in conjunction with an Operational Group to attack

Japanese forces on the Arakan coast of Burma. They jointly conducted reconnaissance missions on the Japanese-held coast, sometimes penetrating several miles up enemy-controlled rivers.

The MU developed or used several innovative devices that would later allow for the creation of a special operations combat-diver capability, first in Army Special Forces (Green Berets) and later in US Navy SEAL units. Perhaps the most important invention in the realm of special operations diving was the Lambertsen Amphibious Respiratory Unit (LARU), which was invented by Dr. Christian J. Lambertsen. The Lambertsen unit permitted a swimmer to remain underwater for several hours and to approach targets undetected because the LARU did not emit telltale air bubbles. The LARU was later refined, adapted, and the technology used by the U.S. Army, U.S. Navy, and NASA. The Army Special Forces Underwater Operations School at Key West, Florida, the home of Special Forces maritime operations, draws its roots from the Maritime Unit.

Lambertsen began his involvement with OSS as a medical student, offering the use of his technology to the secretive organization in 1942. In 1944, he was commissioned as an Army Officer and later joined the OSS as an Operational Swimmer. Lambertsen himself led the OSS Maritime Unit on covert underwater missions to attach explosives to Japanese ships. Dr. Christian Lambertsen is remembered today as the 'Father of Military Underwater Operations'. Along with all the members of the OSS Maritime Unit, he was made honorary Green Berets and recognized by organizations like the UDT Navy Seal Association for their heroic and critical work.

In May 1944, Colonel "Wild Bill" Donovan, the head of the OSS, divided the Maritime Unit into four groups and approached General MacArthur and Admiral Nimitz about using OSS men in the Pacific Gen. MacArthur had no interest at all. Adm Nimitz looked at Donovan's list of units and also said no thank you, except he could use the swimmers from the Maritime Unit to expand the UDTs. He was primarily interested in them for being swimmers, not their military training. The interest in the tactical applications of the OSS Operational Swimmers' training only developed later, but most of Group A's gear was put into storage as it was not applicable to UDT work. The OSS was very restricted in operations in the Pacific. ADM Nimitz approved the transfer of the five officers and 24 enlisted men of Maritime Unit Operational Swimmer Group a led by Lieutenant Choate. They became part of UDT 10 in July 1944. LT Choate would become commander of UDT 10. The rest of MU Group A would fill most of UDT 10's command offices, as would many of the swimmers. Five of the OSS-trained men participated in the very first UDT submarine operation with USS *Burrfish* in the Caroline Islands in August 1944. Three of the men failed to make the rendezvous point for extraction. They were reported captured in Japanese communications and identified as "BAKUHATAI" – explosive ordnance men. They were never seen again and are listed as MIAs.

The first units, designated underwater demolition teams, were formed at the Pacific Theater. Rear Admiral Kelly Turner, the Navy's top amphibious expert, ordered the formation of Underwater Demolition Teams in response to the failed invasion at Tarawa and the Marines' inability to clear the surrounding coral reefs with Landing Vehicle Tracked (LVTS). Turner recognized that amphibious operations required intelligence of underwater obstacles. The personnel for these teams were mostly local Seabees or others who had started out in the NCDUs. UDT training was at the Waipio Amphibious Operating Base, under V Amphibious Corps operational and administrative control. Most of the instructors and trainees were graduates of the Fort Pierce NCDU or Scouts and Raiders schools, Seabees, Marines, and Army soldiers.

Carp. W. H. Acheson Silver Star ceremony for UDT 1 action at Engibi where he stripped down to swim trunks and did reconnaissance in broad daylight on a hostile beach, becoming a role model of UDTs being swimmers.

When Teams 1 and 2 were initially formed, they were "provisional" with 180 men in total. The first underwater demolition team commanders were CDR E.D. Brewster (CEC) UDT 1 and CDR John T. Koehler UDT 2. The teams wore fatigues with life-vests and were not expected to leave their boats – similar to the NCDUs. However, the protocol at Kwajalein, Fort Pierce, was changed. Admiral Turner ordered daylight reconnaissance and CEC. ENS Lewis F. Luehrs and Seabee Chief William Acheson wore swim trunks under their fatigues, anticipating they would not be able to get what the Admiral wanted by staying in the boat. They stripped down and spent 45 minutes in the water in broad daylight. When they got out, they were taken directly to Admiral Turner's flagship to report, still in their trunks. Admiral Turner concluded that daylight reconnaissance by individual swimmers was the way to get accurate information on coral and underwater obstacles for upcoming landings. This is what he reported to Admiral Nimitz. The success of those UDT 1 Seabees not following Fort Pierce protocol rewrote the UDT mission model and training regimen. Those Seabees also created the image of UDTs as the "naked warriors". At Engebi CDR, Brewster was wounded, and all of the men with ENS Luehrs wore swim trunks under their greens.

After the operations in the Marshall Islands, Admiral Turner restructured the two provisional UDT units and created 7 permanent units with an allotted size of 96 men per team. In the name of operational efficiency, the UDTs were also made an-all Navy outfit, and any Army and Marine corp engineers were returned to their units. Moving forward, the UDTs would employ the reconnaissance method made successful in Kwajalein - daytime use of swimsuits and goggles instead of the Scouts and Raiders method of nighttime rubber boats. In order to implement these changes and grow the UDTs, Koehler was made the commanding officer of the Naval Combat Demolition Training and Experimental Base on Maui. Admiral Turner also brought on LCDR Draper Kauffman as a combat officer.

Lt. Luehrs was one of the 30 Officers from the 7th NCR that staged for UDTs 1 & 2. He and Chief Acheson were the first UDT swimmers. His Corps insignia would have had a Seabee on it,

Seabees made up the vast majority of the men in teams 1–9, 13, and 15. Seabees were roughly 20% of UDT 11. The officers were mostly CEC. At war's end, 34 teams had been formed, with teams 1–21 having actually been deployed. The Seabees provided over half of the men in the teams that saw service.

The UDT uniform had transitioned from the combat fatigues of the NCDUs to trunks, swim fins, diving masks and Ka-bars. The men trained by the OSS had brought their swim fins with them when they joined the UDTs. They were adopted by the other teams as quickly as Supply could get them.

These "Naked Warriors", as they came to be called post-war, saw action in every major Pacific amphibious landing, including Eniwetok, Saipan, Kwajalein, Tinian, Guam, Angaur, Ulit hi, Peleliu, Leyte, Lingayen Gulf, Zambales, Iwo Jima, Okinawa, Labuan, and Brunei Bay. By the fall of 1944, the UDT's were considered an indispensable US military special operations unit, and Navy planners in the Central Pacific relied heavily on the UDT's reconnaissance reports and demolition activities to clear the way for landings.

The last UDT operation of the war was on 4 July 1945 at Balikpapan, Borneo. The rapid demobilization at the conclusion of the war reduced the number of active duty UDTs to two on each coast, with a complement of seven officers and 45 enlisted men each. However, the UDTs were the only special troops that avoided complete disbandment after the war, unlike the OSS Maritime Unit, the VAC Recon Battalion, and several Marine recon missions.

Because they were so integral to the success of missions in the Pacific during the war, the U.S. Navy did not publicize the existence of the UDTs until post-war. During WWII, the Navy did not have a rating for the UDTs, nor did they have an insignia. Those men with the CB rating on their uniforms considered themselves Seabees who were doing underwater demolition. They did not call themselves "UDTs" or "Frogmen" but rather "Demolitioneers," which had carried over from the NCDUs and Lt Cmdr. Kauffman's recruiting efforts from the Seabee dynamiting and demolition school. The next largest group of UDT volunteers came from the joint Army-Navy Scouts and Raiders school that was also in Fort Pierce and the Navy's bomb disposal school in the Seabee-dominated teams.

For the Marianas operations of Kwajalein, Roi-Namur, Siapan, Tinian, Eniwetok, and Guam, Admiral Turner recommended sixty Silver Stars and over three hundred Bronze Stars with Vs. for the Seabees and other service members of UDTs 1–7That was unprecedented in U.S. Naval/Marine Corps history. For UDTs 5 and 7, every officer received a silver star, and all the enlisted received bronze stars with Vs. for Operation Forager (Tinian). For UDTs 3 and 4, every officer received a silver star, and all the enlisted officers received bronze stars with Vs for Operation Forager (Guam). Admiral Richard Lansing Conolly felt the commanders of teams 3 and 4 (LT Crist and LT W.G. Carberry) should have received Navy Crosses.

LT Crist (CEC), LCDR Kauffman, and LT Carberry right-left at the UDT Silver and Bronze Stars award ceremony. Seabees in both UDT 3 and 4 made signs to greet the Marines assaulting Guam. However, Team 4 was able to leave theirs on the beach so that the Marines could see that the Seabees had been there first. UDT 4 posted this sign again on the Hotel Marquee for its 25-year reunion.

As the first to often make amphibious landings, the UDTs began making signs to welcome the Marines, indicating they had been there first, to foster the continued friendly rivalry. In keeping with UDT tradition, UDT 21 created a sign to greet the Marines landing in Japan. For Operation Beleaguer , UDT 9 was deployed with the III Amphibious Corps to Northern China. In 1965, the UDT 12 put up another beach sign to greet the Marines at Da Nang.

Operation Crossroads UDT 3 was designated TU 1.1.3 for the operation. On 27 April 1946, seven officers and 51 enlisted embarked at CBC Port Hueneme for transit to Bikini. Their assignment was to retrieve water samples from ground zero of the Baker blast.

The Korean War began on 25 June 1950 when the North Korean army invaded South Korea. Beginning with a detachment of 11 personnel from UDT 3, UDT's participation expanded to three teams with a combined strength of 300 men. During the "Forgotten War," the UDTs fought intensely, employing demolition expertise gained from World War II and using it for an offensive role. Continuing to use water as cover and concealment as well as an insertion method, the Korean Era UDTs targeted bridges, tunnels, fishing nets, and other maritime and coastal targets. They also developed a close working relationship with the Republic of Korea Underwater Demolitions Unit (predecessor to the Navy Special Warfare Flotilla), which continues today.

Through their focused efforts on demolitions and mine disposal, the UDTs refined and developed their commando tactics during the Korean War. The UDTs also accompanied South Korean commandos on raids in the North to demolish train tunnels. This was frowned upon by higher-ranking officials because they believed it was a non-traditional use of Naval forces. Due to the nature of the war, the UDTs maintained a low operational profile. Some of the missions included transporting spies into North Korea and the destruction of North Korean fishing nets used to supply the North Korean Army.

As part of the Special Operations Group, or SOG, UDTs successfully conducted demolition raids on railroad tunnels and bridges along the Korean coast. The UDTs specialized in a somewhat new mission: Night coastal demolition raids against railroad tunnels and bridges. The UDT men were given the task because, in the words of UDT LT Ted Fielding, "We were ready to do what nobody else could do, and what nobody else wanted to do." (Ted Fielding was awarded the Silver Star during Korea, and was later promoted to the rank of Captain).

On 15 September 1950, UDTs supported Operation Chromite, the amphibious landing at Incheon. UDT 1 and 3 provided personnel who went in ahead of the landing craft, scouting mud flats, marking low points in the channel, clearing fouled propellers, and searching for mines. Four UDT personnel acted as wave-guides for the Marine landing. In October 1950, UDTs supported mine-clearing operations in Wonsan Harbor, where frogmen would locate and mark mines for minesweepers. On 12 October 1950, two U.S. minesweepers hit mines and sank. UDTs rescued 25 sailors. The next day, William Giannotti conducted the first U.S. combat operation using an "aqualung" when he dived on the USS *Pledge*. For the remainder of the war, UDTs conducted beach and river reconnaissance, infiltrated guerrillas behind the lines from the sea, continued mine sweeping operations and participated in Operation Fishnet, which devastated the North Koreans' fishing capability.

President John F. Kennedy, aware of the situation in Southeast Asia, recognized the need for unconventional warfare and special operations as a measure against guerrilla warfare. In a speech to Congress on 25 May 1961, Kennedy spoke of his deep respect for the United States Army Special Forces. While his announcement of the government's plan to put a man on the moon drew most of the attention, in the same speech, he announced his intention to spend over $100 million to strengthen U.S. special operations forces and expand American capabilities in unconventional warfare. Some people erroneously credit President Kennedy with creating the Navy SEALs. His announcement was actually only a formal acknowledgement of a process that had been underway since the Korean War.

The Birth of the NAVY SEAL

The Navy needed to determine its role within the special operations arena. In March 1961, Admiral Arleigh Burke, the Chief of Naval Operations, recommended the establishment of guerrilla and counter-guerrilla units. These units would be able to operate from sea, air or land. This was the beginning of the Navy SEALs. All SEALs came from the Navy's Underwater Demolition Teams, who had already gained extensive experience in commando warfare in Korea; however, the Underwater Demolition Teams were still necessary to the Navy's amphibious force.

The first two teams were formed in January 1962 and stationed on both US coasts: Team One at Naval Amphibious Base Coronado in San Diego, California and Team Two at Naval Amphibious Base Little Creek, in Virginia Beach, Virginia. Formed entirely with personnel from UDTs, the SEAL's mission was to conduct counter-guerilla warfare and clandestine operations in maritime and riverine environments. Men of the newly formed SEAL Teams were trained in such unconventional areas as hand-to-hand combat, high-altitude parachuting, demolitions, and foreign languages. The SEALs attended Underwater Demolition Team replacement training, and they spent some time training in UDTs. Upon making it to a SEAL team, they would undergo a SEAL Basic Indoctrination (SBI) training class at Camp Kerry in the Cuyamaca Mountains. After SBI training class, they would enter a platoon and conduct platoon training.

According to founding SEAL team member Roy Boehm, the SEALs' first missions were directed against communist Cuba. These consisted of deploying from submarines and carrying out beach reconnaissance in a prelude to a proposed US amphibious invasion of the island. On at least one occasion, Boehm and another SEAL had smuggled a CIA agent ashore to take pictures of Soviet nuclear missiles being unloaded on the dockside.

The Pacific Command recognized Vietnam as a potential hot spot for unconventional forces. At the beginning of 1962, the UDTs started hydrographic surveys, and along with other branches of the US Military, the Military Assistance Command Vietnam (MACV) was formed. In March 1962, SEALs were deployed to South Vietnam as advisors for the purpose of training the Army of the

Republic of Vietnam commandos in the same methods they were trained themselves.

The Central Intelligence Agency began using SEALs in covert operations in early 1963. The SEALs were later involved in the CIA-sponsored Phoenix Program, which targeted Vietcong (VC) infrastructure and personnel for capture and assassination.

The SEALs were initially deployed in and around Da Nang, training the South Vietnamese in combat diving, demolitions and guerrilla/anti-guerrilla tactics. As the war continued, the SEALs found themselves positioned in the Rung Sat Special Zone, where they were to disrupt the enemy supply and troop movements and in the Mekong Delta to fulfill riverine operations, fighting on the inland waterways.

Combat with the VC was direct. Unlike the conventional warfare methods of firing artillery into a coordinate location, the SEALs operated close to their targets. Into the late 1960s, the SEALs were successful in a new style of warfare, effective in anti-guerrilla and guerrilla actions. SEALs brought a personal war to the enemy in a previously safe area. The VC referred to them as "the men with green faces," due to the camouflage paint the SEALs wore during combat missions.

In February 1966, a small SEAL Team One detachment arrived in South Vietnam to conduct direct action missions. Operating from Nhà Bè Base, near the Rung Sat Special Zone, this detachment signaled the beginning of a SEAL presence that would eventually include 8 SEAL platoons in the country on a continuing basis. SEALs also served as advisors for Provincial Reconnaissance Units and the Lein Doc Nguio Nhia, the Vietnamese SEALs.

SEALs continued to make forays into North Vietnam and Laos and covertly into Cambodia, controlled by the Studies and Observations Group. The SEALs from Team Two started a unique deployment of SEAL team members working alone with ARVN Commandos. In 1967, a SEAL unit named Detachment Bravo (Det Bravo) was formed to operate these mixed US and ARVN units.

By 1970, President Richard Nixon initiated a plan of Vietnamization, which would remove the US from the Vietnam War and return the responsibility of defense back to the South Vietnamese. Conventional forces were being withdrawn; the last

SEAL platoon left South Vietnam on 7 December 1971, and the last SEAL advisor left South Vietnam in March 1973. The SEALs were among the highest decorated units for their size in the war, receiving by 1974 one Medal of Honor, two Navy Crosses, 42 Silver stars, 402 Bronze Stars, two Legions of Merit, 352 Commendation Medals, and 51 Navy Achievement Medals Later awards would bring the total to three Medals of Honor and five Navy Crosses. SEAL Team One was awarded three Presidential Unit Citations and one Navy Unit Commendation; SEAL Team Two received two Presidential Unit Citations. By the end of the war, 48 SEALs had been killed in Vietnam, but estimates of their kill count are as high as 2,000. The Navy SEAL Museum in Fort Pierce, Florida, displays a list of the 48 SEALs who lost their lives in combat during the Vietnam War.

Chapter 35

It is a beautiful Monday morning, November 2023. The Director of the Central Intelligence Organization of Zimbabwe is driving to work in his Toyota VXV 8, the latest off the rack, limited edition. Toyota made this car for high-powered, politically exposed persons who were at high risk, but it did not require an escort on the road. The idea was for the car to have capabilities that allowed a person driving it to protect themselves while back up is on the way.

Inside, it had Internet, Circular magnets to jam the Internet and radios should the need arise. The Internet was powered by Star link Communication Technology, the most efficient on earth. The seats in the VXV 8 could be converted into a comfortable bed. Right behind the Driver, there was a collapsible demarcation that divided the front and back parts of the car. A meeting could be held, and celebrations could be done with music at high volume without the driver noticing or having the slightest hint of what's taking place at the back of the car, as the mechanism has 100% sound proof that even those outside cannot hear a thing.

From the back of the car, the passengers could see the entire exterior of the car through pinhole cameras dotted around the car and neatly covered up.

The VXV 8 Limited edition used Nitrogen instead of ordinary pressure from a gas station. Inside each of the tyres was a jelly-like substance that could stop any loss of nitrogen pressure levels should there be any tyre puncture or perforation on the tyres. In the event that a major tyre collapses, the tyres could run flat for 10 kilometers before the car can come to a total stop.

The car had laser technology that could pop out right at the top of the vehicle and destroy a target without having to destroy the entire infrastructure.

The car came with a smart Drone, bigger than the entry-size camera drones, with the only difference being that this one carried four grenades that explode upon contact, two small bombs that detonated on the target and a small cylinder of Nitrogen that could be deployed at the enemy scene. The Drones were controlled from the car and had an effective range of 1,000 meters. Should the occupants of the vehicle fail to control the drone, the CIO intelligence room would be alerted and immediately take over. The drone takes more than 2000 photos per minute, and using artificial intelligence, it follows sounds and analyses actions and movements such as lifting up hands and throwing things.

The system in the VXV 8 is capable of intercepting emails, SMS, Radio, audio and video transmission messages considered hostile. It uses artificial intelligence to scan through languages and immediately translate them into English, and it recommends appropriate action to be taken.

The VXV 8 Limited edition comes with a freezer. Also comes with Radio mounted equipment that allows satellite communication when all communication channels have failed.

The Director was a man of few words, a man who was shy of the Cameras, a razor-sharp intelligent man with a degree in software engineering and a degree in phycology, a master's degree in War strategy and a PhD in War Strategy with research focused on air to air and ground to air combat. He joined the military in high school, specifically from Fletcher High, where there was a special Air Force young cadets program. Some opined that the team of young lads carried around an air of "we have arrived" at school grounds and around as they went about their business. The team was highly disciplined, and there was never a point where any one of the lads was found offside for an offence deserving punishment. The Director had joined the military through the "normal channel," where he completed the running and physical examination.

Soon after training, he was seconded to the Air force, where he studied for a degree in software engineering and a diploma in Radio telecommunication and modern communication, becoming first in his class.

In the war that broke out In Mozambique, he operated as a squadron leader, rising to Wing Commander. He was seconded to numerous assignments in Africa for peace keeping before returning home with Military honors. The Director was left with one year to retirement; he had discharged himself professionally, yet this new assignment he had to chair came at a time he was slowing down, slowly handing over the reins to his deputy, who was primed to take over from him.

Director General Innocent Kizito Zhiradzago Muchemwa Mavima was a goal-getter, a smart man both in his choice of Cloths and most importantly, his intellect; he had a high intelligence as well as Emotional Quotient.

He drove from his house in Emerald Hill, and for a man who wore an emerald ring, it was tempting to be persuaded to think that the neighborhood was named after his ring. He sped off to the intersection of the Chase and Second Street extension as if though in a high speed chase with the Police, leaving Ash-Brittle on the right quadrant, he tuned into second street extension at high speed with tyres screaming loudly expressing their disapproval, the VXV 8 peaked speed at 180km per hour hobbling over two humps that were within a few meters apart before coming to a brisk stop at the intersection of Lomagundi and Second Street Extension, he swerved to the right turning into Lomagundi Road and driving a little over 100 meters he filtered to the left into King George street peaking at 180 km per hour before stopping at the amber flushing lights at the intersection of Aberdeen and King George before piecing the mist at great speed with the wind whistling around the rear view mirror, went past Avondale Police station and going a little further he approached the merge were he filtered to the left speeding past Emirates office on the left speeding through the shopping center hobbling at the ridge right at the center of the road, he proceeded straight ahead leaving Mass market Purple Bank on the left, he meandered through the road as he avoided pot holes that were dotted all over the road missing some in the process sending the Beast of a car tumbling but immediately steadying due its built.

He cruised towards Parirenyatwa Group of Hospitals, a giant of a Hospital, a heritage asset; a once revered Health and teaching center that is still perhaps responsible for releasing a number of Doctors into the SADC region as well as Austalia, Canada and the UK. He Crossed Cork road, and up until now, he had not paid much attention. He had not paid attention as the car was driving itself most of the time as he was consumed by the latest stories in local and International newspapers; every paper he opened, there was a story of a missing Ambassador in Zimbabwe and one story after another, he felt a huge responsibility was placed on his shoulder.

He lifted up his head and saw the wonder of Harare, a breath taking Jacaranda trees forming an Arch; these plants are said to have been planted in fort Salisbury (now Harare) in 1899. The trees are such a beauty, and each year tourists travel from the UK to see such a wonder; however, the beauty was blinding to Innocent as he was allergic to the jacaranda tree flowering or whatever happens during the flowering process. The fact that the windows were open sent tears flowing down; he immediately asked the car to take over driving as he struggled fighting off tears. Despite the challenges, he asked the car to take some photo withthe lady's voice responding with a, "yes sir, how many do you want" and Innocent replied, "take as many as you can and send them to my phone and send some to my wife."

He turned into Tongogara Road, a road named after Zimbabwe's Finest decorated Soldier who led the armed liberation struggle in the Second Chimurenga War that Brought Independence to Zimbabwe, a man who was fearless and courageous and yet humorous when he chose to. As he crossed second street, he slowed down as he approached the uneven plane where a Musasa Tree had been left to grow right in the middle of the road; the tree carried a historic symbol as historians narrate that it was on that tree where Mbuya Nehanda (Grand Mother Nehanda) had been hanged by the British settlers after she resisted and called upon the people to resist the rule imposed by the white people. The Woman is the beacon of hope and an example of how women can contribute to society. Nehanda's story that she asked the Natives to take up arms and fight the white colonial rule gave courage to the guerrillas, and even now, as the country fights the devastating 'illegal' economic sanctions, the Name of Nehanda continues to be brought to the fore.

He drove straight ahead, and as he approached the state house, he replayed how the First Lady had been crying and the President had been still and being as strong as he could, but inside, he was hurting. This created a sense of frustration in him. Innocent had only slept for 2 hours as he spent the entire time coordinating the investigations with the Police, INTERPOL, AFRIPOL and all the Pols. He drove into Borrowdale road, then turned right, then left into KG6, aka King George the 6th.

The meeting started at 08:00 and all members were seated. The Director of CIO took to the podium, and after ordering the national anthems for the two nations, he started addressing the team members.

"I have played our two national anthems so that you are reminded that we serve our very two great nations, that we are carrying the hopes of our nations, and that our nations have given us this responsibility to rescue the Ambassador and his family, the girls as well as hunt down the drug lords."

Recently, I have seen our two nations setting aside their differences as they sought to tackle a common enemy that has ravaged our societies. We believe from the intelligence we have gathered that the three objectives we seek to accomplish may involve the same characters.

We have had an exchange of life for life with the Notorious JBZ. He had kidnapped one of our detective's Wife, and the detective had preempted his move and secured his son, which we agreed to release in a life for life exchange. It was agreed that moving in on him at the time was too risky as little is known, and so we took the opportunity to record his voice and learnt his negotiation skills and his temper and mannerisms.

We have heightened security at the ports of entry and exit, all entry points to holiday resorts have been closed, and Inter City travel has been limited, with checkpoints established every 30 kilometers. We have raised the alarm with INTERPOL AND AFRIPOL within the SADC, and all neighboring nations are on high alert. The recent opening of the Forbes Border post on a 24/7 basis creates a high risk of escape.

The team will be chaired by myself, and under me will be three Vice Joint Chiefs. I will be deputized by the Chief of Military Intelligence, Deputy Chief of Police Operations as well as I know that the Police have their sentiments regarding their role, but this is now a matter of national security; this is not a pissing competition here, but two nations are at risk of going to war, and the world is watching our every move. We believe that we are in the best position to share and cooperate with Other Nations; however, the Police will be critical in their Investigation skills and their proximity to civilians.

The three Vice Joint Chairs will be will be as follows:

1. Joint Vice Chair 1: Eagle 1 To lead the Ambassador's Case and be the lead on all matters related to same.
2. Joint Vice Chair 2: To lead Vasikana (Girls) – The Girls' case
3. Joint Vice Chair 3 to Lead Team Manyama focusing on the Drugs case.

Each team was given a place to work from; there was an hourly reporting time to the Vice Joint Chairs where they would share any conformation gathered, including sharing and referring information regarding leads that could be more useful to other team members. The meetings were attended by the Chair if he so desired to do the same.

Earlier on, three team members from the United States had been denied visas on the basis of them being LGBTQ, and despite any attempt by the US Government, the lads turned women were still denied visas and had to be dropped from the team. The actions by Harare were met with mixed feelings in the USA Diplomatic Corridor, yet the US could not allow such a matter to divide the team and divert attention, given the extensive work that had been done to thaw the frosty relationships that existed between the two nations.

The selection of Dr. Innocent Zhiradzago Kizito had drawn criticism as some believed that the Police Chief needed to handle the matter; however, the matter was classified as a national security issue and given that the CIO had high-level access to classified information, it allowed decision making to be fast without the need to frequently seeking access to classified Information. The Military Intelligence Supremo was placed on standby and ready to serve in any way possible. Given the manner in which the guns were handled, the Zimbabwe National Army, and the Air Force were on standby given the nature of kidnapping, where expert Marine Corps were ambushed and killed on the spot. The ZNA, US Marine Corps coopted from US military establishment in the SADC region, started Military drills together. This was meant to ensure interoperability and to agree on communication protocols, radio channels, and chain of command, as well as to make sure all are familiar with the geography of the country.

The Big Cat was appointed to lead the Ambassador's Case; Noel Jones was assigned to lead the Girls' Case, while Silver was appointed to lead the case related to drugs.

Detective Mike was asked to take a leave, a decision he disagreed with, but despite having been appointed by the president initially, he had to agree to the command. He had been asked to support his wife, who went through a traumatic experience under the hand of the Drug Lord.

Chapter 36

In the dimly lit room, tension hung thick as diplomats fiercely debated the rescue priority. The clock ticked relentlessly as the urgency of the situation increased. Innocent girls' lives were on a fragile thread, hanging by the whims of ruthless captors. To make matters worse, there was a diplomatic impasse stemming from whether to prioritise the ambassador's family or the girls. This deadlock posed potential political and international ramifications if they failed to safeguard a leader's kin. As the verbal sparring escalated, the negotiators struggled to find common ground. The ZRP insisted that every life held equal value, while the CIA feared the repercussions of prioritising one life over another.

Amid the heated discussions, a covert operation unfolded. The special task forces from both countries collaborated in a daring rescue mission. Stealthily infiltrating the kidnappers' lair, they aimed to liberate all hostages simultaneously, defying the diplomatic deadlock. With the clock ticking down, the rescue team faced obstacles and unforeseen challenges. Meanwhile, the argument in the diplomatic room reached a fever pitch, with neither side willing to yield. The fate of the kidnapped girls, including the president's daughter, teetered on the edge of uncertainty. While the two parties were cooperating, there were always some egoistic team members who were overzealous and aimed to outshine others and receive all the credit for heroic feats. With the likes of one Joe Billiat from the ZRP, it would need a miracle of some sort to avoid a dramatic turn of events and allow the rescue team to successfully liberate all hostages.

#

In the heart of the teapot-shaped country, chaos ensued as the president's and minister's children found themselves unintended victims of a ruthless drug dealer's twisted game. A heated conflict of objectives emerged as the ambassador, torn between his duty to his nation and his personal anguish, advocated for the immediate rescue of his wife. Simultaneously, the president grappled with the dilemma of prioritising his own daughter's and other girls' safety over the ambassador's wife. It was a case of the saving five over saving one paradox. That is, would you rather lose one to save many than lose many to save one? This paradox was coined the "trolley problem" as articulated by Foot and Thomson, and it is when people are forced to make a moral decision between two ethical judgments, that is, harming one person or letting many people die. Respectively, that is utilitarian judgments versus deontological judgments. In the rescue discussions, there was a moral dilemma as whether to prioritise the general populace or the elite. There were no privileges for the general public, but for the elite, they were privy to freedom of choice. For instance, the poor can only go to public hospitals such as Sally Mugabe Hospital, while those with means can visit private hospitals locally or abroad. The president had a choice, and so did the minister. He had an obligation to his people, the people he led, to bring all remaining girls safe from captivity. It was unfortunate one of them was already confirmed dead. The other two found in Newlands were undergoing medical checkups. Kidnappers are prone to do anything to instil pain, regardless of their motive. It was protocol to conduct medical tests.

Meanwhile, at the police headquarters, Detective Mike spoke in a low tone, seemingly sounding defeated even though he tried to mask it with a fist pump, "We're doing our best, but this guy operates like a ghost. It's like he's always ten steps ahead of us." He looked ahead and waited for his boss to speak, but instead he stared at him nonchalantly.

Detective Mike continued, "So, I still maintain that we should listen to what Roselyn is saying. She is a vengeful sidekick of the drug dealer, harboring a personal vendetta, and her willingness to engage in covert communications to tip off the rescue team will benefit her, and she is also asking for immunity. Despite her personal revenge goals, she seems remorseful for all the cruel acts they did under the guise of power.

The boss raised his eyebrow, and Mike answered as he knew that look signaled "what about consequences" question.

"I know that her cooperation will create tension within the criminal network, and her safety will be of paramount importance as she may also need to testify against him for all those crimes. However, Gross has agreed to offer her witness protection and that she may be transported to South Africa or Botswana once the finer details emerge. They need her too to nail Martinez, you see. It would be a win-win if we sided with Roselyn. She is not aware of this arrangement yet.”

The boss strode to the interrogation room and walked over to Roselyn with a straight face. One hand in the pocket and the other scrolling on his phone as if she was a nonentity.

She sulked, but he did not flinch. She then cleared her throat, but still, he remained fixated on his phone, feigning to be busy. He was finishing his game of Candy Flush. Games can be addictive.

She punched a fist on the table, breaking the silence. The boss finally looked in her direction.

 “I've had enough of his games. I'll help you, but you need to promise me some freedom; I wasn’t a willing accomplice.”

He answered, “Listen, young lady and hear me well; I don’t repeat my words. I speak once, twice, you won’t like it. We do not make deals with criminals, but if you provide valuable information, we'll consider leniency.” He continued, “You see, crime can be addictive; you won’t pay heed to the consequences of your actions until you hit a brick wall. That point is when you reach the end of the road. Nowhere to go. Nowhere to run to. Nowhere to hide. Games can be addictive, too. They make you lose focus if you let them. Like you did. You don’t even have a single property in your name, not even a bedsitter. Yet you smell like a million dollars.” He weighed her with disdain from head to toe and shook his head while frowning. He was, by all means, a no-nonsense man when it came to ladies. He particularly ignored those who offered him services of a sexual nature.

Roselyn burst into tears.

“Tears and fears don’t move me. Instead, I move fears and cause tears. That is the call of duty.” Without giving her a chance to respond, he banged the door, leaving her to wallow in her misery.

Chapter 37

As the days turned into nights, Zimbabwe became a battleground of conflicting interests and hidden agendas. Already, the USA had escalated its intelligence efforts as there were possible leads to bringing Martinez down. Charles Darwin said that human beings, like animals, thrive on the "survival of the fittest" principle. That statement is still relevant today even so as either state had its sovereignty to protect. Zimbabwe officials, now fully aware of the drug dealer's insidious presence, faced a reckoning. The diplomatic tensions, which had recently transformed into cooperative efforts to dismantle the criminal empire that had exploited the nation for far too long, marked a new chapter in the fight against corruption and crime. Special appreciation went to the Zimbabwean Ambassador to the US, who remained assertive and astute in the face-off with the US Secretary of State. It was a remarkable feat for the Zimbabwean diplomat to pull that off as he was often in the local papers for his captivating dance moves of "*ndombolo*" (fast-paced Congolese dance movements consisting of gyrating the hips). He patted himself on the shoulder for scoring this one, and he intended to see the rescue mission succeed at all costs. He had faith in the local police force, and he kept giving them positive reinforcement. Coupled with the US security teams, he was confident that success was imminent. It was unfortunate that one girl had been lost to suicide. They had to continue racing against time to save the girls not only from the kidnappers but from themselves, too. Traumatic conditions can be debilitating to the point of being irrational. Any more fatalities would symbolize failure on the rescue mission's part. They would have failed their daughters, their nieces, their sisters and their future mothers.

The rescue operation of the girls, now two days old, unfolded with a delicate balance of precision and urgency. The intertwined fates of the kidnapped young girls and the pursuit of justice were woven into a high-stakes narrative that demanded collaboration across borders. This meant saving the girls by hook or by crook. No time to waste. News that they had been auctioned was rubbished by some men in the task force, while others argued that it was true. Any leads and all leads were treated as serious. As such, when the estranged drug dealer's ex-wife, Nobesuthu, came forward, she was given attention.

In the midst of the intricate rescue operation, Nobesuthu, driven by a thirst for justice, presented her conditions to the authorities. She was abandoned by JBZ, and when he returned after fifteen years, she seemed to have forgiven him. Nobesuthu was touched by the innocent girls' kidnapping. Also told the police that JBZ was a unit of measurement, of stealth, enigma and cruelty. That unit could mean anything to anyone at any given point of time, depending on one's need for the unit. In short, there were many shades of JBZ; hence, it would be difficult, if not impossible, to apprehend him. Consequently, that would make finding Martinez harder, too. Mission impossible.

Nobesuthu, clad in designer sunglasses, ripped jeans, a sheer blouse and a white blazer, leaned closer to Detective Mike and puffed her cigarette smoke to his face, saying, "I'll help you uncover the drug dealer's identity, but I want assurances that my involvement won't be used against me in our custody battle. My focus is on justice, not personal disputes." She had a son with the man she called JBZ, who lived with him. Nobesuthu had recovered her health and looked plump and radiant, unlike the time when her so-called husband re-entered her life. As written by William Congreve, an English author of the late seventeenth and early eighteenth centuries, it is true that "hell hath no fury like a woman scorned." The fundamental message in this story is a lesson for life, especially for all ill-intentioned men masquerading the streets as gentlemen to lure naive ladies.

Put off by Nobesuthu's arrogance, Detective Mike answered, staring at the window, avoiding her gaze, "We can work on an agreement. Our priority is bringing down those responsible, whatever and whoever they may be."

A radio message intercepted his response, and he left Nobesuthu with other attendants while he talked. It was news that a lady named Roselyn, an apparent vengeful sidekick-cum-side chick was also seeking retribution for past grievances and wanted to help uncover the truth behind the girls' kidnapping and unmasking of JBZ. However, she had laid out her own demands during a tense exchange with the rescue team. Mike was made to understand that she wanted to provide critical information, but she demanded protection. The drug dealer would not take kindly to betrayal. She had seen enough bloodshed.

While witness protection was discussed, both ladies were made aware of the consequences of their actions. As the conditions were negotiated, Nobesuthu's bitterness swelled, revealing underlying tensions and conflicting motivations. As a result, the Chief of Operations emphasized that the two women should never be in the same room since a verbal or physical clash could easily erupt between the ex-wife and the sidekick. Well, that instruction was too late, as an overzealous officer led Roselyn into the room without following protocol. Roselyn glared at the leader who had rubbished her off hours earlier and treated her with disgust. Mike could not figure out why his boss had acted so strangely with her earlier.

Seeing Nobesuthu's disapproving look, Mike was quick to explain, "She is here for the same reasons as you. No drama; otherwise, the cells are open."

Nobesuthu gave a crooked smile and answered, staring at Roselyn from the top of her sunglasses, "You may be helping us, but don't think for a second that I've forgotten your role in all of this. Redemption isn't a simple path for a slut like you."

Roselyn retorted, "Save the moral high ground, Mrs. ex-wife. We're all trying to survive in a world tainted by corruption. My actions might be stained, but at least I'm trying to make amends. He never loved you anyway."

The heated exchange was cut short by the Head of Operations, "Enough! This is not the place or time for sex-starved runts. Vent your sexual frustrations elsewhere." The rescue operation, already teetering on a delicate balance, faced additional challenges amidst the verbal sparring. In the ensuing drama, the ex-wife's conditions and the sidekick's demands became integral factors influencing the course of the mission, adding more complexity to an already intricate narrative of rescue, justice, and revenge.

Chapter 38

In the high-stakes diplomatic chamber, a tense dialogue emerged among the rescue team members as they grappled with conflicting priorities in the rescue operation.

"Our citizens are in immediate danger. We must prioritise the girls' safety over political considerations."

The ambassador's wife and son are also hostages. Our nation cannot afford to be perceived as weak. We must prioritise their rescue."

As the debate reached a boiling point, the rescue team received intelligence that led them to a clandestine location where the kidnapped girls were held. The urgency of the situation heightened as they prepared for the mission.

The rescue mission leader said, "We can't wait any longer. Every moment counts. Our lintel suggests they're being held here," he finished pointing on the big screen at a location about 254km from the capital city, Harare. "That is Mukumbura. They could easily be in Mozambique. All stations ready!"

#

Meanwhile, within the grim confines of the captors' lair, tension among the kidnapped girls escalated. One of the captors targeted a sick and vulnerable girl, prompting a disturbing exchange with his colleagues. This girl pleaded for access to medication as she had a chronic condition that required her to have a daily dosage of medication.

"We don't have time for weak links. If she can't keep up, we might as well leave her behind. Her buyer would be so disappointed and angry. I am certain he will finish her off. I might as well do that now," yelled the mean man.

"I say we teach her a lesson. A slap might straighten her out. This is not home where you spend the whole day changing TV channels or scrolling on Instagram. Welcome to instant reality," another one chimed in, smoking weed in the corner.

A third captor chimed in, "Leave her alone! She's sick. Have some humanity. What's with you? You won't get any extra money for beating her, you know." shouted another one, also smoking weed, pacing about. Two more rogues agreed to leave her alone, and one gave her water. Complete mayhem broke out, and this internal strife among the captors threatened to escalate into violence as the rescue team closed in on their location.

As the diplomatic impasse had been broken, the rescue team, driven by a shared mission to save innocent lives, continued the daring operation, venturing into the heart of danger to confront the captors and bring the kidnapped girls to safety. Within the high-profile search operation, the rescue team implemented a series of meticulous procedures and code names to maintain operational security and confidentiality.

"Operation Hippo is a go. I repeat Operation Hippo is a go. All teams, maintain radio silence until further notice," the mission leader announced over radio messaging. The use of code names like "Operation Hippo" was crucial to avoid detection by potential infiltrators or those monitoring communication channels. There was suspicion, but no leads from the culprits have been revealed yet.

In a few minutes, the second command officer said, "Initiate phase Ethos. We need eyes on the ground without arousing suspicion. Beta team, you're clear for insertion."

The tech specialist added, "Commencing PRISM protocol for satellite surveillance. We'll have a real-time visual on the target site in T-minus five minutes." Once activated, the prism surveillance system would provide a 360-degree view, feeding real-time data to the command centre. Thus, with each encrypted image and audio stream, intelligence analysts would examine the situation, identifying the number of captors, their armour, and potential escape routes. With all this in place, everything seemed to flow with ease according to plan. The degree of coordination and cooperation between Zimbabwean and US police was outstanding, given the earlier deadlock and arrogance from the leadership. As the rescue team neared Dotito, they referred to the kidnapped girls with specific code names to protect their identities.

The rescue mission leader announced instructions to focus on retrieving the targets using code names. Amidst the risky operation, the rescue team's adherence to procedures and code names showcased their commitment to executing a mission of utmost importance with a keen understanding of the need for discretion and security. However, unknown to them, the wicked abductors operated under coded identities, and an internal threat within the police force posed a grave risk to the mission. The lead kidnapper enquired over the radio, "Prime, this is Falcon. Status update on the merchandise?"

"Falcon, all systems normal. They're clueless about our plans. Over," said Prime, the police mole. Prime was the defense attaché whose real name was Ray Bundt.

Meanwhile, the rescue team remained vigilant, unaware that their every move was being monitored by an insider within the police force. The rescue team leader shared a coded message telling the team to keep an eye out for any unexpected interferences; they could not afford any leaks on such a delicate matter. However, the attaché within the police force continued to provide crucial information to the enemy, jeopardising the secrecy of the operation.

Chapter 39

Men paced about the room, staring at each other with subtle spite. Whether some were happy or not was a mystery. The urgency of finding the girls alive and well was real, but for the aggrieved, it never seemed enough. Some of the girls' parents took to social media to express their disgruntlement at the lack of speed and demanded immediate answers. Since the parents of the kidnapped girls awaited the safe return of their daughters, a compassionate support network, including counsellors and law enforcement liaison officers, was established to guide the parents through the excruciating wait. The delicate balance between providing information and managing their anguish became a crucial aspect of the rescue operation. One of the girl's parents was angry about social media influencers leading to these senseless extravagant parties and the lawlessness prevailing among adolescents in the country.

The distraught mother fumed, "This wouldn't have happened if it weren't for those influencers and their wild parties. They glorify lawlessness, and our children pay the price!"

A senior law enforcement liaison officer attending the mission responded with great calm, showing maturity and years of experience dealing with frantic clients, "I understand your frustration, but we can't solely blame influencers. Our focus is on the rescue operation, and we're doing everything in our power to bring your child back safely."

"Power? Where was the power to prevent this in the first place? These influencers create a culture of recklessness, and now my daughter is suffering because of it!"

A counsellor in the room chimed in, "I hear your concerns, and we can address them once the immediate crisis is over. Right now, we need unity and strength to support the rescue team and each other. Here, we are dealing with a potential case of post-traumatic stress disorder (PTSD); as such, our priority will be to address that while the blame game will be secondary. It will be dealt with, yes, right now is not the time."

Unity? Our society is crumbling under the influence of these so-called influencers. They promote parties, drugs, and now my child is a victim of their toxic culture!" She grabbed her phone from her handbag and scrolled for a few seconds. Then she flashed it to the counsellor's face before rotating it to everyone's faces.

"What unity? You call this, right? Look at these orgies! Despicable. How disgusting! That, right there, is your problem."

Somewhat angered by this lady's rantings, another parent who had been silent all along responded. "Was your daughter forced to follow these social media influencers? Did anyone hold a gun to her head for her to log in, create an account, and follow social media madness? In law, we say, 'Was she under duress?'" There was mumbling among the parents, and some nodded while others shook their heads.

"Another lady added, "You should be meek and not give the authorities a headache over your ignorance. I see you are the type who delegated parenting duties to social media. Now you are crying foul and want to make noise about it. My daughter is in this mess because of her own doing. She is a party animal. I tried my best to raise her well. Nowadays, children have so many rights, unlike back in our days. Slap a kid, and you will go to jail for child abuse. What more could I have done? She sobbed.

Seeing her apparent lack of support, the loud lady asked, "What is this PTSD you mentioned?" Her head remained bowed down while she waited for an answer.

"Good question. PTSD is a mental health condition often triggered by a terrifying event, either experiencing it firsthand or witnessing it. People with PTSD may display symptoms which include flashbacks from the event, nightmares, severe anxiety, as well as uncontrollable thoughts about the event. These symptoms may go away on their own within the first few weeks or months after the trauma, but if left untreated, they can last for many years. The good news is that treatment will be available free of charge for your kids at designated clinics and will include different types of psychotherapy and medications. Of course, all girls will be treated depending on their specific symptoms and experiences. We will share leaflets with you on PTSD."

That said, the senior law enforcement liaison officer added, "You see, we are all here for you. We share your concerns, but let's channel our energy into supporting the rescue mission. Blame won't help us now. We need to focus on bringing all the girls home."

"Fine, I understand. Bringing them home is just the first step. We must still address the root cause – these influencers are poisoning the minds of our youth. They need to be held accountable before it's too late!"

The counsellor answered, "Correct. We can discuss measures to address these concerns once we ensure the safety of the kids. Your voice is important, and we'll work together to make changes." The anguish and frustration subsided, and the senior law enforcement liaison officer reassured the whole party that the focus would remain on supporting the rescue operation and addressing broader concerns once the immediate threat was mitigated.

Meanwhile, outside the police station, the boyfriend of one of the girls paced about the car park. The girl's father had barred him from entering the station. He blamed the boy for misleading his daughter by dating her for two years with no serious intentions with her. He said if he had married her, she would not be chasing parties, and she should be home tending to household duties and raising kids. He was even more angered by his dress style. It was a peculiar fashion trend the world over. He walked around wearing his pants slung so low that one would wonder if gravity had suddenly intensified. This unveiled a curious sight - a parade of boxers and briefs in various colours and patterns, proudly on display for the world to see. If one saw him with his friends, it looked like they were having an exhibition of undergarments. A fashion *faux pas* that defied all logic. The girl's father always expresses his disgust when he talks about this boy. Now, seeing him dressed like that while he was dealing with his daughter's kidnapping made it all worse. He spat next to the boy's shoes, shook his head, and then walked into the station.

However, the boy remained unfazed, his confidence unwavering. He always defended his sagging trousers as a form of self-expression, a rebellion against the stifling norms that dictated how one should dress. To him, it was a symbol of nonconformity, a flag proudly flown in the face of tradition. He maintained that the times had changed and stereotyping others based on their dress sense was wrong and insignificant. The more the girl's father and his own parents showed their distaste, the more determined he was that he would turn out to be a successful businessman and raise a noble family. Time will tell.

The boyfriend grappled with the sudden disappearance of his girlfriend. Initially, he told his friends that it was a lie and that she might have found a way to dump him. Later, reality struck that it was not a prank or a pretend game. He confided in one of his uncles that he had taken the girl for granted and that the terrible incident was a wake-up call for him. He would set things right and do what was needed. However, he said he would not change his way of dressing. He had no updates about his kidnapped girlfriend except that which he read in the public domain. All he had was her picture in his wallet.

Chapter 40

Back at headquarters, the rescue team leader announced, "Gather everyone; we need to discuss our next moves. The situation is escalating, and time is of the essence."

One man added, "The captors are demanding immunity, and JBZ's and Martinez's involvement adds another layer of complexity. How do we proceed?"

The intelligence analyst answered, "We have the ex-wife Nobesuthu and the sidekick Roselyn cooperating, but we need to tread carefully. This man is playing a dangerous game, and we can't underestimate his reach."

The rescue mission leader went on, "Our priority remains the safety of the hostages. We won't compromise on justice, but we need a strategic approach. Suggestions?"

The Zimbabwean representative from the state security office also responded, "Let's leverage the diplomatic channels. The presidents need to coordinate their efforts and present a united front. Publicly condemn the captors while assuring the safe return of the hostages."

In agreement, the intelligence analyst said, "And we should intensify efforts to unveil JBZ's network. His personas, the disguises – we need to expose them to weaken his influence."

Another senior police spokesperson added, "The public is growing anxious. We can't keep them in the dark. We need to address their concerns without revealing sensitive details."

In response, the rescue mission leader said, "Transparency is key. We can provide updates on the progress without compromising the investigation. Keep the public informed, but cautiously so."

Another official asked, "What about the demand for immunity? We can't entertain that."

The intelligence analyst was quick to answer, "Instead of outright refusal, propose conditional terms. Promise a fair trial but emphasise that immunity is off the table. It might buy us time and keep the captors engaged."

In conclusion, the rescue mission leader said, "Good. Assemble the diplomatic teams and gather intel on JBZ's known associates. We're dealing with a shadow, but shadows can be pierced." After saying that, a message was received from Falcon via encrypted communication saying they had 72 hours to agree to their terms for the release of the hostages. This message intensified the pressure on the rescue team, diplomatic officials, and law enforcement agencies.

The rescue team leader responded with a straight face with no trace of panic whatsoever, "We're on the clock. Every moment counts. Let's mobilise quickly and gather as much intel as possible. Our men are closing in on them in Mukumbura. This could be a decoy." As the clock ticks, the rescue team faces heightened urgency, racing against time to locate the captors and secure the hostages.

In that instance, the rescue team leader announced via radio, "We've got an update. Another team found the ambassador's family. They are alive and well, and no ransom was paid." That news was a huge relief as the men high-fived each other. It was a victory worth celebrating. As per protocol, the ambassador was notified immediately. There was an urgent need to reunite them and gather any information they might have about the captors. Of course, the first point of call was the medical examination. While it was good news that she was found, they had to cease their celebration and focus on the kidnapped girls. The rescue team leader sensitised the team that it was absolutely important to maintain momentum. He closed off by saying, "The captors won't get far, and we're closing in."

The captors, aware of the pressure mounting against them, made another bold demand for immunity in exchange for the release of the kidnapped girls. Their leader, via encrypted communication, said, "Listen carefully. We have your precious hostages. If you want them back alive, grant us immunity from prosecution immediately."

The rescue team's response was defiant yet tactful. The whole team agreed that they had crossed the line by even demanding 'immediate immunity'. They were not willing to negotiate with criminals. Meanwhile, the captor leader, codenamed Falcon, insisted that they had 24 hours to agree, or the hostages would suffer the consequences. On the other hand, the rescue operation still maintained that they would not entertain their demands. They had to find another way to resolve the matter without compromising justice. The presidents were notified. As the rescue team grappled with the captors' demands, the countdown began, intensifying the urgency of the mission to secure the hostages without conceding to the criminals' request for immunity.

Chapter 41

News reports and social media were awash with the developments of the kidnapping case. On the state television channel, they reported the following breaking news, "In a shocking turn of events, the captors of the kidnapped girls have demanded immunity from prosecution in exchange for their release. Authorities are facing a difficult decision, balancing the urgency of rescuing the hostages with the need for justice."

Another news reporter said, "The international community is closely watching as the diplomatic and law enforcement agencies navigate this crisis. The demand for immunity has sparked debates on the ethical and legal implications of negotiating with criminals."

Also, social media had mixed reactions. An X user wrote, "Immunity for criminals? Are you kidding me? Justice should prevail! #HostageCrisis #NoImmunity."

On Facebook, a comment read, "This is a tough call for the authorities. On the one hand, we want the hostages safe, but on the other, granting immunity sets a dangerous precedent. What would you do?"

A user on Instagram posted a picture of a praying person with the caption, "The tension is palpable as the world watches the developing hostage situation. Praying for the safety of the hostages and hoping for a resolution that upholds justice. #HostageDrama #JusticePrevail."

As the news unfolded, public opinion on social media platforms became divided, reflecting the complexity and moral dilemmas surrounding the demand for immunity in the ongoing hostage crisis. The global community watched and debated, hoping for a resolution that prioritised the safety of the hostages while addressing the broader implications of negotiating with criminals.

#

In the conference room, the rescue team leader was so focused on analysing the latest clue that he barely noticed his phone vibrating on the table. Within a few seconds, his wife entered the room, where he was immersed in documents and maps. "You've been at this for two days straight. The kids miss you, and frankly, so do I. You can't even answer your phone."

Looking up, momentarily breaking free from the web of information, he said, how did you get in here? You shouldn't be here. Well, I know, and I'm sorry. This case is complex, and every second counts." He tried to usher her out, but she remained still.

Folding her arms, expressing both concern and irritation, she replied, "I understand the importance, but your family needs you too. The kids are starting to think you've moved to the office."

Sighing, he closed the laptop and signaled everyone else to leave the room. "I can't neglect my responsibilities here, but I also can't neglect you and the kids. It's a delicate balance. Besides, this case is not permanent."

Softening her expression, she said, "We're not asking you to choose. Just find a way to be present, even if it's just for a moment. The kids need their dad, and I need my husband."

He nodded, stood, and put a hand on her shoulder. "You're right. I need to take a break, and spend some time with all of you. This case won't be solved in a day, but I can't let it consume everything." However, he abruptly stands away from his wife.

Taken aback by his sudden movement, she asked, "Where are you going?"

"Woman, I will see you at home. I love you, but I don't have time for this right now. We're dealing with a critical situation, and every moment counts."

Angry and hurt, she sobs. "And what about our family? Do we not count? You can't keep treating us like an afterthought."

Storming towards the door, he answers, "I'm doing my best to handle both, but I can't be everywhere at once."

With frustration boiling over, she wipes her tears and shouts back, "Your 'best' isn't enough for us. We need you here, present. If you can't see that, maybe you should reconsider your priorities." Then she left.

Chapter 42

In a house in the high-density suburb of Epworth, a couple were overwhelmed by the uncertainty surrounding their child's safety. This girl was one of the wannabees who had attended the party and had met the unfortunate encounter. She had often gate-crushed at extravagant and exclusive parties without drama included. Over the months, she also became a favourite to one of the popular bouncers, "Bigaz," with whom she exchanged favours in exchange for entry into the posher parties. Her mother turned to her spouse, "I've been thinking... maybe we should seek help beyond what the authorities are doing."

Raising his head from the comfort of his pillow, he asked, "What do you mean?"

The wife paused before proceeding, "I was thinking of seeking guidance from a traditional healer. They have a different perspective; maybe they can provide insight or spiritual guidance that we're not getting elsewhere. I can't stand this anymore. The uncertainty is eating me up."

Startled by her suggestion, he sat upright and stared at her with intent, "But what about our pastor at church? Wouldn't seeking help from our faith be more appropriate in times like these?"

She nodded, being the submissive she always was, "That's true. Maybe we should talk to our pastor first. But I also believe in exploring all avenues. We're dealing with something beyond our understanding, and maybe different perspectives can help us make sense of it."

Her husband pulled her closer to his chest, "I just want our child back safe. If seeking guidance from both traditional sources and the clergy can bring comfort or answers, I'm willing to try."

#

On the other side of the city, where the roads were pothole-free, and the neighbours did not know each other because the yards were so large, a couple was on the verge of fighting. They quarreled, blaming each other for their daughter's partying and subsequent kidnapping. The frustrated husband paced the room. "This wouldn't have happened if you were stricter with her! You let her attend those wild parties without setting proper boundaries!"

The wife, crossing her arms, retorted, "Oh, please! This is not solely my fault. You were never around, always immersed in your work. Maybe if you were a more present parent, she wouldn't seek attention elsewhere!"

He pointed at her with an accusing finger while scowling his face. "She learnt it from you! Your leniency, your lack of discipline. Now look where it's gotten us. Our daughter is missing, and it's because you let her run wild!"

She clenched her fists, and with tears welling up, she glared at him, "You can't pin this on me. You were never there to support me in parenting. I had to make decisions on my own. You can't just waltz in and blame me now!" Her lips trembled, and she clenched her fists tighter.

Her husband raised his voice, "Blame you? I blame both of us! We failed as parents, and now our daughter is paying the price. If only you had been stricter, if only I had been more present – maybe she wouldn't have ended up in this mess!"

Her voice was shaking with emotion, and she said, "I did my best, and you know it. You can't rewrite history now. We need to focus on finding her, not pointing fingers."

Just as the dust was settling, he brought up their family backgrounds. "Maybe if you hadn't come from such a dysfunctional family, our daughter wouldn't have turned out like this. Your lack of structure influenced her behaviour!"

The husband's remark was a personal attack, and he made her temper flare again, "Don't you dare blame my family! Maybe if your overbearing parents hadn't suffocated you with rules, our daughter wouldn't have felt the need to rebel."

"At least my family had values and discipline. Yours was a free-for-all, and now we're dealing with the consequences. Nonsense."

With angry tears streaming down her face, she stared at him, "Your so-called 'values' stifled her. She needed room to breathe, to make her own choices. But no, you couldn't see beyond your rigid upbringing!"

"I provided stability, something she clearly lacked from your side of the family," he snapped back, punching the wall.

Pointing at him, she said, "Stability is not control. She needed understanding, not your oppressive rules. You are lucky I don't cheat; no other sane woman would stand that." As the exchange delved deeper into each other's family backgrounds, the argument intensified, revealing long-standing issues that had simmered beneath the surface of their relationship.

Still angry, the husband said, "Maybe if you had a proper role model growing up, you would've known how to handle parenting!"

This incensed his wife, who yelled, "And maybe if you had a heart, you would've known how to connect with our daughter on an emotional level!" Without responding further, the husband went outside for a smoke, banging on the door.

Chapter 43

Falcon, the captor leader, spoke via encrypted communication, "Prime, any updates? We need to remain ahead in the game."

Prime replied over the radio, "Falcon, they're closing in. I'll feed you the coordinates once they breach the perimeter." The rescue team, relying on their high-profile search procedures and code names, pressed on with the mission, unaware of the imminent threat from within their own ranks. As the rescue operation reached a critical juncture, the mole maneuvered to provide the captors with real-time updates, creating a tense race against time for the rescue team to navigate the perilous situation and bring back all the girls unscathed.

The rescue team leader said, "Our country has its own complexities. The roads, the neighbourhoods – we know them intimately. Our local expertise can be the key to navigating this operation successfully."

The head of the US team answered, "Absolutely, and our resources can complement that. Our advanced technology and training bring an extra layer of capability. Together, we're stronger." Their collaboration was an opportunity to exchange skills and learn from each other. He added, "Understanding our high-tech equipment can be as crucial as knowing the Harare's back alleys, and vice versa. Your understanding of the local culture and potential hideouts is something we can't replicate. It's a two-way street, making us a more versatile team." The whole team nodded despite being spread among three cars. The messages over radio wiring were loud and clear.

A member of the team from ZRP asked, "We need real-time updates on their movements. Can we speed up the information flow?"

But the communication officer from the US wing answered, "Our protocols require verification. We can't compromise on accuracy. It's a balancing act."

"But speed is crucial here. We can't afford delays."

"We'll find a middle ground, but we need to stick to our procedures for everyone's safety." With that said, the mission went on in silence.

In a pulse-pounding sequence, the rescue team initiated a high-speed chase through the narrow roads, racing against time to reach the captors' location. However, the challenging road conditions added an extra layer of intensity to the operation. The rescue team leader announced via radio, "Hold tight, everyone. We're approaching another pothole. Keep an eye out for potential obstacles, too. Impalas are common in these parts of the country."

As the convoy of sleek vehicles tore through the uneven roads, potholes became treacherous obstacles, testing the skill and precision of the drivers. A driver in the leading car gritted his teeth, "Pothole at twelve o'clock! Hang on!" The vehicles skillfully swerved and dodged the road imperfections, but the erratic movements caused the rescue team's progress to slow, intensifying the urgency of their mission. Meanwhile, the rescue team leader via radio encouraged the team to maintain pursuit and not let the road conditions compromise the mission. The pockmarked roads posed a significant challenge to the rescue team's pursuit. The same driver gritted his teeth again, "We've got a rough terrain ahead. Hold on tight!" The potholes, camouflaged by the darkness and the urgency of the chase, lurked like hidden traps, creating an unpredictable course that tested the limits of the rescue team's cars. Nevertheless, in the midst of the high-stakes operation, a commendable display of cooperation unfolded between the local officers and their counterparts from overseas. Despite their differences, they seamlessly worked together to navigate the complex mission, showcasing resilience and dedication. Their seamless coordination reflected a shared commitment to justice and the rescue of innocent lives. Their collective spirit exemplified the power of collaboration in the pursuit of a noble cause.

As the convoy left the main highway behind and ventured onto the dust roads leading to Mukumbura, the atmosphere went through a transformative shift. The transition was marked by the crunching sound of gravel beneath the wheels and the billowing clouds of fine dust that rose and hung in the air, catching the muted glow of the moon. The dust road, narrow and winding, meandered through the untouched wilderness. The three vehicles' headlights cut through the obscurity, casting long shadows that playfully danced along the edges of the road. At certain points along the route, the reflective eyes of nocturnal creatures briefly caught the gleam of the headlights. The highway revealed glimpses of the surrounding landscape – fields stretching into the distance, the silhouette of distant hills, and the occasional outline of a solitary homestead. All this scenery sped past as the rescue team was not on a sightseeing tour nor a night trip across the savanna. They were racing against time. Their only companions were the faint glow of the vehicle's headlights and the occasional gleam of stars overhead. Harare's night skyline dotted with city lights had long disappeared beyond Harare Drive and Lomagundi Road. Also, the highway ended in Mount Darwin and the cars sped onward to Mukumbura, leaving the growth point of Dotito behind. Mukumbura was a village in Mashonaland Central province under Mount Darwin district in the northern region of the country. The journey to this sleepy village spun across the mesmerising Zambezi Escarpment's Mavhuradonha Mountain range. The journey through the Mavhuradonha Mountains was an immersive experience for the senses. The gentle hum of the engines was accompanied by the soothing sounds of nature – the rustling leaves, the babbling brooks, and the distant echoes of nocturnal wildlife. As the cars navigated the twists and turns, the Mavhuradonha Mountains became more alive in the darkness, with the moon casting its shadows. Each treacherous bend along the mountain range unveiled a new facet of this natural masterpiece. It was a passage to the untamed beauty of the African wilderness. As the cars continued along the dusty path, a silhouette emerged under the moonlight. It was the unmistakable outline of Mukumbura. The village awaited, veiled in shadows and surrounded by the natural symphony of the African night.

Mukumbura was nestled amidst the undulating hills and lush landscapes. It was tranquil village where Zimbabwe and Mozambique shared a border post. On the Zimbabwean side, it was called Mukumbura, while on the Mozambican side, it was Mecumbira. These border posts were separated by the Rio Mukumbura River. For the rest of the villagers, time seemed to move at its own unhurried pace in this remote enclave. However, for both the kidnappers and the rescue team, time was of the essence. There was no time to waste. Even the massive baobab tress seemed to watch as the drama unfolded with cars arriving at such odd hours of the night. Business had ended around 5pm, and most people were already relaxing in the comfort of their thatched huts. Yet, beneath the surface of this idyllic setting, Mukumbura harboured a sinister plot whose battleground was set and ready to be fought.

Once stationed near the growth point where GPS had led them, the rescue team leader deployed prism surveillance drones to scout the perimeter. The prisms silently hovered, relaying crucial information about the exterior layout, possible traps, and any signs of the kidnappers' presence. This technological advantage allowed the team to strategise and coordinate their approach as they closed in on the e location of the hostages. Every move was informed by the real-time data provided by the prisms. They approached a small, abandoned store. The team leader spoke via radio, "Let's proceed with caution." The team then approached the darkened store, careful not to alert the captors.

One officer relayed, "I've got movement inside. Looks like we're in the right place."

The mission leader instructed, "Prepare for entry. We don't know what we're walking into." While attempting to gain entry, they found themselves in a sudden and intense shootout.

Falcon, the captor leader, shouted, "This is our way out! Don't let them take a single step!" Gunfire erupted as both sides exchanged shots in the now dimly lit store.

The mission team leader, crouching, spoke into his radio, "We're under fire! Secure the hostages and find cover!" Bullets continued to ricochet off metal surfaces, creating a discord of echoes within the store.

The US head of mission also chimed in, "We need suppressing fire! Keep them pinned down!"

The rescue team leader agreed, "Flank them from the left! We can't let them escape."

Amidst the chaos, the rescue team maneuvered strategically, aiming to neutralise the captors while ensuring the safety of the kidnapped girls.

A sidekick from the perpetrators shouted, "This isn't over! We won't let you take them!" meanwhile, the intense shootout continued, with the rescue team exhibiting a combination of tactical expertise and determination to overcome the captors.

The rescue team leader encouraged his team, "We have to end this. Move in and secure the area!" As the gunfire intensified, the rescue team advanced, determined to bring the captors to justice and bring the kidnapped girls to safety unscathed. Amidst the chaos of the shootout, the rescue team maneuvered to minimise casualties while dealing with the panicked reaction of some of the kidnapped girls. They screamed so loud it annoyed the captors. Then, the rescue team leader shouted, "Hold your fire! We need to secure the area without harm to the hostages."

One of the ZRP officers added, "Some of the girls are panicking! We need to get them to safety." To this, the team leader gestured to the men behind to move into the girls.

The US leader then said, "Focus on de-escalation. We can't afford any more injuries. Secure the perimeter." As the rescuers worked to subdue the captors, a few of the kidnapped girls, frightened by the gunfire, still attempted to escape.

The rescue team leader shouted, "Hold your positions! We're here to help. Stay calm!" The girls seemed to listen, although most of them were still screaming and shaking. Seeing the police's apparent victory and their sophisticated weaponry, Falcon Captor Leader moved back in retreat, "We're outnumbered! Fall back!" His team, realising the situation against them, retreated as the rescue team regained control.

The team leader said, "We've got the situation under control. Attend to the injured and secure the girls. Let's get them out of here." In the aftermath of the non-fatal shootout, the rescue team tended to the wounded, ensuring the safety of the kidnapped girls and highlighting their commitment to resolving the crisis without unnecessary harm. On the other hand, the culprits were apprehended as they did not reach far. They were outnumbered in every sense of the word. They may not have anticipated that their hideout in transit to Mozambique would be discovered, especially with a police mole on their side. JBZ would be angered by such recklessness. Nevertheless, they were all under oath to protect their own, and no snitching or consequences would be dire to the third generation. They did not call him JBZ for nothing.

Chapter 44

After the rescue team successfully retrieved the kidnapped girls, they proceeded back to Harare for comprehensive medical examinations to assess their well-being. A general practitioner (GP) addressed the team, "We need to conduct thorough medical tests on each of the girls. Check for injuries, assess their mental health, and screen for any potential health issues they may have encountered during captivity." Their overall safety was still a top priority, and the rescue team vowed to ensure that they received the best care they could. The medical examinations encompassed a range of assessments, including physical injuries, psychological well-being, and any potential exposure to health risks during their time under hostage. The GP and other medical professionals examined the girls. The GP then said, "Physically, they seem to have endured stress, but no major injuries. However, we should monitor their mental health closely, considering the trauma they've experienced. Individualized plans for PTSD, depression, and eating disorders to be considered where necessary."

The rescue team leader added, "Arrangements are already in place for counselling and support services. We need to ensure they have the necessary resources for recovery without delay. They will reunite with their families once all security checks are ticked."

The girls went through more comprehensive medical evaluations to address both physical and psychological aspects of their well-being, emphasizing the importance of holistic care in the aftermath of their traumatic experiences. After the successful rescue operation, the girls were provided with nourishment and care. It was emphasized by the doctors that they needed food and sustenance after what they went through. They were given a proper meal. The rescued girls were then brought to a secure location where a dedicated team ensured they received nutritious meals.

The lead counsellor advised that it was important to consider their mental well-being as well. A comforting environment and a good meal could contribute to their timely recovery.

The girls, having endured a traumatic experience, were offered a chance to replenish their strength and begin the healing process. The rescue team leader then arranged for them to meet their parents and guardians. They were still important to the investigation as the detectives needed to know what conversations they overheard and anything that could aid the arrest of the notorious JBZ and Martinez. The provision of food, medical attention, and emotional support became a crucial aspect of post-rescue care, aiming to restore the physical and emotional well-being of the girls after their harrowing ordeal.

Following the successful rescue mission, the debriefing process revealed the conditions the kidnapped girls endured, including their access to food during captivity. The girl whose parents blamed each other's upbringing for their daughter's kidnapping spoke, "They didn't feed us well. It was sporadic. Sometimes, they gave us just enough to survive. Just morsels. Some of us are used to having English breakfast or Continental. The food was disgusting and cheap." In turn, the officials exchanged subtle puzzled looks, and the rescue leader asked if anyone else wanted to share their eating experiences. A few girls took turns to speak while others remained only sniffled while biting their lips. It was crucial to document their experiences for the investigation; hence, the rescue leader, together with the counsellors worked together to retrieve details from the girls.

The revelations about irregular and limited access to food during their captivity underscored the difficult conditions the girls faced. The GP, in conjunction with a dietician, raised the issue of malnutrition. As more information emerged, it became clear that the girls' nutrition was compromised during their time in captivity, highlighting another aspect of the challenges they endured. Other important tests revealed no evidence of sexual assault. Moreover, the GP announced weighty news, "During the medical examinations, we discovered traces of substances in the systems of some of the rescued girls. It seems they were exposed to drugs during their captivity."

The rescue team leader's eyes bulged as he said, "Drugs? This complicates things. We need to determine if it was voluntary at the party or if the captors were using substances to control them."

The GP replied, "It's challenging to ascertain the exact circumstances, but the toxicology reports suggest exposure to substances commonly associated with illicit drugs, namely cocaine MDMA (ecstasy), GHB, ketamine, and Rohypnol. Here is a detailed report on each of the girls' drug profiles. It is not severe, but it is concerning."

The US mission leader added, "If the captors were drugging them, it adds another layer to JBZ's. We need to uncover the motive behind this. Already, one cut her life short. Selling the girls is one thing, but drugging them is another. Inform the parents and provide counselling support. This revelation may be difficult for them to process." As the team grappled with this revelation, the implications of drug exposure during captivity further intensified the already complex and harrowing ordeal for the rescued girls and their families. Whether the girls consumed the drugs willingly at the party or not was a question time would tell through more counselling. Some of the girls took drugs casually at parties to fit in and boost confidence, especially when attending orgies. Most of the parents were shocked to learn about these parties their children often attended only that this party became breaking news.

#

While most people were happy with the rescue outcome, Detective Mike was overjoyed despite being absent from the operation. No doubt, Mike was a seasoned detective who had dedicated countless hours to fighting JBZ. He beamed with joy, talking to his wife, Lisa, "I can't believe it. We got them back. After all this time, they're finally safe. This may shed light on unmasking JBZ. I need to be back on that case, babe."

***

The next day, in the evening, around 4.30pm, a press conference was organized to provide updates and address the public regarding the successful rescue operation and the ongoing investigation. Smiles beamed on most of the attendees' faces, with the exception of a few melancholic individuals and those from the intelligentsia. Perhaps it was the nature of their job to mask their expression no matter the situation. They stood erect like statues.

The chief spokesperson of the rescue party straightened his moustache and began his address. "Ladies and gentlemen, thank you for joining us today. We're here to provide an update on the recent hostage crisis. The rescue team has successfully retrieved the kidnapped girls, and they are now safe."

Reporters in the room eagerly raised their hands, seeking more details. The first journalist spoke, "Can you share any information about the captors and their demands?"

"Due to the sensitive nature of the ongoing investigation, we cannot disclose specific details at this time. What's important is that the hostages are safe, and we're actively working to bring the perpetrators to justice, and we will bring them to justice."

Another journalist sought information about the condition of the rescued hostages.

The reporter cleared his throat and asked, "How are the girls doing? Have they received medical attention?"

"The rescued girls are currently undergoing comprehensive medical examinations to address any physical or psychological concerns. Their well-being is our top priority, and we're providing them with the necessary care and support." Questions continued regarding the timeline, collaboration efforts, and the overall strategy of the rescue operation.

The spokesperson dismissed the more sensitive questions and those that were meant to spite the rescue operation's response time, as some were of the view that the operation should have taken a maximum of 24 hours. The spokesperson was an astute man with an overbearing presence. He managed the presser well without any commotion. He continued, "We appreciate your questions, but we ask for your understanding as we cannot compromise the ongoing investigation. Rest assured, we are committed to transparency and will share information as soon as it is reasonably possible." He continued, "Before we conclude, I'd like to express our deepest gratitude to the dedicated members of the rescue team, law enforcement, and all those involved in this complex operation. Their tireless efforts and unwavering commitment made this successful outcome possible."

A reporter raised a question about the diplomatic implications between USA and Zimbabwe. "Can you elaborate on the diplomatic collaboration between the two countries during this crisis?"

"Certainly. The cooperation between our two nations has been crucial in navigating this challenging situation. Diplomatic channels have remained open, and both presidents have expressed a shared commitment to resolving this crisis while upholding the principles of justice and international collaboration."

As the press conference continued, another reporter inquired about the captors' demand for immunity. "The captors demanded immunity for their release. What is the government's stance on negotiating with criminals?"

"Our position is clear – we cannot and will not negotiate with criminals. Granting immunity sets a dangerous precedent. Our priority is to ensure the safety of our citizens and bring those responsible for this heinous act to justice through legal means."

More questions came. "Can you share any updates on the progress of the investigation and when we can expect more information?"

"The investigation is ongoing, and we appreciate the public's patience. As soon as we can responsibly disclose further details without jeopardising the case, we will do so. Transparency remains a key principle in our approach."

As the press conference unfolded, the spokesperson took a moment to acknowledge the emotional toll the prevailing crisis had taken on the community and nation at large. "We understand that this incident has deeply affected our communities. Our hearts go out to the families involved, and we assure you that support services will be available to help them cope with the aftermath. We are stronger together, and we will overcome this challenge as united people." In his concluding remarks, the spokesperson emphasized the resilience of the community members and the importance of standing together during difficult times. "In closing, let us remember that even in the face of adversity, our nation has demonstrated remarkable strength and unity. We remain steadfast in our pursuit of justice, and we thank you all for your continued support and understanding. Updates will be provided as the investigation progresses. Thank you."

The press conference concluded with a sense of cautious optimism, leaving the public informed about the ongoing efforts and reassuring them of the government's commitment to a just resolution. One gentleman in a cap and tinted glasses immediately reached for his phone. One of his questions had been rejected, while another on the well-being of the girls was answered. Little did he know that the eyes of the security team were on everyone like hawks. A signal was sent to seize him and inspect his phone on his way out. Like the rest of the journalists present, he had a lanyard with his accreditation details.

Chapter 45

The Big Cat had spent the night at the US Embassy using their facilities; he had gone there to look for information, hints, records or anything that could lead them in the Right direction. He interviewed everyone at the embassy and asked them to take a polygraph; one of the Marine Corps failed, and his name had been noted, but after it was realized that even three more staff members, including the defense attaché had failed the test, it was decided that perhaps everyone was not in the best state of mind to take the test as they were still in shock after the kidnapping of the Ambassador.

Big Cat ordered all the files of all staff members and their activities. While that information was being gathered, he accessed the system for the same information; he was aware that, in some cases, there were information gaps between the system and the physical files. Though the nature of information that is usually omitted in files is not considered critical, it sometimes gives hints to some events and activities when analyzed in aggregate.

The Idea was to send information to the US for further analysis. He called Innocent and requested access to the database for the Cargo Manifest, a record for all flights detailing the number and dealt as well as seat numbers and who they sat next to and their destinations and any other movements that may need analysis. The Big Cat requested for the Zimbabwe Republic Police and SWAT teams under his team to request all VISA applications that were ever made from any non-African Country and pay particular attention regarding VISAS that were applied for at the port of entry, including those that were applied for at the physical border post. They were to concentrate on any visitors who dropped off in the neighboring countries and crossed into Zimbabwe by Road. The Big Cat had sent the files for all Embassy staff to the FBI for further analysis. Earlier on, The Big Cat asked for information to be sent to all SADC and COMMESA member countries, requesting landing and takeoff information for visitors who flew private jets and helicopters.

The Big Cat requested an annual events Calendar for the Ambassador for all the events scheduled; he requested information on the security teams on each team that was responsible for his protection, including the advance team members. Details of all Minutes of meetings that were held, as well as the Radios, sent daily, was requested for analysis. The Big Cat requested for all events registers and images captured at each event, and these were sent for further assessment in the USA.

Locally, the Big Cat requested the details and movements of all prominent businesspeople and their known associates. There was a sharp disagreement between Samuel Luckson, a Marine Corp, who escaped from the scene of the kidnapping of the Ambassador's wife and son. Samuel did not take it lightly that Big Cat was slinging accusations to the staff in the middle of a crisis.

Samuel believed that the Embassy worked as a closely knit family and that the kidnapping of the Ambassador's wife, son, and the Ambassador himself was devastating enough.

Big Cat demanded, "We need information for all staff members to be taken for further analysis."

Samuel Luckson snapped at him, "We are in the middle of a crisis, and all you want to do is bayonet the wounded? We are the victims here; we are the ones who are in trouble here."

Rubbing his moustache, the Big Cat continued, "It's a routine procedure to ensure that we get rid of any mall that may be among us or anyone who may be blackmailed by some terrorist organisations out there."

Samuel Luckson sulked and added, "That's bull ship, man why the hell do you think that we are working in cooperation with some terrorist organisations here."

Big Cat remained calm and bellowed, "Protocol requires that we eliminate all possibilities starting from inside."

Samuel Luckson raised his voice and lifted his head up, glaring at Big Cat, "Protocol, my ass, I ain't giving you shit; go fuck yourself."

Big Cat still calm said, "Look man I really understand that this is the most frustrating process after what happened to you, but I urge you to cooperate with the investigation process or else I will designate you as a suspect in the case."

Samuel Luckson went berserk, "What if I refuse? What are you going to do? You think you are in America? Babe, you are a *loooooooong* way from home, and your arresting powers do not apply here. Welcome to Africa, where human and investigator's rights are cut to shit size."

Big Cat sneered, shaking his head, pitying the ill-informed challenger, "I will have you transported to the USA, where you will be court Marshalled; meanwhile, the joint operation here has jurisdiction, and you will be arrested under Zimbabwean Law for obstructing justice."

Samuel Luckson guffawed like one at a beer hall, "You are one ignorant goat; we are not subjected to local laws here bitch."

Big Cat stood up, charging towards Samuel. At that point, the Defense attaché rushed to stop the imminent fight. Samuel walked away, and the Big Cat instructed him that he should be arrested as a suspect in the ongoing investigations. The Defense attaché quickly asked, "What was that about man?"

Big Cat tuned his back from him as if hiding something and spoke over his shoulder, "What are you talking about?"

Defense attaché seemed to emphasise, "The man has been very short tempered since the kidnapping; he needs help, not harassment."

Big Cat ignored the feigned empathy and spoke without remorse, "He is a key suspect. He was part of the security team that failed to protect the ambassador's family, but now you think he is a hero? If he talks now, we can even have a deal for him, but if not, he will face the chair."

Defense Attaché lifted his chin and put a straight face. "If you're going to start slinging accusations about failure to protect the Ambassador and his family, then I suggest you bring those accusations to me, and I'll deal directly with them."

Big Cat retorted, "Is that a threat?"

"I don't make idle threats," he chortled.

"Then I shall report that you and your team are obstructing justice, and have you secured here as key suspects in the case; my name is Big Cat, remember that."

"Maybe you've dealt with enough drug cases to be high for the rest of your life."

"Watch me!"

"Listen here, busy bee, Big Cat. It's easy to come here in fancy pants, speaking civilian English. I've lost men in this incident, and I do not appreciate you coming here with the head office mood and a holier-than-thou attitude, pissing on my team. Get that? You have your warning."

Chapter 46

BigCat sat at his desk at the US Embassy, staring at the wall covered with photos and notes related to the kidnapping case. He rubbed his tired eyes and let out a frustrated sigh. "There's something off about this whole situation," he muttered to himself. Just then, his phone buzzed. It was a message from his informant, warning him about a possible leak within the police force. BigCat's heart sank. Could it be true? Were his suspicions true that someone on the inside was working with the drug lords?

Big Cat stared at the message that had just popped up on his phone, his brow furrowing. Without a word, he pushed away his untouched cup of coffee and hastily gathered his belongings, stashing his laptop in its bag while he rushed out. His colleagues glanced up, surprised by his sudden departure. "Hey, Big Cat, everything okay?" some called after him. He was already halfway out and slammed the door. He left his coffee untouched, and that was so unlike him. The beefy man loved his coffee so much that he had about five cuppas a day. BigCat's love affair with coffee was legendary among his colleagues. He was rarely seen without a steaming mug in hand, his robust brew fueling his relentless pursuit of justice. Some joked that he had a direct line to the coffee machine, while others marveled at his ability to down cup after cup without batting an eye.

But Big Cat knew the truth – his addiction to caffeine was both a blessing and a curse. It kept him sharp and focused during long hours on the job, but it also left him jittery and irritable if he went too long without his fix. With the electricity shortages calling for frequent load shedding, he was struggling in Harare to maintain his habit or, rather, addiction. He almost bought a flask, but then again, the fear of being poisoned made him ditch the idea. Maybe the assignment to Zimbabwe also meant some life-changing positives. Perhaps he could live without that much caffeine dependence after all. In the same way, he convinced himself that he had had enough of women, well not all, just brunettes and blondes. Big Cat often joked with his fellow agents that if anyone ever wanted to take him down, they'd have to infiltrate his coffee supply first. It was a light-hearted quip, but deep down, Big Cat knew that his dependence on caffeine was no laughing matter.

As he stepped out onto the car park, Big Cat scanned around with stealth. It was common to be watched, spied upon, and every instinct required one to be extra cautious. As he glanced around, scanning any sign of tempering or danger, he thought the universe offered no answers, only a sense of foreboding that hung heavy in the air. He drove off fully aware that whatever awaited him on the other end of that message could change everything. With a steely resolve, he squared his shoulders and drove off.

A few minutes after reaching the residence where the embassy housed him, he left in haste, driving back to the embassy. He went into his designated private office, and soon enough, there was a knock on his office door. He looked up to see a striking woman standing there, her confidence evident in every movement. How may I help you?" he asked, trying to hide his surprise at her sudden appearance. It was his first time seeing her.

The woman sauntered in, a seductive smile playing on her lips. "The iconic, legendary, husky Big Cat, I've heard so much about you," she purred, her voice dripping with honeyed charm.

Big Cat arched an eyebrow, his instincts on high alert. "And who might you be?" he asked cautiously.

She leaned in closer, her perfume filling the room with its intoxicating floral scent. "Call me Nana," she whispered, her eyes sparkling with mischief. "I'm here to offer you a deal you can't refuse."

BigCat's grip tightened on his pen as he studied her carefully. "Reaching this far implies you have security clearance at reception, fine. And what kind of deal would that be? I don't have all day, missy."

Nana leaned back, crossing her legs provocatively. "I have information that could help you crack this case wide open," she said, her voice low and enticing. The mole, the hole, the ball, but it'll cost you."

BigCat's heart skipped a bit at her confidence and apparent resolve. Could Nana be the spy he had been warned about? Or was she just a pawn in a much larger game? Either way, he knew he had to tread carefully.

"Alright, Nana," he said, masking his suspicions with a smile. "You've got my attention. Let's talk. Ten minutes is all you have; otherwise, don't waste my time."

As Big Cat listened to Nana's tantalizing offer, his recorder was on. He stole a quick glance at his phone as if the SMS with the warning was flashing in his face. Additionally, Nana's sudden appearance only fuelled his suspicions further. But he needed to gather more information before jumping to conclusions.

"Tell me what you know," Big Cat said, his tone firm but measured. "And remember, I'm not one to be trifled with. Right here in this room, you may never set foot on earth if you play with me."

Nana chuckled softly, her eyes glinting with amusement. "Oh, I know exactly who I'm dealing with, Big Cat," she said, her voice dripping with confidence. "That's why I came to you. I don't deal with babies."

As they continued to talk, Big Cat searched for signs that Nana could be playing him. But try as he might, he couldn't ignore the tantalizing breadcrumbs she dangled in front of him – clues that could potentially break the case wide open.

Minutes passed as they delved deeper into the intricacies of the syndicate's operations. As Big Cat became more relaxed around Nana, there was a loud knock on the door. Startled, Big Cat glanced at Nana, who merely shrugged in response. Before he could react, the door swung open, and the CIO boss, together with the defense attaché strode into the room, the boss's expression stern. "Big Cat, we need to talk," he said, his voice devoid of its usual warmth.

Big Cat sighed and muttered, "Shit, you slut," as he realized what was about to happen. He had been so consumed with the case that he had forgotten about the delicate balance within the force. "Wait, I can explain," he began, but the boss held up a hand to silence him. The defense attaché made a sly smile.

"I'm sorry, Big Cat, but I've received some troubling information," the boss said, his tone heavy with regret. "You're being suspended from the case with immediate effect pending an internal investigation." BigCat's jaw clenched as he struggled to maintain his composure. This was exactly what the syndicate wanted – to remove him from the equation. As he gathered his things, Big Cat shot a meaningful look at Nana, who watched the scene unfold with a satisfied smirk. It was clear now – she had been sent to seduce him, to distract him from the truth.

But Big Cat wasn't about to let them win. As he left the room, he stared at the defense attaché and turned to Nana saying, Remember, I said right here in this room, so it ends where it starts."

Special Agent Carter: A mysterious figure from the FBI, Special Agent Carter had been quietly observing the syndicate's activities for months. With his sharp wit and keen instincts, Carter quickly became an invaluable ally to Big Cat in his quest for the truth. But as the investigation took a dangerous turn, Carter's true loyalties remained shrouded in mystery. As Big Cat navigated the treacherous maze of lies, deceit, and betrayal, he realized that he couldn't trust anyone but himself. With the clock ticking and the stakes higher than ever, he would need all the allies he could get to uncover the truth and bring the perpetrators to justice. In Harare, he had made a few allies.

BigCat's reputation preceded him wherever he went – a formidable investigator with a razor-sharp mind and a confidence that bordered on arrogance. His ego was as expansive as his track record of solving cases, and he made no effort to hide it. When it came to his history with the ladies, Big Cat was known for his charm and his penchant for keeping things casual. He had a long list of ex-girlfriends who could attest to his magnetic personality and his reluctance to commit to anything beyond the thrill of the chase. Despite his reputation as a ladies' man, BigCat's relationships were often fleeting, and his focus was always on the next big case. He was a lone wolf by nature, more comfortable prowling the mean streets of the city than navigating the complexities of romance. But deep down, Big Cat longed for someone who could see past his tough exterior and understand the man beneath the badge. He just wasn't sure if he was ready to let his guard down long enough to let them in. Perhaps that's why he let coffee be his companion. With his suspension in place, he set to exonerate himself by hook or crook with urgency. He was Big Cat, after all.

hapter 47

ilver was leading the team responsible for drugs; he had earned his name from an incident in which he intercepted a consignment of drugs in a joint operation between the Military and the Zimbabwe Republic Police. By mid-morning, after the briefing by the CIO boss, Silver had called on his team members, and they went to work. Chiminsky, a US SWAT member, was placed in charge of Radio communication. His duty was to manage all Radion-related communications and advise on strategies related to radio communication. He was a short man with a face that looked tired, I suppose from listening to a lot of crap over the radio in his 20-year career.

At 11 am, after the briefing, Silver assigned the ZRP plain cloths team to deploy teams in all places like Bars, street corners, hooking paces, lodges, and trucking stop overs in all towns. Phase two was to arrest street corner drug sellers; this was a more complex operation given that word was in the street that drug Lords were being hunted down like dogs.   The goal was to bring rain, not the usual rain but shit rain.

Silver himself visited Chikurubi Maximum Prison, where he had interviews with hardcore criminals serving various sentences for drug trafficking, among other crimes. These fellas would demand between USD2000 to USD5000 just to point the police to the right place. Silver knew who to go to and talk to. He had three interviews, all of which yielded nothing.

As Silver was leaving the Prison, he was almost at the gate when he heard a voice calling him; it was a junior prison warden. He stopped the car and lowered the window; the warden politely asked, "Are you getting into town? I need a lift". Silver was annoyed and closed the window, but as he started moving the car, Wesley, the FBI team member, shouted, "I like this girl," Upon hearing that, Silver was elated and stopped the car and picked up the warden.

They drove in silence for 100 metres before Silver greeted the lady and introduced herself. The Lady Introduced herself as Precious Mudiwa Makoni.

Precious said, "So, you're the one leading the investigation regarding drugs, right? Specifically, you're the one looking for JBZ?"

"Who told you that? Where did you hear that from?" Silver asked.

"Answer the question, boss," Precious insisted.

"I don't know what you're talking about," Silver replied.

"Then please, drop me off here," Precious requested.

"What does that have to do with your trip to town?" Silver inquired.

"I'm disappointed in you. How were you selected to lead this operation? We're aware of all your moves, including the hit on the hawkers you ordered. You won't see any for the rest of the week. Anyway, they don't have to stop their trade," Precious retorted.

Silver was stunned as Precious revealed what was happening, realizing that all his actions and instructions were now public knowledge.

"Who told you about that?" Silver demanded.

"The inmates told me," Precious replied.

Silver asked, "What time did they tell you?"

"I would say real-time, maybe not exactly real-time, but say 5 minutes after the meeting," Precious replied.

Silver questioned, "How come?"

Precious explained, "All street operations are coordinated. You don't just send people into the streets. The operation needed to be aligned with Harare Operations, Bulawayo Operations, and so on. If you issue such information in the morning, that's what you get."

"I am aware of that," Silver acknowledged.

"The following conversation never happened; do you understand?" Precious stated.

"You could say," Silver responded.

"I need a yes or no from you, Sir," Precious pressed.

"Who the hell are you asking me to answer yes or no to?" Silver demanded.

"I have already told you my name, but if you insist, I am a woman who is about to save your ass; that's my other name. Satisfied?" Precious retorted.

"How so?" Silver questioned.

"Answer yes or no first," Precious insisted.

"What's this game all about? I can report you to the police for being a nuisance and for obstructing justice," Silver threatened.

"Silver, Silver, Silver, where the hell is the silver lining here? Clearly, there is nothing Silver about you, Silver Sir," Precious mocked. The FBI agent who was in the car could not help but laugh aloud.

"What's your point?" Silver asked.

Precious said, "The police is not particularly happy with the way they've been put on the backbench. This will be a war of territory, and you have to talk to your bosses to fix that. They are threatening to initiate their own investigations. In fact, they may have started the process already."

"And you know this because?" Silver questioned.

"I am far ahead of you in everything that matters," Precious asserted.

"For example?" Silver pressed.

"Like the mix-up of colors. That short court will go well with a black, not a grey jacket. Satisfied?" Precious countered.

"We do not have time for this. We are dropping you off here; we have important business to take care of," Silver declared.

"Dropping people is what you're known best for," Precious retorted.

"Young Lady, you don't know me at all. I will call your superiors and…" She handed him the phone with a curse, pointing at the Commissioner of Prisons.

"Call him now and get me arrested if you wish to do so," Precious challenged.

"Here is your phone, and please get out of the car," Silver instructed.

"No, Dad, this time I will not let you go," Precious insisted.

"Dad? I am not your dad," Silver corrected.

"Remember, Precious, you dated 18 years ago when you were posted in Nyamapanda. You stayed at her house, and when your mission ended, you left her and promised to come back for her, but you never did. She died when I was 10 years old, and I did menial jobs to send myself to school from a young age. I have been looking for you. I have your photo," Precious revealed.

"Nice try," Silver dismissed.

"Is it true that you have a bullet wound on your right thigh which could not heal for years and that my mother healed it?" Precious inquired.

"It was not your mother," Silver affirmed.

Precious stood there, clenched her fists, and said, "Yes, it wasn't her, but she took you to the house of an old granny who healed the wound over a week. You were almost dismissed from work for AWL, but after you revealed the healed wound, you were pardoned.

"Enough," Silver interjected.

Precious asked Silver to open the door. Stepping out of the car, she circled around to the driver's side and handed him a paper. There, in bold letters, was a name: "The Big Dhara" – a notorious criminal Silver had put in prison years back. He was now a free man somewhere in the country, but nobody knew where. Rumor had it that he was now a businessman keeping a very low profile.

With a solemn expression, Precious continued, "Good luck, Daddy. Mom would have been proud to see us meeting. She loved you so dearly, and you abandoned her. She never gave up hope of meeting you again. She called your name for a week before she died, and she had hoped that you were somehow going to come before she died."

"Life is more complicated, Precious," Silver began, "I fell in love with your mom upon arrival at my workstation, but she turned out to be..."

"...the daughter of a criminal you were hunting?" Precious finished his sentence, her tone heavy with accusation. "There was love between the two of you, and you had no right to abandon us."

"You are right," Silver admitted with a heavy sigh. "I had no right to do that."

Exiting the car, Silver closed the door. As he approached Precious, she instinctively moved away, her body language guarded.

"If you think we can make up for the lost time here, you are mistaken," Precious asserted firmly. "You are going to start by throwing me into the air, holding my hand, pretending to teach me how to walk, carrying me on your back, on your shoulders, teaching me to eat. Then, we can talk."

Chapter 48

It was 6 pm, and Silver decided to go to the streets himself to observe if what Precious was saying had any substance; the streets were empty, and the hawkers were not in the streets that particular day. There were none in pubs either. At that point, he reported to Innocent, and the Chief of Police was called for a meeting where the Chief of Police denied the allegations that the Police was sabotaging the operations on the streets because they felt undermined. The CIO boss then gave an order that any communication and Interactions between the civilians and the investigation team was to be specifically handled by the Police. The Police were given the go-ahead to round up prostitutes, and that night, about 322 Hawkers were rounded up. It turned out that the Police were even aware of where to get them from. They were both men and female prostitutes; some protested that they had licenses to operate as commercial sex workers, but no one was willing to listen to them that night.

All unlicensed prostitutes were threatened with arrest and were detained in police custody unless they cooperated with the police. Approximately all street drug retailers were netted, but all of them were selling sexual stimulation drugs. They were to be released, but on second thought, they decided to press charges unless they lead the police to some credible information where they would find drugs in the class of cocaine and drugs in that category.

Chapter 49

I t was 9pm, and the teams were gathered at the KG6 for an update meeting. The CIO boss wasted no time and went straight to the point. I have received your reports, and I applaud the groundwork we have covered so far. I wish we could celebrate that, but the pressure we have faced is unprecedented. We have made great progress, but we are not able to share all the information we have at the present moment, as doing so could jeopardize the operation and put a number of people at risk. We are urged to press hard. I want results by tomorrow morning.

That night, a special Unit of the FBI started monitoring multiple places for unusual movements. At first, they were frustrated by the many activities in multiple cities, but as time went on, only a few cities were observed as having activities, and the police were sent to check out these places, but most of them were either holiday resorts or fishing. The surveillance went on, and this time, Radio experts were sent to sights flagged as having unusual human activity.

The FBI Cyber security team was deployed to areas with unusual activity and cracked the nearest systems to view all email and related transactions; there were coal mines and gold mines that had some activity. The team used AI to get into the system, search through it, and report areas where there was constant communication. These reports were sent to the US for further analysis, with results to be released in the following 30 minutes or an hour.

Chapter 50

At midnight, the CIO boss called for a meeting at the KG6, and the FBI and ZRP, working together with the Civil Aviation Authorities, acted swiftly on information on a plane that requested an emergency landing for fuelling in Kariba; the Plane was spotted by Radar flying at very low altitude in the Kariba dam, It the requested emergency landing, this prompted jets to be sent there to assist the ground staff to intercept the plane; however special Agent Montgomery of the FBI insisted that it was a diversion and that the real criminal activities were likely to attempt a landing at places far away from Kariba. At exactly the same time that the plane was landing at the Kariba to fuel a plane, it was said to have landed at the Gonarezhou Trans frontier Park Zimbabwean side in Malilangwe. This prompted a swift reaction, activating the Military, Police Support Unit and the Rangers operating in the Park to react to the emergency. Some troops crossed through the now defunct bridge that was destroyed during the liberation struggle.

When the reaction team arrived, the Plane had just landed, and the passengers were loading some bags, which were later found to be bags of gold weighing 50kgs and USD 120 Million Cash. The crew did not resist arrest; they complied with all the orders that were given. The cash and gold were transported to Harare by air, and the criminals were transported to the nearest Police post for processing before they could transported to Harare.

The fourteen-member team was handcuffed and transported to Chiredzi Central Police station. As the convoy was about to approach the main road coming from the National Park, there were grenades thrown at the car in front, and the one at the back was also attacked through heavy fire. Machine guns could be heard churning out bullets nonstop, and the support Unit and the Military demonstrated their skill and managed to return fire for fire; some of the fighters fled, but four surrendered; three were taken alive but injured, but there were six fatalities. Three men were down, one from the support Unit, One from the Military and one Ranger who had accompanied the convoy as part of the witness. The remaining three suspects managed to flee into the bush, and an armed search party was called. Both

Mozambique and South Africa were alerted of the armed assailants who had run away from the country. Trans frontier is a park between three countries Zimbabwe, Mozambique and South Africa. The Concept is that wild animals can be allowed to move freely in the part of the park where the countries intersect.

Like they say, get the drugs and see the runner, but get the cash and see the boss himself. Soon after the cash incident, the CIO received a call.

Innocent greeted, his voice steady despite the tension in the air. "Hello."

JBZ chuckled a hint of surprise in his tone. "Innocent, I am told you are leading the operations. I must say I had underestimated you."

As the FBI team worked fervently to trace the call, the CIO Boss urged, "Keep him talking. We need to pinpoint his location." Mobile phone operators stood poised, ready to provide crucial information as required, backed by an advance court order.

"You must really think that I am daft to call you while I am in Zimbabwe," JBZ remarked, a sardonic edge to his words. "Anyway, your FBI guys can trace all they want."

Innocent inquired, his voice calm but firm, "What do you want, JBZ?"

A knowing undertone coloured JBZ's response. "You know the answer to that, don't you?"

"Why don't we do it nice and easy?" Innocent suggested, his tone diplomatic yet resolute. "Nobody gets hurt in the process. I give you back your money and gold, and you give me the girls, the Ambassador, and hand yourself over to the police. Then, we all go home."

JBZ leaned back, his voice smooth with a hint of amusement. "I am happy to be talking to you. I have been told that you are an intelligent man, and had my doubts, but I am liking it already."

Innocent reciprocated with a nod of appreciation. "Thanks for the compliment. I am told you are a master planner, a tactician."

"Master Plan, my ass," JBZ retorted with a scoff, his tone laced with disdain.

Innocent raised a hand in a placating gesture. "No profanities, please. The kids are still awake. Let's stick to family language."

"Hang on a moment," JBZ interrupted abruptly, his demeanor shifting. "I need to show you something."

With a swift motion, JBZ dialed a number and engaged in a conversation for three minutes, speaking in what sounded like Arabic or a similar accent. He returned to the call, his voice composed. "I am back, Sir. Please check your phone."

Innocent glanced down at his phone and watched a video unfold—a bus engulfed in flames, passengers scrambling to escape through the windows. It was a chilling warning of the potential consequences.

"I figured that you are all about evidence," JBZ remarked casually. "This can happen to anyone here. By the way, my condolences to the three men who died in the line of duty. It was very brave of your military to take on such a group. Ex-Marine rebels are not easy to fight with."

Innocent's expression tightened with concern. "What's the plan then? Where do we exchange?"

"Why do you want to rush to the conclusion?" JBZ countered, his tone smooth yet loaded with implications. "We have not even buried the dead, and you are already talking about an exchange."

Innocent spoke between gritted teeth, "Don't speak like you fucken care."

JBZ smiled, clapping his hands, "Wow, temper, temper, let's stick to family language and family like tempo; the kids are still awake like you said."

Later on, the captured suspects were taken for questioning; due to their condition, they had to be transported in an ambulance to Harare into a Military Clinic. Three ambulances were transporting the suspects, and they were spaced for two hours each. About six hours into the journey, the first car was near Beatrice, and the other two were following. A car emerged from the woods, hitting the first ambulance by the side and sending the ambulance rolling like a salt sea crocodile drowning prey, displaying its signature drowning style.

The escort team responded by opening fire on the car, yet no one emerged from the car. The driverless car was being remotely controlled; it took pictures of the scene and was asked to look for one of the suspects and drop a target-specific micro Bomb. The car released a small drone with a (TSMB) hanging at the bottom, and after scanning, it matched one of the people thrown into the grass and immediately threw the TSMB, reaping the suspect's head with only the shoulders visible.

The escort team made attempts to seize the car, but it was all in vain. They attempted to call for support, but all the communication channels, including cell phones and Satellite communications, were down. The attack vehicle had a communication system that jammed communication within 1 1-kilometre radius. The attacks were carried out at the same time, and all of them could not comprehend what had just happened. Nobody had seen such firepower, and the level of organisations, and execution was on point with no loose ends left, no DNA to extract. It was a perfect plan, the best lain plans on motion. Innocent had to admit that whoever attacked was loaded for War. Innocent received a call from JBA soon after the attack.

"I gave you three witnesses, and you lost all of them?"

Innocent yelled, "Your world is becoming smaller boy; this was your last dance on the stage. Soon, you will be narrating these stories in hell; I am going to hand you, in fact, I want to strangle you myself."

"How about we meet face to face, you and me and talk it through," JBZ's voice was a little shaken.

"I do not talk to terrorists; now that your world is shrinking, you want to talk? I would rather hunt you down like a dog and kill you myself."

The FBI managed to crack into the complicated communication systems that "JBZ was using" he was in a boat floating around the new Bridge connecting Botswana and Zambia near the Quad Point, the location of JBZ or whoever he was caused many challenges as the Quad Point is where Botswana, Namibia, Zambia, and Zimbabwe meets. Any attempt to carry out operations without express authorization and cooperation of the member states involved was likely to spark diplomatic outrage and tension.

An emergency Team meeting with INTERPOL was followed by AFRIPOL and subsequently by commanders of the military and chiefs of Police in the QUAD point nations, where a cooperation agreement was reached, and the Zimbabwean team was to lead the mission. The US was requested to assist with the release of their Marine Corps operating in the Quad Point nations as well as advanced air to air combat. After waiting for four hours, two F-22 Raptors and one Apache Helicopter were cleared for the mission. The US also requested an Hourly update on the matter, which the Zimbabwean counter parts could not confirm, deciding to sound like Nigerian Movie stars with the signature saying of "We shall See".

The following morning, three Boards with fisher men entered the Quad Point waters and started their fishing routine; these were ordinary boats which, and the crew members were from the Quad Point nation supported by the FBI and the US Marine Corps. Once everyone was in position, Innocent was asked to call "JBZ," and he answered after three rings, preferring to go on top of the yacht where a helicopter landed on the other end. He spoke with ease and never interjected each time Innocent was talking.

The coordinates were confirmed, and the teams moved; JBZ went into the Helicopter, and the Hitscop was immediately started; just after taking off it was two F22 Raptors emerged, performing the signature spin and showing off their weapons; they escorted the Helicopter to a secure Military Airbase, the People's Liberation Air Base (PLAB).

JBZ was arrested together with the two pilots.

Innocent: I told you that I was going to hunt you down like a Dog.

JBZ's eyes flashed with a mix of defiance, "You have nothing."

Innocent was quick to reply, "I thought you were far ahead of me for centuries."

JBZ's voice, cutting through the tension like a whip, said, "Look around you, Innocent. The storm is coming, and it's coming fast; look around you. You are in valley, and it's failing apart; rocks will be tumbling, snakes rattling, trees breaking debris splashed everywhere; survive that you will be worse in the battle."

He continued, "You seem to be in denial that you are under arrest; give it a minute or two, and it will sink in."

Calm, JBZ spoke, "You have never been able to see the bigger picture."

Innocent's eyes narrowed with impatience. "Where are the girls and the Ambassador's Family?"

JBZ leaned forward, a faint smirk playing on his lips. "Did you not forget to ask about the JBZ, who is supposed to lead you to Martinez? Isn't that the third objective?"

Innocent's frustration boiled over. "Answer the damn question, will you?"

JBZ's gaze remained steady, his voice calm amidst the rising tension. "Temper, temper," he taunted, a glint of amusement in his eyes. "Why don't we stick to family-like language and family-like tempo?"

Innocent's jaw clenched, his hands balling into fists. "I am a very kind man, but the team that's coming is not," he warned, a dangerous edge to his tone. "So, we can either do it here, no one gets hurt, or we wait for the teams coming through."

JBZ's expression hardened, a defiant glint in his eyes. "You think I am scared?" he challenged, his voice cutting through the air like a knife. "I have endured pain of the highest degree, and I do not fear anything at all."

As JBZ was talking, a team of three detectives arrived at the scene lead by Detective Mike. They had gone through vetting and security checking, as no one was taking any chance. Innocent walked out of the interrogation room; he had a small chat with the team of detectives, who brought them up to speed with the progress and the confessions they were seeking to extract from him. The Detective went into the interrogation room, where they introduced themselves and asked for the information. Detective Mike introduced himself, accompanied by Detectives Lesly and Bob, and then turned to JBZ, asking for his identity. JBZ confidently replied that he was Detective JBZ. Detective Mike's eyebrows arched in mild surprise at the response. "Detective JBZ," he echoed, "That's a new one," he remarked, a faint hint of skepticism in his tone.

JBZ's lips twitched into a half-smirk, his eyes glinting with a hint of amusement. "That's right," he replied, his voice carrying a subtle air of confidence. Detective Lesly exchanged a quick glance with Detective Bob, a silent acknowledgment passing between them. This was shaping up to be an interesting encounter.

Detective Mike's expression remained unreadable as he continued, his voice taking on a more serious tone. "Where is the Ambassador and his family? And the girls?"

JBZ's lips curled into a smirk, a flicker of amusement dancing in his eyes, his jaw tensing as he considered his response. "I ain't telling you shit," he shot back.

Detective Mike's gaze hardened, his patience wearing thin. "I was hoping you would say that," he retorted, a steely edge creeping into his voice. "Looks like we have a man who likes it rough here. So rough it shall be." Detective Mike leaned over and whispered into JBZ's ears saying, "It is going to hurt, but you will be fine."

Detective Mike and his team swiftly restrained JBZ, securing his hands over his legs with handcuffs and leaving minimal room for movement. They then hoisted an iron bar to a height of 1.5 metres, clipping it securely at both ends before exiting the room. JBZ's cries rang out, echoing like the urgent warnings of monkeys sensing the presence of a cheetah prowling in the neighbourhood. The pain radiating through his body was excruciating, each moment stretching into unbearable agony. Despite the torment, after just two minutes, JBZ found himself craving a cigarette, but the detectives remained resolute, ignoring his pleas.

Detective Mike moved closely and asked JBZ one more time for the information, but JBZ decided to keep quiet. Detective Mike took a set of pliers and started plucking off JBZ's nails, starting with the right foot and then moving to the left foot. This process produced a piercing pain that saw JBZ screaming, much to the attention of Innocent and the rest of the Investigation Team on site. JBZ was in pain but did not budge. The Detective was not going to yield either; he proceeded to the fingernails, starting with the left and then to the right. Still, JBZ was not talking but asking for a lawyer.

Detective Mike called in a nurse and a reinforcement team; they held him to the ground and circumcised him with a blunt knife. He was now sweating and asking for water, but nobody responded to him. Detective Mike looked at him and asked him to talk. When JBZ remained silent Detective Mike took a pair of pliers are clipped JBZ's mouth, and when he opened it, Detective Mike uprooted JBZ's tooth. He spat blood into Detective Mike's face. Detective Mike was not bothered by the spit.

JBZ eyed Detective Mike warily. "What do you want?"

Detective Mike's gaze remained firm. "Answers to the questions I asked."

"My name is Hassin Ibrahim Fayez Sheriff," JBZ declared.

Detective Mike leaned forward, pressing for information. "Where is the Ambassador?"

Hassin hesitated briefly before responding. "They are with JBZ."

Detective Mike's brow furrowed. "Why did you identify yourself as JBZ if you are not? Maybe Hassin is not your name as well?"

Hassin's voice held a hint of urgency. "We responded to black market information that a US ambassador and his family were at an auction, so we brought the required amount of money."

Detective Mike's gaze hardened as he pressed for answers. "And where did you get the money, and where do you come from?"

Hassin's reply was delivered with a chilling calmness. "From Yemen, the money—we got it from Zambia and South Africa through our contacts and operations there."

Detective Mike's jaw clenched, his next question hanging in the air like a heavy cloud. "What did you want to do with the Ambassador?"

"The wife, I wanted to take her as my sex slave; the boy would work in my fields, and the Ambassador would be killed in retaliation in a televised interview."

Detective Mike's brow furrowed with concern. "Where is JBZ right now?"

Hassin's response was unsettling. "You can't find him; he is everywhere."

"How?" Detective Mike pressed; his tone edged with frustration. "What about the one who was feeding his local community and ex-husband to that Nobesuthu and sleeping with his aide Roselyn?" The two women had been granted safe passage to Zambia as immunity for their significant cooperation in the matter, yet they were, in fact, in the dark about JBZ's true identity. They had both loved the way he lied without realising they were actually living a lie.

Hassin's lips twisted into a sinister grin. "That's just another version. Are those two ladies still alive? They have thick skin. Anyway, it is through a system called Eagle. It sees the entire world, and it sees everything that you are doing. He listens to all your conversations. That's where everyone who buys drugs and human slaves will log in; payments are done through Bitcoins."

Detective Mike's jaw tightened, but he chose to table his questions for now. "We will come back in twenty minutes," he declared firmly, signaling to his team to follow him out of the room.

After twenty minutes, Hassan was dead, his throat was slit open. This puzzled the investigation team; there were no cameras to replay, and the interrogation room had been set up in haste to collect information as fast as possible.

Chapter 51

The ZRP was leading investigations, and two prostitutes had led the law enforcement to one Casper, a man in his early Forties living at 12396 Gunhill Avenue. The house has 22 bedrooms, three sitting rooms, a helipad, and a cinema that can accommodate 60 people. The house was sitting on 2500 square metres on a 16,500 square metre stand. It could not be seen from the gate, but there was a friendly game, such as zebras, antelopes and rabbits. At the gate, the police asked Lizzy, the prostitute, to talk to Casper nicely, but if all failed, the ZRP and SWAT teams were already in position; the Support Unit and the Military were on standby two blocks away.

The driver of a small white car with the blue-beam taxi written on top came to a stop and rang the intercom. Casper bellowed, "Who the fuck is this?"

Through the crackle of the intercom, Lizzy's voice broke through. "It's your girl Lizzy here."

Casper's hand paused over his work as he listened intently. "Which Lizzy are you talking about? I am busy."

There was a hint of laughter in Lizzy's tone. "There's only one who gives you peri- peri chicken position."

Casper chuckled, his voice tinged with amusement. "My acids are too high today. I don't want no peri-peri today."

Lizzy's voice was filled with playful suggestions. "How about the apple juice position?"

Casper's laughter echoed through the room. "Apples are acidic, too."

Lizzy persisted, her tone teasing. "How about tongue out and water landing airplane?"

Hearing this, Silver was not sure if this was going to work; he was growing impatient as Lizzy and Casper continued their apparent banter. As Silver was processing the situation and looking for an appropriate way to respond, there was silence as Lizzy kept talking, with no response coming through. After a moment, there was the sound of a Bell Jet Ranger taking off; Silver figured that Casper was seeking flight take-off and landing details from the authorities the entire time. The flight aspect posed a new challenge, as nothing could be done without the involvement of the Air Force of Zimbabwe. In Zimbabwe, every plane that takes off and flies in the sky with the intention of landing, whether on land or across into other national airspace, is required to seek approval before they may be shot down by the Air Force. Silver quickly updated the Chief that they needed urgent access to the Air Force high-level team to provide stand-by assistance. After 3 minutes, the Chief Vice Air Marshall was on the line.

Chief Vice Air Marshal Rodrick's authoritative voice resonated. "My name is Rodrick. I am the Chief Vice Air Marshal. I am told we can be of help with the current investigations?"

Silver's demeanor shifted, acknowledging the senior officer's presence. "Yes, Sir. We are looking to—"

Before Silver could finish, Chief Vice Air Marshal Rodrick interjected, his voice firm and decisive. "I have set up a team of six officers to be on standby and to grant you all the requests." A few minutes later, a call was placed to Silver, and a wing commander spoke, repeating what the Chief Vice Air Marshall had said to him. The Wing Commander gave assurances that all the information needed was to be supplied. Silver immediately asked for credentials of the Helicopter that took off at the supplied address, the names of the owners, the location it was going to, the names of the Pilots flying it and their ETA. He also requested a flight schedule for the past year, the times and frequencies of flies and if the Hit scope was being flown by the same Pilot or different Pilots. The Wing Commander took note of the request and promised to get back to them in a few minutes and to start releasing whatever information would have been made available.

The ZRP and the SWAT team forced entry into the Gunhill house, where the Alarm went off, and dogs went mad chasing the officers around the big yard. The police battled with the violent dogs and in the process, decided to kill the dogs as they were mainly German Shepherds and violent ones, for that matter. The team entered that house forcibly, mainly from the front; soon after opening the door, there were a number of venomous snakes, which could easily be identified as the black mambas, two giant pythons and some spitting cobras. These snakes seemed to have been randomly released to slow down the police. There was a shootout, and the team went inside the house. There were voices of ladies screaming in other parts of the room, and when the police moved in, they saw young ladies from 18 years to 23 years old packing drugs into small packets. They were visibly drugged, wearing only undergarments. There were three ladies who were counting money and packing it into seals. They continued what they were doing till the police ordered them to stop.

Silver picked up the phone and spoke briefly to the CIO chief, who was excited that there was tangible information to take to the press and that the power was shifting. The drug teams were being pushed to the corner bit by bit. Silver called experts on drugs to the scene, ranging from forensics, narcotics, ballistics, parks and wildlife, human trafficking experts and homicide. One SWAT member was going through the other rooms when she heard a sound what sounded like a bomb ticking; she peeped to have a better view, and there it was only left with 10 seconds; she immediately yelled for people to evacuate, and as they attempted to do so, there was a gas fire that came from the Kitchen causing panic. The police managed to escape, and a few of the ladies moved; the police saw at the last minute that the girls who were counting cash were sitting on bombs, and it was too late to do anything.

The explosion started from the main safe room, and there were three more strong explosions with blood mixed up in the explosion and screams of "Innocent souls" who were trapped in the inferno. It was a terrible site to see, yet a usual one, especially for the SWAT teams. The area was cordoned off, bomb experts were called in, and forensics made their way to the place; the fire brigade could be heard screaming all the way, but by the time they arrived at the scene, there was nothing to save, there were many bodies that could not be identified.

Innocent's voice boomed over the phone line, a mix of concern and disappointment. "I hear you have started World War III, son. What's going on over there?"

Silver's voice came through, tinged with urgency. "We walked into a trap, Sir."

Innocent's tone turned stern. "What did you expect, son? You really think you were going to walk into the house, arrest the suspect, and collect evidence?"

Silver's response was swift. "No, Sir. I might have misjudged the situation, but we did not have much time to react."

"You're damn right you didn't," Innocent retorted sharply. A pause followed, the weight of the situation hanging heavy in the air. Innocent's voice softened slightly. "Clean this mess and come to the meeting place. I want to talk to you."

Later, at the meeting place, Silver approached Innocent with a respectful greeting. "Good evening, Sir. You called for me?"

Innocent's voice carried a mix of admiration and concern. "That was brave of you to be in the line of duty like that, but I want you to manage the investigation from the office and get some reports. The US authorities have insisted that the Defense attaché be a part of the investigations, especially regarding drugs."

Silver's response was immediate and firm. "No way."

"Yes, way," Innocent countered firmly. "These teams need balance."

Silver's tone hardened. "I would say it's a bad idea, Sir. Everyone who was at the embassy when the kidnappings started should be considered as a prime suspect until they are cleared. Bringing them here may give them access to further tamper with evidence."

Innocent's voice remained resolute. "These are decorated soldiers. They are working to serve their nation, and they will do everything to protect it."

Silver persisted, his voice tinged with urgency. "What if there are some who are not happy to be here? This is a tough call, Sir. Make your assessments."

Innocent briefed Silver that SWAT experts had traced the phone call of a person calling to ask for money. The money and gold was traced to a series of armed robberies that were done over three months ago. The person who called was not JBZ; in fact, the police were acting on Information, and after giving a press conference bout the money and Gold, many victims came through and Identified the suspects we have in our custody as being part of the robbery. They have since cleared more than 50 cases of robberies. Public relations say that they are receiving numerous anonymous calls from people who are either claiming to have seen JBZ, are aware of drug scandals, or have information about the ambassador.

Silver kept playing the scene at the house in Gunhill, and he could tell that there was something very wrong. Could it be that Lizzy was using a language that they could not understand? Silver asked the team to bring Lizzy for questioning, but they had just dropped her off at her house after making some statements. 20 minutes later, there was a fire at the flat where she stayed, and when police arrived, they were shown her body, burnt beyond recognition.

Silver spoke to one of the prostitutes who worked with Lizzy; he managed to establish that Lizzy always used one driver to go to her "Big" client in Gunhill; she had bragged that they used a special language when communicating and that it spiced things up.

Chapter 52

The Big Cat received the results of the staff analysis, but they did not seem to show much detailed and meaningful information. The analysis was a summary of days at work, leave days taken, the number of days before leave days were taken, who each of the members met and where they went when they were off duty. Samuel had taken too many sick leaves than anyone, and he usually attended African cultural festivals. He had attended most of the social events escorting the Ambassador's wife and son. He had a close and professional relationship with the Ambassador's wife and son. Samuel disliked American policy, especially the imposition of economic sanctions on Zimbabwe. He had grown to like the country, and in private meetings, he had mentioned that he would not mind to take a wife and settling in Zimbabwe. In fact, it was rumoured that he was dating a Zimbabwean girl; the girl was an artist and activist who spoke against sanctions against Zimbabwe.

At that point, the Big Cat placed Samuel under arrest and designated him as a possible suspect. He went on to appoint the defense attaché as one of the team members. This process required clearance from the head of the operation, and Innocent had no problems with that at all. There was confusion about what to do with Samuel; he was a suspect in a kidnapping case, yet their rules of engagement did not allow them to be subjected to the local laws and regulations. Their conduct is governed by the laws of the USA, and where there is misconduct, they are sent to a military-specific court.

Innocent's tone was stern as he addressed Big Cat. "I understand that you have designated Samuel as a key suspect based on a series of credible associations with anti-US groups in the country."

BigCat's response came swiftly. "Negative, Sir. Samuel is still at the Embassy, serving his duties as usual."

Innocent's voice grew sharper. "Is that so?"

Big Cat hesitated, his words measured. "Yes, Sir, we are—"

"I am not the Head of CIO by chance, young man," Innocent interrupted firmly.

"We may have flagged his movements, but we have not done anything beyond that," Big Cat clarified.

Innocent's frustration was palpable. "We are in the middle of an investigation, and when we get a credible lead, you decide not to share the information?"

"No, Sir, we are still trying to make further assessments to determine if these statistics and events mean anything or if they are just there," Big Cat explained, his tone respectful yet firm.

Innocent's frustration simmered beneath his words. "Do you realise that you take us back to the negotiating table, a process that could take forever to find common ground?"

Big Cat shrugged his shoulders while keeping a straight face. "Sir, this is above me. I have no authority to hand him over. He may be in Zimbabwe, but he is on American soil per international laws."

"So, the Embassy is harbouring a key suspect, and you won't hand over the suspect for questioning?" Innocent's tone was skeptical.

BigCat's voice remained firm. "International law prohibits you from even going to the Embassy and interviewing him. He has immunity by virtue of the laws and agreements we signed as the two nations."

"I want to interview the suspect," Innocent insisted, his voice tinged with determination.

"I'm afraid it won't happen, Sir," Big Cat responded firmly.

Innocent's frustration boiled over. "Look here, I do not care who you are. I will give a press briefing of a US Marine Corps who is a key suspect, and the investigation team has no access to him."

BigCat's tone softened slightly. "I will seek authorization from my superiors, but I make no promises that it may go your way."

Innocent's gaze hardened. "You do that."

The Big Cat went to the Embassy holding cell where Samuel was being detained and found him dead; he hanged "himself" using tyre cables; he had written a confession note that he was responsible for the Kidnapping of the Ambassador's wife and Son and that he had received large sums of money in exchange for the information about their whereabouts and that on the day he had been spared deliberately.

The Big Cat had to activate Protocol; he wanted the Zimbabwean Authorities to hear nothing about Samuel's Death or the so-called note. A radio was sent, and a request was made for advice on the steps to take. Since the Zimbabwean Authorities were not aware of who Samuel really was, a plan to swap and send his body to the US and send a man similar in stature to Harare and pretend like nothing ever happened. The Big Cat entrusted the defense attaché with the report writing and all the arrangements that were to be made. There was to be no report of death to the authorities in Zimbabwe as such information would further compromise and bring to question the circumstances leading to the death of a highly trained Marine Corp.

Somehow, there was no secrecy at all. Information that is considered confidential was now shared and made public to the staff, and there was a somber mood at the Embassy; people could not openly mourn as Samuel was not supposed to have died.

The Big Cat received a call that he needed to attend to a scene at Westgate where Samuel's girlfriend had committed suicide by throwing herself into the road where she was run over by a Jeep Cheroke; she was pronounced dead on arrival to the Parirenyatwa Group of Hospitals.

The police recovered a letter where the deceased claimed to have been a part of a team that had planned to kidnap the Ambassador's wife and Son; the note claimed that the girl worked together with Samuel. The Big Cat asked the ZRP and SWAT team if any of them had prior communication with the deceased and how they were alerted of the accident and the time. The times were confirmed, making it clear that both the Embassy and the Police were alerted at the same time. This raised more questions about the intention and involvement of the informer. The Big Cat did not want to admit it, but what he was facing was even bigger than him; it was a complicated scheme, and someone senior at the embassy was involved, but who? How were they involved, and with who? While he was thinking about this, the acting Ambassador was informed of the matter and the possibility that there was a mole at the Embassy.

The Big Cat devised a plan to weed out the mole; he told the defense attaché that all the information was to be shared with only three people at the embassy due to lack of trust. This was to continue till the mole was discovered.

At nightfall, a vehicle left the embassy and got into Chinhoyi Road. It was a sprinter. The driver had 1 passenger who was willing to bribe his way through to Makuti; the idea was to somehow make it to Kariba and hire a boat that would be driven across the waters crossing international waters into Zambia, where the body would be sent to a mortuary and the paperwork done. Or at least smuggle the deceased into Kariba Overnight Ferries, a boat that ferries people and cars from Kariba to Victoria Falls. This option would lead to the Kazungula Border.

The whole journey went well, and just before they got to the main street in Kariba, there was a roadblock mounted. Three policemen, six heavily armed soldiers, and the Police Support Unit were at the site. The driver panicked and was somehow suspecting that the plan had been leaked to the police and that he was facing imminent arrest. The car came to a stop, and the police were stern and demanded to see the inside of the truck. The driver hesitated, his eyes darting nervously as he surveyed the heavy police presence. He began to ask questions, his voice tinged with confusion, but the officers were in no mood for explanations. With stern expressions, they proceeded to search the vehicle meticulously. Ignoring his inquiries, they searched the vehicle thoroughly but found nothing. Turning their attention to the driver, they grilled him with questions, deeming him a person of interest but lacking evidence to charge him. Reluctantly, they let him go, suspicion still looming.

The car served as a decoy, but the mission was abruptly aborted as the police were tipped off by an unknown informant. This plan was shared with the defense attaché. Meanwhile, Samuel's body was negotiated between US and Zimbabwean Authorities, and an agreement was reached that the matter be kept under wraps and that a replacement be brought per plan.

Chapter 53

It's a Saturday morning, and mourners are gathered at 1644 in Kuwadzana phase 3; Monalisa had died of an overdose of cocaine. Her body had turned green for some reason. She was a girl who grew up from a humble beginning, an intelligent girl who had managed to defy the odds. While most young girls were hooked on drugs and prostitution, she decided to focus on her school. When she finished her Advanced Level, she earned A stars in Physics, Chemistry, Mathematics, and Biology. She had been a prefect from primary school to high school, becoming a head girl and still balancing her activities and coming out the best in class. She carried the hope of many.

To the grannies, she was an example of how a child can be well-mannered and to mothers, she was an example of other young girls. Society saw hope that one could grow up under painful and difficult circumstances, but they could overcome and rise to become the hope of society or perhaps the entire nation.

During the speech time, the family explained how their daughter was found unconscious in her room at the university; it was difficult to believe that their hero was on drugs. Many questions were raised; her friends disputed that she was on drugs, and college mates, even from different faculties, gave testimonies that she was a composed girl who was well-behaved. The story was difficult to accept, and even the police were confused as none of the people they interviewed confirmed that she was a drug addict.

There was a letter on her bed that simply read, "It didn't have to end this way; all you needed to do was work for me, a lesson to all." The message was difficult to understand, who wanted to work with her, to do what, why kill her, was the cocaine forced on her, who was behind the evil act. The police had asked for more time to investigate the matter, but they had to recommend burial as there was no fresh evidence. There was no one talking or saying anything that was credible enough to construct an investigation. When the time for body viewing came, it was a heart-wrenching moment when friends and families fainted, some fainting, to comprehend how their hero had died through an overdose of drugs. Never before had society felt robbed and cheated on by death. It was a very painful moment. The mother cried aloud till she had no voice. The question was why, why my daughter, why at this point? The father was speechless; with his walking stick held firmly in his right hand, he walked slowly to the with tears flowing uncontrollably; he did not attempt to wipe the tears. It was such a sad moment for him, his princess, and a top global student in International Science and Chemistry. He never believed that his daughter was a drug addict. What troubled him the most was the violation. The postmortem showed that she was abused sexually several times. Then, the gory part was one of the breasts were outright removed, and the other's nipple was missing. This was no easy part, and for the parents who had identified the body, it was a very tough time. Pain, agony, and anguish spread a dark cloud over the community; all the young girls and boys, the grannies and mothers, were in mourning. Their hero was taken away from them. As the coffin was being closed, there was loud wailing. It was a complicated time, and the family was inconsolable. The Pastor who did the message had to stop the message three times as he was moved and became emotional. What a sad ending.

The Minister of Science and Technology was there to pay his last respects. He had travelled with the girl for an international awards ceremony, and he was proud of her. His mood and mannerisms' showed a man who was in deep trouble; his chemistry teacher fainted twice during the three-day mourning period, he was given the podium but failed to speak as tears clouded his eyes, paid held his brain from thinking, and he became tongue-tied.

Chapter 54

Silver left his house and picked up three team members, two FBI and one ZRP; they drove to the RESTORENTE DIPOPOLIS, a popular place with a certain type. They had been tipped by Precious that the Big Dhara would be there. They reverse parked at a distance from the entrance just in case things go bad. The restaurant was full, and there were no tables. Silver wanted to walk to the waiters and just ask for the Big Dhara, but he decided against the idea.

While Silver was still thinking, a man came from behind him and shouted, "Silver, my tormenter, is it true what I hear? They say you are making such a mess around town? I used to have a lot of respect for you. I hear you are all over the show with very limited success."

Silver turned and faced the man he had put in prison; the harsh reality was that he was now a son in law of a hardcore criminal. They faced each other eye to eye in an intimidating way and non-seemed to back off from the standoff. No words were uttered; the Big Dhara started shaking with anger and clenched his fist.

Big Dhara snapped, "So you are not so clean, hey. You and I are the same; you are just a criminal like me."

Silver shot back, "You are the criminal, a thief in the night stealing shit that does not belong to you."

Big Dhara lifted his hand, "Careful, son, I am not as soft as I was before. This time, I will kill you with my bare hands and bury you in a plain box, an unmarked grave and an unregistered grave."

Silver nonchalantly answered, "It takes more than talking to kill me; I am a mammoth. I don't go down that easy."

"20 years, you still coming with the same sorry-ass speech. Do people actually believe it, or have you listened to your lie several times, and now think it's actually true?" Big Dhara forced a laugh.

Silver looked him straight into the eyes. "Yes, from time to time."

As Silver stood before Big Dhara, the tension in the room was palpable. Big Dhara fell silent, his thoughts consumed by memories of his daughter and the man who had once put him behind bars. With a surge of pent-up emotion, he swung a punch at Silver, igniting a sudden brawl that was quickly subdued by the team.

"You have some serious balls coming here demanding information and talking to me as if I am under arrest or investigation," Big Dhara growled, his voice dripping with contempt.

"This is a national crisis," Silver retorted, his tone firm.

"And you are the saviour, the guardian?" Big Dhara scoffed.

"I am merely doing my job," Silver replied evenly.

"Then go ahead and do it," Big Dhara challenged.

"I hear you're a businessman now. I need your assistance," Silver pressed on.

"Go to the university if you want a business master class. Why would I do a damn thing for you?" Big Dhara shot back, his tone laced with bitterness.

"It's the right thing to do," Silver insisted.

"You lost your moral compass and the right to preach morality when you abandoned my daughter. You took advantage of her, and now you come crawling back," Big Dhara accused, his voice filled with anger.

"I'm sorry. I was young and made wrong decisions. Please forgive me," Silver pleaded, his voice tinged with remorse. Silver knelt down and begged for forgiveness, and while he was kneeling, Big Dhara took a moment and struck again. With a loud thud, Silver fell to the ground, landing headfirst. The sudden blow left him unconscious, sprawled out on the ground amidst the chaos of the scuffle. An ambulance was quickly called, but just as it arrived, Silver began to stir. He opened his eyes to find Big Dhara holding him in his arms, tears streaming down his face like an endless supply of beer at a party catered for by the government. Silver asked to be released, and Big Dhara reaffirmed that he was the only family he had and that they should stick together.

Silver quickly changed the subject, "Tell me about the drugs and the kidnappings."

Big Dhara was playful yet playing it tough, "Pay damages for impregnating my daughter first, then we will talk."

Silver was taken aback. "Are you serious right now?" Big Dhara demanded that he kneel down and greet him properly, as a son-in-law should do. Silver could not believe that he was kneeling before the man he had put in prison. He regretted neglecting his daughter's mother, but that was a little too late. The damage was done. He reached out of his pocket and handed over a USD100 as a token. Big Dhara grabbed the bill and shouted with so much joy as if he had been given a million dollars. To him, holding a USD100 note from a son-in-law was a dream that had come true; he immediately burst into tears as he wished that his daughter was alive and that they could have been a proper family.

Big Dhara pointed to the back of the restaurant; they sat in the garden chairs with Silver's team, quiet and observing the drama unfolding. The food was served, and they ate it in haste. As they were done, Silver was about to leave when his host asked him to stay for ice cream. Silver was now confused about whether there was a genuine prospect of getting any information; the FBI members were following the proceedings, showing a great deal of patience, and taking some notes in the process, and so was the ZRP team.

Silver explained to Big Shara that they were on the hunt for the Ambassador and JBZ despite being tasked with focusing solely on a drug-related case. Big Dhara, impressed by Silver's ambition, warned about the elusive nature of their target, known for running illegal operations ranging from drugs to robberies and money laundering. This individual, surrounded by bodyguards and flaunting luxuries, remained a mystery, with rumours suggesting connections to Mexican or American entities. The challenge lay not just in finding him, but in crafting a convincing story to approach him, given his notorious temper and tightly controlled operations. "Where can we find this guy?" Sliver asked, intrigued.

Big Dhara explained, his gaze fixated in the distance, "You can't find him unless he wants to be found, and you better have a good story; he has a bad temper, and moves with bodyguards all the time. The man has changed. Now wears a USD300, 000 watch just to see the time."

Tell me, "Who is he working with?" Silver pleaded.

"No one knows; some say he works for Mexicans or Americans, but whatever is happening is well planned, like they have their shit together, it's like they turned the whole drug business into a real company."

Silver leaned forward, his eyes narrowing with curiosity. "Who leads them?" he asked, his voice laced with determination and a hint of urgency, his gaze fixed intently on Big Dhara, awaiting his response open-mouthed.

Big Dhara's response was matter-of-factly. "No one, really. People toss around JBZ's name, but JBZ isn't a person; it's more of a concept. The current leader, whoever they are, takes on the name JBZ. It's like a shadowy figure, elusive and ever-present, haunting every corner of the operation."

Silver's brows furrowed with intrigue as he leaned in closer. "What's the name of your friend you mentioned earlier? Can you get us close to him for questioning?" he asked, his tone laced with a sense of urgency.

Big Dhara's expression turned solemn as he weighed his words carefully. "The man is like the god's eye system," he began, his voice tinged with a mixture of admiration and caution. "He has eyes everywhere, sees everything. He has people in all high places: corporates, government departments, and everywhere."

Silver's eyes flickered with a glint of determination as he absorbed this information. "Tell me about his family," he pressed, his voice low and calculated. "Does he have any weakness I can exploit?"

Big Dhara spoke as if in a trance, "He has a son enrolled at Stonewall International School; he drops him every morning on his way to work. You will have trouble knowing which car he drives. It's said he never rocks up with the same car in a month."

Silver's gaze sharpened as he absorbed Big Dhara's words. "What's the name of your friend's son?" he inquired, his tone focused and intent.

Big Dhara's brow furrowed in frustration. "How on earth am I supposed to know?" he snapped, his voice tinged with annoyance at the unexpected question. Silver remained undeterred, already seeming to piece together the puzzle. "All I know is that the son is in the school rugby team and that he is holding the current 1st place for tennis," he stated firmly, his determination evident in his voice.

Big Dhara implored Silver, "Please don't get killed; come back to us, at least to your daughter; you are the only surviving parent she has."

Silver and his team took off at a high speed and headed to Stonewall International School. They were met by the school caretakers, who pointed them to the school head's office. The school head was an imposing figure, a firm and intimidating man. Silver greeted the school head and indicated that he wanted to talk to him in private. The school head had insisted that if it was about school places, then there were no places. Silver nodded as if accepting defeat.

Silver sighed, a hint of frustration in his voice. "My friend will be disappointed that I couldn't find a place here. He really wanted his son to have some real competition."

The Head's eyes widened in recognition. "Jefferson Makuvise is your friend?"

Silver nodded. "Who else would I be talking about?"

The Head leaned back, tapping his chin thoughtfully. "Makuvise, huh? He's always sending his money our way, but he's never around. We only ever deal with his PR manager, who's just as icy as he is."

Silver's lips tightened in agreement. 'Yeah, Makuvise is a cold one. Keeps to himself, doesn't want any interference."

The Head leaned in, his voice dropping to a whisper. "He's been sick lately, you know. Heard his son and wife have been showing up instead. They say he barely leaves the house, only takes walks at night."

Silver's eyebrows raised in concern. "When did this start?"

The Head shrugged. "A few weeks back, I reckon."

Silver rubbed his temple, realizing his dilemma. "I seem to have lost my phone. Could you help me with Makuvise's latest number?"

The Head chuckled, a smug grin spreading across his face. "You're such a luddite, Silver. Why don't you have all your contacts backed up on the cloud?" Pulling out his sleek iPhone 14, the Head scrolled through with practiced ease, showing off his technological prowess. "Here," he said, tapping the screen. "But I've never actually had to call Makuvise myself. Everything's always been well-organized."

Outside in the school grounds, Silver dialled Jefferson Makuvise's number, the phone ringing three times before it was finally answered. He asked the tech team to check the current location of the phone; however, they did not have anything to pin him down, so they could only track the phone.

Silver spoke first, "Good afternoon, Jefferson." There was a long silence, and after some 30 seconds, a voice came to the phone.

"Silver, what took you so long to call? You didn't need to bother the school head; now, his life is in your hands. He has broken the school confidentiality rules. Go and give him the phone. I want to talk to him." Silver hesitated, and as he started to move to the head office, he heard a loud explosion. It was somewhere close within a 10 km radius. He kept walking towards the office, and he saw the school head with a knife at the back of his head; the radio was playing "Killing Me Softly."

Silver decided to go and check on the Big Dhara, but it was too late. As he arrived at the scene, the Restorente Dipopolis was reduced to ashes, and witnesses say a man had smelled gas and asked people to leave the restaurant, but unfortunately, three people could not make it. The Big Dhara was injured; he was in a critical yet stable condition and taken to the hospital by ambulance. Silver received a call from the CIO boss in charge of the operation, who summoned him to the station right away.

When he arrived at the station, the Big Cat was there, along with all other team members. Silver was informed that his house was set ablaze and that everything was burnt to ashes. The house was actually bombed, though no one was injured.

In other news, security at the hospital managed to arrest a man who had come pretending to be a medical doctor; they wanted to transfer the Big Dhara to a private high-end hospital. The security got curious when they saw that the same man had been driving an ambulance that he parked at casualty, a deviation from the normal procedure.

Chapter 55

Silver rushed to the hospital to see Big Dhara, which was now heavily guarded. Big Dhara was in a ward overlooking the Brooke Hotel right by the corner. In the morning, there were unexpected construction works that started the day after Big Dhara was admitted into the hospital.

As Silver came close to his bed, the Big Dhara started coughing and sweating; he held his hand firmly and said, "There is a tape recording at my house; there is a disc under the carpet just as you get into the house. Please be safe."

Silver left the Hospital in a huff, took off into Seventh Street, and rushed to the streetlights before swerving into Chitepo Avenue, sending the car screaming in disapproval of the fancy driving and making tar marks in rage before meandering as he overtook cars from both left and right sides of the road breaking at least 10 traffic rules in the process overtaking from the left, doing 70km in a 40 zone, hooting to scare other drivers to give him way, overtaking on double continuous lines among other offenses. He picked up speed, and without slowing down, he curved into Enterprise Road, now moving at 180km per hour, ignoring the streetlight at turnoff KG6 and speeding ahead at 180 Km/hr. He came to a complete halt to give way to a freight liner that was making its way towards the direction of town. Jack Jacobs was making its usual sound as it tried to slow down the commercial truck. Silver could not take chances, so he decided to stop. He turned into New Lands Shopping center, driving right through before circling the roundabout, where he took the fourth turn into Princess Drive. He drove up at Formula One speed hobbling at the two-speed humps but maintaining the speed. He turned left into Little Fontana Road and parked at number 3.

Inside the gate, a fire had just started, but he managed to grab the USB but could not locate the recorder. He tried the second time to enter the house, but there was now a thick smoke engulfing the house. He tried one more time, but this time, objects were being thrown around. A beam fell behind him, closing his escape route. He tried looking for other exit routes, but all he could see was thick smoke, and he was fast running out of oxygen; in a last-minute attempt, he summoned all his strength and broke the glass, narrowly escaping as the other beams fell right where he was standing.

As Silver and his team were leaving Big Dhara's house, a grey Toyota Hilux GD6 and a Ford Ranger screamed to a brisk stop. Without a preamble, two men emerged from each car, both carrying assault rifles, and then the rain started, the rain of bullets; this is one time one could sing the kindergarten song "Rain, rain go away, come back another day."

Silver's FBI, ZRP Support Unit and the Crimes Department were equal to the task. One FBI agent threw a Rocket-propelled Grenade (RPG), and two more which reduced one of the cars to shit size mixing blood and flames in the process. The other car took off in a huff at a high speed. One suspect was arrested on sight, and backup had been called for. The suspect was taken in for questions but needed medical care. He had sustained injuries on both legs, but he was going to live. He was taken to the safe house clinic where the other arrested suspects who needed medical care were being held.

Silver received a call from Jefferson. Jefferson spoke, "You are one hard to kill mother fucker I have come across; why won't you just die, and we all go home?"

Silver murmured, "Then this world will be boring for you. Who else can give you the adrenaline I give you?"

Jefferson sniggered. "You make a very important point right there. The world will be a boring place without guns, bombs, conspiracy and smart people like you to outsmart."

Silver sulked and spat, "Save that many people are dying needlessly, and it's something you can't be proud of."

Jefferson lacked sympathy in his answer, "Some people die so others may live; there are people wasting our God-given right to life, just existing instead of living."

Silver clenched his fists. "Yet you never seem to do any of the dying."

Jefferson showed no remorse as he continued, "All those who died were supposed to die; their time had come."

Silver was trained not to show emotion, but he was becoming irate and struggling to remain composed. He paused to recollect himself, then spoke with a renewed sense of calm yet marked with harshness. "I have been employed to stop crimes, and sometimes with a shoot to kill order from my employers, and I will gladly kill you for free." Silver waited for a response, which never came. "You have killed many men for? What's the benefit to you?"

This time, Jefferson wasted no time responding, "I will kill anyone who stands in my way."

Silver nodded with a grin; if you are still ordering hits and overseeing the streets, my take is that you are someone's chess piece. A pawn, I should say."

Jefferson leaned back, a smirk playing on his lips. "You're on point, but you're forgetting something here," he countered confidently. "I established this market single-handedly, so I am the boss here. In any case, pawns do graduate to much more important pieces, such as knights, bishops, castles, or even a queen."

Silver's expression turned steely as he checked the timer on his phone, noting how many minutes they had been on the call. "You're halfway across the chessboard, pawn, and it's my duty to ensure you never graduate. You'll always be a pawn."

Jefferson's voice lowered, his tone dripping with superiority. "What do you know? I'm smarter than you and will always be ahead of you by 100 years."

Silver's voice remained firm. "So says a man who's busy handling dirty work while real bosses are in the comfort of their homes, counting cash and making online transactions. Far away from danger."

Jefferson's voice carried an edge of intensity as he leaned closer to the phone. "The struggle starts from the streets," he countered sharply. "You can't learn the ropes from the office."

Silver's lips curled into a sardonic smile. "Looks like the ropes are too long for you. You'll never get to the endpoint." With that, Silver ended the call. His team had extracted the information they needed.

#

Back at the hospital, the construction works had started, and in a surprise turn of events, the crane was lowered to the fifth floor where the Big Dhara was admitted, while people were wondering what was going on, a steel ball was thrown and dragged to the corner ward where at least three beds were dragged injuring patients in the process. The Big Dhara was swift; he ducked and took the fire escape, where he met a man in a black suit waiting purposefully with guns in both hands. He quickly covered his head, and at that moment, more patients and staff started pouring in, much to the frustration of the man in black.

Silver was stunned when he got to the Hospital; Big Dhara's house was up in smoke, the ward was destroyed, and the restaurant was set on fire. Someone wanted to kill the old man, but for what? The old man had to be protected as he was now very vulnerable.

Chapter 56

The US government was concerned about the involvement of its Embassy staff and had asked that a full-scale investigation be done. A special team was assembled in Washington and was to be reporting to the President its findings. Rumours had started swelling in the media that the USA embassy staff had betrayed their own boss to the drug Lord. This was devastating news, and the Pentagon was trying its best to ensure that the intelligence community reached out. In the process, all the US relations were activated, and nations were to share their own intelligence with the US, and of course, this came at a cost. Surprisingly, even North Korea, Russia, and Red China cooperated on this matter and agreed to share any intelligence briefings about what they would gather. In the Pentagon, a high-level meeting was taking place; the president wanted to hear what was happening on the ground.

The information that had been sent to the US in the wake of the death of Samuel, the suspected traitor and mole at the Embassy. Their analysis results came through, and only the Big Cat was allowed access. When the Big Cat opened the files, he was expecting to see the usual circumstantial evidence, which required a series of assumptions that would require further analysis for months. However, there was a file for the defense attaché, his history, a detailed analysis of his movements and a clear indication that he had many reasons to be angry with the government of USA. The report was cleared to be shared with the Zimbabwean authorities to manage a further escalation in case the authorities get wind that another high-ranking authority has been designated as a suspect, but with no information released officially.

The defense attaché had visited Cuba under the "support for the Cuban people visa"; he visited Iran, Iraq, and Afghanistan, among other nations. A series of bank accounts in enemy territory was traced to him directly or indirectly through companies where he was an eventual beneficiary. He closed some bank accounts after the Zimbabwean government enacted a law that required all the eventual owners to be disclosed, even when the banks and securities companies were holding shares as nominees.

Using Artificial Intelligence, the AI reported activities where the defense attaché could have been involved; this was achieved through information gathered on the internet showing places he had visited, the time he had spent there, the phones he called and numbers and names of people he was in close proximity with. The information was assessed, and one of the people came up as Jefferson, among other names.

The defense attaché was an official suspect who could give information. There was confusion about what and how to charge him as most of the information constituted suspicion in the USA, especially when visiting enemy territory under different names, but Zimbabwe had no jurisdiction over the matter. There was no evidence linking him to the kidnapping of the Ambassador or the girls; however, it was enough to question him.

Later on, the Big Cat went to the Embassy with the view to question the defense attaché, but he was not there, a very worrisome turn of events as no one leaves the embassy without clearance, especially the Marine Corps, let alone the defense attaché.

In the meantime, a man named Hamdi Sheriff, an Iranian who was born in Ethiopia was on his way to the airport, the Robert Gabriel Mugabe International Airport; he had five applications from which to book a taxi. After realizing that using an app would create a permanent trail, he decided to hire a conventional taxi and paid cash.

They drove to the airport in Silence; they approached the Air Dzimbahwe hangers circling the roundabout before crossed over into the airport, avoiding the pricy parking lot, they drove to through passing the domestic terminal on the left, slowing down in front of a giant recently renovated airport, the biggest sign of China Zimbabwe cooperation after the Parliament of Zimbabwe.

It was often whispered in closed-door meetings that the West was increasingly getting worried about the growing influence of the Red China in Africa and in particular, in Zimbabwe, where the Chinese had penetrated into mining, construction, retail and tourism, just to name a few. Advisers to Western governments believe that the continued isolation of Zimbabwe from the multilateral institutions and exclusion of its financial system was benefitting China, with the West getting no reward from the isolation.

Hamdi Ismail Sheriff walked to the counter and produced his passport for check-in; the staff at the Intercontinental African Airline checked him in as he was one of the last passengers to arrive. There was a heavy presence of police and plain clothes FBI Agents working in a coordinated way, looking for any suspicious passengers. Hamdi did not have any bags to check-in. He had no hand language or any extra things to carry. He went through to the security checkpoints, and upon producing his passport, he was asked to remove his cap. He passed all the points, and the last was the immigration desk, where his passport was stamped. The moment he stepped into the walkway, he was asked to accompany two security Agents.

"Good afternoon, Sir," the Airport Security greeted Hamdi, his tone professional yet firm. "Kindly follow us to the office by the corner there."

Hamdi's brows furrowed with suspicion. "Am I under arrest, Officer?" he questioned, his voice tinged with concern.

The Airport Security shook his head reassuringly. "No, Sir, just carrying out security routine," he explained, trying to ease Hamdi's worries.

Hamdi's patience wore thin. "Then ask everything you want to ask right now or else charge me," he demanded, his tone firm and assertive.

A hint of authority crept into the Airport Authority's voice. "I can detain you for 48 hours on account of suspicious behaviour," he warned, his expression stern.

Unfazed, Hamdi stood his ground. "Then take me now; I am your prisoner today," he declared defiantly, his resolve unwavering.

The Airport Authority let out a sigh, his frustration evident. "I hate paperwork and all the trouble that comes with it," he muttered, expressing his reluctance to engage in bureaucratic procedures.

As the two were conversing, the FBI and ZRP were closing in; they rushed over to him with a gun pointed into his head and at that point, there was a radio asking everyone to stand down as Hamdi was not a suspect and that the police had nothing on him, it was a bunch of wild conspiracy theories.

Hamdi was let go, and in less than a minute, there was a beep followed by the girl announcing. This is a security announcement:

"Please do not leave your luggage unattended; if you see any unattended luggage, report it to security immediately."

A moment later, she was back again. "This is a final boarding call for all passengers on "Intercontinental African Airline." Please proceed to gate number GSP16 for boarding."

Hamdi was running now; he produced his boarding pass and was ushered into the corridor; he proceeded straight to the 460-seater plane. He was almost there; he was going to leave the country and never come back to Zimbabwe again. He reached the door and presented his boarding pass, then proceeded to his seat. His heart pounded, and his feet felt clammy and nervous. He let out a huge sigh of relief. He glanced around, the tension easing slightly as he waited for the plane to take off, hoping to leave behind any further potential unpleasant surprises.

The police were waiting for Hamdi, and the moment he seemed relaxed in his seat, they apprehended him. He was taken out of the plane, and his passport ceased. The suspect was taken to a secure facility for questioning.

The Big Cat was the first to address him off the plane, "Hamdi? Is that your terrorist name? What's wrong with you?"

Showing no remorse, Hamdi replied. "I have worked hard to protect my nation, and when I was due for promotion to one of the top diplomatic positions in our foreign missions, you launched a full-scale investigation based on falsehood just so you could get rid of me?"

The Big Cat remained calm, "You are a soldier; your number one duty is to protect our great nation; your duty comes ahead of your personal ambitions."

Hamdi spat behind him, "That's bullshit, and you know it, I was this close, and I was framed, and the entire investigation took forever; the allegations raised against me, I will never recover from them."

The defense attaché was the one responsible for framing and killing Samuel; he had written the note in Samuel's embassy holding cell, and ordered the death of Samuel's girlfriend. The Big Cat continued to question him, "Where is the Ambassador?"

The Defense attaché responded casually, "This matter is above your pay grade; it's too late to save him; he has been airlifted already."

The Big Cat was resolute, "What do you want, man? Release the man, and you will be treated with leniency. We will show you mercy."

The Defense Attaché: I need to talk to the Zimbabwean Authorities; they are the ones I want to cut a deal with, not the US."

"So, you are cooperating with an enemy?" Big Cat quizzed him.

"I have nothing to lose," said the Defense Attaché, "I take my own chances."

The Big Cat spoke sotto voce, "Think straight man, there can be a way if we can get the Ambassador, we can work a way for you to be out of this mess; give up while you still can."

The Defense Attache chuckled, "I will make an offer to the Zimbabwean Government that they will not refuse."

The Big Cat tried to reason with him. "But you can't be a civilian here. You came here under a military cooperation agreement, and Zimbabwe will not protect you."

The Defense Attaché laughed loudly, "You are late, my dear; by now, he is in Yemen, or god knows where they will soon be conducting a televised interview."

The Big Cat snapped his fingers with a smile beaming on his face. "Not really; we have intercepted the plane before an exchange could take place."

Shrugging his shoulders, the Defense attaché rolled his eyes. "Let me guess, and you brought the money and suspects, it never occurred to you that the money and the Ambassador exchange was to take place in the same place. How bad are you guys?"

Soon after the discussion with the defense attaché, the Big Cat attended a briefing meeting. So many things were happening, and there was a lot of tension over the preferential treatment of suspects and prisoners. A total number of 105 suspects had been rounded up as a result of the operation where the prostitutes gave leads to distributors of drugs in the streets. Six street suppliers were rounded up, but they were still to be taken to court to face charges of possession and distributing illegal drugs. The court cases were to be a priority, but the investigators wanted confessions and cutting deals to get to the kingpin. After "interviews" with the drugs section, there were six confessions that led to the supply of information about the local suppliers of drugs. Most street corner drug sellers had agreed to cooperate with the investigation team, but their confessions were left to lower-level police staff to handle and document the paperwork. There was not much strategic information.

LANDING IN 15 MINUTES

Elliot Chatima

And

Rumbi Chen

Chapter 1

It is 15:45 pm on a Thursday afternoon, Captain Smith was headed home, he had flown a number of planes in his career with a total flying hours of 52,000 hours he was considered a seasoned pilot. The Captain was now headed home after a long flight from Australia Canberra to the UK London Airport and from the UK to Kenya to Zambia and then now to Zimbabwe which happens to be the last leg. He was operating a DM 747 Max operated by Sahara Africa Airlines, the leading airline operating commercial passenger and cargo planes across the world with more than 300 destinations worldwide, the plane was made by Euro Martin. The Plane was a giant with a carrying capacity of a staggering 980 people on two decks. The DM 747 Max was the most powerful machine overtaking Airbus 340 and Boeing 747 -8 Intercontinental both with a carrying Capacity of 600 people and Airbus 380-800 with a carrying Capacity of 800 people. Captain Smith came to the mike to make an announcement; "Ladies and Gentlemen we shall be starting our descending shortly, weather is cool with clear skies, temperature 25 degrees Celsius. We are estimated to be landing in 15 Minutes. Please return to your seats and fasten your seat belts".

At that moment the plane was lifted abruptly with wings turning violently threatening to send the plane into cigarette rolls. The Captain steadied the plane but there was another problem, clouds formed and from nowhere it started raining the plane was tumbling, there was severe thunderstorm and blinding lightning which threatened to interfere with onboard communication infrastructure. The screams of women and children were heard while some decided to pray with some folk shouting what seemed to be a prayer in tongues "Zibro sakata" while others were yelling what sounded like "Zibrosakata karibosakara" whatever that means others were praying in English and some in Shona. There was commotion as hand luggage compartments opened with the hand luggage items thrown around hitting passengers in the process. The Captain came back to the mike with a form voice "may we take our seats and remain seated until we have landed. Do not attempt to assist anyone, let the cabin crew do their job. May we offer maximum cooperation to the Cabin Crew".